THE
FAMILY
FRIEND

Also by C. C. MacDonald

Happy Ever After

THE
FAMILY
FRIEND

C. C. MACDONALD

Harvill *Secker*

LONDON

1 3 5 7 9 10 8 6 4 2

Harvill Secker is part of the Penguin Random House group of companies
whose addresses can be found at global.penguinrandomhouse.com

Penguin
Random House
UK

Copyright © Chris MacDonald 2021

First published by Harvill Secker in 2021

A CIP catalogue record for this book is available from the British Library

penguin.co.uk/vintage

ISBN 9781787301566 (hardback)
ISBN 9781787301573 (trade paperback)

Typeset in 13.5/17.5 pt Bembo Std
by Integra Software Services Pvt. Ltd, Pondicherry

Printed and bound in Great Britain by Clays Ltd, Elcograf S.p.A.

The authorised representative in the EEA is Penguin Random House Ireland,
Morrison Chambers, 32 Nassau Street, Dublin DO2 YH68.

Penguin Random House is committed to a sustainable future for
our business, our readers and our planet. This book is made from
Forest Stewardship Council® certified paper.

MIX
Paper from
responsible sources
FSC® C018179

For Mum.

1

Erin's heels clack along the uneven pavement like castanets. She got off the train eighteen minutes ago. She bought a vanilla doughnut from the delicatessen opposite the station and ate half of it before dropping it in a bin. She filmed herself doing all of this, told her smartphone camera why she was throwing it away – too much sugar – and why she bought it in the first place – it was luminous yellow and made her smile. But when she watched the footage back, she came across a little irritated, probably because she was thinking about having wasted £1.20, so she decided not to post the video.

Erin runs her fingers over the ridges of a long fence that hems in the gardens of a row of bungalows, nausea bubbling up from her stomach, giving everything she sees a filter of unpleasantness.

She rounds the corner and emerges onto a wider road, where most of the cars drive over the speed limit, and spots the memorial opposite to a little boy who was one of its victims some years ago. Broken shards of old CDs hang from the tree at the memorial's centre to ward birds away from the dutifully tended floral display and sun-bleached Arsenal shirt. The story goes that the boy's mother was chatting on the phone and didn't see him step out. The road is one back from the sea, protected from the harshest ravages of the North Sea wind, but not far enough away to escape the ice water in the air that seems to seep through Erin's merino-mix cardigan as the light dies away.

Glancing up at the houses, the dusk reveals who's in and who's out. The colours glowing from the windows remind her of the blinking lights of a Christmas market. The strobing blue of a humungous flat-screen; pink warmth coming through a mid-range red Ikea roller blind upstairs; the ochre tint of an open fire, shadows licking a paved driveway.

A cloud must have moved as the sky turns from a muted purple to Technicolor terracotta. She stops outside one of the houses, a bungalow with a dormer stuck out of its roof. The square bay window that stretches over most of its frontage emits a golden hue that gives Erin a swell of warmth and she touches her chest as if she can feel it. She gets out her phone, scans the screen for a moment and posts something before dropping it back into her coat pocket. The January air makes her eyes water. She blinks them dry, scratches her right ear with her shoulder and walks towards the bungalow with the purpose of someone prepared to face the music.

She nudges the house's cast-iron gate gently with her knee and heads up the path. She glances through the window and stops.

A man sits at an oval dining table at the back of an open-plan living-kitchen-dining room, smiling. He's looking at a baby boy with copious dark hair, plumed up in a loose Mohawk, being held out by a striking red-headed woman with a face so chiselled it could have been drawn on a computer. She lifts the baby into the air, staring at him and, is she singing? It seems to Erin like she might be singing. She has the boy stand on her knees and makes him dance, using the hand that isn't supporting him to move his arms and legs like a marionette. The man glances at the woman and the baby, looks down and his face cracks into a slow smile.

The woman puts the baby back into the crook of her arm and looks straight out of the window. Erin knows that she can't be seen now that it's darker outside but she ducks away from the woman's gaze anyway. The man tickles the baby's palms as he reaches towards him.

It looks like something from an advert for a gas company. The happy family laughing with each other in the warmth of the home. The woman holding court, mother, friend, lover. Perfect.

Except that's not her family. It's Erin's.

2

BRAUNEoverBRAINS

358 posts   36.2k followers   1,321 following

ERIN BRAUNE

Mum to Bobby. Salty sea-dweller. Bright up your life. Reformed thespian.

These are my hangover shades. Because this is my hangover.

Banger of a #gifted mini-break @digidetoxglamping. Huge thanks. The cocktails were ting. Not entirely convinced about not having my phone for twenty-four hours. Felt a bit like I'd had a frontal lobotomy. Not the best. BUT my first night away from Bobby-boy was surprisingly fun. I can't wait to see him but feel racked with guilt and nerves about having left my baby boy behind. IS THIS NORMAL? What if he's pissed off with me and doesn't want cuddles?! All your good wishes yesterday made leaving him a lot easier. This piñata was in the bargain bin of a shop at the station (everyday travel essential, sure). Not convinced big-Bob will know what to do with it but will look lush hanging by the window in his nursery and maxing out the Frida Kahlo vibes. WISH ME LUCK.

#thehungovergames #toooldtosayting #mumsofinsta #absentmumsofinsta #hotmessesofinsta #haveabreakhaveameltdown #willyoustillloveme tomorrow

AnnaMaitron HE'LL BE SO EXCITED TO SEE YOU
salveno33 'thehungovergames' LOL
Fran_Tony98 i'd never leave my son at nine months and certainly wouldn't come back still drunk.
motherhubbardglittercupboard Erin, you make it look easy but you still deserve time away. Hope you got my @mysteryboxes to celebrate 30K followers.
Tontonteron some people have real problems

3

'Here she is,' the woman says in an Australian accent as she spots Erin standing at the open door frame to her living room. Erin's fiancé Raf stands up and gives her a flat-palmed wave and a crooked smile that references the strange woman in their front room. The woman gets up and walks towards Erin, still holding baby Bobby, who's scanning his mother's face to try and make sense of it. Erin knows she should put her arms out for her son but finds herself leaning against the in-built shelving, fingering the frayed top edge of a hardback.

'Erin, Amanda,' Raf says, having edged around the table, a note of weariness in his voice, 'an old family friend from back in Oz.'

'I think this might be yours?' the woman says with a muted laugh as she gets to the door. Erin comes forward to take Bobby, but his little monkey paws cling to the edge of Amanda's summer dress so she has to prise them off before handing the baby over. Erin is unbalanced by the sudden weight of her son as he attaches himself to the crook of her arm. He squeaks, then buries his head into Erin's neck, his wedge of hair tickling the underside of her chin.

'Amanda's mum used to work with my dad at the university,' Raf offers, leaning on the last word and giving Erin a look warning her to be tactful.

'It's just so great to meet you,' Amanda says, clapping the tips of her fingers together to emphasise how great she's finding it. 'The woman who captured Raf's heart.' Erin catches her fiancé's eye over her shoulder. He shakes his head, a hint of a shrug, eyes hooded.

'When did you get in?' Erin says, trying to sound casual.

'This morning,' Raf answers. 'I called but you were, you know, uncontactable.' Erin looks at Bobby. His over-round cheeks are dappled with patches of red, his eyes look raw, sunken and the dribble rash on his chin seems angrier than it did yesterday. It looks like he hasn't slept for days. Teeth, probably. He cries out several times every night until Raf goes in to soothe him and they always blame teeth though she's no idea if that is the real reason.

She spends longer than usual taking in every detail of Bobby's face, assessing how much he's changed in the thirty-six hours since she's been away. Guilt aches in the pit of her stomach. How could she leave him for so long? It must have been so unsettling, and on top of that, another woman, here in their house when his mum's away.

'Raf said you've been at some thing in the woods where you're not allowed to take your mobile? Sounds wonderful. I wish smartphones had never been invented.' Erin spots Raf smirking as he takes some mugs from the table over to the sink. Erin's often said to Raf how pretentious she finds people who bang on about how phones are to blame for everything. She notices that there are still plates with the crumbs of some kind of flapjack on the table. They've been having tea and cake in her absence. The house seems calm, composed, even the often-screaming Bobby.

'It was fun, yeh.' Erin thinks of being stacked around a huge wooden table in the most beautiful forest just outside Sevenoaks with seven other mummy-bloggers; being fed espresso martinis and a smorgasbord of vegan nibbly bits. How much they laughed guiltily every time Anna Mai (74k followers) barked that she missed her phone way more than any of her kids, the way the whole gang giggled every time Erin asked the guy who'd done the food if he had any bacon bits she could sprinkle on top of the food. The blissful silence, the empty space in her head where the bubble of stress around how Bobby's going to sleep normally resides as she put her head on the crisp Egyptian cotton pillow in her luxurious yurt.

She feels a sharp pain and looks down to see Bobby grabbing a clump of skin on her shoulder. She yanks his hand away. Amanda's watching with a strange intent, pupils large in paper-white eyes.

'You must have missed this one so much.' Amanda tickles one of his feet.

'Yeh, course.' Erin waves Bobby's hand drowsily in the air. The action feels insincere and she has the thought that she's somehow trying to copy Amanda dancing Bobby around the table, so she stops and lets the boy's arm fall to his side. She scans the room. Her colour-coded play texts, her blocky modern prints, her fiancé rinsing things in the sink in the orangey light of the kitchen. It's all the same as it was when she left, but this stranger's presence makes her feel like she's been gone for months.

Raf sidles over to them while Bobby discovers his mother's jawline with a pudding fist, eyes doubtful as if he's never seen it before. Raf leans towards her, takes the back of her neck in his long fingers and gives her a firm kiss somewhere between her cheek and her ear. Amanda's eyes seem to grow bigger and she smiles on in wonder as if she's at an immersive theatre production.

'Does he need to nurse?' Amanda says, nodding at Bobby who's grappling at Erin's top and headbutting her chest.

'Ah, I don't know?' She looks to Raf.

'He'll be due a feed,' he says. 'He's done great on the bottles though.'

'Great,' Erin says, trying not to feel too aggrieved that Raf seems to have taken his day and a half of solo parenting in his stride while Erin knows how difficult she would have found it. She has Bobby every day during office hours and often during the day at weekends, but Raf's never been out of the house overnight and she probably wouldn't sleep a wink if he was. She knew Raf would be fine without her, he never gets het up about anything, but she wishes it didn't seem like everything had gone quite so well in her absence. She takes Bobby over to the table and tells him in a doting baby voice, 'Can't be grabbing at ladies' dresses, can we? We're going to have to teach you about consent, aren't we, Mr Handsy?' Amanda makes a strange noise and Erin turns to see her catching a laugh in a clenched hand.

'Sorry, you're just so funny, Erin,' she says, shaking her head, amazed. Erin affects a grin at Amanda's compliment as she sits down and scrabbles for the app that tells her which breast she's pumped from most recently. It was only just before she got on the train but she's doesn't trust her memory for such things at the moment.

'Shit,' she says before she can stop herself as she sees that she has more than 400 notifications to attend to on her Instagram.

'You all right?' Amanda plonks herself in the chair next to Erin as Bobby's fingers pincer at her shirt.

'Yeh,' Erin says, 'just, you know, stuff to do.' She puts her phone face down on the table, squeezes each breast to see which is fullest before pulling her top up and shoving her baby towards her nipple. Amanda leans forward and watches more closely than seems appropriate, as Bobby latches onto Erin's nipple like a cartoon vampire.

'You must be so relieved,' Amanda says.

'What's that?' Erin voice catches, her spit tastes acrid. She needs her bottle of water from her bag.

'It's the first time you've left him?' Erin nods. 'Sometimes they can be a bit fussy, doctors call it nipple confusion but I think babies are cleverer than that. I think it's their way of saying "I don't want those toxic-chemical plastic bottles, I like my milk straight from the udder", but he's doing fine. Beautiful boy.' She squeezes the pudge that sits above his elbow. Erin gives her a wary smile.

'Could you get me my water, babe?' she says to Raf.

'I'll go.' Amanda hops up from her seat and heads over to the discarded bag by the door. Erin feels ambushed by this woman's presence. She almost wishes Bobby would tussle away from her nipple, distracted by the light and the hubbub, so she could make her excuses and take him to his room to start tackling the Everest of Insta-messages she knows she'll have to deal with into the night. She won't be going on another phone-free weekend, she thinks to herself, regardless of which ex-model turned mixologist is making the cocktails.

'Amanda,' Raf says, as he plucks their plates up from the table, 'had been emailing my old address for years, the stupid "phoneypony" one from back in the day.'

'We used to be close,' Amanda says, a sudden thinness to her voice.

'From when we had to move up to the north for a bit,' Raf offers from where he stands in the low lights of the kitchen. 'I will have mentioned Amanda and her mum, Ez, when I gave you the director's cut of my nomadic teenage years but there was quite a bit of data to take in, Mand, so don't be offended if she's forgotten.'

'Yeh, a lot,' Erin says, summoning a laugh.

'Formative years though,' Amanda says, handing Erin her bottle of water. When was it Raf moved north? Erin thinks. His dad was a doctor who worked at universities so they lived all over Australia, and although she knows the various places he lived, she's never quite got a handle on when he was where. Amanda sweeps crumbs from the table into her hand and goes over to deposit them in the bin that she doesn't have to ask Raf the location of. She wears a string of thick brown beads as a belt over her beige dress. With her bare feet and her hair falling in copper waves far beyond her shoulders, she reminds Erin of a goddess depicted on a ceramic pot.

'Do you still live in Australia?' Bobby comes on and off Erin's nipple, pulling it painfully as he does. She rests her hand on the back of her phone, a ticker-tape machine running in her head as she thinks of all the things on there she'll have to catch up on.

'I do. I mean, I did. It's – it's actually this –' she goes over to the far corner of the living room and indicates a painting with open hands as if presenting a magic trick – 'that brought me here. Someone I worked for, she's really into that social media stuff and she was showing me your Instagram and I saw this.' Erin looks over Amanda's shoulder at the painting. It's a shrouded figure sitting among orange-red rocks with a vivid pink sky behind her. Erin's never liked it, but Raf wanted it up, it added some colour to a dark recess of the room and, crucially, it didn't cost them anything. 'I recognised it from Raf's dad's house, used to be in the dining room?'

'Mm-hum,' Raf mumbles in affirmation. Erin glances over to him leaning against the kitchen work surface. She knows he's had the painting for a while but she didn't know it belonged to his dad and is a little surprised that he'd want something of his father's up in their house. Perhaps even someone with an unhappy childhood wants little mementoes of it in their adult life. Amanda comes and sits back down next to Erin. 'So then I saw pictures of this little beauty.' She tussles Bobby's thick hair, 'and with Mercury in retrograde, I knew it was a sign.' She flicks her full eyebrows up and 'hahs' a chuckle to herself.

'Amazing,' Erin says, trying to catch Raf's eye but not wanting to seem rude.

'I was going to message you, on the app, to get in touch, set up a visit, but it felt like if I didn't just book a flight and do it then I might chicken out.' Bobby comes off Erin's nipple and then lurches back on, fledgling teeth pinching the skin, making her want to grab him off her and put him on the floor.

'Amanda's going to stay in the garden,' Raf says.

'Only if that's OK.'

'Course,' Erin says with fabricated gusto. She glances out the window above the sink at the anthracite-grey and glass studio flat that takes up the furthest portion of their narrow garden.

'I've got the name of a B&B in town that looks nice so I'm super happy to go there. I didn't expect you to have space for me.'

'No, no, it's fine,' Erin says, Amanda interrogating her with swift eyes to check she's really as welcome as they've said she is.

'That's the sweetest thing,' Amanda says, squeezing Erin's wrist. 'I've wanted to see Europe for years but, you know, big scary world, thought I'd start myself off visiting a friendly face.' She gives a little shrug before cocking her head to look at Bobby from a different angle, a faraway smile on her face.

Erin looks into Bobby's eyes, Raf's Italian heritage show-ing in the deep brown of them, and wishes she could feel as misty-eyed when she looks at him as their new guest seems to.

'I've got something for you!' Amanda blurts out, clapping a hand to her throat, excited like a child. If she and Raf grew up together, Erin thinks, she must be a few years older than her, but with her Disney-princess eyes and girlish clothes she seems younger. She skips past the table and out the sliding doors towards the studio.

Raf comes and leans over Erin to give Bobby a kiss on the top of the head.

'Hello, mate,' he says. He pulls back and puts his hands on Erin's shoulders and squeezes. 'She won't stay long,' he says. Erin flips her phone over and looks at the screen, ripe with hundreds of notifications. 'You don't mind, do you?'

'No, it's fine,' she says, fighting the urge to dive onto Instagram. Since she's got into the tens of thousands of followers, responding to all the messages has become overwhelming and she won't be able to sleep unless she's made inroads, but she knows how upset Raf will be if she goes on so soon after getting home.

'Mercury in retrograde. You got the tiniest clue what that's meant to mean?' Raf says. She gets distracted by the sight of another message arriving. 'Ez?'

'Sorry, what?' she says, placing her free hand on his and craning her neck round to look into his perma-stubbled face.

'You must be tired after all that partying.' Raf huffs out a sigh as he takes his hands away from her shoulders. The sliding door clicks open and Amanda comes to the other side of the table and faces them like a candidate for an interview. From an embroidered bag covered in Chinese symbols she produces a large pink crystal and places it on the table in front of them.

'Rose quartz,' Amanda says, making it sound like the name of a person. It's the colour of coffee cups in trendy cafes, millennial pink they've started calling it, but translucent. It's formed of two columns, alongside each other, like twin towers, that grow out of a mass the shape of a large bread roll. Erin looks over to the shelving unit by the entrance to the room, immediately thinking about where to put it. There's a stack of books with pinkish spines and a speckle-glazed pot in a similar shade – one of the many primo charity-shop buys that make up her Insta-adequate interior. Although maybe the stone should go somewhere less prominent – she might not want someone seeing it in the background of one of her Insta-stories and making a thing of how she's into crystals. These are the things she has to think about now. 'It has a very feminine energy.' Amanda runs a finger around the base. 'It opens the heart chakra and I just thought, with your whole positivity thing … Anyway, it's for you.' Amanda glances at Raf and looks down, embarrassed. Raf rests two fingers on the large vertebra at the top of Erin's spine. It makes her feel anchored for the first time since she saw Amanda through the window.

'I love it,' Erin finds herself saying, feeling bad that she and Raf have given Amanda the sort of reaction to her talk of crystals and energy that's popped her former bubbliness, 'you really shouldn't have because you've come all this way to visit, but I love it.' Amanda's eyes spark again, pleased. There's a nervous energy to her, like a skittish animal.

Bobby reaches over to the crystal but he overbalances out of Erin's arms and knocks his head on the edge of table. He erupts into a wall-shaking scream as Erin, infected by panic, tries to juggle him back to the safety of her chest. He arches away from her and it seems as if she might drop him before Raf swoops in and takes the baby from her. He jigs the inconsolable Bobby over to the mantelpiece and lowers the boy's eyes towards the tendrils of a spider plant that he swishes around with his elbow. Bobby's quickly distracted and the cries disappear as suddenly as they arrived.

Erin stands paralysed, riven with her own ineffectiveness, a hurricane of self-flagellation beating at the doors in her head, attempting to blow in. She's been feeling more connected to Bobby recently, not as much as she pretends, but better, and now she's abandoned him and undone all that progress. Amanda has gone to the kitchen and arrives over at the mantelpiece clutching a bag of frozen edamame beans. Raf tries to put the bag on the baby's head but it riles him so Raf hands it back. Erin watches as he murmurs his thanks as if he were a surgeon in a hundred-year-old war and Amanda his Florence Nightingale. She turns and sees Erin staring at her.

'You must want to catch up, find out how the little one's been coping.' She weaves her neck in the air, halfway between a dance and a stretch. 'The first time you leave a baby can be incredibly unsettling.' Erin fingers the spires of the crystal on the table. Amanda swishes the door into the garden open. She's about to walk out into the darkness when she turns round, her angular face breaking into a beatific smile.

'I can't wait to get to know you all properly,' she says, eyes dropping towards Bobby's head then up to Raf. 'It's been too long.' She sweeps out of the room, sliding the door shut behind her and walks towards the studio in the garden, the lanterns on the pathway lighting up one by one as she passes them.

4

14 October 1998

I talked to him today. I found him in the art department. He told me to call him Donny.

He started at school about six weeks ago and has smiled at me in the hall four times since. Each one more nourished with meaning than the last. On Monday, we saw each other in the corridor that runs parallel with where the principal's office is, and he didn't smile. He didn't blink. His face did nothing. I know now it was an invitation.

He told me about a trip he'd gone on with his dad to Kakudu Park to see the Nourlangie cave paintings. He talked about the Lightning Man and his wife and how inspiring he'd found it. He showed me a sketch he'd done while he was there. A huge figure of a woman and a smaller man figure, their skeletons visible, with a crowd of smaller figures below them. He said he found it incredible that these primal people still celebrated the union of two souls over the unconnected rabble below them. The woman the goddess, the man her protector, her devotee.

Then the bell rang and the spell was broken, but I believe something commenced today. I could feel something vibrating between us. Something small. Something precious. An energy that felt almost divine.

5

'She got our address from Lydia's daughter Anya,' Raf says from their en suite bathroom. Erin's perched on the end of their bed, stress fluttering in her chest as she scrolls through the seemingly never-ending list of notifications. A mum asking for advice of which mindfulness app to use, another asking where she gets her fake plants from, a few trolls, a few people telling her how beautiful they think she is. What's become, since she got into Instagram less than a year ago, the usual. 'She said she called her to ask last week and Anya just gave it up to her,' he says as he squeezes through the narrow bathroom doorway, drying his face on a towel. Erin hums to herself, pleased. Carly Reagan (113k followers) has liked the selfie she took on the train that she posted when she got back on Wi-Fi seconds before she saw them all through the front window.

Raf knocks into the chest of drawers and a tube of something clatters off it. Erin glances up to see him making his way towards her, craning his neck under the sheer eaves of the room. Raf's six foot three so the attic room feels tiny when he's stood up in it. When they moved down to the seaside from Croydon, Erin imagined they'd be able to afford a roomy three-bed but, with her not having a salary and Raf's earnings as a graphic designer, decent enough to live on but not consistent enough for the tastes of mortgage providers, this converted bungalow was the most they could extend to. Two bedrooms, theirs in the attic and Bobby's just off the open-plan ground floor.

Raf sits down next to her and puts his hands over hers, over her phone.

'Please can I look at these?' she says.

'You've had the whole train journey.'

'Had to leave our sim cards at home for this stupid "detox" and the train Wi-Fi wasn't working.' She slides her hands out of his. A comment on her post from one of her regular communicators, Florri-Bourne, grabs her attention – *You CANNOT be hungover. You look incred.* She has to put her tongue on the roof of her mouth to stop herself smiling. Raf, wearing nothing but a pair of running shorts, coils his sinewy arms over each other in his lap, eyes down, radiating his being ignored, so Erin slides her phone face down onto the bed's coverlet.

'Amanda seems nice.'

'Yeh,' he says, his tone a shrug almost.

'You don't seem very excited to see her.'

Raf puts his hands behind him and spreads them backwards onto the bed.

'I don't know. She was my dad's friends' daughter. We got on pretty well but we didn't even know each other for that long. After I left Oz, I didn't give her much thought to be honest. She was a lonely kid, didn't get on with her stepdad. I probably should have stayed in touch, a letter or something. But, you know, halfway across the world, trying to get over the fallout of the stuff with Dad. It's just one of those things.' Raf doesn't talk much about his life back home and Erin's had to come to accept it. His father was a serial philanderer and it ground his mum down so much that, when Raf was eleven, she ran away from the family. So he was raised by his dad who, ostensibly, made little effort to hide how much he resented the task. A few years later, it emerged that his father was having a relationship with an undergraduate student. The girl's parents found out and the ensuing scandal got so combustible that Raf was sent to England where his dad's old colleague Lydia kept an eye on him. Raf told Erin the whole story one deep and meaningful night soon after they got together, but in the following four years, the subject has never really come up. And with her conventional upbringing in the suburbs of London she doesn't feel she has the right to drag him through what sounded like a traumatic childhood.

'She's very – I don't know – more open than I'm used to. Not very British.'

'No,' he says, a laugh in his voice.

'Lovely though,' Erin says. 'Bit oogly-boogly maybe? With the crystal and stuff.'

'Fair to say she had that in her locker when she was a teenager.'

'And an interesting outfit for January.' Erin expects Raf to laugh with her but he doesn't. 'Suits her though. She's in great shape – yoga I bet. There's this "five-minute stretchify" hashtag that's going around. I should probably get on it.'

'Yeh, for sure,' he says, reaching his arms out until his right hand rests next to her bum. It's meant to be affectionate but it only makes Erin aware that her bum spreads now in a way it never did before she had Bobby. She looks at her upper arm in her vest top, not fat but the flesh is looser, less toned than it used to be. Amanda's arms look like the cables of a lift.

'I don't know. Doesn't feel like what we need at the moment,' Raf says, his fingers moving up onto Erin's hip, 'her turning up. For you, it's not fair on you at all.'

'What does that mean?'

'You know, with Bobby.'

'What are you trying to say?' Heat has poured into her throat. It feels like he sometimes says things like this just to provoke her. She shifts herself away from him, dragging her phone into her pyjama pocket.

'You know, you're not –' He hesitates, trying to find the operative phrase, the one that won't prick the balloon that's barely containing her anger. 'You're still trying to get your head around Bob.' She shoots him a glare of disbelief before jolting off the bed to the corner of the room where she rifles through a pile of cardboard boxes until she pulls out a heavy obsidian pot of 'Night Cream enriched with Seaweed and Carbon Chips' and heads into the bathroom. Although all the free make-up and baby gadgets she's been sent since passing the 30k follower threshold don't help much when she's trying to stretch her weekly budget at the supermarket, she's loved using premium products again, and spreading the thick blue cream onto her cheeks has the desired effect of cooling her annoyance at Raf's suffocating concern for her mental well-being.

About a month before her due date, while sat on a bench on the seafront glancing through tabloid red-carpet shots of a girl, Kara, she'd been friends with at drama school, Erin was hit with the sledgehammer of her impending motherhood and it shook her out of what she now realises was intense denial. It felt like someone had twisted the focus on the lens of a camera and she could look at her life with absolute

clarity. She was thirty-three. She had no semblance of an acting career. She'd been bailed out of crippling credit card debt
by her fiancé and, with no job in their new town and thus
no maternity pay, was now reliant on him for money. She ran
her finger down the list of her life choices and found them
all wanting. Going to university before drama school so that
by the time she emerged she was not only saddled with two
lots of student debt but also twenty-five and too old to play
the ingénue roles that were the only ones going for new
graduates. Trying to keep up with a group of girlfriends with
tastes so extravagant they stretched even their corporate pay
packets. The last-minute holiday to Ireland she agreed to go
on that led to her missing the chance to step in to play the
lead in a low-budget movie that went on to be an indie hit
and a huge launch pad for a girl called Rhia Trevellick, who
looked great but was nowhere near as good an actor as Erin.
And then moving down here for a simpler life, crucially, a
financially less demanding life, the sort of settled provincial
life that she'd never ever wanted. And, as she sat hyperventi-
lating on that bench, these crushing epiphanies brought on
a panic attack. She was certain it was her heart and she was
dying so she called an ambulance and was rushed to A&E.

After Raf had brought her home from the hospital, he
told her that all of her feelings, all her fears were completely
normal. Big life events like having a child often held up a
mirror to where you wanted to be in your life and he didn't
think anyone felt like they had everything sorted. He didn't,
he said. But he was happy, he said. He was excited for their
future, he said. No one ever feels ready to have kids, he said.
But it feels like from the moment he saw her, pale and drawn
on the hospital bed, he's treated her like this, like a Victorian

invalid who has to be cossetted and worried over and she finds it exasperating.

Raf clears his throat. She hears him go over to the boxes to tidy up the mess she's made with her rifling. She gets her phone out and sees that, as a result of Carly's like, an additional forty or so people have followed her just in the past couple of minutes. Bar the hashtags, it wasn't even a good post. She needs to work harder, she thinks, every post has to be as funny, as relatable, as shareable as possible. She's on the crest of something, she can feel it. She can't get distracted now, a few bad posts could be enough to undo all her hard work.

She hears singing coming from their garden and glances out the small Velux window at the studio. A sliver of light shows through a gap in the blinds that obscure the world from the glass-fronted box. She reaches over and clicks the window open to listen. It could be Joni Mitchell, high and haunting. Amanda is singing. As she was when Erin first saw her through the window holding her son. She blinks and an eyelash catches a clot of cream getting some of it in her eye. Erin goes back to the sink and rinses her face with cold water.

Raf appears in the door frame and stops for a moment, one eye squinted in the direction of the window. They listen to Amanda for a moment, neither breathing for a good few seconds, but the sound of Bobby coughing through the monitor snaps them back into the room. Raf notices the Instagram app open on her phone in her hand and huffs back into the bedroom. She looks down at the plughole in the sink, sees a coil of her hair in the depths. Her breathing shallowing as the air raid of Bobby's crying begins to wind up. He's awake. Three hours, he never sleeps for a longer spell. It's beyond exhausting. She hears Raf grabbing his dressing gown off the back of the door and leaving, the floorboards of the stairs playing their three-note melody as he descends.

A sharp spike of cold rushes into the room. She looks out the window again and sees a shadow moving behind the garden studio's blinds. Goosebumps spear up on Erin's skin and she clunks the window closed, the singing snuffed out like a church candle.

She settles herself into bed and switches off the light. Ten past ten. Bobby's first feed of the day is 4 a.m. so she's normally asleep much earlier than this. She listens to see if he's still screaming down in his room but she can't hear him. Raf sleeps down there most of the time so she can sleep undisturbed. She misses having him next to her, his pepper-scent, playing her fingers over the network of veins on his arms that stand out so clearly that she can see her thumbnail stopping the blood flowing around his body.

Erin switches the white-noise machine on. A facsimile of a hairdryer fills the room though she can still make out the sound of Amanda's singing. But the window's closed. The tune must have got stuck in her head. She closes her eyes and pictures Amanda, cross-legged on the pulled-out sofa bed, eyes closed, singing. Her dress now a brilliant white tunic, a crown of shells in her hair. Erin smiles to herself.

Her mum always used to say that when you're a parent of young kids, it's best to have people around as much as possible because it forces you, the parents, to be nice to each other. Perhaps Amanda's presence, her self-possession, her Zen-calm, will bring a counter-melody into their house that will bring Erin and Raf's relationship back to some kind of harmony. With a guest around, she might be a bit more judicious with her phone use, something she knows he's really struggling with. Perhaps having Amanda here will force them to inject some brio into their everyday interactions and sharpen some of the flatness that Raf seems to have projected towards her since Bobby was born. He didn't seem flat tonight. He seemed heightened, on point.

Erin's exhausted. She's been thinking about putting her head to this pillow, of being alone in her bed, since she dragged herself out from under the embrace of the faux-fur coverlet inside her yurt this morning. But she can feel the buzz behind her eyes. The flickering LED dots in her head of all those unanswered messages, all those people demanding she engage with them. She pulls her phone up out of the covers from where it was, clenched in her hand next to her collarbone, sits up against the headboard and sparks it into life.

6

Bobby sneezes and two thick trails of snot spurt out of his nose with such alacrity that the shock makes him burst into tears. Erin apologises to a mum she's talking to whose name she can't remember, gets down on her knees and hoists Bobby up from the gym matting into her arms. She wanders away from the people she'd just been telling about her digital detox retreat over to her stuff. She roots around the compartment under her #gifted buggy but she can't find any tissues. How can she never remember something as fundamental as tissues? She looks over to a circle of bearded dads, a number of whom she knows to say hello to, and wills one of them to sense her plight and come and help, but they're too busy laughing at their toddlers scrapping in front of them like tiny gladiators.

She glances around the church hall, polystyrene ceiling tiles and walls of corkboards laden with colourful flyers for colourful church events. Bobby's mewling is obviously not drilling into anyone else's temples because no one seems to have noticed. Abi, a ruddy-cheeked local mum who lives up near the library, glances at Erin, widens her eyes in sympathy before turning back to a lady who resembles a pumped-up Dolly Parton whose legs two toddlers seem to be trying to topple like Samson in the temple. This group used to be one

or two grannies on childcare duty and a dozen or so beleaguered local mothers, but since Erin posted about it a month
or two ago it's become almost unbearably busy with most
of the former attendants crowded out by a flood of down-
from-London migrants and their exotically named children.

The old dear, Megan, who helps out at the group, arrives at
her shoulder with a huge box of tissues. Erin wipes Bobby's
nose despite him trying to dodge the tissue like an amateur
boxer, but as she goes again to pinch a rogue trail that she
missed before, she clunks the back of his head with her wrist.
He arches his body. There's a moment of deafening silence
before he erupts into an indignant scream. Erin swallows and
holds her eyelids shut hard for a moment as heat flushes all
over her skin.

When she opens her eyes it feels like the whole room is
now looking at her. She summons a wide smile and gives
eye-rolls to anyone who makes direct eye contact with her.
She notices Sophie Delauney (6.4k followers), a heroin-chic
twenty-eight-year-old singer with eighteen-month-old Abel
and a tiny beach-ball pregnant belly, standing with her gaggle of music-scene friends. One of them, Kristina, glances
over at her. Erin puts Bobby up in front of her, tries to make
him dance his legs around, just as Amanda did yesterday, but
the screams don't abate. She mimes pulling the trigger of
an imaginary gun at her temple for anyone still watching.
Kristina grimaces; another mum, Amina maybe, wrinkles her
brow in disgust, making Erin instantly regret the gesture.

She cradles Bobby into her and makes a shhing, soothing
sound, but she may as well be singing the cucaracha to the
boy for all the difference this show of mothering ever makes
with him. Bobby screamed when he first came into the world

and it feels like he hasn't stopped since. Erin's convinced he doesn't like her. And sometimes, particularly times like this when she just can't seem to stem the flow of his anguish, she's not sure how much she likes him. Something for which she wears a near-constant millstone of guilt around her neck. He's her baby, she loves him, she's meant to love him. But it's not easy to love a wailing ball of rage.

Glowing red filament heaters rain artificial heat down on the hall. She wishes her friend Caz was here. Caz used to come to this group with her before it became a cool 'hangout'. Caz would just whisk Bobby out of the room and somehow bring him back calm. Caz has a son a couple of years older than her daughter Imogen so Caz knows how to be a mother.

Erin decides to do what her friend would do. She grits her teeth as she forces the bucking Bobby into the straps of his buggy. As the screaming carriage parts the Red Sea of people on its journey towards the exit, every parent turns and gives Erin a look of commiserative support. She responds to them with comical eyebrows, apologetic waves at not having had a chance to catch up, an ironic thumbs up. To them she's breezy, chilled out about Bobby screaming, nailing it, for those that follow her Instagram, very much on brand. They have no idea that, now she's outside on her own in a battery of cold air and the boy's shrieks are even louder than before, if someone offered her a flight to the other side of the world right now, she might just hand Bobby to Raf and get a cab to the airport.

She pushes the buggy down the road towards the sea. Clouds sit low in the sky and the air, pregnant with the threat of rain, clenches around her like a cold hand. Erin tries to take her mind to a place of Zen as Bobby's cries become gurgled up with the phlegm he never seems to be able to shift. Has he got enough clothes on? she thinks. Is this my fault? Do I take him out too much? It's fucking January by the sea. I'm such a selfish bitch, she thinks. She's doing the calming breathing she got off a YouTube video someone posted in her comments but it's having the opposite effect and she feels near hyperventilation and she's reminded of her panic attack. No, she thinks to herself, I'm fine, Bobby's just hard, it's teeth, it's reflux, it's a phase, this isn't me, there's nothing wrong with me. She looks through the clear window in the buggy's hood. Bobby's little round head is beetroot-coloured and he's thrown his blanket off.

She gets to the promenade, having to shove the right-hand wheel of the buggy hard over a protruding mound of concrete from where someone has driven into a metal bollard, and the jolt, or it could be the sea view, seems to calm Bobby momentarily.

She glances over at the greasy spoon cafe to her left populated by the blue-rinse brigade. The stinking wheelie bin dedicated to dogshit that stands by the steps to the beach. The middle-aged man giving his crumbling beach hut a coat of brown paint. She puts her hand on her phone in her coat pocket. She could do something for her stories. Talk about how challenging Bobby's being, talk about how when he screams it makes her insides feel like they've been thrown into a deep-fat fryer. She could weep into the collar of her coat. But she won't. Grace Fentiman, an influencer's agent she's been talking to, said that her sunny, funny tales of new motherhood by the seaside are exactly what the world needs right now. The sky is grey, the sea is grey, the air is heavy with the stench of rotting seaweed. Sunny, funny.

Bobby rears up his footmuff and coughs out the beginnings of a new bout of crying. Erin pushes the buggy roughly to the right, onto the small bridge that goes over an inlet. Machine-gun bursts of agony still. Maybe his underdeveloped digestive system isn't coping with the feed she gave him forty minutes ago, but even though she knows it's wrong, Erin can't help but blame Bobby for how insane his screams make her feel. Her phone is in her hand now. She scrolls through Instagram. Unreal sunlight of people on holiday, the elegant tones of magazine-worthy interiors, minimalist plates of work-of-art food.

In the distance she sees a woman she knows, Lorna Morgan, walking along the promenade towards them with her mothership double buggy and accompanied by her daughter, Clara, bedecked in head-to-toe hot pink, on a Barbie-pink scooter. Lorna, the twins and their older sister are all identical. Very pink skin. The same length straw-blonde hair. Their shoulders go straight into their heads and whenever Erin sees them all together she has to try very hard not to think of Tennessee Williams's description of children – no-necked monsters.

Erin hides her phone under the buggy's handle as they approach and puts on a blank expression, a hint of a lazy smile even, as if her son's screams are water off a duck's back. As they pass, Lorna creases her face at Erin in some pretence of concern. Erin smiles and walks on. Erin's pretty sure Lorna doesn't like her much, but at this moment in time, she's struggling to care about it.

Thirty seconds onwards she pulls the buggy's cover back. Bobby's face almost fluorescent, more and more mucus sludging out of his face. She looks around her before shaking the buggy, hoping to surprise him into silence. Another howl.

Stress billows around her head like someone's set off a flare. Erin swallows, looks round to see Lorna heading away, far in the distance. She darts her eyes around the beach to see if anyone's looking before picking up the pace, driving the buggy uphill onto a grassy mound, the fronts of her shoes slipping slightly in the mud. She pockets her phone. Both hands on the buggy. Bobby splutters, the cries going to a higher register, more strained now but just as forceful. Her head feels like it's going to burst. She shakes the buggy again. More screaming. Shakes it again with such ferocity she almost lifts it off the ground.

She stops. Comes round to face Bobby, kneels down on the wet ground and tries to get her hands round her baby to pull him out. But he's still strapped in. She attempts to twist him around his restraints but he buckles in the opposite direction.

'Fuck,' she intones up to the darkening sky. Then someone's there. A burgundy flash comes between her and the buggy.

'Have a breather. There you go, lovely boy.' Erin blinks round to see Amanda clicking Bobby out of the buggy and into her arms. She wraps her maroon coat around the boy, who's arching his back away from her like Alien trying to burst out of her body. Erin wheels away towards the sea, does exactly as she's told and takes a moment. In the periphery she can hear Bobby ramping down a little, bursts of pained crying becoming further apart. Erin presses the tips of her fingers into her eye sockets but her skin is still vibrating as the stress courses out into the air.

A black dog races across her eyeline on the beach. She turns back to Amanda who's wearing tight yoga pants and trainers under her coat. She's dipping her head behind the collar of her coat, playing a game of peekaboo that's confusing Bobby into calm.

'You OK?' Amanda asks as Erin returns.

'Fine now, thanks.' Erin's embarrassed, not sure how much Amanda saw. There's warmth in her eyes so hopefully she came along at the end and didn't see her shaking the buggy. Erin offers her hands to take Bobby back.

'It's OK,' Amanda says, pulling Bobby towards her, going in for a mock bite on his neck. 'Sometimes you need someone else to take over for a minute. That sort of screeching, it's so much worse for the mums. It's evolutionary. Like a bolt of lightning. Meant to make sure mum stops everything she's doing to help baby.' Erin thinks of herself scrolling through Instagram, trying to numb herself to her baby's screams. Guilt pinions her deep in the gut. 'When we were back in caves though, poor mums had all the other women around to help out when it got too much. Not having to deal with little demons like you, all on their own.' She nuzzles into Bobby's nose as she says this to him. 'Your mumma needs a break I'd say.'

'I'm fine,' she says and Amanda nods, examines her, seeming to look at the space around her, weaving her head in the air like a dancing python.

'I know,' Amanda says to the boy, with enough meaning for Erin to think that perhaps she saw a bit more than she thought. Rain starts to dot Amanda's coat. 'Shall we head back?' she says, taking control.

Erin clenches her hands, feels nails press into flesh as she and Amanda walk past the three newly built houses where builders call to each other under a flapping blue tarpaulin. She's lost her temper before with Bobby. She's never done anything that would hurt him. But being caught at that level of chaos, that pitch where you've lost control of what's considered normal, civil, with your own child, is chilling to experience. Like someone listening in on your darkest thoughts.

'Are you doing anything for you?' Amanda asks.

'What do you mean?'

'Acupuncture, meditating, yoga, a hot bath even.'

Erin smiles. 'No time. Nice idea though.'

'You'll be amazed how much more you'll appreciate him if you've had a break.' Erin clunks the empty buggy up the kerb and onto the pavement of her road, Bobby still cocooned inside Amanda's coat.

'Do you have kids?' Erin asks. She assumed she doesn't because she's here on her own, but perhaps they're at home with her husband or ex-husband.

'I was a teaching assistant for a while, been a childminder for years, babysitting as well. Even the hardest kids I've had, the real pain-in-the-posterior ones, once you've had some time away from them, you realise they've always got their hooks in you, energetically speaking. It's only when you see them again, you feel how much you've missed them, how much you need them.' Amanda's gooey eyes are fixed on Bobby. Her words make Erin wonder whether there's something wrong with her because she didn't feel a surge of gladness when she was handed her baby last night. When she looked down at his closed eyes as he fed first thing this morning it didn't feel like he had his energetic hooks in her, it didn't feel like there was anything between them. But he's chained to her, stuck with her poor boy. 'Anyway, it's just a thought. What do I know?' Amanda says as Bobby places a hand on her freckled cheek. A lot more than I do, Erin thinks.

She clicks the brake of the buggy and goes to open her front door. Amanda flicks her rain-darkened hair into Bobby's face and it looks like he might actually be enjoying it. Erin's phone buzzes in her pocket. The long vibration of an email. Something lights up in her at the thought of some news, something tantalising from the outside world and Amanda catches it. She looks at the baby and back at Erin then she bursts into a beaming smile, eyes moistening. Erin swallows spit, ashamed, because she was excited to get an email and Amanda thought the three of them were having a moment.

7

22 October 1998

Had the shock of my life this afternoon. I came home from school and there, in my kitchen, sipping on a glass of ice water, was Donny. He was wearing overalls that were spattered with lilac paint.

He said he'd been going house-to-house offering to do a little decorating on the cheap and Mum had said that the front fence needed a going over. I asked him if he knew I lived here and, although he said no, I think he kind of did. A few days ago he said he needed to see me outside of school, but I knew, with Craig being like he is, that might be difficult for us, so now he's here. It's so romantic.

When Mum came back in from the garden, I went straight upstairs to do my homework because I was sure I wouldn't be able to hide the connection that's growing between us. It feels so strong, so intense, even though Mum's not exactly the most switched on in terms of reading energies, I just know she'd sense it. But I watched him from my room. He painted the fence with meticulous strokes, took time over it, prepared his tools before moving to each section. He didn't look up at my window, not once, even though he must have known I was there. Not until Craig came back from work, and when he glanced up at me watching down, Donny's eyes followed and we looked at each other for a second before I ducked into the shadows of my room. I expected Craig to tell him to go home but, I don't know how Donny did it, he must have told him a joke or something, which he never does with me, because Craig looked like he didn't mind him. And when Craig saw how good a job Donny had done on the fence, he seemed happier than I've seen him for ages, which is still barely smiling, but still.

Since he moved in with me and my mum two years ago, Craig's always warned me off boys, told me I'm too young, that they're all out for the same thing. But Donny isn't like that. Craig hasn't got the capacity to understand the purity of what's developing between him and me. But seeing the two of them together in the yard, Craig not telling him to 'piss off' instantly, gives me hope that one day, maybe, we can let our devotion to each other shine out in the open.

8

'He OK?' Erin peeps over the beautifully ornate wrap-scarf that's tying her baby boy into Amanda's chest.

'He's watching the world go by. Go walk over there.' Amanda shoos Erin off with a schoolmistressy finger-point. Erin accepts her mock castigation with a smile and almost skips over a rock to walk closer to the shoreline. Amanda found Erin after Bobby's nap and almost forced her to come out for a walk on the beach. It's not that she didn't want to go, but wearing Bobby in their structured sling for any longer than five minutes gives Erin the shooting hip pain she's had ever since giving birth to the huge-headed little man. She also didn't fancy spending an hour pretending she was chill while Bobby clambered and scratched at her trying to get out, which was his current mood when it came to being in any form of transport apart from her arms. So Amanda offered to take him. She went to the studio to grab a scarf she had and, like an illusionist doing some kind of disappearing act, wrapped Bobby onto her front and they set off.

Erin skips up onto a little clump of rocks and hops down onto the wet sand. She half jumps and walks backwards, sees the moment her footprints change direction as if two different people have walked towards each other and embraced.

'Having fun?' Amanda calls over to her from up near the cliff where she's more sheltered from the wind.

'I cannot tell you!' Erin says as she turns round and walk-jogs towards Amanda, falling in step with her fast pace. 'A walk, with another adult, not having, you know, that weight on me. This is better than sex!' Amanda smiles but there's a hint of an embarrassed blush that reminds Erin she probably doesn't know Amanda quite well enough for that sort of comment. She could be religious.

'I'm amazed you and your mates aren't out here all the time. What a place to bring up a bubba.'

'It's always talked about but never really happens.'

'I'd have thought everyone would want to go for a walk with a famous Insta-mumma – that is what it's called?'

'Insta-mum, usually. I don't know, it's – I don't hang out with my followers, that's not how it is.' Erin hears a note of sadness in her voice. She probably knows north of fifty mums locally and there are many, many more that know who she is, she can tell by the way they look at her, but she still wouldn't really call any of them friends, apart from Caz, and they met the old-fashioned way. 'And he – he can be so hard. I find it more stressful being with people when he's kicking off, you know, them seeing me, not calm.' Amanda gives her a sympathetic smile, this morning on the grassy bank implicit in her words. Amanda was wonderful when she stepped in to help and hasn't mentioned it since, no judgement. Seeing so much of other people's approaches to motherhood through the window of social media, Erin has started to forget that there are people in existence who don't judge.

'Have you not got family close?' Amanda asks, Bobby reaching an arm out of the sling and leaning on it so he looks like a Lothario cruising for girls in his soft top. He is cute, crazy cute. Those dark, dark eyes, all that hair, tiny Kirk Douglas dimple in his chin. All Raf, Erin sees none of herself in her baby boy, maybe it would be easier to forgive him for his screams, for his need, for his desperation if she could.

'My mum's in Croydon, my brother lives in west London.'

'Is that far? London's not too bad, is it?'

'Not too far. But we're not that close any more. Mum really didn't want me to move away, and Alex, my brother, he and I have drifted apart.'

'That's so sad.'

'He's quite down the line, you know? Good job, capable wife, perfect kids. He's happy with how everything's turned out and I get the impression that he and Beth, his wife, find me a source of unnecessary drama.'

'You are an actress.'

'Exactly. Beth's very, partner in a law firm, power suits, you know, "lean in", that sort. Probably thinks I'm a bit of a joke.'

'No!'

'Anyway, it was getting me down, and Raf, level-headed as always, said that it would be best to accept that we were in different places in our lives, so we made the decision to just –' Erin makes a cutting action in the air.

'And with your mum?'

'I think she thought I'd live a five-minute walk away from her forever. For months after we moved, every time I rang she'd make me feel so awful and, I don't know, her and Raf, she's always been pretty rude to him.'

'Really?'

'She has this thing about Australian men, thinks they're all machismo.'

'Couldn't be less like Raf.'

'I know. She never made much effort to get to know him and, he never mentioned it, but I know it bothered him, so I stopped ringing and she was far too proud to be the one to reach out. Makes me sound stubborn.'

'Not at all.'

'I was always an obedient little girl, teacher's pet, those roles from when we're kids, we're expected to be like that forever. Families! Fuck.'

'It won't be forever. These bonds we have, especially ones from when we were kids, they don't just end. They're part of us, they develop in our genes, in our DNA. All of you are still connected here.' She touches her heart like Erin's seen yogis do and she hopes Amanda's right. Erin misses them. Her big brother's the only person that could ever really make her belly-laugh and she misses the euphoria of that. But every time she'd leave their beautiful Victorian house in Richmond after a visit, with its vast basement kitchen and its two well-adjusted if a little obnoxious children, her life choices, all those bad decisions would run around her head like a minia-ture train set for weeks afterwards. They've barely seen them since they moved to the seaside, and although Erin's mum came down to meet Bobby when he was born, she made a point of not staying and hasn't been back since. She used to be supportive of anything Erin did but she couldn't under-stand why they were moving away, just at the time that they might need her help, and because it was Raf's idea to move, she's childishly taken it as Erin choosing him over her. And with everything going on in Erin's head, the constant shame she feels for still not loving her baby enough, the financial drain she's become on Raf, no sight of a career on the other side of this year of nominal maternity leave, she just didn't have broad enough shoulders to bear her mother's disappointment as well. She's learned that sometimes you have to make difficult decisions, to end difficult relationships, just as a form of self-preservation.

'I've not spoken to my ma for nearly twenty years,' Amanda offers, eyes fixed on the horizon, 'but I still think about her every day. And I know she does me.'

'Do you have other family?' Erin asks, up near the cliff now, feeling the chalk dry-rub onto her hand as she runs it along the sheer face. Amanda leans her head to the ground slightly, only for Bobby to shove a hand up under her chin. She laughs.

'Not family, no. There's a – there's someone,' she says, smothering a sheepish grin, 'someone significant, who's come back into my life recently.'

'A boyfriend?'

'It's not –'

'Sorry, that's so nineteenth century of me. Girlfriend? Dolphin-friend? Sorry, I shouldn't even be asking. Just ignore me. I'm a nosy bitch.'

Amanda laughs at Erin's flustering. 'No, it's – it's fine. It's just there's a lot of water under the bridge, so, you know. We're taking things slowly.'

'Well, I think you've pulled a seriously flair move,' Erin says, mushing a waterlogged pebble of chalk between forefinger and thumb.

'Oh yeh?'

'Flying halfway across the world from him is the ultimate in playing hard to get.'

'Guess that's right.'

Erin stares at the side of Amanda's face, those cheekbones like cut crystal.

'I needed to leave Oz to, to know, you know?'

'Time apart, get some perspective.'

'Things between us have always been complex and I can't have that energy coming back into my life without knowing that this time things can be different.' Amanda must feel Erin staring at her because she whips her head round to her, the suggestion of a tear at the corner of her eye. She smiles it off, reaches a hand out and grabs Erin's wrist, squeezes it and then lets it go. 'It's so lovely to be here. The colours.' She thrusts her arms out wide, the action shocks Bobby and he puts his Puffa-coated arms back in within the wrap. 'It's so beautiful! I love it!' Amanda shouts out to the sky. It prompts Erin to look up at the vast blue above, makes her see the golf-course green tops of the brilliant white cliffs, and it makes her grin and throw her arms out as well and she almost, almost whoops along with Amanda. When the moment dies and their arms are back down by their sides, they both notice Bobby glaring at Erin. His unsmiling mouth seemingly more fixed in an angry pout than ever at these two women enjoying life so much when he has no intention of seeing anything positive about it. And spontaneously the two of them guffaw into laughter until it dies away and they look at each other and something passes between them, a quiet wave of mutual satisfaction at having each other in this place, in this time Erin feels a warmth spread in her stomach like she's just eaten a bowlful of stew on an icy day. And for the first time in a long, long while she feels nourished.

9

'Can you not take Bobby with you?' Grace Fentiman asks, her voice made nasal by the speaker on Erin's phone.

'To London?'

'Uh-huh.'

'Er ... ' Erin stands in front of the kitchen sink, watching thick rain obscure her view of her garden. Bobby's hit-or-miss in the buggy and trying to manage a two-hour train journey, the Underground and a sodden metropolis with him in the hip-crippling sling is an impossibility. 'He's got a chest thing, if it wasn't raining ... '

'Course.'

'Shit. This is *so* annoying.' Erin scours away a patch of mucusy sick from the top Bobby's just been wearing with scalding water. She flicks her wrist under the stream and wrinkles her nose at the pain.

'I could suggest you call in, but don't think Ally's producer would go for it. I had to do a big pitch for them to go for you.' Erin and Grace haven't yet formalised their working relationship, but when someone called the agent from Ally Thornton's MotherBoard podcast saying their guest had dropped out and they needed someone to step in, Grace had put Erin forward. Ally's a hip, young radio presenter and her guests are usually celebrities and mega-influencers, so, as

Grace has now said three times, this could be a huge thing for Erin's profile. She's called Raf a few times but he's not picking up. He's having to take freelance projects on top of his agency work to cover the mortgage so she couldn't ask him to take time off anyway.

She hears a bump and looks over to see Bobby has keeled over on the Winnie-the-Pooh blanket he's playing on. Mercifully, he's avoided the minefield of loose building blocks and doesn't seem to have hurt himself.

'What can I tell them? Their recording session's running until six.' Erin spots a figure in white emerging from the studio at the end of the garden. Amanda lifts her head to the rain, it looks like she's drinking the water. She's holding an orange bucket that Erin recognises from their garden shed.

'Give me two minutes,' Erin says to Grace. 'I'll call you back in two minutes. Less.' Erin goes to right Bobby and finds him a cuddly butterfly with various rubber and plastic appendages that he can shove into his mouth. She clicks open the door and sprints out into the downpour as she sees Amanda walking out the back gate.

'Amanda, I need the biggest favour ever,' she shouts after her, no time to dice in niceties. Amanda comes back down the alley behind their house. Erin runs under the cover of the studio's porch where their house guest joins her.

'We just don't get weather like this at home. It's New Moon, crazy low tide, it's elemental. I was going down to see what beasts came out in something like this. Crabs, oysters, muscles. I thought I could cook. You guys want to come down?' Erin creases her eyes. Amanda can't have heard her.

'Can you do me the hugestest favour ever?'

'Sure,' she says, a hint of ambiguity in her inflection.

'Can you watch him?'

'Bobby?'

'Yeh.' A globule of rainwater pools into one of Erin's eyes and she blinks it away. 'I've got to go and do a thing in London. Last minute. I'd never normally ask but it could be a pretty big work thing for me and you've worked with kids.'

'Is he on his own in there?'

'I don't mean to spring it on you.'

'We shouldn't leave him.' Amanda heads over the muddy grass towards the house as Erin stepping-stones her way across the patches of paving behind her. She glances at her phone, trying to do the sums of timings and trains and Tubes. Erin needs to either go or stay and she has minutes to decide. As they get in, Bobby swivels to see them.

'Have you spoken to Raf?' Amanda asks, going to the kitchen and drying herself with the tea towel before throwing it over to Erin.

'Not been able to get him.' Erin dries off the bottom of her hair. There'll be photos at the podcast. Ally Thornton has a black bob with a white-and-red David Bowie streak on one side of it. She always looks immaculate. Amanda blinks her long eyelashes and cocks her head to the side. 'I'll text him though. He won't mind if it's you.' Amanda looks at something in the garden and Erin can't make out her expression. She feels edgy with the need to be somewhere else, like getting stuck behind a tractor on a single-lane road. Bobby's brow creases and he grizzles at being ignored for so long. Erin picks him up and takes him to Amanda. 'It's so much to ask and I wouldn't dream of it if I didn't know how totally amazing you are with him.' Bobby reaches towards Amanda as she twists her hair into a bun. 'And look, he's sick of me anyway. Give you some time to get to know each other.'

'All right,' Amanda says, 'no worries.' She takes off her slick winter coat, letting it fall to the floor. She's in one of her tunic tops, this one a pale blue. Bobby holds his arms open to Amanda and she takes him to her chest, cuddling him like a much tinier baby. 'How can I say no to you, eh, my darling boy?' Erin smiles at them, gives Bobby an affectionate pat on the head, touches Amanda's elbow and then she's off upstairs where she tears her clothes off and tears on a new outfit, does a thirty-second make-up job, before tearing back downstairs to the hall.

She rifles through her £400 #gifted baby backpack and finds her keys, phone charger and headphones and puts them in a green glittery clutch before giving herself a moment to look in the hall mirror. The vintage trench she got from the Cancer Research shop opposite the station makes her look tall, powerful, her hair up, professional, the forest-green eyeshadow, fun-loving and it goes with the bag. For a two-minute job, it's pretty bloody good, she thinks. She grabs a wide-brimmed black hat from the shelf above the coat hook behind the door and tries it on. It looks great but in the rain could give her the appearance of a wader so she puts it back.

This feels like a step up and she's ready for it. She can still see the thin tributaries of stress that crease around her eyes through her foundation but there's more light in them than there's been for months, not the sparkles she tries to generate for her photos, this is real, shining excitement. She taps the shabby-chic hall table three times with the tips of her fingers and turns back into the living room. Amanda's stood exactly where she left her over by the sink, Bobby still cradled in her arms like a newborn. He's quiet, calm, and they're just staring at each other. Erin feels spit catch at the top of her throat and a shard of envy at the effortless calm Amanda seems to have with Bobby splices into her enthusiasm. A tiny sound, Amanda singing, humming, an ancient sound, drifts across the room. She was going to go over and give Bobby a kiss on the head, the sort of thing she's seen on a thousand television shows and films. A mother's parting gesture of love, of propriety, but she decides it's better not to upset the apple cart by making it too clear that she's leaving him.

'Good luck,' Erin says weakly. 'I'll be forever in your debt for this.'

'Happy to help,' Amanda says in a theatrical whisper, before restarting her song and turning back to Bobby.

Erin picks up an umbrella from the stand and strides out into the deluge, leaving Amanda inside clutching her baby boy.

10

BRAUNEoverBRAINS

372 posts   39.7k followers   1,377 following

ERIN BRAUNE

Mum to Bobby. Salty sea-dweller. Bright up your life. Reformed thespian.

This is my podcast pantsuit. Because we did a podcast.

ALLY THORNTON IS A DREAM. We had a hilarious chat. Well, tbh, cos Ally is so bloody good at her job it wasn't just a thrill ride up the lollercoaster. We talked how hard it was giving up acting, keeping things Zen on two hours' sleep, the anxiety that comes with getting a biblical deluge of DMs, and a whole lot of other shiz. But most importantly, we provide you with the definitive guide to what different condiment combos work best on toast and plans for our Carbicide Cookbook. SPOILER ALERT: Ally has a penchant for a rice sandwich. 😂

BUT. Who is that standing next to Ally and me? If you don't know her or her extended prosecco-drinking pinky finger, this is the pocket rocket that is Grace Fentiman. Grace is agent extraordinaire and THE Svengali of the influencer world. And she's offered to represent me! I couldn't be more delighted to be working with this wonderful woman. She's a positivity-head too and as soon as we started chatting – about the worthy topic of how we managed to survive before the invention of four-minute microwave mug-cake – I could tell she was full of great ideas and integrity. I'm so excited about working together and everything the future holds.

Also. Promise to stop posting pictures of me boozing. I'm a good mum and my baby does see me every now and again. Honest, guv.

#i'mnotdrunkyou'redrunk
#BRAUNEoverBRAINSmegaglobalworldtour.net
#notarealwebsite
#ifitwasarealwebsiteweneedtofirethebrandingperson
#doineedawebsitenow
#grace?
#doi?
#seriously

theparentalist this is HUGE. @bubbleagent is a FORCE. Instagram better reinforce its walls cos you guys are gonna tear through it like a Scud missile.

Annamaitron SHIT THE BED. This is mega. My two favourites under one roof. Snuggles?

jeremyforbes wow. drinking. groovy. you must be such a laugh.

bubbleagent I have no words. After a turbulent pregnancy and a pre-birth freak-out, @Brauneoverbrains was terrified of succumbing to post-natal depression, but she took action and took control. She dressed bright, exercised and tried to laugh through some tough times with her gorgeous baby boy. And Instagram has taken her to its surgically enhanced bosom. Erin is such an inspiration and I'm so proud to be working together. Besitos supermum.

Ghiie288 How do your children ever see you? You're always mooning around like a teenager. Mums should be at home looking after their children. Disgusting.

11

Erin's key trips to the side of the lock. It's seven forty-five and she's had a premix G and T on the train to celebrate signing with her agent. A couple in fact, on top of the prosecco or two she had at the studio when Grace showed up. She puts her phone back in her coat pocket and tries the door again. The key slides home, but when she goes to turn it, it sticks. For a moment she thinks the locks have been changed before she gives it a wiggle and lets herself in. She drops her bag down onto what was a pile of coats behind the door, but it clatters onto the laminate flooring. The coats have been hung up somewhere else.

The house is charged with the pungent smell of a Middle Eastern souk. Cooking spices mixed with some kind of citrus aroma, lime or lemongrass. The hallway is dark, the living room dimmed. There's a candle she's never seen before flickering on the hall table, the mirror behind creating its double. This doesn't feel like her house.

She hears movement upstairs. Raf must be giving Bobby a bath. His responses to her multitude of texts about leaving the baby with Amanda, checking that he was OK with her doing the podcast, telling him what time she was going to be back, have been uniformly utilitarian. *That's fine, Good luck, Hope journey OK.*

'Whatcha.' Amanda's voice from the kitchen. Erin dips into the main room and sees her leaned over the kitchen surface chopping something. She's wearing Raf's navy apron over a pale grey dress, hair in two French braids. 'How did it go?' She turns, kitchen knife turfed in chopped coriander. 'Should I ask you for an autograph?'

'Wouldn't bother,' Erin says through a polite chuckle. She looks past Amanda at her kitchen. It's pristine and a floor lamp has been moved to the side of the bookshelf so, with the spotlights from the kitchen ceiling turned off, the space looks warm and intimate. The sofa that Erin leans her leg into appears to have been hoovered. There are no toys on the rug, no crumpled nappy bags in a pile on the console table by the doorway, no mugs of half-drunk instant coffee filming over on the coffee table.

'The place looks amazing.'

'Bobby had a long nap an hour or so after you left.'

'Here? In the house?'

'In his room, yeh.'

'Wow,' Erin says, through half-clenched teeth. She pinches one of her eyelids together like there's dust in it.

'Know you said to take him out in the buggy for naps but with the rain … He was so tired after we'd played for a bit, I thought I'd chance it.' Amanda turns back towards the pot that's steaming up the window in front of her.

'And … ' Erin can't quite form the question. Bobby's never slept in his cot for her, not during the day. He just screams and screams until Erin picks him up and shoves him in the carrier or the buggy and out into the world. 'Did he not, er, protest? To being left?'

'We'd had a pretty intense peekaboo session, I read him about three thousand stories, then we practised some standing up against the wall. He was knackered.' Amanda must see the defeat coming into Erin's expression because she adds, 'Between you and me, I think he was sick of the sight of me. Wanted to sleep away the minutes until he could see his mum-bear again.'

Amanda takes the lid off the bubbling stockpot and releases a dry-ice puff of steam that collects underneath the kitchen cupboards. She sweeps the chopping board of herbs into whatever she's cooking. There's a thud from upstairs and a sloshing and then Bobby cries out. Erin feels the familiar punch of panic, the relaxation from the booze and the train instantly wrung out like a wet flannel, and she turns towards the narrow staircase, climbing two at a time. As she gets to the top, the cries have gone. Erin pictures Amanda lying on the floor next to Bobby on the Berber-style living-room rug, face in balled hands like a teenager, fascinating Bobby with her games and attention. Not sitting behind him, staring at a phone screen, but actually engaging with him, and she can almost taste how shitty it makes her feel.

Erin stops at the door of their bedroom. In the bathroom she hears Raf shhing their son as he heaves out snotty breaths. She waits, picks at a turned-up corner of wallpaper and it comes away. She scratches at a hole in the plaster, white dust collecting under her nail. The carpet in this upstairs hallway needs replacing. She doesn't take any photos for her feed up here so it's still as they bought it. The choices of a pensioner. Concentric shades of brown. Decor that sparks zero joy. The studio near King's Cross where she recorded with Ally earlier was beautiful. Spotless glass, dark red iron girders on the ceiling, a huge coffee machine so golden and gleaming it could have been from Greek mythology. Ally told her to take her shoes off to experience the carpet, and when she did, it felt like each of her toes were being given a shiatsu massage. An assistant offered her a beer or a gin and tonic. She asked for a sparkling water, professional, and it arrived with a cold frosted glass, crushed ice, a slice of lime and a small bowl of cashew nuts. Ten years of learning lines and recording tapes, sleazy meetings with sleazy nobodies for short films, fringe theatre, viral marketing campaigns all in the hope that one day she might be treated like someone that deserves a free drink with all the trimmings. It was exhilarating. As a small lump of the wall comes away and drops onto the floor, dust around it powdering the carpet, she wants to be back there. The space, the quiet, the focused energy of a workplace.

The truth is she's scared. Not just of Bobby screaming when he's handed back to her. She's scared of how Raf will be. Ever since the post-interview elation melted into the synthetic train seating, she's felt the fluttering wings of worry about what he's going to say about her leaving their baby with Amanda for the day. Before Bobby was born, Raf talked about how he didn't want his children raised by nannies and boarding-house matrons like he was, and she knows this is different, Amanda is his friend, but concern for how he'll react steams inside her nonetheless.

But when she rounds the corner and stands in the door of the bathroom, bubbles and water sloshing on the lino, her fiancé turns to her with a huge smile.

'Hello, Mum-mum,' he says, lifting Bobby into a towel and onto his chest. He comes over and wraps his arms around her, Bobby's wet hair leaving a dark mark on her jacket. He hands the baby into her like they were playing rugby, a wedge of bubbles still stuck in the thick rolls off his neck. She wipes them away with a corner of his towel and pulls his bunny-eared hood over his head. He looks well rested, jolly, the sort of baby you'd see on a poster. The clenched feeling in her chest whenever she's holding him seems to slacken a little. He's not smiling, of course, but he almost looks pleased to see her.

'How did it go?' Raf asks, moving past her to make space in their cramped bathroom. She comes through and places Bobby down on their bed where Raf's laid out a nappy, the pack of wipes and his sleepsuit like they were surgical implements.

'Really well, I think. She was nice. Lovely, in fact.'

'I'll do him.' Raf brings a tube of organic moisturiser from one of the #gifted boxes and squirts it onto Bobby's naked belly, making him squirm. 'Have you seen the house?'

'What do you mean?'

'Can't believe Amanda had time to do a whole spruce-up while looking after the Bobmeister.'

'He had a really long nap, she said.' Erin thought she'd made a simple statement but her tone must have been tinged with protestation because Raf turns to her, a little shocked.

'I didn't mean it like that. Don't take it personally, babe, she's got nothing else to think about.' Erin smiles, comes over to her unusually content baby and helps Raf keep him still by dangling her necklace over his face. Raf seems different, more energetic. When they first met, four years ago or so, she was entranced by his self-assured poise. His charisma, the enigma of him. This tall man, with his own sense of style, kaftans and loose-fitting linen trousers like a character in a Bond film. His voice was insouciant, he had a smile that played behind his lips but rarely came out, always calm, self-possessed. But when you got past his veneer of cool, which in itself felt like you'd been let into a secret club, he'd reveal this megawatt sparkle in his eyes when you got him onto something he was into, revealing that there was a passion, a fire inside the stillness. But in the last eighteen months, so much of that has gone. He'd never complain about his life, often the opposite, telling her how perfect things are now, but there's a heaviness about him that was never there before. Erin knows it's stress, the pressure of having to provide for them, to make a life for them, and, although he would never want her to, she feels responsible for the dulling of her boyfriend. But tonight he seems to have some of his former zip back.

Erin doesn't want to puncture it, but she decides to rip off the plaster.

'I signed with the agent, Grace, the one that'd been emailing me.'

Raf picks Bobby up and stares at her.

'Oh, right.' He nods, keeps nodding, not aware he's doing it. He wriggles Bobby into his sleepsuit and takes his wet towel over to the radiator by the window. He holds Bobby up, showing him the view, although there's no moon, nor stars visible to light the sliver of sea they can normally see through the gap between the flats opposite.

'I know we should have talked it through,' she says, leaning against the frame of their bathroom, 'but she's really good, like really impressive, and she doesn't represent many people. So I didn't think I could say no, and at the end of the day if I don't get any money, then she doesn't get any money.' She comes over to him at the window, thinks about threading her arm through his but decides against it. 'And, I don't want to get ahead of myself, but this could be – people earn a lot of money doing this stuff. Like, a lot. Wouldn't it be so great, you know, take some of that pressure away? Bobby and money stuff, sometimes feels like all we talk about. I know how hard it is, how hard you're working, providing for us all. I want to be the one who brings home the bacon for once, it can't be all on you forever, it's not right. And at some point, maybe you could ease off a bit, spend more time with the little guy.' He huffs a laugh out to himself. She catches muscles moving in his face, inscrutable. Is he angry? She's overstepped the mark. After all he's doing, all he's done for her, is it ridiculous to expect him to look after Bobby while she goes off to work? He sweeps his nose against Bobby's bath-fresh, glowing cheek.

'As long as you don't forget about us, big shot,' he says, almost a whisper. They stare at the black, rain-dappled glass for a moment. The halogen buzz of street light fighting through the weather, the pounding sound of thick waterfalls onto the flat roof above the bay window from their overburdened guttering. He reaches his arm round her waist squeezing her into him. 'Smells amazing, doesn't it, whatever Amanda's cooked?'

Bobby seems to take his words as a cue as he lurches towards Erin, forcing her to catch him in the crook of her arm.

'Wait, his tummy, you're –' Raf's warning comes too late as a scrambled-egg slick of thick vomit spits out of Bobby's surprised lips and onto the arm of Erin's gleaming white top. 'Shit.' Raf takes Bobby back. 'God, you have to be so careful with his tummy, don't you?' he says. Erin smiles as she tries to pinch the sick up in a tissue without spreading too much onto the cotton. She looks at Bobby's face staring at her from Raf's arms. His brow pinched together, molten-brown eyes devoid of sentiment. She smiles inside because Raf seems to be OK with her getting an agent, he seems fine with her taking a job, something that will give her a little respite from the boy staring blankly at her. She glances down at the tissue. There are little nuggets of green in Bobby's sick, cucumber, courgette perhaps. Amanda managed to get Bobby to eat some greenery. If she has to be away for work, something that Grace seemed to suggest might become a fairly regular occurrence, he'll be in great hands, she thinks, better hands than hers.

She sits on the bed and takes off her top, her milk-engorged boobs cupped in a bobbled peach maternity bra. Raf gives her a cheeky smile and hands the boy over to her. Bobby latches on, his eyes closed as he goes about his mechanical feeding. She tries to breathe through the pinch of his teeth, the ache of the milk emptying out of her ducts. Raf's OK with it, she thinks, and, even if it's just a few hours a week, she's going to have a life outside of these four walls, a break from this delicate little boy whose arrival has only ever made Erin feel like she's got everything wrong.

12

23 November 1998

Donny left me an orange Post-it in my locker on Friday afternoon that had the word 'tomorrow' and an address on it. There's some sort of colour code to the notes he leaves me but he's told me I have to work it out and I haven't managed to yet. The address lead me about half an hour out of town and finding the exact location took much longer. And when I eventually found it I was amazed to discover that he lived at the old plantation house.

He said he hated the huge house so we walked down to the creek at the end of their estate. He brought pâté and figs. I didn't like the pâté but didn't tell him. He can be abrupt sometimes, a bit frosty. But it only makes me want to please him more.

We sat among rocks at the edge of the water. I didn't know what to say to him and he didn't speak. Just stared at me, a tempest of thought swirling in his eyes. After some time, quite a long time, of saying nothing, I stopped feeling stupid and managed to join him in the meditative state he seemed to have fallen into as he just looked at me. We were silent for almost an hour. And in that precious time it felt like something shifted even deeper between us.

When he finally opened his mouth, it was to tell me to sing. He'd watched me rehearsing in the school choir, I hadn't seen him at the back of the room, and he said I had a beautiful voice. I was embarrassed but I wanted to make him happy so I sang 'Torn' by Natalie Imbruglia. He stopped me and told me to sing something beautiful instead. I made it up. He closed his eyes to listen and I felt like I was making him happy. He looked at me and smiled. I stopped holding my body, felt my muscles relax. I uncoiled my hair from its plaits and lowered the ends of it into the creek.

Then he jumped into the water, just like that, and I jumped in after him, both of us fully clothed. He said that we should leave school together. He laughed as he said it as if he was joking. He said he'd watched me with the people in my class, smiling as they mock me, trying to ingratiate myself with them, joining in their inane conversations about TV or music. He said it makes him furious to see me debase myself to fit in with their small-minded world. He's worried that they'll drag me, my soul, down to their level unless we get away. I'd never put it into those words but I suppose I've always felt the same.

He got out, and while I was coming out of the water and drying myself, he started sketching something in a notebook. I asked to see it. It was a version of one of the primitive women he'd shown me on the postcards from his trip. Spines of rib dominating a stick figure, features exaggerated, monstrous even. I asked him if that was how he saw me and he laughed. The figure was holding something in her arms, a bundle. I asked him what it was in her arms. He told me it was a baby.

13

Forty-six more people have liked Erin's post about Grace since she last checked, 3,476 now. There are twenty-eight new followers. Not a lot. She puts her phone on the table behind the sofa and carries Bobby over to the fridge. She opens the door and sees a bag of tired supermarket parsnips being squeezed into the side by an enormous box of glowing organic vegetables that Amanda's clearly bought.

When Erin first joined Instagram she was sometimes staggered by how excited she got when someone would like her post, or she'd look through the profile of a new follower to see that they weren't some lonely loser but a vibrant young mum with an exciting life, a chic house and attractive friends. And when there was a deluge of followers, after the big mummy-blogger Aisling Strang (376k followers) told her acolytes to have a look at Erin's feed, it felt like a hit of hard drugs. Hundreds of strangers telling her how great she looks, how funny she is, how much she's smashing motherhood. It's intoxicating. The only downside is that she's now hooked to that feeling of validation, and although she acquires new followers every day, when she looks at her phone, she's always disappointed when the steady flow hasn't burst into a torrent.

She grabs a large carrot out of the box, snaps the greenery off, goes over to the tap to wash the mud off, all while holding the baby on her less-painful right hip. She bites into the carrot. It's delicious. Just like all the food that Amanda's made them since arriving. It's been a few days now and she's been the perfect guest. It's not just that she's helped out with Bobby, but also the acts of unasked-for thoughtfulness like refilling the basket where they store the nappies; she's bought candles, reed diffusers and a large succulent she's put by the fireplace that looks superb. But she hasn't been under their feet during the day, constantly trying to spend time with Erin. She walks a lot, has gone on a trip to a castle further down the coast on the train, she's borrowed a bike from one of their neighbours. If anything, Erin would like to see more of her. The times where she's accompanied Amanda, to town for a coffee, the old underground grotto covered in fake cave paintings done by an Elizabethan eccentric, have been some of the best times she's had while looking after Bobby, but she seems determined not to impose. And Erin has to respect that. She's often caught her deep in thought and, although they haven't talked much about her new-old boyfriend, it seems that Amanda's genuinely taking some time for herself away from him to try and figure out the future of their relationship. Erin's in awe of it, slightly jealous even, the sort of studied contemplation of a major life decision that she's never even countenanced herself doing.

She looks out into the garden and sees their guest through her window, sat on the floor, eyes closed, meditating. People used to take the piss out of meditating, bald people in robes chanting 'umm'. But now it's another thing that it's decreed you're meant to try and carve out the time to do. Erin's tried, in the aftermath of her various freak-outs over being a mother, it always seemed to be the Internet's most consistent catch-all for that kind of thing, but she's not sure she's doing it right. She can't turn the thoughts off, no matter how many times she scans her body.

It's raining again. Hammering down. The room feels wet, the mossy smell of damp wafting in and competing with the citrus of one of Amanda's diffusers. It's coming up to midday and she and Bobby still haven't left the house.

Maybe she should try and meditate now. Grace was meant to be calling her this morning and Erin's concerned she's forgotten. She hasn't been able to concentrate on Bobby, waiting for her phone to ring. Not that she ever feels she can fully focus on him when she sits with him, going through the motions of playing. Stacking coloured blocks on top of each other, trying to encourage him to join in, dangling a set of plastic keys in front of him to try and make him smile. That's meant to be the thing that makes all the sleepless nights and stress worth it, when your baby smiles at you for the first time. But Bobby's really making her wait. Perhaps he never will. Maybe her frowning, grumpy baby will grow up into a frowning, miserable adult.

As if on cue, Bobby grabs at the neck of her T-shirt and makes a sound like a baby seagull. He grunts. Pain, a fart, a poo, she never knows how to make him feel better because she doesn't have a clue what it is that's wrong with him. He shoves his fist into his mouth and gives her an agonised expression. Teeth.

She swishes him around the room, a flying tour of the four walls that are beginning to feel like a prison. She drops his eyes down to a banana plant by the entrance to the hall but he wriggles his displeasure. She flies him across the room to the large window, the view of the olive tree outside in the middle of their front garden. The hammering rain doesn't seem to relax him either so she bounces him over to the mid-century black wire and teak shelving unit at the far side of the living room. He reaches for the shiny foil lettering of one of Raf's art books before grabbing a clump of her thin Shakespeare editions and tumbling them to the floor. Erin moves him over to the crystal Amanda gave her that now sits on the top right corner of the unit. He runs his fingers over the dual columns of the rock, the surface sparkling like it's covered in matt glitter. Bobby wants to grab it but it's too heavy for him and Erin doesn't want him to break the thing. Although she doesn't remotely believe in the power of crystals, you still don't want to be destroying things like that, must be twice the bad luck of cracking a mirror.

She swings him up away from it and stops in front of the picture that used to be in Raf's dad's house. Bobby likes the bright colours but there's something about it that unsettles Erin. The person wrapped up in a shawl, looking away into some bleak, arid future. The piece is childish. As if the act of putting this enigmatic figure, a nod to the Renaissance, in some sort of *Mad Max* dystopia would be automatically profound, but it falls flat. Erin's placed the crystal in this part of the room, next to the painting, because it doesn't get much natural light from the window and thus she doesn't often have it as a backdrop in any of her Insta-content.

She puts Bobby down and lets him shuffle around her legs and back towards the rug where a new wooden train set has been cracked open from the box of #gifted toys they keep under the console table behind the sofa. She recalls Amanda going over to the painting on that first night she was here and declaring it the reason for her visit. That and Mercury doing something, her motivation for booking a flight across the world to visit her old friend. But now Erin thinks of it, she can't remember ever taking a photo or filming one of her stories in this corner of the room. It wouldn't make sense to because it's pretty much the only part of their downstairs she hasn't put any effort into curating because the lighting is so bad.

Her phone buzzes on the kitchen counter. As she rushes across the room to answer the call, she glances back at the picture. It must have been in the background once when she was monologuing for her 'stories', she thinks, before blowing her lips out and shaking her head like a horse, stretching her face to relax the muscles, an old drama-school warm-up, readying herself to sound happy and breezy for her agent.

'Hi, Grace.'

'Erin, hi. You OK?'

'All good, yeh. How goes it?' *How goes it?* She's trying too hard. Bobby cries out, indignant at being ignored, and bashes a toy egg on the mat next to him.

'Are you OK to talk?' Grace asks. Erin swings Bobby up and sinks down onto their puffy sofa, bouncing him on her knee while she clutches the phone under her chin.

'Yes. Yes. Sorted now. Bobby.'

'Have you looked at your phone?' There's an edge in Grace's voice.

'Not for a few minutes.' She infuses the words with a knowing laugh to try and smooth over the instant thought that she's somehow posted something that's so bad Grace has decided to stop being her agent after less than a week.

'You've just missed it then. I've sent you an email. Have you got an iPad to watch something on or shall I call you back?'

'I'll get the iPad.'

'Put me on speaker.' Erin does as she's told and swivels round to the table behind the sofa, nearly knocking over a vase of lilies Amanda must have put there. Bobby jiggles off her knee so she drags him to her side next to her on the sofa.

'Ali-Crow −' Grace enunciates the words − 'do we know who an Ali-Crow may be?'

'Never heard of Ali-Crow.'

'Have you got it yet?' Erin clicks onto an email from Grace, with a video attachment.

'Is everything OK?' she asks, her voice breathy, artificially breezy.

'Someone called Ali-Crow posted the video I've sent you. Are you watching it yet?'

'It's buffering, just starting now.' A bank of green. Granite-grey sky behind. The sea. The sound of wind battering the camera's microphone.

'Let me know when it's finished.' Grace's voice, though she barely hears it because on the video she sees that it's her, Erin, pushing their buggy, the morning of the church group, look-ing around, eyes haunted like she's on drugs. The 'her' in the video shakes the buggy and as she and Bobby watch it from the sofa Erin's stomach lurches like she's on a roller coaster. The woman in the video shakes the buggy again, her face contorted with the effort, wind-buffeted strands of dark hair making her look like Medusa. Erin feels spit pool at the back of her throat, she could be sick. Erin in the video stops the buggy with a violent dig into the muddy grass and bounds round to the front of the buggy, her arms grab at baby Bobby. The video stops. She reaches forward, puts the iPad on their wooden coffee table and closes her eyes.

'Is it finished? Erin? Have you watched it?'

'Yeh,' she croaks. Bobby gives her a quizzical look. 'How –
Did you say someone posted this?'

'A brand-new account. No followers, no following. Just
@mentioned you. We managed to get it taken down in less
than two minutes. There's been no engagement or mention
of it on your feed so I doubt anyone's seen it.'

'Right, thanks. I'm–' Bobby's got his bottom to her, scratching his way across the sofa. 'I'm so sorry, Grace. It was – He
wouldn't stop screaming.'

'Erin, it's fine. You're allowed to get frustrated.'

'I know but –'

'Don't beat yourself up for this. You're a great mum, you
know that. People wouldn't be so into your feed if you
weren't.' Erin swallows. She feels nauseous.

'You OK?' It's Amanda, standing by the door into the garden, sun breaking through the thick clouds behind her. Erin
takes her agent off speaker and puts the phone to her ear.
How long's she been there? She looks over to the window,
scrunches her eyes up and nods, trying to smile off any of the
tense conversation she may have overheard. 'You want me
to –?' Amanda mouths, pointing to Bobby who's clamber-
ing over his mother's knee towards the edge of the sofa. Erin
nods an emphatic yes as Amanda swoops down, Erin puts a
grateful hand on Amanda's upper arm before she soars Bobby
into the air and towards the fireplace.

Erin goes out into the garden. She has trolls spitting bile at
her feed every day but she's always been able to write them
off as lonely old arseholes fighting their own private war
against the world by meting out insults to strangers. But this
is something entirely different. Someone has posted a video

of her, minutes from where she lives. A video they know will damage her. Erin begins scratching the inside of her wrist, trying to blink away the shock of it.

'That being said –' Grace's tone shifts – 'as we grow your followership, more people will be watching and – I've had it with a lot of my clients – some people can be quite vindictive with influencers, more so perhaps than with others in the public eye. So it's just important to be aware. When you're out and about. Assume everyone has their camera on you, because they might. I really am so sorry about all this. Just glad we were onto it before people started sharing.' Erin looks inside. Amanda's still got Bobby hoisted up looking down at her from a great height. Erin nods to no one, pinching the ligaments in her wrist together. 'Any idea who it might be?' Grace asks.

Erin shakes her head to no one. 'Er, no,' she says, unable to demist her foggy thoughts. 'There were a fair few people out down by the sea. A church group I was at that morning would have been finishing.'

'It's most likely to be someone you don't know to be honest. This sort of stuff. Trolling. It's the anonymity they get off on. Most likely a man, looking to polish up their self-esteem by taking people like us down a peg or two.'

'Right.'

'There's a guy we use sometimes in these sorts of situations. He's a digital security expert. He'll try and get to the bottom of who Ali-Crow is – though, unless he pops up again, I think it's unlikely we'll find anything. But I do want you to know, we're taking this seriously.'

A gaggle of seagulls shriek overhead making Erin hunch away from them. 'Thank you, that's so great to know.' Bobby is sitting up on the table inside. There must have been some form of leakage onto his vest as he's now bare-chested. Erin turns her attention to her bamboo hedge. The video's hollowed her out. The image of that terrifying woman, her, shaking the buggy, groping and pulling at something so tiny, so defenceless. Loathing courses around her and she's freezing cold.

'It's horrible stuff, Erin, but as your visibility increases I'm sorry to tell you this sort of thing can become par for the course.' The afterlife of a shiver runs down the base of Erin's spine. 'Now, we've got some meetings booked in for the end of this week and the beginning of next. Does that still sound OK?'

'Yeh.' Amanda's said she's happy to help on the days Erin has to go to London and telling her new agent that she's totally free to meet brands and production companies should feel wonderful but now she's seen that, seen herself behaving like that, everything tastes sour.

'We'll talk strategy when I see you. I'll make sure we carve out some time for a cocktail at some point during the day too.' Grace leaves the conversation and Erin with her thoughts, standing in her garden eyes locked onto the bamboo as it swats gently in the breeze. The sliding door shushes open and the air is blasted by the sound of Bobby's screaming.

'Somebody's hungry,' Amanda says, appearing at Erin's shoulder, serene in spite of the racket the baby's making in her ear. The boy lands in Erin's arms and she turns him towards a hanging cluster of flowers that hangs down from a planter high up on the fence. She puts a string of petals into his hand, which distracts him briefly as he takes time to yank on it like a tiny Tarzan. She pulls him a little closer to her. It's an apology to her little boy for every time she's raised her voice with him, every time she hasn't understood that he's confused and in pain and that, to him, the world is a terrifying place. If her new friend weren't standing behind her, Erin would cry into the blue woolly cardigan Amanda's put him in.

'All this attention all of a sudden?' Amanda's voice is quiet, respectful and full of purpose like someone offering support at a funeral. 'Must be a lot to deal with.' Erin turns, Bobby still attached to the greenery over her shoulder. The winter sun behind Amanda makes her red hair shine gold and, in her long green cardigan, she looks like some sort of beneficent wood sprite. She leans forward and squeezes the thick fold of chubby skin on Bobby's ankle, hard enough that the boy looks round at her in indignation.

'This is too much, isn't it?' Amanda says, putting her teeth together in a biting gesture. 'I could just eat him, couldn't you?'

'Yeh.'

'Lunch?'

'How long do you think he'll take to cook?' Erin says. Amanda cocks her head in that way she has, it feels like something adults might have found sweet when she was a child that's become part of her physical lexicon.

'You're so quick, you and Raf must be just laughing all the time,' she says, mouth pursed in a tight smile and Erin hasn't got the heart to say that Raf's never really been much of a laugher. Perhaps he was as a kid, she'll have to ask some other time.

'Lunch would be amazing, thanks.' Erin shifts Bobby from one side to the other. Amanda flicks a lock of hair behind her ear and pirouettes back into the house. She was there, the thought bursts into Erin's head fully formed. When someone was filming her aggressively shaking her baby's buggy, Amanda was right there.

14

'Who you think it is then?' Caz says, through a mouthful of chips.

'Not a clue,' Erin says, nudging her friend's knees with her own.

'Come on, you've got a working theory, for sure.' The potential for beef that comes with Erin's news of the troll seems to have amplified Caz's Glaswegian accent, both 'for' and 'sure' spelled out in two belligerent syllables.

'Such a weird thing to do,' Erin says, 'I genuinely have no idea.'

Caz pokes a hand into the bag of chips that's resting on Erin's lap, the greased warmth pressing into her jeans. They're sitting on the high wall of the harbour arm, the masts of dozens of sailing boats swaying like reeds in a breeze. Bobby sits in his buggy facing them, not sleeping, but not unhappy, gnawing on an oversized fluffy squid like a caveman with a brontosaurus bone.

They've just been at a mums' coffee morning at a brand-new restaurant just up the road that curves down to the harbour. It was heaving, every inch of the room populated by a mother and at least one young child crawling around the floor, banging their heads on chairs and table edges and screaming intermittently. Erin had had no idea that so many people would turn up but she'd posted about it and after what happened at the church group she shouldn't have been too surprised. Erin was struggling to focus as a range of different mums vied for her attention. Two days since the video and she hasn't been able to keep it out of her mind. It was a raven-haired older mother telling Erin that she'd never do some of the #gifted promotional posts she'd done recently – she clearly had a bank balance to match her high-mindedness – that precipitated her catching Caz's eye and their escaping the coffee morning as quickly as they could. And now they're sharing a bottomless bag of chips, watching a smattering of fishermen and older gentlemen tinker with their boats. It's only eleven o'clock but Caz knows the man in the chip shop so he fired up the fryers early. Erin hadn't intended to tell Caz about being trolled but she blurted the whole thing out before the chips were cool enough to eat.

'Well, I'd say there's about thirty-five stuck-up mums round here who I'd put in the "massive twat" category, but not sure which of them's got the onions for something like this,' Caz says and it makes Erin smile. She's missed her so much since she's gone back to her job as a social worker. On the mum scene they were inseparable, Erin quick to laugh and make an effort, Caz almost the opposite, they formed a good cop/ bad cop double act.

Erin catches Bobby staring up at her from under his brow and it reminds her of Amanda being right there, swooping in to save her as she lost her temper on the grassy verge that overlooks the sea. They had lunch after Erin got the call from Grace. Amanda didn't ask any questions about the phone call she'd heard snatches of and Erin didn't elaborate. She doesn't want Raf to know. He'd overreact. And she doesn't know whether it would be to the fact she's being trolled or the way she was behaving in the video but she fears the latter. It took minutes rather than hours after Grace's call for Erin to decide that it might be best for everyone to keep him in the dark. She dropped Grace an email and agreed that there was no point making a mountain out of a molehill.

'I've watched the video twenty or so times, been down to the mound to try work out where it was taken from.'

'And what do the forensics say?' Caz says and Erin hums out a dry laugh which must be pregnant with misgiving because Caz adds, 'Erin?'

'Well, um, Raf's family friend who's staying with us, Amanda, she was there.'

'What?'

'She was there, on the grassy knoll,' she says, trying to make a joke of it, 'she came and helped with Bobby, helped calm him down.'

'You think it's her?'

Erin clears her throat and wipes salt off her fingers with a paper napkin. 'No. No, she's lovely, and she was with me pretty much the exact time the video ends so it can't have been her.'

'Right, well, that's good.'

'I don't know, something like this happens and you question everything. It could be anyone. Literally anyone. That's the thing.'

'I met her, Amanda. End of last week at Millie's Movement.'

'Thursday?' Caz nods. 'I was meeting someone from Channel 5. Jesus, listen to me.'

'She's not a laugh a minute, bit starey, glazed, you know, head in the clouds, but friendly. That hair though, eh? Thick as a rope.'

'You could sleep in a bath of hair mask every night and you wouldn't get hair like that.'

'Put it in a fucking Gro-Bag every day.'

'Inject each strand with anabolic steroids.'

'You could, er – No, I've not got another one,' Caz says, defeated, leaning the chip bag over to Erin who dips her hand in and brings out a thick clump of them.

'I know she seems pretty out there,' she says, 'but she's good fun actually, and amazing with Bobby, been an absolute god-send in terms of Insta-stuff that's kicking off. I've got all these events lined up and there's no way I could do it without her helping out with Bob.'

'What sort of events?'

'Well, it's erm – speaking at a MotherLoving Institute thing.'

'Really?'

'Do you follow them?'

'Aye. That's –' she looks down, scratches at her waterproof jacket – 'that's impressive.'

'I can't believe it really.' The MotherLovingInstitute (178k followers) is a big new collective of bloggers who have banded together to campaign for mothers' issues, particularly relating to loneliness and mental health, being more openly talked about.

'You not want any more no?' Caz says, hoisting the chip bag off Erin's lap as she stands up from the wall. 'Can I see the video?'

Erin's shoulders hunch and she shakes her head. 'I'm going to delete it. Sorry. I don't want anyone to see me like that.' She stands up and leans forward with a paper napkin to wipe a spoonful of sick that's dribbling down Bobby's chin towards the collar of his Eskimo-style bodysuit.

'It happen a lot? Losing your temper with Bobby?'

'Never,' Erin says, a little forcefully. 'I'd barely slept. He wouldn't stop screaming.'

'No judgement here,' Caz says, bending down next to Bobby's buggy to pick up the squid he's dropped. 'Once, when Stanley was screaming like that, I grabbed his ankle, gave it a squeeze. Pretty hard. Got agonising guilt straight afterwards, questioned whether I was a fucking psycho or whatever, so that's good at least.' She wipes the crumbs of tarmac off the toy and hands it back to Bobby.

'It's not me at all,' Erin finds herself saying. Which is something she's not certain of. In the early stages of her pregnancy she started to feel a constant edge of rage buzzing behind her forehead like an electric flycatcher. When she was out and about, she was good at suppressing it, but at home she wasn't so successful. She could see Raf's love for her, his devotion, chip away in tiny fragments every time her anger bubbled over and he found himself scalded by it.

But perhaps this is the real her. The real her that's shouted at Bobby, that's twisted his limbs into clothes harder than she should, that's hissed at him through gritted teeth for him to just stop crying when she desperately needed a moment to reset her head. When she was a kid she'd never dreamed of being a mother and maybe that was her instinctively knowing that she shouldn't be, that she didn't have the constitution for it. 'The idea of it going viral −'

she shudders as she says it – 'and everyone seeing the sort of person I am.'

'All parents have lost it once or twice. That's not who you are.'

'If something happens in a video that goes up on the Internet, it's more real than reality.' An empty nappy bag blows in the wind and sticks to Erin's leg.

'Well, no one saw it, not even me. Get some pics up of Bobby in some of those neon dungarees you've got, eating avo toast from one of those fancy black plates and watch the "likes" flood in.'

Erin slugs some water from Bobby's sippy cup, to wash away the oily residue in her mouth.

'Probably get told avocado's got too much fat for babies.'

'Aye, then the Chilean government would send you two thousand avocados so that'd make up for that. You're very lucky, remember.' The ice wind swirls into the harbour so Caz gets a blanket out from under the buggy and wraps Bobby up in it like meat in pastry. Her two children are at nursery. Stanley's four and Imogen's seventeen months. With her riot of dark curls, wide hazel eyes and her tattoo of an eagle feather on her wrist, Caz is the sort of mother Erin would like to be. Cool, confident, no-nonsense. Happy to laugh at how much of a nightmare her kids are but still rampant with love for them. She'd march through walls for her children. Erin barely puts her phone down for Bobby. The video has affected her, touched a nerve far more than it should have. Caz is right. She's very, very lucky.

Sunbeams reach around a batch of cumulus clouds that hang above the town in front of them. The dappled sunlight brings out the colours in the painted facades of the old

Victorian terraces that overlook the harbour. When the sun shines you can imagine this place, its fish and chip shops, ice-cream parlours, its kiosks and sea-view pubs, teeming with life as it does in the warmer months.

As they walk back up the hill towards their cars, parked on the far side of the restaurant, away from the harbour, Bobby grows bored of being constrained and begins arching his back against the buggy's strap like Frankenstein's monster. Caz rounds the buggy and coos into his face, reaching her hand for something. Erin understands she means a snack and panics to find something. She hands over a shard of rice cake from a packet in her rucksack and it placates the boy. As Caz pushes the buggy up the hill, Erin dashes onto her phone quickly. Twenty-three followers just since she left the coffee morning. Bobby has got a great outfit on under his snowsuit, plus fours and a bright green T-shirt like a clown-golfer, and she'd posed him with two giant croissants instead of ears so he looked like Big-Ears from *Noddy*.

A gaggle of mums, various shades of bright dyed hair, come out of the coffee morning as they pass the restaurant. They stop Erin, though she's only met them once or twice before. One asks where she's going to be tomorrow morning. One if she has any tips for day trips. One congratulates her on the new agent. Caz hasn't stopped walking so Erin tells the women she'll see them all around before skipping up the cobbles to catch up with her and Bobby.

'Sorry,' she says, threading an arm through hers and putting her hand next to Caz's on the handle of the buggy. She leans her head on her shoulder.

'Price of fame,' Caz says. Erin spots an old man with yellowing hair standing on the stern of his boat staring at them.

She looks back towards the restaurant, the three mothers are looking up at her, one waves. Erin unlinks herself from Caz, suddenly paranoid about how someone taking a photo of them could spin it. She gets a flash of that angry woman, her, almost launching the same buggy they're pushing now across the patch of grass. The price of fame.

15

8 January 1999

So now we're bound.

I want to write it down, everything that happened, so that when we're old we can remember it all in vivid detail. Everything has changed.

During the day I found a Post-it. Orange, which I know now means that it's an instruction. 4:00 a.m., Central Bus Station. And then a stick sketch of one of the indigenous women from Nourlangie. This was it.

I snuck out of the top window and had to jump the roof of the porch so I didn't wake Mum and Craig. We arrived at Kakudu when the sun was high and the dark mass of rock stood against it like a sleeping animal. We hiked around the perimeter. We drank from pools. We ducked away from the path to walk in and out of shallow caves. I ran my hands over the drawings, depictions of love, of dedication to the perfect unity between two souls that ancient civilisations seemed to understand far better than we do. Donny'd brought food. Water. He'd thought of everything. Then we found what we'd been looking for. A wide gully of rock protected from the wind, flat, and totally private.

I drew a small circle with a piece of chalk I'd brought with the pair of compasses he packed. I placed the chunk of rose quartz I'd stolen from my mum in the middle of the circle. Then I set about smudging the area to purify it before the ceremony. We couldn't get wild sage so Donny got a large bag of dried sage from the supermarket. I put it in a little crucible and lit it before wafting the pungent smoke into all the gully's nooks and corners. I've seen from Mum how negativity can cling to relationships so I wanted to do everything I could to purge the negative energy before Donny and I start this new phase.

He'd found a ceremony in a book he'd studied – *Magick in Theory and Practice* by an Englishman called Crowley. We'd gone over what we had to do on the bus, but still, as we sat opposite each other and tied our wrists together with his silk scarf, it was frightening. The air felt charged, heavy like before a storm, though there wasn't a cloud in the sky. The wind seemed to be moaning through the gully, singing to us, whispering to us. And then I laughed. And he laughed with me. It was silly, we both felt it, tethered together, a pyre built around a pink rock sitting between us. But we have created something, a connection we share that makes us more, makes us greater than everyone else. Since school ended for the summer, every time I've been able to get away, I've gone to him, and when Craig started asking questions about where I was going, Donny started coming to me, doing more odd jobs for us for a pittance. Craig was delighted. Donny's work was good, he relished the idea that he was getting a good deal and underpaying the little city boy. I almost enjoyed those times more than when we could just be together unwatched, the stolen glances, touches behind Mum's and Craig's backs. The summer has been like a blissful dream, and if life were to end now, it would be enough. So with school starting up again soon, it felt we had to consecrate what's grown between us. To make it official.

Donny lit the pyre. The kindling went up quickly. I lowered my side of the scarf into the flames, probably too quickly, because I was scared the fire would burn out and I wanted everything to go right. The silk took some time to catch, but soon we stood up, the flames having freed us of our physical bonds, but holding hands still above the fire. We took off the burning cuffs of silk and put them on top of the quartz. Then Donny stoked the sticks and I blew on the pyre we'd made and the fire began to lick the sides of the stone.

As the sun plummeted we sat across the fire from each other. Donny was silent for some time, he seemed bored, distracted. I lowered my top so he could see me, he'd never seen that much of me. He told me I terrified him. He drew me towards him and held me there, arms surrounding me, enclosing me. It felt like my whole body had been dragged inside his. He asked me to sing for him and I did and he smelt my hair and said it was the feeling of home. It felt primordial.

I had thought we might consecrate things in a different way, the way the girls in the top year are always talking about. A real wedding night. I am terrifying. The way I feel about him is terrifying. It terrifies me. He rubbed a hand over my bare midriff and whispered into my ear what an incredible mother I'd be.

Mum was furious with me when I got back but I wouldn't tell them where I'd been. I stood silent as Craig ranted and slammed hands on tables at me. He grabbed me at one point, I think he might have hurt me if Mum hadn't been there, but I still couldn't stop smiling.

Now I'm in my room. Without him and with him. Always with him.

16

BRAUNEoverBRAINS

Contact: grace.fentiman@rfgtalent.com

389 posts   41.6k followers   1,438 following

ERIN BRAUNE

Mum to Bobby. Salty sea-dweller. Bright up your life. Reformed thespian.

This is my waste management athleisure. Because, these days, I mostly work in waste management.

This is Bobby's poo face. Tongue out, beetroot complexion, and even though the eyes look crossed, they somehow follow you while the deed's being done like a painting in a horror film. Maybe eye contact helps him relax?

I'm honoured to be talking at the MotherLoving Initiative party tonight at Claridge's. (FEARNE COTTON IS GOING TO BE THERE.) I know there are mums way more amazing than me, far more qualified to talk about the way a baby turns your life upside down and how to rebuild positively. BUT I want you all to know, and I know you know, that if I post something in my stories where I'm posing with A-list or more likely Z-list celebs, or if me and @annamaitron are singing 'Total Eclipse of the Heart' at midnight, that nights like tonight are the outliers and that 99% of my time is spent dealing with this boy and his poo face, and his sick face, and his angry face and, so far, zero smiles. Unlol. Bonjours to you all. Will post some shiz in my stories.

#everydayi'mshovelling #lookintomyeyes
#nappynappyjoyjoy
#iloveyoufearne
#sorryinadvancefearne #supermumsofinstagram
#moonlightingmumma

@varyafinn whoop, whoop, poop.
@motherlovininstitute can't wait to have you. We are PSYCHED. FYI @fearnecotton is bringing extra security
@gossamer we'll be there! #1stnightoffin6months
@julesspurn women have been bringing up kids for thousands of years without going to talks about it. What a load of shit.
@aleister have a nice night away

17

Erin can't get reception on her phone in the chemist so she bats the rubbery phone case on the handle of the buggy. Their part of town is dominated by seafront flats with elderly inhabitants who treat the little pharmacy like a social club. Erin's record waiting time to get the medicine for Bobby's reflux is forty-five minutes. At least there's usually a large supply of purse-lipped old dears to swoon at Bobby and today's no exception. A lady in her eighties, in great shape and wearing a very elegant plum coat that Erin would consider wearing, leans over the sunshade making goo-goo noises at him. She makes a comment about how sweet his little serious face is. Erin tries to catch the harassed-looking chemist's assistant she gave her prescription to ten minutes ago but the girl's working hard to avoid making eye contact with any of the people piled around her desk. Erin's train up to London is in an hour and she needs to get home, drop Bobby off with Amanda, get showered and changed, put some make-up on and then get to the station.

She spots two women in the queue for the post-office desk at the back of the chemist's looking at her. They're both in their late thirties, one wears a green beret and thick-rimmed glasses and both have chunky knitted scarfs on, typical BRAUNEoverBRAINS followers. One of them steals another glance and turns back again, pretending she wasn't looking. Erin enjoys these moments of recognition. It's thrilling that people are excited to see her, that she's a talking point, a story for those who follow her to tell their friends. More often than not they might approach her for a chat or vice versa. But Erin won't talk to them today. Now they just remind her that she's being watched, that there's someone who probably lives nearby that wants people to know that she's not a fun, sunny mum who dresses her super-cute, olive-skinned baby in out-there outfits. Someone who wants people to know that a lot of the time Erin feels so out of her depth, so out of control, she thinks that her super-cute, olive-skinned baby should probably be taken away from her.

'Hiya.' Erin looks round to see Lorna Morgan wearing a coat that resembles loft insulation, stood in front of a double buggy blocking the aisle behind her. Erin looks over at her twins. Sleeping serenely as always. Erin sometimes wonders whether that's the reason she's taken a dislike to Lorna, her boys seem so easy in comparison to Bobby, but no, Erin doesn't like Lorna because she's not very easy to like. 'Was your little boy alright the other day?'

'What?'

'The other morning when he was very upset. We passed you both on the prom or have you forgotten seeing me?' Her voice comes right out of her nostrils, but she's right, Erin hadn't remembered that, a few minutes before she went up onto the grass, a few minutes before she was filmed shaking her son's buggy, Lorna Morgan had been there with her horde of pink children.

'I did. Yeh. Thanks.' Erin peers to the back of the dispensary willing someone to arrive with Bobby's drugs. As they stand there side by side, silence breeding between them, Erin thinks about whether it could have been Lorna that filmed her. She had the kids with her and was walking in the opposite direction. But she could have circled round and been standing across the road from the grass as it's on the route back towards her house. But could she do something like that? Lorna was one of the first people she met when they first moved down here. Erin was five months pregnant and they organised a coffee and a walk on the beach. Lorna is Kent born and bred and talks as if she's always trying to beat some personal best for words per minute. There was always a gossipy element to the stories she told Erin, an icicle core of mean-spiritedness. Everyone she mentioned, those Erin vaguely knew, those she didn't, were, in some way or other, conducting themselves incorrectly, in her plentiful opinion. So when Lorna suggested another mum-date, Erin prevaricated. Which, when they saw each other with their new babies at baby-groups, Lorna seemed to have taken to heart as a snub. Then, two months ago, Erin soured things further by intervening in a conversation Lorna was having with a criminally underslept-looking mum called Jules. Erin very calmly suggested that Lorna ease off on doling out her 'infinite wisdom' to Jules that morning. The word was that Lorna had taken that very personally indeed.

'Saw you got an agent.' Her inflection soars but it's not a question.

'That's right, yeh.' Erin nods and smiles to Bobby's elderly entertainer as she heads past them towards the door.

'Bet they're sending you *loads* of free stuff now.'

'No more than before really.'

'Look at this.' Her shellac scratches at a patch of dirt on the hood of her huge buggy. 'Got it on Buy, Sell, Swap. Mould. Actual mould. Twenty quid though. Couldn't say no.' Lorna doesn't look down at Erin's gleaming #gifted Bugaboo Buffalo, but her meaning's more explicit for it. 'Anyway, must be nice.'

'It's a lot of work, and you've seen at the church, he's not the easiest baby.' Jesus, Erin thinks to herself, sweating now, why am I playing the victim in front of this woman?

'I've not been to the group for the last six weeks.' Lorna peers her head over her buggy to check the boys are sleeping. They are; she folds her arms and stares straight ahead. Her coat is enormous, far too wide for her slight figure. Erin can't help herself thinking that she looks like when multiple children put on a trench coat in a cartoon and pretend to be an adult. Lorna's dislike of Erin seems to squeeze out of her pores, olfactible almost. For someone who feels the need to denigrate everyone in order to inflate her own status and who probably saw herself as the queen bee in waiting for all the various children's groups, it must be galling that someone living two streets away, a woman new to the town, is, both at the groups and by the clear metric of Instagram followers, far more popular than she has ever been. But would Lorna troll her? It's such a strange way to attack someone, and if she did would she hide behind anonymity? Wouldn't bringing down the mighty BRAUNEoverBRAINS be exactly the kind of thing someone like Lorna would get off on?

'You Airbnbing at the moment?' Lorna asks.

'Um, no, no. I've not really got that sorted yet.' Lorna runs holiday rentals for second-homers and has a couple of holiday-park rentals she owns so Erin must have mentioned her and Raf's plan to rent out the studio in the garden at some point. The chemist's assistant finally arrives with Bobby's prescription.

'Oh. Oh, right,' Lorna says, turning back to face the counter. She looks shocked, though she has very fair eyebrows so it's hard to tell whether that's just her face.

'Hope you're not here too long,' Erin says, executing a three-point turn that gives Bobby the scope to grab at a clutch of toothbrushes and knock them to the floor. Erin considers leaving them, a quick glance at the clock above the door, but she can't face Lorna's judgement so bends down to pick them up. From the floor she clocks the woman looking down at her, making a strange face, eyes wide, cheeks sucked in like she's chewing a sherbet. 'Is there something wrong? Erin doesn't mean to sound so confrontational, but she doesn't want to get dragged into nudges and winks.

'I … ' She puts a hand up to her mouth. 'I don't know, I probably shouldn't say.'

'I think you kind of have to.'

'Well,' Lorna feathers her chest with her hand, 'I saw a red-headed woman coming out of the back of your house.' Her head wobbles like a toy dog in the back of a car as she waits for her response. 'If it's not an Airbnb guest –'

'Raf's old friend from Australia.' Erin enunciates each consonant to crush whatever *Desperate Housewives* fantasy the woman's trying to allude to. 'She's staying with us for a bit.'

'Oh, thank goodness,' she says, hugging her padding tighter. 'I've seen her with your partner, Raf is it? Out walking together with Bobby on the prom –' Erin flushes with heat – 'and I thought it was a bit odd. That's a relief.' Lorna's not relieved.

'What do you mean, seen them?' Erin asks. 'When?' Bobby's trying to lift himself up to grab more things from the shelf.

'One time earlier this week, and once last week as well.' Lorna shrugs but keeps her eyes front, suddenly far more interested in the activities of the team of chemists up behind the counter. 'Can't remember what day. She wears such funny clothes, like something out of *Merlin*.'

Erin 'hmps' in reply. She looks around the chemist, the sea of grey heads in their brightly coloured coats seeming to merge into each other. Raf's the busiest he's ever been. Erin's never seen him so stressed with work. He's going back to it after Bobby's down and they've had dinner, sometimes until one in the morning he says, and yet he's taking time off work to go for walks with Amanda. He hasn't mentioned that to her. He hasn't said anything about it.

'Well, it's lovely that he's got company if he's holding the baby for you.' Erin wants to get away from here. She doesn't want to know what Lorna thinks of her fiancé going for walks in the middle of a workday or her opinions about Amanda's Arthurian get-up. Raf works in London one or two days a week and a studio in town the rest of the time, so it's not like he's necessarily been skipping whole days, but why wouldn't he mention it? Erin wheels the buggy back towards the chemist's desk, seeing a woman with a Zimmer frame now blocking the aisle she was planning to escape down. 'Funny old time to visit.' Erin wants to get home, get changed and get out of this incestuous little place for a few hours. 'Bridget, do you know Bridget? Has the three huge cats, lives on Plandell Road?' Erin nods though she's not listening as her eyes dart around the lines of pensioners, desperate to find the quickest way out. 'She said she saw her doing some exercises, as the sun was setting a couple of afternoons ago. Must have been about four degrees. Australians are very outdoorsy so that does make more sense.'

'I've got to go to London,' Erin says, seeing a window to the exit.

'Course,' Lorna says, giving her a three-fingered wave as Erin shoves the buggy towards the photo booth, nearly knee-capping an older gentleman who's staring at a selection of combs.

18

Erin stares at the three cherubs playing their gold-plated instruments looking down on her from above the open double door frame. She slurps about half her flute of champagne. Her friend Anna Mai (89k followers) is telling a story about this wine-tasting holiday some company #gifted her and her family. Erin wasn't listening fully but it seemed to be a cautionary tale about checking the travel company's credentials before agreeing to go on their trips. 'It wasn't quite as bad as the Fyre festival, but not far off,' a phrase she's fairly sure she's heard Anna use already tonight.

The French Salon at Claridge's is the venue for her speech tonight. It's astoundingly beautiful but its ostentation makes Erin feel sad, mournful almost for a life she hasn't lived. The bald reality is that she'd imagined spending her life at places like this. When she played Nora in *A Doll's House* at university, her director said she'd be a movie star, no doubt about it. An agent who'd come to see her told her to go to drama school, that he'd see her on the other side. She directed herself in a production of *The Seagull,* not at the university theatre but at the Theatre Royal in town, that caused such a stir that she had university tutors and bigwigs in the regional theatre scene buzzing around her like flies at a butcher's shop. Drinks parties at Claridge's were the least she was expecting. But they never materialised, the career she had been promised by teachers at secondary school, by self-aggrandising tutors at her drama school and any man over the age of forty who worked 'in the industry', never materialised.

Success was meant to pool around her like molten gold, so she spent years in denial, still believing something would switch and the industry would realise that she'd slipped through the net. So she refused to get a full-time job in case it stopped her auditioning, paid intergalactic rent to live close to the West End, went drinking with her old uni theatre crowd who'd all realised the creative pathway was a torrid and self-immolating one and gone and got jobs in PR and advertising but, ten years later, would still tell her she should keep at it because she was so good in their first-year production of *Blood Wedding*.

It was Raf who saved her from it all. He saw her playing a too-old Isabella in *Measure for Measure* above a pub and got talking to her afterwards. She fell quickly for him. He was tall, she'd always had a thing for tall, and so kind. He put her first. She'd never had a boyfriend that had done that before. A nice guy as it were. From very early on he focused his life around hers but there was nothing desperate or clingy about it. He was matter-of-fact about his feelings for her, his desire for her. He wanted to spend time with her more than he wanted to do anything else, it was that black and white for him. There was none of the neuroses of actors or writers she'd been out with. He didn't put her on the manic pixie dream-girl pedestal like some of the corporate wonks she'd dated. He was remarkably comfortable in his skin, something that Erin hadn't been for seven or eight years. She was drawn to his stillness, a serenity, the sense that no matter how turbulent the sea was, he'd always stay anchored near the shore and she was delighted to tie herself to his strength, his solidity.

After about eighteen months he said he couldn't take seeing how low she was as her auditions, the attention from her agent, from her friends dried up. He tried everything to dig her out of the trench of disillusionment she'd dug herself into. He paid off her numerous credit cards to give her a chance to do something different, got her prospectuses for evening classes, but she railed against it, told him he was trying to crush her dream. When he suggested that he thought she seemed especially low after she'd spent time with certain groups of her friends, the actor crowd particularly, she nearly broke things off with him entirely. But then, after the brutal serendipity that led to her being on holiday when a chance to lead a film came up, an actual feature film that would have led to people knowing who she was, knowing her talent, she realised that she'd moored her ambition to something that was based around blind luck and that Raf was right, she didn't have the temperament for it. And that in still trying to be an actor, she was hanging on to some childish desire, chasing the same feeling of adoration she used to get when she did shows for her mum's friends.

And she was one of the lucky ones, she had a wonderful man who was offering her a fresh start. She rang her agent and said she was giving it all up. And a few months down the line, when Raf asked her if she wanted to have a baby, it seemed like it could be the right thing to do. The purpose she'd always had, the meaning she'd sought through fame, craft, acclaim, ridiculous abstract nouns that had meant so much to her for so long, had delivered only misery. So although she'd hadn't been planning to have a baby until much later, when Raf suggested it might be something they could do, the thought of having something concrete, something that was hers, that was known the world over as providing joy, made it seem like a no-brainer.

'Erin, do you want to come and get ready?' Philippa, the lady who is 'looking after' her this evening taps her on the shoulder. And it's having a baby, with a little help from her mother's put-on-a-smile-for-the-world attitude and Erin's high, photogenic cheekbones, that has brought her here. Here to talk in front of a crowd of amazing, beautiful, inspiring mothers. Acclaim, applause, adoration. What she's always wanted.

She downs the rest of her flute, gives an expression of mock nerves to Anna Mai and Daisy Froome (21k followers), and follows Philippa into the drawing room next door. Rows of seats begin to fill up as she's escorted to the front. She hears snatches of conversation. Nap times, poonamis, flexible working, mastitis, mumpreneur conferences, Bach for babies orchestral concerts. These are not the topics that Erin's interested in, this is not what she likes talking about, and yet, she finds herself posting about them, talking about them to people she meets at groups and cafes. She doesn't talk about rage, about loneliness, about frustration, about her abject boredom and how much she misses the roller coaster of hope and disappointment of her old life. She talks about positivity, and online sisterhood, and moments of overwhelming love and her style tips and baby fashion. Because, just like every performance she's ever given, probably the real reason she never made it, she can't help but play to the crowd.

She reaches the corner of the room, a lectern in the middle of a small temporary stage in front of her. She looks out at the audience. On the far side she catches a middle-aged lady with spiky grey hair leaning into her neighbour, their heads rolling back in laughter at something one of them's said. Another two women in the front row, nodding together, four hands balled together in the younger one's lap. Some words to bolster her through some difficult time, Erin thinks, some sage advice from one superwoman to another. Her relationships with her new Insta-friends are more jovial, more banterous. They talk about having a few drinks, laughing at their hilarious, disgusting children, what they're wearing, where they bought it. The superficial side of being fabulous. What these two women have seems to be deeper, more intimate. Caz aside, despite the tens of thousands of followers and the eyes of all the mums where she lives being on her, she doesn't have that simpatico with anyone.

Erin thinks of Amanda. She thinks of the two of them walking her sleeping baby down by the front, getting to know each other, talking about their families, laughing, bonding. But, since that first walk they had, Erin hasn't been able to do that. Her fiancé has. Amanda and her fiancé, with their shared history about which she really doesn't know much.

Erin leans back on the heels of her new #gifted ankle boots. The leather's stiff and her feet hurt in them. It's a good pain that snaps her out of her treacherous thought process. This, tonight, is a big deal. She will smash this speech because this is her opportunity and she's learned the hard way that you don't get many. She looks at her audience, so luminous that the chandeliers seem to sparkle brighter with their vitality. Their eyes glisten, their shoulders low with a sense of release. They're powerful and successful and Erin is one of them.

Philippa gets up on the stage and asks for everyone's attention. Erin feels a fluttering at the base of her stomach, she breathes out through her nose, the air feels colder than it should. This is fine, this is normal. This is good.

The seats are full now and the room smiling. She spots another cherub looking down from the door opposite on the far side of the drawing room as she walks up onto the stage and goes up to the microphone. She swallows a lump of saliva, takes a sip of the glass of water that someone's put in front of her. All eyes are on her and she couldn't feel more comfortable. Her eyes dart to Bobby again, the cherub, it's not Bobby. She blinks away the guilt she feels at being here, among these strangers instead of being at home with him, caring for him, bonding with him, she shouldn't need these people to love her, his love should be enough. But it isn't. She looks out at the expectant faces, looks down at her typed words in front of her, takes a deep breath and decides to give a different speech.

19

Erin speed-walks up the ramp away from the station, nodding to the good mornings of various faces she recognises from her regular circuits of their village's small high street. For the first four months of his life, Bobby would only nap in the sling, so almost every day, during a particularly rainy late summer, she would walk up and down the section of the street that's covered by rusted corrugated roofing, trying to stay dry.

She catches her reflection in the window of the shop that sells mobility scooters. She doesn't look too bad. The dry shampoo she bought at St Pancras has done a decent job of making it look like she didn't roll out of her hotel and race to catch the train back home. Despite going to bed at 3 a.m., she woke at seven with a rabid compulsion to get back to see her son. She must have still been drunk at the time to make such a gallant decision because, right now, she needs total silence and to sleep off her hangover. Something that definitely won't happen with Bobby around. Her skin feels greasy, scented with tequila. The post-boozing regret flows up inside her like the contents of a blocked drain.

The speech went well, really well. She had planned to run through her story, putting everything on Insta, putting out an account of herself to the world, how this livestream journaling saved her from what she thought was an inevitable dive into some form of mental health spiral. But when she was up there she sensed a hunger in her audience for something else, a desire to be galvanised. So she went full St Joan and gave a rousing call to action. She went for the jugular of gender equality and how it affects mothers, the hypocrisy and contempt that society seems to have towards them. She talked about a new mother's loneliness and the many practical, institutional and financial factors that reinforce it. And it went down like a basketful of Labrador puppies.

The whole of Claridge's seemed desperate to speak to her afterwards. Grace told her she'd played the room perfectly and, judging from how it felt when she was up there, it didn't feel like her agent was flattering her. Fearne Cotton made a point of coming up to her before she left and asking her if she'd like to come and do a short segment on her podcast. The whole thing was pretty overwhelming.

A feeling which led her straight to the free bar and an evening with Anna Mai, Daisy and Elana Clarkson-Wells (134k followers) who Erin had never met but was as much fun in real life as on her Insta. Amid the mood of jubilation, egging each other on, they steamed into the drinks, ending up at a private members' place called Black's, on Grace's company membership naturally. There were celebrities, old English gentlemen in three-piece suits and the most beautiful bar staff and hostesses she'd ever laid eyes on. Erin got caught up in it, drinking espresso martinis and quaffing late-night mix plates of cheeses and charcuterie.

And now her tongue feels like an offcut of carpet as she scrapes it against her teeth. She rounds the corner onto her street, pulling her keys out of her bag, swearing as she catches her hip on the latch of their half-open gate. She puts the key in the lock and stops, squeezing her eyes shut and popping them open. Unsurprisingly she doesn't feel magically better and ready to face her screaming baby. Remorse squeezes through her pores like playdough spaghetti. She needs to spit but someone will probably film it and put it up online.

When she pushes open the front door she's surprised to be met with silence. It's Friday morning. Raf's at work but she expected Bobby to be here with Amanda. Erin glances at the station clock on the back wall. Quarter past ten. There are no groups on now and the buggy is by the door. But he's safe with Amanda, she thinks, and thankfully not her responsibility yet.

She hangs her coat up, shoves her holdall behind the door, goes to the kitchen sink and runs the tap. When it's as cold as it'll go she dips her head down and drinks. She glances out the window at the studio in their garden. The lights are off.

She imagines Amanda babywearing Bobby along the beach to Chalk Mantle or another stack on the coast near them that Erin, to her shame, still hasn't been to. Amanda spends a lot of her time walking when she's with Bobby. Then it hits her, maybe Raf's with them now. She sees him in the maroon beanie hat he lives in in the winter months, Amanda by his side, flaming hair blowing in the wind, swapping war stories from their schooldays while Erin drinks out of the tap like a dog.

She shudders. She's always had the most horrific paranoia after boozing. In her late twenties, almost overnight, she seemed to become that person, the one that would take it further than everyone else on nights out. It was like all her university friends got together and had a meeting somewhere, complete with flip chart and thought-through agenda, to decide that their partying would become collectively more conservative and forgot to send Erin the memo.

Since she woke up, 'Raf and Amanda, together' has been the subject title of a thesis that's being badly written in her head. Although she managed to suppress the thought in order to focus on last night, she can see now that it fuelled her speech with anger, because now it hurts to think of them walking together. Erin and Raf haven't taken Bobby for a walk together on a weekday since his two-week paternity leave ended. He's always said how much he wanted to hang out with them but he's always had too much on. She'd love to walk arm in arm with her fiancé along the seafront as their son sleeps in the buggy but it hasn't been possible. But now, for Amanda, it is.

Erin sinks down into the ancient fabric sofa she inherited from her mum and feels it work its charms on her hangover which, now she's a hundred per cent sober, is throbbing inside her like a pulse. She pulls a blanket off the arm of the sofa, but when it's in her hand she sees that it's not a blanket at all but one of Raf's jumpers. Navy blue, cashmere, incredibly soft to the touch. She pulls it over herself anyway.

The dishwasher beeps to finish its cycle. Erin hadn't noticed its swishing hum when she came in. In the renewed silence she hears a moan.

There's no other word to describe it. The sound of a single, open-mouthed moan. From a woman. Erin hauls herself out of the depths of the sofa and perches on the edge, listening. The same sound again. A quiet moan stifled somehow, as if she were trying not to be heard.

The sound comes from down the hall. Erin stands up, balling the jumper in her fingers. The moan again, it seems louder although the tone is almost identical. She tenses her jaw, cursing herself for having such a strong coffee on the train. She goes towards the sound. When she reaches the end of the corridor she sees a yellow piece of clothing on the lilac carpet, a cardigan maybe, just outside Bobby's room. Amanda's.

The sound once again. It's coming from Bobby's room. As Erin takes tentative steps, she hears words as well. The same voice. A whisper almost, coming from her baby's room. A wave of sickness sweeps up from her stomach, spit gushes into the back of her throat. She twists the jumper between her fists, stretching it out like a garrotte. Then she looks down at it, Raf's jumper. Amanda's cardigan is on the floor outside the room.

She takes a sidestep that puts her in line with the gap in Bobby's door and looks in. The room's gloomy, blackout blinds down, nightlight on. The underlying hiss of static. The sound she's hearing isn't live. The words come from a recording, they could be Indian or Latin, punctuated by the release of a high sigh, the sound she'd interpreted as a moan. It's the same passage of words, then the sound, repeated on a loop. A chant.

As she opens the door and steps in she sees a phone on the bedside table that the chant's playing on. There's a shape in the single bed, the bed Raf sleeps on when he's in with Bobby overnight. Erin tiptoes over, breath held. She stands over the bed and there's Bobby, fast asleep, his features so delicate in repose they could almost be porcelain, lying on his side nestled into Amanda's chest. Amanda's sleeping too.

Erin watches her breath move Bobby's wedge of thick hair once, twice, three times.

Amanda's covered by the duvet but Erin can see she's not wearing a top or a bra. Her hair cascades down arms that enwrap Bobby, holding him into her. The contrast between Amanda's pale skin, her freckled shoulders and Bobby's dark mop of hair, his olivey rolls of flesh, makes the scene look like an image from an Athena poster.

Erin blinks hard, as if there were something stuck in her eye. She feels like she's intruded on some sacred scene of motherhood, except that's not Amanda's baby. The chant continues. Is this how she's been getting him to sleep so easily? Whenever Erin's asked, Amanda's said that he's not always gone straight off but it's never seemed to be the twenty-minute screamathon Erin has cope with. This is how she's being doing it? Chanting MP3s and topless cuddling. She imagines Amanda, this woman who seemed to come along like Mary Poppins, bringing peace to a tempestuous home, someone she thought was becoming her friend, whispering the words of the chant into her baby boy's ears until he falls asleep, filled with calm, filled with Amanda's overpowering contentment and something proprietary begins to churn inside her, a heat that expands in her until she thinks her ribcage might pop like a balloon.

Erin steps back, feeling that if she keeps holding her breath, keeps trying to stay still, her legs may crumple beneath her. She loses her balance and knocks into the nightlight, sending it back into the cot behind her with a clatter. One of Amanda's eyes bursts open. She looks over Bobby's head, straight at Erin. Her face is blank, no guilt, no concession at being caught in bed nuzzling someone else's baby. If anything, she looks irritated. The back of Bobby's head begins to wheedle round and then Erin hears her little boy gearing up to scream but Amanda holds him closer, whispers something into his ears and seems to abate his fury at being woken up. Amanda smiles at her with the side of her mouth that's visible and raises an eyebrow that seems to be saying to Erin 'thank God I'm here to save you from yourself'.

20

Erin looks over at the collection of about twenty desks in the middle of a vast poured concrete floor. The Lookout, the co-working space where Raf rents a desk, is in a converted nightclub that's been stripped back to the brick. Although its members have done their best to conceal it by hanging prints and filling it with house plants, it still has a hint of the building site about it and has barely changed since the only other time she's popped in to see Raf here six months ago. She's wanted to come here more, to break up her day with Bobby, but she didn't get the sense from Raf that a young baby would be particularly popular with the seemingly industrious freelancers.

She looks to the back of the room where there are studio spaces and sees hirsute men in hats, the artists, milling about and laughing at each other's jokes. Raf's in the main body of the first floor. He shares the space with a mixture of graphic designers, writers, Amina, who owns an online kids' clothes shop and who Erin's become friendly with, and even a landscape gardener. But Raf's face isn't squeezed in behind the double monitor where she remembers him being.

There's some movement at the back of the room and there he is, emerging from where the toilet must be because he's wiping his hands on a dishcloth. His eyebrows narrow in surprise at seeing her and she locks him with a challenging glare as he swerves through the workspaces towards her.

She'd had to get out of the house and felt she needed to go to Raf but hadn't really thought why. After Bobby woke, she went and fed him in the living room as Amanda got dressed. Amanda offered to make her a cup of tea but Erin suggested she go and do her own thing after looking after the baby last night and all morning. Erin didn't reveal how unsettling she'd found it but as she walked into town towards Raf's workspace, she was shaking.

'Wasn't expecting you back till after lunch.' He leans in to give her a kiss on the cheek. 'Bloody hell, boozy one, was it?' He backs away quickly, wafting his nose. 'Good night though?' He's nonchalant as he leads her by the elbow towards the wide window out to the sea that's given the space its name. He goes to unclip the sling and get Bobby out but Erin bats his hand away.

'When's she going?'

'What?'

'Amanda – do you know how long she's staying?'

'Is everything OK?

'Just thought you might have talked about it on one of your walks.' Raf sucks his lips in so his mouth is a line.

'You want to go downstairs and get a coffee?' he asks, looking over his shoulder at his co-workers, most of whom are still plugged into their headphones, fixed on their screens.

'I thought you were "the busiest you've ever been"?' Bobby slightly undermines her airquotes gesture by grabbing at her fingers. A few of the freelancers look up from their computer screens. She gets Bobby to do a little wave to Amina. 'They've got baby toys in the place downstairs?' she mumbles to Raf. He nods, before throwing a chivalrous arm out, *after you,* putting his hand on her lower back and leading her and Bobby out the door.

Raf collapses into the cracked leather sofa opposite her. Bobby is at the end of the coffee table between them, manhandling metal cars against the table, making Erin flinch with every clatter. Raf reaches forward for his macchiato and sips it.

'You're pissed off because I didn't tell you?'

'Every day since you've gone back to work I've wanted to text you, wanted to call you, wanted you to come home and be with me, to be with us, because it's boring and lonely and awful, mostly, looking after a baby. But I didn't, because you have to work, I know you have to work so I didn't. But to find out from fucking Lorna Morgan that you've been swanning around with Amanda. That is why I'm pissed off.' Raf looks around, self-conscious, and catches the eye of someone he knows who's sitting in the corner with a MacBook and an overlarge glass teapot filled with mint leaves. He cheerses his little cup into the air. The cafe is painted white but sells houseplants and hand-painted pots, so has the feeling of a very chic greenhouse. He turns back to her and sighs.

'I didn't want you to feel guilty.'

'Me feel guilty?'

'About me having to take time out to check our baby's safe.' Erin swallows. 'We don't really know Amanda, and you left Bobby with her, without asking me, then it just became an arrangement. We never discussed it and, I don't know, I don't think we should be leaving our only kid with a stranger.' Raf runs his fingers through Bobby's mop of hair. The baby looks round at him, one eye a bit lazy, before going back to his cars. Erin goes into her bag and gets out some lip salve and puts it on. She wants to be angry with him. After the shock of thinking that they might be doing something, together, in flagrante in Bobby's room, she planned to interrogate him further about their relationship. But what he's saying makes sense. And, is he right?

'She's not a stranger,' she says.

'I've not seen her for twenty years. I'm not sure we should just trust her to look after our not even one-year-old. Maybe I'm more risk-averse than you.' He says it with a smile. She came into this cafe puffed up with righteous indignation but now she feels like a burst lilo.

'If you didn't want her looking after Bobby, why didn't you say anything?' Raf leans forward and runs a hand over the back of his head. Shreds of silver in his dark hair catch the light from an old-school film lamp.

'Honestly?' Erin shakes her head, *Of course honestly.* 'I thought you'd say I was being "obstructive".' His turn to do air quotes but he does it only with his tone. 'Back when you were still trying to act, every time I suggested you study something else or get a job or whatever, you told me I was being *obstructive*. And the couple of times recently, I've said that I thought your social media stuff is getting a bit much, like the other weekend when Bobby's rifling through the cleaning cupboard, manhandling bottles of bleach while you're staring at your phone, and I innocently pointed out that we might need to watch him a bit closer now he can move around more, you told me I was being obstructive. It's been your word of the week for every week for as long as I can remember. So yeh, I didn't feel like I could "obstruct" you from getting Amanda to watch our son.'

Erin can't handle this. She gulps at her can of ginger beer, hoping its fieriness will somehow spike her into some sort of response. He's been lying to her, at least not telling her, that he's been skipping work to go and spend time with his family friend and yet she's the one who's somehow on the end of a character assassination.

'Sorry —' she bites the side of her lip — 'what has this got to do with me being on my phone?' Her hand thrusts forward, stiff, aggressive and she has to wrap it into a fist and bring it back into her lap.

'I wanted to be around, for the first few times. I went out with them once or twice but mostly I've been upstairs in the bedroom working, just to be on hand. You don't find Bobby easy, it didn't feel responsible just handing him off to Amanda and expecting her to get on with it.'

'So now I'm irresponsible.'

'And this is why I didn't tell you.' He speaks through a laugh. She notices the snagged indent on his canine tooth, a result of too much fingernail biting, he told her once. His other teeth are pristine, shining white against the black of his beard. 'It's not a judgement on you. You want to do this stuff —' he points to her phone on the coffee table — 'I don't fully understand it but —'

'It's a job. We can make money from it.'

'Because that's your motivation.' Sarcasm courses through his words. Bobby grizzles so Raf lifts him up and stands him on his thighs, facing Erin. The boy jiggles his head in her direction. She widens her eyes and pastes on a smile to try to cheer him up.

'I was thinking of you, not saying anything. Thought you'd be appalled I was having to catch up on work in the evenings. What with money as it is.'

Erin grabs a napkin off the table and blows her nose into it. She smoked last night and it's bunged her up, made the hangover feel about twelve times worse. She hadn't really thought about the implications of Amanda looking after Bobby. When Grace called about the podcast the only thing going through her mind was a strategy to get to the recording studio without her screaming baby. After that, it just seemed fine. Amanda's always delighted to look after Bobby, shooing Erin off, saying 'get going now, don't miss your train', whenever she's lingered with them before going up to one of her meetings. And Raf hadn't said anything. As far as she was concerned, he was OK with it. But now he's said it, she knows he's right. Erin doesn't know this woman and she couldn't have been more delighted to leave her baby with her.

'Has it been nice?' she asks, trying to keep the bitterness out of her voice.

'What?' Bobby tries to make a goalkeeper's dive off the sofa so Raf spins him around and jigs him up and down in a galloping motion.

'Spending time with Amanda?'

'I wasn't doing this to spend time with her.'

'I know, but has it been nice? She's here to visit you. You thought it might be weird. Is it weird?' Raf moves his head in a figure-of-eight motion, Bobby still bouncing on his legs. Erin takes a bite of her shortbread.

'It's been all right. Good to catch up.'

'Reliving the glory years?' she says, spitting a crumb into the air in front of them.

'I left everything –' he seems uncomfortable – 'left Australia completely behind after what Dad did. So yeh, I guess it's nice to hear bits and bobs about how things are now.' He puts his aquiline nose in Bobby's face who squirms away from it as if it were a small animal. 'Mainly been good to spend a bit more time with this little legend, hasn't it, mate?'

'She's great with him, isn't she?' Erin can feel the acid seeping up through her words. After seeing her baby with Amanda, snuggled up with her, she feels the need to hurt herself more, to curdle her hangover with a double shot of self-loathing.

'It was a late one last night. Finished up late, didn't it?' His voice is firmer, his smile gone, and she feels like she's talking to a teacher.

'Quite late, yeh.'

'Drank a lot?'

'The speech went really well, like really well. Thanks for asking.' Urgh, she thinks, she sounds like a stroppy teenager. He sighs, an almost imperceptible shake of his head. Perhaps she doesn't have a right to be angry with him for taking time out to be with Amanda and Bobby. She entrusted their baby to someone because she was an old friend of his. That's not enough, that's not enough for a conscientious parent, for anyone. But, with all of Grace's plans for her swirling in her head, half of which Raf knows nothing about, it felt like she'd dropped into their lives like manna from heaven. And the fact that Amanda was holding her child close, there's nothing wrong with that. A nursery nurse would do the same, Erin thinks. But the image of Bobby squeezed against Amanda's naked chest swims back into her head. Raf catches her eye, the side of his mouth smiles. What would he think if she told him about how she found Amanda and their baby in his bedroom? Would he double down on his needing to be around? Would he suggest that she ease off her trips to London? Erin's got to go at least twice next week to try and firm up some brand partnerships. She can't pull away now, just when she's on the verge of getting paid, money she's earned, going into her account for the first time in forever.

'But, you know what,' he says, 'I was being overcautious. You were right not to be worried, she's amazing with him.' He would be fine with the napping, Erin thinks. He'd love it in fact. She's always got the sense he wanted her to be more motherly. 'Skin-to-skin' contact was something the antenatal classes had always banged on about being a way of getting an angry baby calm. Raf would probably think that Amanda had found that the solution to their problem baby is to simply act like his mother.

21

Erin stands swaying on the decking outside what's become Amanda's lodgings. The blinds are up but there's no sign of movement. Most of the front of the building is glass, revealing a sofa bed, small table and chairs, and a wood burner in the corner. There's wood panelling on either side of the frontage that conceals a kitchenette on one side and a small shower room and toilet on the other. Everything visible has been kept very tidy. Amanda has accessorised the gunmetal-grey sofa with a colourful scarf, her backpack is propped next to the thin wardrobe, a yoga mat leans against the back wall, but otherwise it could be unoccupied.

She comes round to the front of the studio and presses her palm on the cold glass of the door, condensation marks spreading out from her fingers. The morning is cloudless but cold. She looks down at Bobby sleeping in the sling, its strap leaving a beaded indentation on his delicate little forehead. It's been two days since she found him and Amanda in the nursery. She hasn't left him with her since and the incident hasn't been discussed. But it's had an effect on her. Although there's been a staggering amount of engagement with her feed since clips of her speech at Claridge's have been shared online, she's made an effort to leave her phone upstairs while she's with Bobby in the day. It's been hard, she's felt like she's been blinking twice as much as before as her thoughts strum around about what she might be missing on there, but it's made a difference. She's found herself getting more engaged in creating little games with Bobby on the rug of their living room, playing simplified versions of theatre games and inventing distinctly accented characters in his animal-infested board books.

Amanda's not been popping her head in as much as she was before either. She spent yesterday morning with some acupuncturist she met, and Erin hasn't seen her this morning. Perhaps it's her acknowledgement that, although Erin had asked her to help with Bobby, she had overstepped the mark a little. But Erin's missing their little chats, Amanda asking about people she had met in town, telling Erin about the history of some natural beauty she'd visited or trying to educate her about a new holistic practice that Erin would almost certainly never try. Amanda not being around as much has also made Erin wonder about how she'll manage when she goes. Grace is finalising negotiations on a contract for a brand ambassadorship that would involve going to London at least once a fortnight and probably far more, and even if she can convince Raf to put Bobby in childcare, it's not something that can just happen overnight. There are settling-in sessions and she knows people whose babies have basically been rejected because they've screamed from the moment they were dropped off. Erin's fairly sure Bobby would be such a baby.

She finds herself trying the handle of the glazed door of the studio, telling herself that she's just checking everything's OK with it for Amanda, as she walks in. But the smell that hits her is so overpowering she thinks it might wake Bobby so she nearly turns round and goes straight back out the door. It's herby, a bit like weed but not quite as acrid. There's notes of a pizzeria, basil, which she's always thought tastes like the smell of fresh-cut grass. On the shelf above the one-burner hob there's a line of small hessian sacks, with various types of dried herbs and spices poking out of the opening at the top of them. Erin wanders over to the kitchenette and studies the labels. The names are like something from *Game of Thrones*. Ginkgo Biloba, Feverfew, Belladonna, Digitalis, Verbena, and then ones she's heard of, Camomile, Echinacea, Eucalyptus, Elderberry. The colours are tantalising and she has a desire to sniff them but, knowing she'd probably manage to spill something all over Bobby's head, thinks better of it.

She opens a cupboard and sees a blue Post-it stuck to the bottom corner of the inside of the door. 'SONNET 116' it says in black biro capitals. Erin had to learn some of Shakespeare's sonnets for their voice classes at drama school but she can never remember which one's which.

As she turns away from the kitchenette, Erin notices that Amanda's arranged a collection of her crystals in a pattern on the table. There's a circle of them intersected by lines of little rocks that lead to a tiny obelisk-like murky grey crystal in the middle, a little larger than the others. There are pale pink stones, the same as the crystal Amanda gave her, but also a brighter pink with lines of white within it, and then some translucent deep red, highly polished stones, like rubies. The whole arrangement is bordered by a square of peach-coloured rose petals with a plain white candle at one corner. Erin's read that crystals are a big wellness trend at the moment.

She picks up a small pebble from the corner opposite the candle, careful to clock where to replace it. She rubs her thumb over the roughness on one side of it. What 'energy', she wonders, does this perfect little pattern indicate? Calm perhaps. Are these the secret to Amanda's effortless tranquillity?

She seems so content with everything. Like every leaf on every tree is the most wonderful thing in the world. It might be she's had a lot of therapy, Erin thinks, her brother had an old girlfriend who was similar. Very level. Very calm. Every word measured. Erin later found out it was down to years of therapy when she was a teenager. The cadence of Amanda is similar. She seems so joyful. Perhaps, Erin thinks, she sees herself like the bus in *Speed*, that if she ever showed anything negative, she might explode.

Erin skips past the window and into the bathroom. The studio was a fairly new addition to the house put in by the previous owners so the room has the grey slate finish and gleaming dark tiles that Erin's seen on various home improvement shows, but the room's tiny. A box of a shower, toilet, small corner sink with a bathroom cabinet above it and barely space for an adult to be able to access any of them. On the ledge above the sink stands a large muddy-green wedge of soap, the sort with chunks of bark in it that you might get from one of those shops that smell so pungent that the staff must be nursing a constant headache. She looks down at a bamboo cup at the back of the sink. A wooden-handled toothbrush, accompanied by a tube of some toothpaste brand she doesn't recognise, but there's something else in the cup. She plucks it out by the handle, it's a small screwdriver. She tries to find what Amanda has been fixing in the bathroom, but she can't see anything. She replaces the screwdriver and tries to reposition it exactly where she found it.

She opens the door of the cabinet and reveals a line of tiny glass bottles containing different coloured liquids and covered in Chinese symbols. She picks out a luminous pink one. On the back there's a picture of a droplet going into an eye. She closes the cabinet, being careful not to clatter it into Bobby in the cramped room, and looks at her bloodshot eyes in the mirror. She leans her head back and shakes a drop into each of them before she has time to think about whether it's a wise move. It stings but once she's blinked away the remains of whatever's in the bottle, and she's regained her ability to focus, the woman gazing back at her looks quite different. The red tributaries in the whites of her eyes have disappeared and her pupils have dilated to such an extent that the ring of pond-green iris that encircles the huge black dot in the middle of each eyeball is barely visible.

She stands in the doorway, blinking at the buzzing feeling in her eyes. When she opens them again she notices something catching the light underneath the sofa bed. She moves over to the middle of the room and bends down as much as she can while still keeping Bobby upright. She sees what looks like an oversized jar of pickles nestling in the darkness in the gap where the mattress folds in on itself. She gets her phone out and shines a light onto the jar and sees something that makes her stumble back and nearly drop her phone. Two black, lifeless eyes were staring back at her from inside the container. Bobby rouses slightly with the jolt of her movements. Her breathing's spiked and she has to get it under control as she shhhes him back to calm. She goes back to the sofa, one knee on the floor, desperate not to bend Bobby's body, but needing to see what it was looking at her from inside a pickling jar. She manages to get in a position, shoulder resting against the wall, to pull the jar towards her.

The sound of the rattle of metal, the lock on the back gate, makes her jump and she bangs her elbow on a sharp corner of the sofa bed, swearing under her breath at the pain. She glances at the contents of the jar quickly. A small doll, naked, head and legs plastic, body made of flesh-coloured fabric. Some rusty nails. What looks like mud. Dots of red – chilli flakes? She hears steps on the wooden patio of the studio and pushes herself up the wall to stand. She sees Amanda's arm reach towards the door and kicks the jar back under the sofa as far as she can without disturbing Bobby.

Amanda's in the open doorway. She wrinkles her brow slightly at seeing Erin and Bobby in her room. She's wearing a chunky cardigan over a peach dress, her hair in a huge braid wrapped around her head like a crown, and she carries a bucket of some sort of green sludge.

Erin opens her mouth, making a show of being about to speak, about to make her excuses, and then she points down at Bobby, puts the side of her face in her palm to indicate that he's sleeping. Amanda's face creases into a loving smile – *that's sweet*.

'You OK?' Erin mouths. Amanda nods, cocks her head to the side, admiring the picture of mother and baby. It's Erin's property but she feels as if she's been caught out in the studio and is suddenly aware of her huge pupils and what she must look like. Amanda uses the drops, Erin just clocks. Perhaps that's why she always looks so bright-eyed and bushy-tailed. Maybe she's always on Chinese uppers. Erin points to the garden, making a gesture that says, *I'll get out of your way.*

Amanda stares at her, her eyes blank like the doll she keeps in a jar. What the hell is she doing with a doll in a jar? Erin thinks. Is she into voodoo as well as crystals? Something to do with the boyfriend back in Oz? As she passes, Amanda leans towards Erin to say something. She smells like Earl Grey tea.

'Sea lettuce,' she whispers, indicating the bucket of sludge. 'Clears heat from the liver. Super important in terms of general balance.'

'Be nice in an omelette,' Erin whispers back, making a mock-disgusted face and tries to go, sure that Bobby's going to wake if they keep talking. Amanda grabs her just above her elbow, a touch firmer than the feather touches of tactility she's employed with Erin since the moment they first met.

'Perhaps I can make you a tincture, be wonderful for you to get everything in balance.' She releases her grip and strokes Erin's upper arm. It sends a shock of electricity up Erin's neck. She swallows, a little disquieted. Amanda blows Bobby's hair and walks past her and into the bathroom.

Erin wanders back towards the house. She glances down at her arm. A band of red remains where Amanda's fingers were.

22

22 January 1999

I have to make a choice.

I found Mum in my room again. Snooping. She's trying to find this journal. I've kept one since I was 11 and even though I told her I'd stopped, she knows I'm lying. But she'll never think to look behind the extractor fan in my toilet. I'm not sure if she knows I can use a screwdriver. She might find out I can if I find her in my room again.

Last week she found one of Donny's Post-its wedged into the pocket-inside-a-pocket of my jeans. It was a sketch of one of his skeleton goddesses. I'd had some trouble from one of the footie boys that morning and he'd given it to me to remind me how powerful I was. He often calls me his goddess. I'm no good at drawing so Mum knew instinctively it must have been from the person I've been seeing.

She's desperate to find out who I've spent all of this summer vacation with. I felt bad to begin with, watching her and Craig losing their tiny little minds over where I'd been, who the mystery boy, they've assumed it's a boy, is. But then I discovered Craig's been getting people to spy on me throughout Palmerston and has even tried to follow me out to the plantation house. So I don't feel too bad about our secret now.

She's tried to ground me, like we're characters in a high school movie, but she's working during the day so I've just not been coming home until late at night, sometimes not at all. She's threatened all sorts of punishment, but I don't have pocket money, I don't watch TV, she doesn't know where I keep my books. She's powerless.

The irony is that this is the most attention I've had from her for years. I know it's not been easy since Dad left. But she hasn't *needed* to go to the pub every Friday and Saturday since I was nine – ever since she's deemed me young enough to be left by myself. She's not *needed* to tell me to make myself scarce the evenings Craig's poker mates come round or she and him need to have their 'date nights', which I know consist of them drinking three bottles of wine and largely failing to have sex. I've seen it from the gallery at the top of the stairs. It's funny, before I met Donny, that's what I thought grown-up love was.

Craig I feel more worried about. He's always done the territorial, alpha male of the house act when it comes to me, but it's getting out of control. He keeps talking about what it's like for him as my dad even though he isn't my dad. He's come into my bedroom, sat on the end of my bed, tried to tell me that teenage boys only want sex and even then they don't know what they're doing. That they don't appreciate how special I am. He got almost emotional the other day when he asked if I wanted to go for a walk with him and I said no.

I feel so blessed that Donny found me. We did alloys at the end of last term, in chemistry class, and that's what it feels like we have. Two elements reacting together to make something new, our spirits fusing into one entity making our bodies, our minds, our souls stronger. I feel three times the person with him as when we're apart.

He's worried though. I can tell. Every time I tell him about what Mum's been doing he clams up and stops talking to me. When I've pressed him he says it's because he's scared of losing me. He's convinced someone will find out and that once that happens, they won't let us be together.

He's not going back to school. He says he can't, not now. He's going to Darwin, he has money for somewhere to live. There's a gallery owner who's taken an interest in his work. He says I could find a job. Mum will disown me if I go. Craig, who knows what he might do, but I know he'd see it as me betraying him, he'd be jealous, he'd poison Mum against me. I know it would be irreversible.

But Donny needs me to go with him. He says that without me, he isn't an artist any more, he's barely human. He needs me. I wish I had the words to describe how extraordinary that feels.

I have to choose. But there's no choice. There's no question. This is the beginning of a life I never thought I could have. This is the beginning of something magical. I never dared to believe in fairy tales before, but now I know they can come true.

23

BRAUNEoverBRAINS

414 posts   54.3k followers   1,638 following

ERIN BRAUNE

This is my Zen poncho. Because I'm the new face of worldwide Zen. 😂

DEEEELIGHTED to announce that I will now be the online, and occasional physical, ambassador for Phibe Digital, home of the incredible PieceOFMind mindfulness app. They're working on a new social networking app specifically designed for mums on maternity leave, providing a one-stop shop for information and booking for baby groups, support groups, mindfulness and just general 'dating' for mums who are trying to stay sane while bringing up their lovely human. AND THEY WANT MY ADVICE ON IT. SO. Please DM me, comment, anything that you'd like to see and I will act as a conduit for all your amazing ideas and suggestions. The girls at Phibe – YES THEY'RE GIRLS – and I want to give every new mum, whether they're struggling with their new

baby or loving every second, a support network living in their pockets. Cos without all the love I've had from you guys, I might not have been able to get out of bed, let alone be standing in the sunshine, baby asleep in the buggy, listening to the Fearne podcast, absolutely loving my life. Huge props to @gracefentiman for getting me and @phibedigital together. I can't wait to get cracking @lydiamanuel
@alicetrenchard

@lydianmanuel YAY. We can't wait to get you back in the office, Erin. Super excited about future plans.
@andywesto this is awesome awesome awesome stuff. What an amazing resource for new parents. (Stay-at-home dads allowed on it too right? LOL)
@lydiamanuel 100 andy. We love anyone that's staying-at-home-to-look-after-bubbas.
@annamaitron HOLY GUACAMOLE. This is going to be huge. I'm sure @phibedigital have it covered, but I will happily invest 20–75 English pounds in this app. What's that in stock options @BRAUNEoverBRAINS?
@crowleypoly Q: She's amazing. How does she do it? A: She doesn't.

24

Caz
Congratulations pal.

> Erin
> Ta babe. Excited.

Caz
Frappuccinos are on you then?

> Erin
> Whenever the contract's
> signed,
> for shizzle! How was Friday
> group?

Caz
Mega. Amanda was there with B-man.
Had a chat. She was wearing a
full-length lace number.
Miss Havisham vibes.

> Erin
> Harsh!

Caz
Lorna was there,
first time in ages.

> Erin
> I missed her. WHAT a shame.

Caz
In full shite-chatting
flow too. Some newbie
was saying how she'd come
to the group cos of your
Insta. Lorna got right on one.
About how it was her that
started the group and
now she couldn't even go.

                    Erin
                    The church group?
                    Wasn't it Jesus's idea?

Caz
She did start it though. Year or so
before you moved down. There was
nothing for mums going on so she
set it up.

                    Erin
                    Not exactly
                    Glastonbury though.

Caz
She was saying how her and
most of the local mums have stopped
going because it's become, her words,
a 'trendy love-in'.

                    Erin
                    What is her problem?

Caz
The group is pretty rammed
but it's not exactly your fault.

                    Erin

It's got nothing to do
with me.

Caz
I don't know. She was
properly pissy about it.

Erin
WTAF

Caz
Small town, small mind.

Erin
She was there, nearby,
when the
the video of me
shaking the buggy
was taken.

Caz
Really?

Erin
Saw her pushing the
twins and Clara. They
were going in the oppo-
site direction, but still.

Caz
Reckon it's her?

Erin
I didn't. But I also
didn't think I'd hijacked
her precious baby
group. Think she's
capable of something
like that?

Caz
She was raging the other day but,
I don't know, seems a bit full-on.
There been any follow-up from
your agent?

> Erin
> She says it's not worth
> getting worried about.

Caz
But are you worried?

> Erin
> It's harmless.

Caz
A lot of weird comments on
your feed atm.

> Erin
> Welcome to the
> Internet Cazabelle.

Caz
What's Raf said?

> Erin
> Um …

Caz
You didn't tell him?

> Erin
> He'd do his protective
> bit if he knew someone
> had filmed me. Not
> worth getting him het
> up over nothing.

Caz
Think it is nothing?

>Erin
>Not been anything
>else. It's just some
>lonely dickhead with
>an axe to grind.

Caz
Let you know if I hear Lorna
slagging you further. It'd be mad
if it was her but you never know.

>Erin
>Yeh, do. Got a call in
>ten.
>Mañana chica.

25

Erin pushes the Bugaboo up the hill, her back almost parallel to the ground as its wheels rumble over the cobbles. Bobby stares up at her, unimpressed. He's tired but also, perhaps, wired as she probably gave him too many titbits of pastry in order to quieten him down in the twenty minutes before she made her escape from the 'mum-summit' at the brasserie at the end of the harbour they were just at. She's not sure he's going to sleep and she gets the drop-in-altitude feeling at the thought of him screaming for the whole walk home. But at the moment he's quiet, looking angelic in the winter sun, and as she gets to the high street, she gets her phone out to treat herself to a quick flick on Instagram.

She swiftly imbibes the thirty-seven new followers she's got since she last looked – she was careful not to check it at the brasserie, hyper-aware of the eyes of the room on her – then ignores the 186 notifications she has and searches for Sophie Delauney's handle. Erin had gone to the summit expecting to see Sophie and her scenester posse because their friend Aleya had organised the event, but they weren't there. Erin's not exactly friends with them but they mostly discuss TV shows and films they've seen, what gigs are coming to town and the best new music, obviously, which makes them far more appealing to spend time with than the normal diatribe of nap times, nipples and weaning advice that underscores most mum-group interactions.

Lorna Morgan was at the summit, however. Erin didn't talk to her but she was constantly aware of her buzzing around at the far side of the room. Erin caught her glaring at her at one point. It seems absurd that she'd be the one that filmed her shouting at Bobby but she has always seemed like someone who carries a heavy sack of grudges with her wherever she goes, so Erin shouldn't discount it.

She finds @sophdelano and clicks onto her 'stories'. Her tattooed music producer boyfriend doing up her kitchen, her cat swiping at their huge TV, and finally a picture of a very beautifully rendered latte and something samosa-like next to it. Erin turns her buggy off the high street and towards the car park that sits behind it. She knows the cafe Sophie's in, if she's still there. Erin went to sleep late last night trying to keep up with the daily deluge of messages she's had since her speech at Claridge's went faintly viral, so she could do with a coffee. Then she could breastfeed Bobby to sleep, put him straight in the buggy and avoid the napping battle on the way home. It's a great plan.

She crosses through the car park and over the threshold into the courtyard of the Beets and Peaches Cafe and it's like crossing over into a different country. Tropical-looking trees hung with Chinese lanterns, lizard-motif murals on the wall next to an outside toilet, metal tables in vivid yellow and pink. She hears laughter inside, and Bobby seems to snap to attention. He begins to struggle against his constraints, bouncing up and down in his seat like he was on a horse. She walks into the cafe and hears Sophie Delauney's elfin voice. Erin sees her sat on the other side of a free-standing bookshelf that's filled with succulents in wonky-looking pots, the people she's with laugh again. Erin pushes the buggy towards the shelf when a voice stops her.

'I think it's really damaging,' the Australian accent says. It's Amanda. Bobby wriggles in his buggy again. Erin glances past the plants in the bookshelf and makes out Sophie's acolytes Mercedes and Kristina sitting opposite Sophie and Amanda, who she's obscured from seeing by a column of doorstop fashion books.

'Instagram specifically?' Kristina asks.

'All of it. In ten, maybe even five years, I think doctors will be talking about it like they did about smoking. The pressure to look perfect, have the perfect stuff, the perfect life. And it's so addictive, way more than any drug.'

'I'm totally addicted,' Kristina chips in.

'I try not to look at it at weekends, but it's hard,' says Sophie.

'Is she on it all the time?' Mercedes asks Amanda and Erin feels her hands grip on the handle of the buggy. She's paused here, hiding behind some cactuses, earwigging in on their conversation because she somehow knows that she's been the subject of this conversation. She considers bursting round the corner to interrupt but she wants to hear Amanda's response.

'She seems so stressed by it all. I want to take her phone off her and just be like "look at the sky, play with your son, talk to your husband", you know? She's so, so lovely, but she's completely in its thrall.' Erin swallows a boulder-sized lump in her throat.

Bobby wrenches his whole body towards where the women are sitting, almost sliding out of the seat. He squawks at still being constrained and Erin hears the women clear their throats and shuffle in their seat when they realise some-one's next to them. Erin pushes the buggy away from them, up towards the counter.

'Erin!' Amanda's voice, elated, betraying nothing of what she's just been saying about her. Erin turns to see her with Sophie's boy Able in her arms and Sophie, Mercedes and Kristina, lounged over oriental scatter cushions on a pair of sofas, assorted kids ambling around the table. The floor's lit-tered with wooden blocks, the table with coffee cups, a board of hummus and pakoras along with three brown, what look like, medicine bottles.

Bobby squawks like a furious seagull so Erin lifts him up out of the buggy. He throws his fist towards Able in Amanda's arms and begins to flip around on Erin's chest like a fish on the floor of a boat.

'Someone's amped to see you, Mand,' Sophie says. Amanda hands Able back to his mother and Erin, flustered, finds her-self depositing Bobby into Amanda's open arms. Her baby nestles his head in the nook between Amanda's head and shoulder. She turns to Sophie and her friends, scrunches her face up in that way she does to indicate something along the lines of *isn't he a darling*. Mercedes catches Erin's eye, a hint of furtiveness gives away some sense of concern at her having heard some of their conversation. Amanda sniffs theatrically towards Bobby.

'Ooo, stinky-dinky bum. Shall I go change him?' Erin nods, still not quite sure what's going on here. Amanda fishes into a black patent leather bag, Sophie's, Erin thinks, for a nappy and wipes and sweeps past towards the outdoor toilet. Why was Bobby so desperate to see her? He'd practically punched

Erin in the face to try and get into Amanda's arms. Sophie and her perfect spherical pregnant belly stand up and beckon her to come and join them.

'Didn't know you were around, love,' Sophie says, pincering Erin's shoulder as she sits down on the seat where Amanda was. 'Has Manda got you on any of these?' Sophie leans over to one of the bottles. Erin shakes her head, looks towards where Amanda's gone off with Bobby.

'What is it?'

'Verbena, fennel, a load of flower oils.' She takes the lid off and offers a sniff to Erin. It smells like sambuca. 'I told her I was feeling anxious the other day so she made me this up. So sweet. I've been looking for a good herbalist for ages.'

'That's what you're all doing here?'

'What?'

'Is she giving you –' Erin searches for the word – 'a herbal thing, a consultation?' Sophie looks over to Kristina whose baby is now attached to a surprisingly large boob. Erin has only ever seen her in workwear, boiler suits and the like, and now struggles to return her attention to Sophie.

'We were just having a morning hang. Amanda brought us all something –' she indicates to the bottles – 'just for things we'd spoken about.'

'Mine's for my back,' Kristina adds. 'Don't know what it's got in it but it's funky as fuck. Think it's got booze in it too because I'm feeling a'ight.' The girls laugh.

'She's lent me this bracelet –' Mercedes waves her wrist showing off a chunky band made of gemstones – 'and sent me a link to this great website. Sustainably sourced, verified healing crystals, quite reasonably priced too.'

'I didn't know you knew each other?' Erin says, trying to seem as enthusiastic as they are about healing crystals and herbal tinctures.

'We've been doing Pilates – she came out to Phoenix Wines the other night.'

'She's tried to recruit us for yoga on the beach,' Mercedes adds, her plummy voice and blackberry-stain lips always making her seem a bit drunk. 'But I'm not fucking touching that till the spring.' The other women laugh again. Erin absent-mindedly picks up a pakora and pops it in her mouth. It tastes like a salsa verde bath-bomb. She looks up at the cafe's decor, prints by local artists, posters of French films, a palm-tree-themed wallpaper, the furniture either upcycled or intended to look like it's been.

'And, shit, actually, God.' Sophie prods her lip-ring with her tongue. She has a pixie cut that she's recently dyed rose gold. It looks great. 'I should have checked it was OK with you, I only just asked her.' What now? Erin thinks. She feels entirely discombobulated by this little gathering. She's just spent the last hour and a half at a dated restaurant soaking up the earnest acclaim of a bunch of strangers, but there was a whole other party going on, the one where the cooler mums were discussing herbal remedies and reminiscing about nights out at wine bars she didn't even know had happened. 'I've asked Amanda to be my doula. Is that OK?'

'I thought you were due in April?'

'End of March. Did you need her for something then?'

'Um, no. No.'

'She's just so great. How she is with Bobby? Must be heaven having her at home. And, I don't know if you get the same, but I feel like I relax, like my whole body just relaxes, being around her. Able's birth was so traumatic. I think it could make all the difference having her to help.'

'Yeh,' Mercedes says as if Sophie's just revealed a unique insight, 'I totally get what you mean.'

'But –' Sophie turns to Erin – 'only if it's cool with you.'

'Yeh, course, I'm not her boss,' Erin says, laughing nervously. It's the beginning of February. The end of March is nearly two months away. Amanda said she was stopping off with them before going on some travels around Europe. Erin hadn't really thought about it because having her around seemed so fortuitous, but surely she was only planning on staying for a couple of weeks. But now she's making plans, concrete plans, the sort that aren't easy to disregard, to stay for another two months. And if she were to stay, how much of a commitment is being someone's doula? Would she still be able to help with Bobby? Is she starting a business teaching yoga, selling herb tinctures to people? Erin feels hot, feverish almost, thoughts tripping, barrelling over each other in her head. She needs to tell Raf. They need to have a discussion. They need to get some kind of clarity on this whole situation immediately.

'Oh my God, look at this. Look at this, everyone.' Amanda rushes back into the room from the toilet. Bobby in her arms, his lower half in nappy only. 'Look!' They all look, Erin almost lifting out of her seat as Amanda stations herself and Bobby in profile like they're about to do a skit together. Then she roars into the little boy's face, not like a lion or a dinosaur but more some strange monster, contorting her face as she does it. Then Bobby does something extraordinary. His face widens into a grin and he laughs. A sucking-in laugh, like a cackling witch, but a laugh nonetheless.

The girls start clapping, someone whoops, like it's the end of a concert. They all look at Erin, excited, delighted. Sophie puts an arm around her. Erin's posted so many times about how, no matter what she does, she can't get little Bobby to smile and how she's trying not to let it deflate her high spirits, so they all know how big a moment this is for her. Amanda glances round at everyone, a bemused Bobby following suit, the hint of happiness glowing still in his shining round face. Amanda fixes Erin with a look, widens her eyes, gives that shrug, an almost imperceptible raising of her eyebrow. Is she checking Erin's pleased, pleased enough that her grumpy little boy is finally smiling? Or is it something else, is there a hint of smugness, a touch of triumph? Amanda breaks her look and grabs Bobby into her, smothers his neck with kisses and sits down opposite Erin.

'Good boy,' Amanda says, 'clever boy.'

26

'Roaharrrr.' Erin finds a guttural sound from deep within her stomach, hands in claw-like pincers in front of Bobby sat in his high chair. He stares up at her like a withering talent-show judge, not the slightest hint of a smile. 'Fuck's sake.'

'Ez,' Raf reprimands her, leaned in the crook of their horseshoe kitchen cabinets.

'I don't get it. What she did wasn't even very good.'

'He's probably not in the mood. I'm not exactly Mr Chuckles when bedtime's round the corner.' Erin walks behind Bobby's high chair, to the other side of the living room, then turns and creeps back towards him. She can feel Raf's concerned eyes on her. She's been trying to make Bobby smile for the last ten minutes, trying to show Raf what she saw in the cafe, trying to show him that it wasn't Amanda that made Bobby smile, but that she just happened to be the person in the right place at the right time.

'Raaaaaaa!' Erin shouts into Bobby's ear, pincering his little shoulders, trying to surprise him. He tenses under her grip, eyes close, face wrinkles like an old peach and it looks like he might be about to cry. Erin steps back, practises a different monster face, puts her arms wider, preparing a different approach. Three years of drama school, she thinks to herself, I can be a much better monster than Amanda. She looks up to see Raf, piercing her with a side-eye like she's lost her mind as he lifts Bobby out of the high chair, back towards the low kitchen lights and into the safety of his arms.

'You didn't know?'

'You said Sophie only asked her to do it this morning. How would I know?'

Erin's in their bedroom going through a box of #gifted breathable athleisure that arrived this morning. She catches her reflection in the window. She looks wide. She knows she's not fat but she's never thought she was wide before. Perhaps she should take this unexpected delivery as a spur to start running. She could document herself doing 'couch to 5K', she thinks – that would be super accessible for her followers.

'How long did you think she was staying?' she says to Raf, who's crouched down on the floor with Bobby who's rolling around on a large bath towel naked, having some 'nappy-off time', reaching into the air and staring at a revolving light that puts stars and planets on the ceiling.

'Don't know.'

'What did she say? I was at the no phones thing when she first got here. What did she actually say about how long she'd be here?' She stretches a boob tube out. It's far too small so she tosses it into a pile on the bed.

'She didn't,' Raf says, keeping his voice low. 'I guess I thought she'd be here a couple of weeks.'

'Exactly, not three months.'

'She's only in the kitchen,' he says in a stage whisper.

'Are you going to talk to her?'

'Er, yeh, sure.'

'You know she's giving out herbal remedies to people. People she barely knows. Sophie was all "I've been looking for a herbalist. Don't let her leave."'

'Right,' Raf says. 'Can you?' He indicates to a squirming Bobby who he's struggling to hold in place while he tries to put a nappy on him. Erin grabs a smartphone running case from among the new delivery and gives it to Bobby to distract him. She holds him in place while Raf secures the nappy and rubs moisturiser into his plump little belly. She feels the rolls around her baby's elbows under her fingers and swells with affection. His eyes, so similar to Raf's, are locked on to his dad even as his mouth and hands attempt to fit more of the Velcro strap into his mouth. Raf picks him up and wriggles him into his pyjama bottoms over on the bed.

'Is this about him smiling?' he says, picking the towel up from the floor and backhand-tossing it into the laundry bin.

'It's about the fact that we have your friend staying at our house and we have no idea how long for.' He flicks his eyes up at her from beneath the canopy of his thick eyebrows. He's got that disappointed look in his eyes that makes her feel like a child and around a thousand times more irritated than she was before. 'I mean, has she told you, in any detail, what she's actually doing here?' He strides over to her and presses his index finger onto her lips, stopping Erin saying another word.

'She'll hear you,' he says through a clenched-teeth whisper. Bobby begins to rankle, an arm reaching towards Erin's neck. Raf hands him over to her and she takes him, shocked at the abruptness of what her fiancé's just done. It felt aggressive and that's not Raf at all. 'Do you know what she's doing here, Erin, most of the time, what she's been *doing* since she's been here?' He hasn't moved, face angled to the floor, voice just above a whisper. 'Looking after our baby when you're in London. That's what she's doing. That's why I don't feel that comfortable saying to her, "Hey, Amanda, how long you staying, mate? Gonna think about slinging your hook? Who's gonna look after Bobby when you're gone? No idea really, his mother doesn't seem to have much interest."'

Erin opens her mouth and closes it again, like a child's impression of a goldfish, as Raf stalks over to the window and opens it. The cold air swirls into the room like a phantom. She can't remember a time that he's spoken to her with such cruelty, so the first thought she has, a thought that seems to become more and more valid as she computes what he's just said, is that she must deserve it.

She sits on the bed. Bobby's crotchety, hungry, so she pulls up her top and presents a breast to him. He turns his head like she's just revealed a bright light, lets out a shrill wail, bats at her sore nipple. Erin shoves his head onto her boob and after the briefest resistance he begins to nurse.

'I'm, I'm sorry, that was not kind,' Raf says, 'speaking to you like that.'

Erin gets her phone out and starts scrolling through Instagram. More than a hundred new followers. An over-whelming number of messages to respond to. But her fiancé's just said what he actually thinks and it feels like being stabbed in the throat. Excruciating pain followed by the feeling of having all the wind sucked out of her. He turns to her, spots the phone. She can see him deciding not to comment as he comes over to sit next to her.

'I saw a bit of that speech you did the other night. You going on about how lonely it is being a mum, how lonely you were, and I just, I thought, I'm working my arse off every day, to put a roof above our heads, time I'd love to be spending with my son and, and you're not doing it anyway. Amanda is. Even though you know that someone else looking after my son is something I never, ever wanted. I barely remember the time before my mum left, any care I got from Dad has probably fucked me up for life, I just wanted things to be different for Bob.' He flicks a finger at one of Bobby's toes. 'She's staying here, probably longer than she wanted, because you've pretty much asked her to. How many times have I heard you tell her she's a "godsend", a "lifesaver"? Maybe she's desperate to get back to her life but she probably doesn't feel like she can.' As if in response, Amanda clatters a heavy pan into the sink.

'What do you want me to do then?' Erin looks at Raf before shifting a cushion under Bobby's bottom. 'Tell me what you want me to do?' He sighs so audibly that Bobby opens his eyes and looks up at his dad.

'I want you to be happy. That's all I've ever wanted. Everything I've done since we met, all I've been trying to do.' He can't hold Erin's look and stares away from them, down at the floor. It's true, Erin thinks, since they first met her happiness has been so much more important to him than his was to her. 'But nothing seems to be enough, the life I'm trying, working, to give us, it's not enough for you.' Erin doesn't know how to respond, so she leaves his words hanging in the air. 'I don't want Amanda living here,' he says, 'not really. I want it to be just us. A family. A new chapter away from the city, like we planned. So if you want me to ask her to go, right now, I will happily do that.' His voice is frail, broken, almost on the edge of tears.

Erin's phone buzzes and it snaps Raf from his thoughts. She glances down at the screen, an email from Grace. Perhaps it's about the contract. Every time her phone does anything she hopes it might be the contract from Phibe Digital, the money finally that step closer to her account. She tucks the phone under Bobby, conscious of the optics of checking it now.

'You're right about the smiling,' she says. 'It should have been me. I'm feeding him.' Bobby pulls his head away from her nipple before Erin clamps him back on. 'I half ruined my body giving birth to the little bugger. I thought he'd smile first for me. It's not Amanda's fault he didn't.' Erin thinks of the email, thinks of the day a week she's agreed to be at the Phibe offices for the next couple of months. She thinks of the chain of London hotels Grace said have expressed an interest in her hosting a monthly influencer's dinner. She thinks of Fearne Cotton's podcast, the four other less esteemed ones she's been invited to be on in the two and a half weeks since Grace's been her agent. She can't bring Bobby and she can't turn it down. They need the money, she needs the money, some of her own. If she can't honour all these commitments, if she can't keep raising her profile, keeping herself in position as Grace's future superstar, she might not get anything. Erin needs Amanda to stay around for a while longer, just until she can start to be a bit more picky, make enough to show Raf that he can start turning work down. But what Amanda said about her in the cafe, the topless cuddling with her baby, the way she gripped Erin's arm when she caught her snooping in the studio. She had seemed so lovely, Erin thought she might have a friend, a confidante, but now she just can't shake the feeling that she might not be able to trust this woman.

'Food's done, guys.' Amanda's call comes up to them, muffled by the carpet on the stairs. 'I'm hitting a class with the girls. Don't wait for me to eat.'

'Have fun,' Raf calls back, not shouting but loud enough to be heard in their small house.

'We have to find out what her plans are,' Erin says. 'For her sake as much as anything else.' Raf nods, puts a hand on her bare knee and squeezes it. 'You're right. It's not fair to make her part of the family then ask her to leave. We need to find out what her intentions are.'

'Yeh,' he says, scratching at the hair on the back of his neck. 'Otherwise she might be with us forever.' He makes a funny face, something to lighten the mood that says *God forbid*, before getting up and going into the bathroom.

Erin looks down at Bobby, his eyelids are drooping closed and then popping open again to suckle some more food every few moments. She experiments with holding Bobby closer into her, pushes the pillow up to support him. He reaches his free arm around her waist, tickling the skin under her vest top. A pulse of warmth runs up her back. The front door clicks shut as Amanda leaves for the evening.

27

6 February 1999

We're here! We made it! We have a flat together like a real husband and wife! AND AND AND

WE MADE LOVE.

We got a taxi from Palmerston bus station in the middle of the night and arrived at our apartment by the Darwin Marina. And there, that first morning, before we'd even unpacked our bags, he took me in his arms, carried me to the bed and made love to me. It was like he'd unleashed all of the emotion that had been brewing within me. I wept and wept and wept and he held me in his arms. It was almost too wonderful. He was quiet afterwards, but when I asked if it was OK, he smiled at me and said I was perfect. Then he got up, got his pencils and began to sketch me just as I was, lying naked, there on the bed.

Before, back home, he always said he was scared, scared of piercing the energetic bond between us, even after our marriage ceremony at Nourlangie. He said that desire could do strange things to spiritual bonds like ours and he was scared it might irreversibly alter what we had. But as he drew me, he seemed so much happier than I'd ever known him to be, so much more relaxed. He looked up from his pad at one point and said, 'Now we can really be. Be how the universe wants us to be, just us, together forever.'

And that was when I knew I'd made the right decision. In the night-time cab ride I'd been scared. Leaving my mum, leaving school, being a fugitive from the only life I'd ever known. It wasn't until the car got to the outskirts of Darwin that the profundity of what we'd done, what I'd done, really hit me. And I can admit, to this blank page, that I had doubts.

But now I don't. We wrote a note for Mum to tell her not to follow us, to be happy for us, and to try and move on with her life without me. Donny said that one day, when I'm older, when they've had some time to get perspective, they'll see that I had to get away. It came to me like an epiphany that Craig's feelings towards me aren't healthy, his trips to my room, talking to me about sex with boys, it's not appropriate. Donny didn't like the way he looked at me. He said he saw hatred in his eyes, and something else. He'd hit my mum before. How long before he hit me, or something much, much worse?

The apartment is tiny, dirty, and a little damp. Donny's been out most of the time, at Richard's gallery, but I've been cleaning and doing as much decorating as I know how to do on my own and, even though we only moved in three days ago, it's starting to fall into place. I've cleared the balcony and I want to plant a herb garden there. I told the woman next door I like crystals and she's given us this beautiful smoky quartz, and I cleaned its energy and polished it up. I was going to make it the centrepiece on our coffee table, but then I thought Donny might want to know where I got it from, so now it's under the sofa.

I want to make our home perfect for him. I've been read-ing in magazines about how to please him in other ways as well. He's sacrificed so much for me. I know, with a little work, I can be everything he needs me to be.

Sometimes I pinch myself hard, hard enough that it leaves a mark, just to make sure I'm not dreaming.

28

Erin turns the corner, past the small stone fortification that sits atop the promenade, and spots Amanda in the distance. She's leaning on the metal pole that blocks toddlers from falling into the sea, head on her forearms. She could be stretching but she's not wearing her yoga pants. As she gets closer she sees Amanda's shaking her head. She slaps the metal with one hand, then grips it, legs wringing around each other. She's upset, Erin thinks.

There's part of her that wants to walk on, Bobby's looking sleepy, and having spent the morning doing a live Instagram Q&A with the whingeing baby locked to her hip, she's desperate for an hour or so's peace, and stopping to chat to Amanda could jeopardise him nodding off. But she's never seen Amanda anything but upbeat so she can't just leave her.

'Hey,' she says as gently as she can muster. Amanda wheels round, blinks eyes puffy with past tears, and sighs out a smile.

'Erin, hello. Hey, baby.' Bobby, eyes half closed, on the edge of sleep, acknowledges Amanda's greeting with a lurch to the other side of the sling.

'Are you OK?' Erin asks. Amanda does a strange nod, like her head's dipping under a set of waves.

'Boy trouble,' she says, voice gravelly, shaking it away as if it's nothing. Amanda notices something, cocks her head at Erin. 'You're so, so beautiful.' Her voice almost catches as she says it. 'Stand there, give me your phone.' Erin crinkles her face in confusion but Amanda's insistent, she positions her to stand against the barrier, a twenty-foot drop down to the beach below, and reaches her hand out for Erin's phone. There's something manic in her eyes, whites too big like an anxious animal. She comes up to Erin, hand still stretched out for the phone. Erin sees the drop down to the rocky beach below out of the corner of her eye and hands the phone over, Bobby enlivening at the activity. Amanda takes a few steps back and holds up the phone and frames Erin and Bobby up in its camera.

'Picture-perfect,' she says, followed by the artificial sound of a camera shutter opening.

29

BRAUNEoverBRAINS

431 posts   65.8k followers   1,712 following

ERIN BRAUNE

This is my loved-up face. Cos I'm in LURVE.

THIS PLACE. THIS BOY. SPREAD MY HEART ON TOAST BECAUSE IT HAS MELTED.

Been such an exciting month, but I've missed this boy more than I can say and having him snuggled up to me, in sunshine like this! It's not always easy-breezy looking after a bubba but what they say is true, value every moment you have with them because the time is so precious. And, as if you don't already think I'm a smug twad already, LOOK AT THAT VIEW.

But wherever you are, whether they're sleeping or awake, love your bubba like they love you. Because, perish the thought, they might not always feel so ardent!

30

Erin concentrates on the ridges of black rock as she steps over them. Five minutes ago she turned her foot on one and it sent a jag of pain drilling into her left hip. Amanda stops ahead, allowing Erin to catch up with her.

'Whose idea was it?' Amanda asks, her schoolgirl-style duffel coat not quite covering the hem of her dress.

'Whose idea was what?' Erin asks, still trying to talk quietly so Bobby doesn't wake even though she's slightly out of breath. They've only been walking for five minutes but Amanda's raced ahead and it's hard going. There's a path at the top of the cliff that leads all the way to the chalk needle on Jessup Bay, but Amanda wanted to walk along the beach. So it's been mostly sucking sand, slippery rocks and knee-deep piles of drying seaweed that Amanda's treating like nature's obstacle course.

'Having a baby,' she says, slowing to allow Erin to catch up.

'It was a joint decision, I suppose.'

'Hm,' Amanda says.

'I felt rudderless, I was blaming Raf for it. I was becoming a bit of a nightmare to be honest. I think we both thought it might bolster things between us.'

'It has.'

Erin gives Amanda a quizzical look. Her tone wasn't questioning, she was telling Erin she was right, that having a baby *has* brought them closer together, despite having only known them as a couple for a matter of weeks.

'Are you sure you're OK?' Erin asks. 'You were – you seemed upset, up on the prom?'

'Just, this guy back home.'

'You spoke to him?'

Amanda nods. 'I'm not sure it's going to work.'

'Has he got impatient?'

'Sorry?'

'You being here, is he not happy to give you space any more?'

'Something like that. I shouldn't be telling you all this.' She dismisses herself with a shake of the head, frustrated, that edge of mania creeping into her eyes.

'It's fine, honestly. If you need to talk to someone, you've helped us so much, it's the least I can do.'

'Look, I don't know. He – he needs me, I know he needs me, but he can't see it.'

'He's broken things off?'

'He doesn't know what he wants. He's a conundrum.'

'Shit, one of those?'

'It's so draining.' Amanda looks at Erin with a wan smile. 'But I can't seem to –' she tenses her two hands into claws and then releases them into the air – 'tear myself away from him.'

'He sounds like a dick.'

'He's not.' Amanda's jaw tenses, she's suddenly defensive.

'No, I just mean, he's probably not half as complicated or interesting as he wants everyone to think.' Amanda's face creases into a tight grin. Erin's phone buzzes and Amanda notices her attention drift into a different universe. The buzzing in her pocket has been almost constant for the last few minutes. The short buzz of Insta notifications, the two pulses of vibration for a WhatsApp, the longer one of an email. She's so used to these mini-shocks of engagement that she hasn't thought to look, but even though she doesn't know what they are, they still give her a little starburst of happiness. The photo Amanda took up on the promenade was lush. Erin was kissing the sleepy Bobby's head, strands of hair blowing artistically in the breeze, the sun reaching through a particularly photogenic band of cloud. Amanda captured something, the vastness of the landscape behind making the moment between mother and child both intimate and essential. She's loath to involve Amanda any further into their lives, but Erin's feed could do with that sort of photography all the time.

She gets her phone out, hoping that it's Grace with some news – she's fishing around a production company that are considering Erin to front an Internet kids' show and, although she's being blasé about it to Raf, she's inordinately excited about the prospect of being on-screen, even if it is just online.

Trying to reach you. Going to voicemail. Please call me now.

It is from Grace. On the email icon she sees she has twenty-three new emails come in. She has forty-plus WhatsApps. And Instagram has gone insane, more than two hundred notifications. Something's happened. Her chest clenches and, despite the wintery air, she wants to take her coat off.

Up ahead Amanda jumps up onto a crop of shining wet rocks and throws her arms up, causing a flock of seagulls to fly up in the air over Erin. She ducks down though none of them are very close to her. Bobby shifts to the side but doesn't wake.

'Fuck sake,' she says under her breath, brandishing her phone in front of her like a lit stick of dynamite. Grace's tone does not commute good news. She needs to call her immediately but she can't risk waking the baby. Erin's first thought is the video of her shaking the buggy. They never found out who 'Ali-Crow' was so there was nothing to stop them from reposting the video.

She goes into Instagram, clicks onto her notifications, scans down the list as fast as her phone will load them. Messages from handles she recognises, but most she doesn't. Then the words: *You have been tagged in four photos by Leister-worcley.* She clicks onto the 'Tagged' icon. There they are. Four photos.

Erin at the brasserie on the end of the harbour, Bobby on her breast, a pained look of disgust on her face as she looks down at him.

Erin dead-eyed at the church hall baby group, ignoring Bobby as he holds out a block to her.

Erin, face into the buggy, contorted in anguish on the patch of grass near the beach, a still from the video from before.

She's not in the last photo. It shows Amanda, sat on a sofa somewhere Erin doesn't recognise, Bobby cradled in her left arm, drinking a bottle. Amanda pouts a big kiss to the baby and Bobby's eyes are shining.

Amanda's there, next to her, and Erin flicks the phone away from her so she can't see the screen. She bends down to the level of Bobby's head, adjusts his hand that's become trapped.

'The stack's just round the corner,' she says and Erin gawps at her. 'All OK?' The heat on Erin's chest from Bobby being on her feels excruciating now.

'Can you, can you take him?'

'He's asleep.'

'Can you get him off me?' Her voice harsh. When Amanda doesn't act immediately, Erin begins to tear at the back of the wrap, desperate to get the weight off her. Bobby begins to crotchet but she doesn't care. She yanks at the knot on her back, pulling the wrong part that abruptly tightens it, waking Bobby with a start.

'Let me.' Amanda goes round the back and unties the wrap and takes Bobby into her arms. Erin walks away from them, looking up at antlike figures on the cliff above. Is whoever it is watching her now? she thinks Because someone is following her around town, taking pictures of her. Someone is trying to make it look like she hates her baby. Like she's a terrible mother. Then rounding it off with a picture of him drinking a bottle, she meant to do a post about him combi-feeding but kept putting it off, but worse, drinking that bottle with sparkly-eyed Amanda, a nanny in all but name that, again, she hasn't even begun to mention on social media.

Amanda disentangles Bobby from the wrap and drops it onto a patch of rock. He's fully awake and not happy to be so. She bounces him up and shows him the sea to try and bring him down from his ratcheting grumbles. Erin stalks further up the beach towards the cliff face, stumbling on patches of seaweed, rage swirling within her like a tempest. She doesn't deserve this. What has she done to be targeted in this way? She's about to phone Grace but she stops and sits down on the wet sand. She goes through the pictures again. The blankness behind her eyes. The joy in Amanda's. She flicks down the comments. 'Inauthentic', 'bullshit', 'breast is best', 'hot nanny', 'betrayal', 'dishonest', 'exploitative'. Incendiary words

boom out of each tiny sentence. She can hear Amanda singing 'wheee' as she swings her baby boy into the air. Erin's eyes
begin to water, but she's not upset, it's the anger leaking out
of her. She turns her phone to face herself and presses the
record button.

'Fuck you, you fucking coward,' she says to a picture of her
own angry face on the phone's screen, the red record button
blinking to the side of her. 'Sneaking around taking pictures
of me and my baby. If I look bored, if I look pissed off in
them, maybe it's because I am bored. Maybe it's because I am
pissed off. Yeh, I'm giving him a bottle sometimes. How else
do you think I can go to events on weekday nights? Should
I have *declared* it to the world? If people don't like it they can
unfollow me. I don't give a shit.' But then the words catch
at the back of her throat like leaves in a drain. She stops the
recording and puts the phone back in her coat pocket. Bobby
shrieks with joy up ahead. Erin puts her head between her
knees.

31

'So, I'm feeling very sad and very, as you can see from the panda-eye mascara debacle going on here, very upset about what's happened today. Someone intruding on me and my family in this way feels very personal and I'm feeling attacked. It does feel like an attack. I know that lots of people with far fewer followers than me have to deal with some of the most despicable abuse online, death threats, rape threats, etc. And I've had a few of those and they're awful when you get them and are one hundred per cent not OK at all, but we're taught to dismiss them as trolls and ignore them. And the fact that society has just said that that's sort of fine is a pretty horrendous thing, but I'm not here to talk about that today. But yeh, the fact that the pictures are of me and Bobby and one of our friends is, it's very personal and worrying. Whoever it is has been near enough to take a photo. And that is not on, at all. So please stop. Stop taking these photos. However, um, this is really hard to say right now but, these photos have actually been a wake-up call to me about what I choose to post and a reminder that I have a responsibility to be as open and transparent as I can possibly be. I should have made it much more explicit that I'm no longer exclusively breastfeeding. For the last three or four weeks, I've been pumping breast milk and Bobby's been

having it in a bottle. There it is. And, to be honest, he's not
been great on the boob recently so we might have to think
about him starting on formula and that is totally cool, and
if it ever seemed like I made a big deal of him being exclusively breastfed, then it was never my intention to shame
those that chose not to. Most of the reaction has been about
the bottle, but people also want to know who the lady with
Bobby is. She's called Amanda. She's an old friend of Raf's
and she's been amazing helping me out with Bobby when
I've had to be in London for work. She's not a nanny that
we're paying, she's not a #gifted childminder from an agency,
she's just doing us a good old-fashioned solid. I didn't want
to feature her because she's not on social media and doesn't
want to be. But again, *mea culpa*, if I ever gave the impression that I was doing everything I was doing while always
looking after Bobby, then that was a false impression and I
apologise for it. What these photos have taught me is that I
am not perfect, my life is not perfect, and I don't always love
all aspects of being a mum. I never thought that my feed was
saying that I did, but some of your responses to the photos
have made me reconsider my own output. I want us all to
be the best caregivers, the most loving parents, the most
satisfied and fulfilled people that we can. If my Instagram
feed EVER made anyone feel inadequate or in some way,
not 'enough', then I'm filled with remorse and if there are
those that now feel I'm some sort of fraud, I want you to
know that I'm not. But if you choose to unfollow me, there
are some wonderful women out there who I'd love you to
fill the void with who I'll link to in the next few frames of
my stories.

'I love you all and hope that you'll be patient with me as I take a day or two to get over the intrusion into my family's life. It's been a very difficult day. I am going to drink gin. Because that is how middle-class women have been brought up to cope with all varieties of distress.'

32

'I thought the album you posted last night was inspired. Tonally, a perfect reaction.' Grace Fentiman jingles a teaspoon around her mug, fishes out a green tea bag and puts it on the edge of the untouched plate of ginger nuts that rests on Erin's dining-room table. At ten o'clock last night, Grace had helped Erin craft a video response to the pictures for her 'stories' and Erin had the idea of posting a selection of blooper photos that she'd taken while trying to make content for her Instagram feed. Bobby writhing around while she tries to take a selfie of them, her with sick all over her top, Bobby incandescent, head thrown back, screaming at her. The sort of photos that seem like a mission statement of authenticity moving forward but nowhere near as questionable as the ones posted by her unwanted paparazzo.

It's late afternoon, the day after. Grace's come down on the train. She wears a Barbour padded gilet over a crisp white shirt with dark fitted jeans, all pristine. It looks like she might have ordered the whole ensemble from Net-a-Porter last night in preparation for a rare trip to the provinces. She's so well put-together she makes everything in Erin's house seem shabby in comparison. Raf plonks a brown teapot with a chipped spout in the middle of the table and sits down next to Erin. She'd been desperate not to tell him about the photos last night but lots of people they know would have seen them so she had no choice. He's put on a veneer of concern, but she can tell, the shortness of his sentences, the way he can't look at her for too long, that he's angry she's invited this into their lives. He smothers her hand with his.

'What do you suggest we do?' he asks Grace, tone businesslike.

'We've informed the cyber-bullying team at the Met and I think you should report it to the police down here.'

'You think they'll do anything? I mean, you get burgled over here and the coppers hardly bat an eyelid.' Erin gives Raf a look. He's barely spoken to Grace since he got back from work but now he seems to want to take out his anger about the situation on her. Erin tried to get him to stay at the studio but he's said he blames himself for not taking more of an interest in her Instagram so he insisted on meeting Grace. 'I was googling it last night. There's nothing threatening about the photos that would tip it off as stalking or harassment or whatever else this bastard is up to. So what can they do?'

'Listen,' Grace says, pushing the handle of her teaspoon on the table from six o'clock to nine. 'You are right. The police probably won't do much. There's an assumption that things on social media are harmless, because mostly they are.'

'Mostly —'

'Which is why we've got our guy, Xavi, on it. We've booked him for the whole of this week to work on this. He's the best in the business.'

'What's his background?' Raf asks, too curt.

'He used to work for the Spanish government. The point is, and it's really important that both of you understand this, the point is that we're taking this very, very seriously. There's nothing more important to me than my client's well-being.' Raf releases Erin's hand, shifting in his seat. 'Erin, is there *anyone* you can think of that could have taken those pictures? Do you want to go through them, all of us, try to work out where you were for each shot, if there's someone you saw at those places?'

'Um.' Raf and Grace both lean in. Bobby pulls away from Erin's boob, pawing at her nipple, turning his nose up at it. This whole set-up is excruciating. Something from a nightmare. But she's also breastfeeding. She shoves Bobby on but he must not be on right because it's painful as he feeds.

Erin has done exactly what Grace's suggesting. She's visited the spots, tried to rack her brains about who was there, what the weather was like, where everyone else was. Lorna was at Colvin's, the brasserie where the 'mum-summit' was, but so were about fifty other mums. Amanda's identified the picture of her and Bobby as being at a cafe called Stornaway, but she's been a few times, so she couldn't narrow down when the photo was taken but there's no reason Lorna couldn't have been there. And she was nearby at the time the video was taken. But the day the picture from the church group was taken, Erin's certain it was last week because of the jumper she was wearing, Lorna's Instagram indicates she was in Maidstone all day visiting her sister so that seemed to discount her. Amanda of course was there at the time of the video, she could have been at the other locations, Erin didn't know how long she'd been coffeeing with Sophie and her pals on the day of the 'mum-summit', and Erin had sat near the window so the picture could have been taken from outside, but firstly, she was with Erin when the troll posted these photos and the video from the mound that they managed to take down and, more pertinently why would Amanda post a picture of herself?

Every rational deduction has led to a dead end which points to it being someone she doesn't know. The terrifying thing is that she has tens of thousands of followers, names on a screen that represent real people she knows nothing about, who see what she does every single day. Erin's never posted her address or anything stupid like that, but it's not a stretch to find out where she lives. She's googled some of the landmarks that have appeared in her feed, the beacon of the lido, the alternate purple and yellow beach huts, and an image search brings up their town's name immediately. Hang around for a day or two and someone would be sure to see her and Bobby in town.

'I don't know,' she says, 'I can't think of anyone that would do something like this really.' She glances out of the front window, as if the culprit will be standing out there taking pictures of them now. 'Could it be some sort of incel guy? Anna Mai —' Grace nods, acknowledging the name — 'said that she'd been having lots of very aggressive sort of "get back in the kitchen" type stuff on her feed. Stuff about how a mother shouldn't dress the way she does.' Anna's a gym-buff and hot with it and doesn't baulk at showing off her body on 'the Gram'. 'She said there'd weirdly been a massive increase in that sort of online abuse in the last two or three months. Maybe someone like that?'

'After your speech, you mean?' Raf says. Grace narrows her eyes. 'Calling out the patriarchy can be pretty inflammatory to certain stupid arseholes.' Grace waves her head from side to side as if balancing out his suggestion like ingredients for a cake. 'Have you had to deal with anything like this before?' Raf asks.

'Not exactly, not personal photos like this,' Grace says, adjusting the starched cuff around her left wrist, keeping her eyes fixed on Raf so as not to be watching the breastfeeding. 'But I've had a few clients who've had some pretty horrible stuff. Death threats, threatened sexual assault, torture. I suppose the most similar is a presenter I had whose address kept getting posted up online. She got sent some odd things, but nothing happened really.'

Erin's about to ask what 'nothing happened really' means but Bobby screeching cuts her off. He arches his back away from her chest. He doesn't want her milk. He hasn't wanted her milk for a week or so now. Not from her breast. Not from her when she pumps it and tries to give it to him in a bottle. He doesn't want anything from her. She feels so hot she wants to put Bobby down on his mat and walk out into the rain. Grace gives her what must be her sympathetic face, but it's not hard to tell that she's not much of a baby person.

'Can you –' Erin stands and expects Raf to stand with her and take Bobby, but he remains seated, picks up his phone and calls someone.

'Could you just come and give Bob a bottle for a minute?' he says. 'Yeh, that's right, yeh.' He puts his phone back on the table. Erin looks through the thick lines of rain that hammer onto the mud-green lawn to see Amanda duck out of the studio and skip towards the house and she's surprised to feel grateful. Even though she's loath to let Grace see Amanda charm Bobby into silence she could really do without him scratching and screaming at her while she has to endure this conversation.

Amanda breezes through the door, wet hair twisted into a lock and swept over her shoulder, an embroidered bag hanging from one arm.

'Come here, babba,' she says, taking the screaming Bobby from Erin. 'Hello,' she says to Grace in the polite way a cleaner would acknowledge their employer's guest as she moves past the table towards the kitchen and flicks the kettle on.

'This is Amanda.' Erin realises she doesn't know how to refer to her. 'Our friend.'

'Erin tells me you've been a godsend?' Grace says, cocking her head.

'The Lord moves in mysterious ways,' Amanda says without turning round. Grace takes her time examining Amanda's lacy purple dress with its billowing sleeves as she warms Bobby's bottle in a bowl of hot water.

'What's the plan of action with threats like this? With your presenter client, what did you actually do?'

Grace swings back round to face Raf. She nods, grimaces into a smile.

'There's no set protocol. With the presenter we reported it all but ultimately just had to let it blow over. It's a horrible part of having any sort of public recognition. Are you feeling frightened at all, Erin?' Grace asks.

'No, not frightened, no. They're only taking photos.'

'So far.' Raf's smartly clipped nails scratch at an old scar on the surface of the table. Grace side-eyes him before returning her laser focus to Erin. She can see how Grace's got to where she is. Her eyes are swimming-pool blue and when she looks at Erin it makes her feel like a significant person, someone who should be listened to, yet conversely, she has such effortless authority, Erin always finds herself deferring to her entirely.

'The reason I ask is, the Phibe thing is a pretty major contract that I'm still trying to hash out, but it does require you
to commit to them, set number of posts per week, days in
the office, all that stuff, over a nine-month period, as discussed.' Erin spots Raf's hands ball up on the table. He knows
about the job with Phibe, knows about the time commitment. He'd been happy for her, but, as always, she could tell
he was thinking about how it would impact them as a family.
'I'd hate to get it all over the finish line,' Grace continues, 'and
then for you to decide, totally legitimately, that you're going
to have to duck out of Instagram for a bit and for us to have
to pay back all that money.'

'I'm not going to leave Instagram,' Erin says, with a vehe-
mence that causes her to check herself. Raf pushes his top lip
out with his tongue. 'I just hate the idea of letting whoever it
is win.' Raf takes her fingers in both his hands.

'I agree,' he says. 'You can't run away.' Erin squeezes his
thumb.

'Good,' Grace says, 'I think that's the right play as well.
We're on the crest of getting somewhere really exciting. So
in terms of next steps…' Over Grace's shoulder Erin notices
Amanda putting something from the counter into her bag.
She scans the surface, a Pyrex bowl of lightly steaming water,
a dishcloth, a spoon. Erin looks up and sees Bobby, limpet-
like on Amanda's hip, slurping on his bottle. How does she
get him to do that? she thinks. How does she get him to
sleep so easily? Erin's tried the topless cuddling technique
but it didn't work as she'd hoped. Perhaps it's stress, the stress
that radiates from her body. Since he's been born, with every
scream, every scratch, every noise he's made, every panicked thought he's demanded from her, her head's felt like a

microscope slide invaded by a rapidly multiplying cell, always on the verge of cracking down the middle.

'Is it possible to download images from Instagram, Ez?' Raf's voice cuts into Grace's strategy that Erin was only half listening to.

'Um–'

'Not easily,' Grace says, 'not from someone else's account. Why?'

'If your guy, Xavi, can get me them as JPEGs, I could probably find out what sort of camera they were taken on.'

'Raf's a graphic designer.'

'I've got software that can go pretty hardcore on an image and there's a lot of photographers work at my office. I mean, we're assuming it's done on a smartphone but, to take images, that many images, without you noticing, Ez, it's possible whoever it was was using a proper DSLR camera. Just a thought.'

'Good idea,' Grace says. 'I'll see what I can do.'

Erin's had the same thought. If whoever it is has some sort of telephoto lens, they could, like a sniper in some horrific war movie, be shooting her from anywhere without her ever knowing. And in that case, what other photos could they have? Have they been outside her house? Taking photos through their front window. She looks at the bay window. They took down the chintzy curtains the previous owners left and haven't got around to replacing them. Likewise, their bedroom window had a blind, but the cord has snapped so they've taken the whole thing off. Raf wanted to fit shutters but said they couldn't afford them yet. Perhaps this might spur him on to do something about it.

'Do you think it's the same person as the other week?' The three of them at the table swing round to Amanda in the kitchen, Bobby lolling across her as he drinks. Erin and Grace catch each other's eye. Grace knows that Erin hasn't told Raf about the video on the bank of grass on the seafront. Bobby's head begins to droop so Amanda shifts him into an upright position and stands staring at them, her elaborate purple dress and wide, innocent eyes making her look almost doll-like. Raf seems to growl as he clears his throat.

'What happened the other week?'

33

Raf's shoulders couldn't be more hunched over if he was scrumming down in a rugby match. He perches on the edge of their sofa, holding Erin's phone out in front of him as if it were a bomb. The only sound in the room is the roar of the wind battering the microphone of whatever the video was recorded on. The video ends. Erin begins to speak but Raf puts a hand up to stop her. He presses play again. Erin feels like she has a stitch. She can hear Bobby squawking upstairs with Amanda. Soon after Grace left, Raf asked her if she'd get Bobby ready for bed. He didn't need to explain why. As Amanda crossed the room to the stairs, Bobby clutching at her neck, she mouthed 'I'm so sorry' to Erin. But it's not Amanda's fault that she lied to her fiancé.

The video ends again. This time Erin decides to let Raf speak first. The hum on the fridge behind her suddenly seems as if it's being played through a sound system, such is the silence that gathers between them.

'What happened after this?' His voice is low.

'He was stuck in the buggy. I couldn't get him out.' A deluge of words tumble from her mouth. 'He'd been screaming all morning, like screaming screaming. It must have been reflux pain. It was horrible. He was arching his back so much that I couldn't get him out to give him a cuddle.'

'So what did you do, give him a slap to shut him up?' He twists his body to her, expression neutral as his words pierce like a stiletto.

'I should have told you, I know I should have told you, but –' She moves across the floor to him, but he doesn't open up the space on the sofa so she's forced to perch on the arm. The wind is throwing sheets of rain at the big window, rattling the frames and drawing Raf's attention back to the halogen glow of the street outside their house. 'I didn't want you to see me like that.'

'Your "team" managed to sweep it under the carpet?' He glances at her and she nods in response. He bites his top lip and closes his eyes. 'You weren't ever going to tell me?' She feels like she's onstage and has forgotten her lines, throat dry, pulse racing. Of course she wasn't going to tell him and her hesitation tells him as much. He sucks air through his teeth, stands up and bangs his shin as he walks towards the hall.

'You're going out?' she says, voice cracking. She wants him to have a go at her, she wants to have it out with him and to be able to explain why she'd behave like that, why she wouldn't tell him about it. She wants to be able to tell him that she feels like she's not the mother he thinks she should be, that no matter how many times he reassures her about how good she is with Bobby she can see in his eyes that he thinks she's failing them. But he's going.

'It's hammering down. Can't we – Talk to me.'

He stands in the door frame, pulling his long grey waterproof over him. He screws his maroon beanie onto his head and pauses, looking at the floor.

'Someone is following you around taking photos, videos of you and our *son*. Think about Bobby. For once in his life, think about him.' Erin stands, she opens her mouth. 'What? What are you going to say? That you were thinking of him? That you *always* put him first? Fuck. I can protect you. My job is to protect you if you're bringing psychos into our life. But how can I do that if I don't know what's going on? And like, what *is* going on? What else haven't you told me?'

She goes to him, she's garbling. 'I'm sorry, I should – I was just so – I felt so –' She's grabbing at his waterproof, smelling the black pepper from his aftershave.

'Or do I need to protect him from you?' His words spread a chasm between them. She looks at him, his eyes dewy pools overflowing with disappointment. He tenses the muscles in his jaw and eases her hands off his jacket. 'I've got work, a mountain of work, that I can be doing.' He slides around her, straining every sinew not to make contact with her, his fian-cée, as he walks out of their house.

She goes into the kitchen and flicks the kettle on almost by impulse. A cup of tea will do nothing to improve her situation but she's grown up in a household where it's the prescribed balm for almost any ill so she goes about rinsing a mug that's been left on the counter. Bobby's half-drunk bottle rests on the side. She squeezes her left breast. It feels flaccid, less pumped up than it would have done at this time a couple of weeks ago. She'd found it so amazing that, after a few painful weeks to begin with, her body instinctively learned her son's eating habits and moderated her milk supply to suit him. Her phone buzzes in her pocket and it reminds her that she's chosen to interrupt this amazing natural process. She's cho-sen to rely on Amanda, on sporadic pumping and a little bit of formula to feed her baby. She's chosen to invite the world into their lives. She's chosen to hide threatening behaviour from her husband, for what? Her phone buzzes again, and again shortly afterwards. For that, she thinks to herself. For the dopamine hit of a thin plastic block of computer chips buzzing in her pocket incessantly. She takes the phone out and looks at the dark mirrored tile in its tan leather case. The thirty-four new notifications don't have their normal effect. She feels the device's insubstantiality in her hand and thinks about how easy it would be to casually drop it in the washing-up bowl, to cram it down the waste disposal unit and listen to it being macerated. Instead she blackens the screen, and just for a moment, she hates it, hates it for how much she needs it.

She picks up Bobby's half-finished bottle, takes the lid off and puts it in the microwave for a few seconds. It beeps that it's finished just as Amanda rounds the corner into the kitchen clutching her son in his monochrome sleepsuit. She spots Erin putting the bottle on the kitchen surface and slamming the microwave door.

'Don't you normally breastfeed him to sleep?'

'Thought I'd have backup in case he doesn't want to have a go on these puppies again.' Erin points to her chest.

'I can do it,' she offers, 'if you have stuff you need to take care of?'

'No, I want to, thanks.' Amanda smiles and hands Bobby over into Erin's arms. As his little hands grip the flesh on her forearm she's struck by how ape-like babies look as they swing from the safety of one adult's arms to another's.

'Are you sure you're calm enough?'

'Sorry?'

'I'm so so sorry, Erin.' Her inflection goes up in that way Australians sometimes do. 'I *really* thought you'd told him.'

'It's fine,' Erin says, holding Bobby's gaze, 'I should have. Not your fault.'

'And, I wasn't earwigging, the other week. You had your agent on speakerphone. I couldn't help hearing.'

'It's fine. Honestly. I fucked up.'

'Let me give him the bottle,' Amanda says, clutching her wrist. 'Go and do a meditation, or listen to some minimal techno, or whatever you do to relax. Spend some time on your social media or whatever.' She glances down to the phone in Erin's other hand. 'I feel so awful about this.'

'Raf'll get over it.' Erin picks up the bottle that feels too hot in her hands. Bobby grabs towards it, so she squeezes it into her jeans pocket, the heat searing her bum through the denim, and heads towards his nursery. 'Go out,' she says to Amanda as she gets to the corridor down to Bobby's room. 'I deserve to do some time in solitary with Sir Screechalot.' Amanda stands bathed in the orange light from under the kitchen cupboards. Her arms are crossed in front of her midriff and she seems coiled in a way Erin's not seen before. She looks concerned. Erin doesn't know why but she feels bad for her, bad to have put her in the middle of this situation. 'Honestly, don't worry. This is my fault,' she tells her.

'I hope he can forgive you,' she says, with the dawn of a smile.

'Thanks,' Erin says, turning Bobby as he grapples over her shoulder to try and get to the bottle before heading into his room. She knows that the video makes her look bad, she knows that not telling the father of her child about something like this is thoughtless, but she hadn't even considered the fact that he might not forgive her.

She gets the bottle out of her pocket once she's darkened Bobby's room and sits in the #gifted ergonomic beanbag chair next to his cot. Bobby's nursery is by far the most beautiful room in the house. Bouji Mumma Boutique had sent her loads of amazing stuff, prints, a rug with a hand-stitched elephant on it and a tepee decorated with Mondrian patterns. She's about to get a boob out to see if he'll accept it, but he's crawling across her lap to the bottle so she decides not to bother. Erin squirts some of the bottle onto her hand, it still feels hot but probably just about OK. She adjusts herself in the chair to get comfortable, knowing that to avoid any screaming, and she really can't handle any now, she might have to stay in the chair for half an hour with him sleeping on her once he's finished. She licks up the milk resting on the flesh between her index finger and thumb.

It's sweet. She's tasted her breast milk before and it's always a little sweet but this tastes like cake icing. As Bobby gets over her legs and reaches for it, she puts it up, out of his reach. She puts her tongue on the hole in the bottle and squirts more out. It's insanely sweet and there's another taste, almost medicinal.

'Baaa.' Bobby calls out a warning of a tantrum at the bottle being withheld from him. Erin blinks, unable to make sense of what she can taste. The room feels too dark all of a sudden and she clicks a lamp on next to her, causing Bobby to shield his eyes from the light. She sucks on the bottle, any squeamishness about drinking her own milk miles from her mind. It's so sweet that she winces as if she's accidentally drunk neat cordial.

Bobby lurches up and squeals out in anger at her. She shoves the bottle into his hands and he collapses down into her arms and drinks it down greedily.

The taste stays on her tongue, the tangy cloy she gets after drinking Coke, which she hasn't done for years, but then that liquorice, medicinal taste. Like herbal cough mixture. The row of hessian bags filled with herbs and spices in Amanda's studio flies into her head. Then she remembers Amanda in the kitchen this evening, while she and Raf were talking to Grace, squirrelling something away into her bag.

Erin grabs the bottom of the bottle and Bobby's closed eyes jerk open, his hands grip it harder, feeling the tension of her hand. Erin wants to yank it away from him and throw it far away but she can't have him go ballistic. Whatever it is Amanda's putting in his bottle, it's nothing that's going to harm him, she feels sure of that. But Amanda has put something in her son's bottle. She's put something in Bobby's milk, the milk Erin has sucked out of her by a machine like a dairy cow for forty-five minutes every morning, and not told a soul about it.

She wants to text Raf, to call him back to the house and tell him what she's discovered, but she can't. Not with how he left. It would seem desperate, a pathetic excuse to try and get him to overlook what she's done.

She looks up at a small piece of rock on Bobby's bookshelf that's been there for nearly two weeks. It's a circle, pinkish-white. One of Amanda's crystals. Erin thought it was a nice gesture when she first saw that it had been placed in here. But now it feels like an invasion, a quiet colonisation of her baby's space. She swallows a lump in her throat and listens to the regular sucking sound of her son getting to the end of the bottle. The milk, her tampered-with milk, mixing with air so it almost sounds like kissing, as his body becomes limp with sleep in her arms.

34

'So it's either deal with angry Houdini in the buggy, or two weeks of agonising hip pain after a morning babywearing. I've never seen *Sophie's Choice*, but I have to assume that this is way worse.' Erin stops recording herself. Bobby's hammering at a toy xylophone as if he's writing a symphony designed to give her a headache. She googles *Sophie's Choice*. It's about the Holocaust. She'd get slaughtered for that. She deletes the video.

Outside the clouds sit latent in the sky, the heaviness of the air threatens the drizzle that's been off and on all morning. Erin's spent the last few hours trying to create content in the house and she just can't seem to get it right. It's two days after the photos were posted and although her heartfelt response seems to have worked and the backlash against her has been fairly mild, now she's been exposed as being a far less breezy and 'chill' mum than she'd previously portrayed, she's overthinking her posts to the point of paralysis.

There are some mums that are popular for being no-holds barred in their parenting journeys. Who cry and confess into their smartphones, locked in the bathroom, while their babies scream outside – people like it, it's relatable. But there's no doubt that Erin's sunny positivity has proved a runaway success in comparison to those. 'There's only so much "poor me" grim reality people can handle before they turn off,' Grace had said to her once. And since Erin first got on any social media, in the frontier days of Facebook, she's agreed with that axiom. When people would write a status update alluding to something bad that's happened, a 'Really tough day today', 'Feeling low' or even an 'FML', when everyone else piled on to send messages of sympathy or support, Erin would always be conspicuous by her silence. She could never understand how it would help the person. She found it needy, a pose of vulnerability, of weakness affected to get people's attention, even if that attention only manifested itself as pity. Her mum was a GP before she retired, very hard-working, very impressive considering she'd not come from an academic family. Her sister, Erin's Auntie Claire, had been ill a lot as a child meaning their parents had lavished most of their time and affection on her. So Erin's mum had learned to get attention by being impressive and that need not to reveal the weak parts of her character was drummed into Erin from an early age.

So this morning she's been trying her best to be 'authentic', but failing miserably. In an authentic post she might be warning whichever cowardly shit is taking pictures not to fuck with her or her six-foot-three fiancé, it might feature her calling out Amanda's gall putting some herbal tincture in her son's milk, or it could feature her doing an Edvard Munch silent scream at her own stupidity at not telling Raf about the video. Because that's mainly how she feels today. Furious with herself, frazzled by the barrage of destructive thoughts pluming in her head, and tired, on-the-edge tired.

The night of Grace's visit she barely slept, trying to solve the thousand-piece jigsaw of everything that had happened in the last twenty-four hours. Raf stayed at the studio working that night, which hadn't been uncommon with him before they had Bobby, but he hadn't done it since. Then last night he came back long after she'd gone to bed and, although she sat waiting for him, he didn't come up to her and left in the morning before she got up with Bobby. She's had moments of being furious with him for the casual way in which he's kept himself away. Going AWOL to come to terms with his wife having lied to him is a luxury that a baby's primary caregiver doesn't have. But she knows she doesn't have a leg to stand on any more. She's fucked up and it's better he have time to forgive her. He's never responded well to her confronting him about anything.

Bobby throws the xylophone's beater into the air and it hits the stem of a plant on the coffee table, scattering soil onto the floor. He begins bum-shuffling towards the mess and Erin gets her phone ready. She kneels down, framing up the shot and watches the screen as Bobby puts a chunk of soil in his mouth. He spits it out, makes a disgusted face and Erin snaps him. She has the money shot, the first image for her Insta-stories for today. She looks at the photo. She'll have to put a caption about how she found him like this otherwise people will be asking why she wasn't stopping her son eating soil, but it's perfect. Funny, relatable, authentic, some nice colours from the bookshelf in the background.

Bobby hauls himself up on the coffee table and knocks some coasters onto the floor. Erin glances outside to see that it looks dry and, not being able to handle the screams of wrestling Bobby into the buggy, decides to endure the pain, throwing him in the sling before she heads out for town.

As she walks along her road towards the front, with Bobby enjoying the fresh air and the closeness of her body, she wants to get her phone out and edit the photo, but she keeps seeing neighbours and doesn't want to be seen on her phone when she's with Bobby now. With the sun threatening to break the stranglehold of cloud, she goes down a ramp towards the promenade, finding it thankfully empty.

The sea is blanket-calm and as Bobby waves his arms in the air at a swathe of seagulls that fly out towards the horizon, Erin breathes in the seaweed air and starts to feel something close to calm. She stops, lets her smartphone fall to the bottom of her coat pocket and gazes out at the water. Eighteen months ago, on the day trip that first gave Raf the idea to move down here, they'd stood somewhere near this spot, his arm around her, and looked at this view together. He'd said something about how much bigger than us it was, how it made you think about what your priorities were. She knew that was a nod to her, a dig almost. Whenever she got frustrated with her career, with another audition that didn't lead anywhere, he'd tell her that she just needed to adjust her priorities. This, the scenery, the peace and quiet, is why they moved here, this is what Raf wanted. A simple life by the seaside, not having to work too hard to pay London rents, being a family. But she hasn't been able to surrender to that and now things feel anything but simple.

Bobby grabs at one of her fingers and grips it, he turns his head up to try and look at her but he can't see past the mass of hair. Perhaps that's the answer. The contract with Phibe isn't signed yet, she could call Grace and say she's leaving Insta, she could suggest Amanda might want to get back home, try to make a go of things with her complicated man,

Erin could dedicate herself to Bobby until he goes to school then she could get a job down here, something that wouldn't take her away from home too much. It wouldn't be exciting, it wouldn't be what she ever wanted, but Raf's not doing what he wants to do, most people don't get to do what they want to do. Perhaps that's what growing up means.

Erin gets the sense that someone's there. She swings round sharply, but the promenade is empty. Nothing but a beautifully rendered white-chalk angel graffitied on the concrete lip at the bottom of the cliff. As she gets her phone out to take a picture she senses movement around the brush at the clifftop and looks up. No one there, but she can't shake the feeling that she's being watched.

She turns and strides towards town. Whoever has taken those photos hasn't just chanced on her. They've been where she and Bobby have, several different locations, Amanda and Bobby as well, and that's just the pictures that have been posted. Even though the town's not huge, whoever it is seems to know exactly how to find them. Is she being followed? Is whoever it is watching her all the time? She hasn't ever noticed anyone, but people look at her a lot now and she just accepts them as her Insta-followers. She hasn't seen anyone taking photos of her, but it's so easy to do inadvertently with a smartphone.

The clouds have smothered the burgeoning sunlight and as Erin rounds the corner into the bay that leads up towards the harbour and the esplanade of colourful houses, the grey promenade seems oppressive by comparison. She searches the cliffs ahead for some way of getting back up to the headland but the nearest ramp up is five minutes' walk away. If someone is following her, if someone means her harm, she shouldn't be trapped somewhere so isolated.

She moves towards the ramp, speed-walks almost. The bumpy motion begins to lull Bobby to sleep. She keeps glancing over her shoulder at the top of the cliffs. There's no one there. It must have been a seagull. Some pensioner's dog dicing with death in the search for salty-sea smells. But she doesn't slow her pace. She looks at the picture of Bobby eating soil and types out a caption:

> Organic. Vegan. Sustainable.
> Soil-based is the new plant-based.

She wrinkles her nose. It's not amazing but it'll do. She's about to post it when she notices the edge of the painting of the woman in the desert-like landscape at the side of the frame. She zooms in slightly to crop it out and gets a strange sense of déjà vu. This is not the first time she's edited it out of her Insta-content.

She stamps onto a patch of broken beer bottle as she turns up a path that leads away from the sea and up to the town. She feels certain that she's manipulated two or three of her photos before to remove the painting. She finds it creepy and assumes others will so she didn't want it featuring and she remembers editing down video clips for her stories to make sure it wasn't in the background. So how did Amanda see the painting she remembers from Raf's dad's house, the thing that spurred her to visit them, if Erin's never posted it online? Erin stops in front of a dark tunnel that leads under the road into the bustle of the town. The floor around the entrance is littered with plastic packaging, a scrunched nappy, mulching leaves. Bobby's arm flinches in his sleep.

She glances up at the cliffs one last time before she heads away from the beach, half expecting to see Amanda's hair flaming above the brush but there's still no one there. No one watching her. That she can see. But it could be her, Erin thinks, this, the trolling, started after she arrived. She steps over the litter and braces herself for the smell of urine as she walks into the darkness and the safety of civilisation at the end of the tunnel.

35

19 April 1999

I've done something I shouldn't and I feel so so stupid.

This is the first time I've written in here for some time. Donny thinks it's childish writing a journal and I'm sure he's right. But today, I'm so low, so alone, that I feel like I could just drink a schooner of bleach.

The first couple of weeks here felt like a honeymoon. We made love every night. When Donny went off to the gallery he'd leave me Post-its with page numbers for poems, he drew studies of me he'd done while I slept in sharpie on the mirror, the Madonna, he loved to draw me like a Renaissance Madonna. It was his joke to me. He'd get groceries sent up every couple of days and I'd always have dinner on the table for him. I felt like a housewife from an old movie. 'Hi, honey, I'm home,' he'd say.

I started doing exercise videos in the flat. The library was just across the street so I snuck out and got books about yoga, calisthenics, meditation, recipe books. Jean, our neighbour, showed me a mail-order directory you could order crystals from. I didn't tell her I didn't have a bank card in case she clocked how young I was, but I'd still have a good time looking at the pictures, reading up, making lists of the ones I'd buy once I could get a job and have some money of my own.

I got lonely in the days. Someone Donny knew at the gallery knew a guy that worked with Craig and said he was on the rampage looking for me. It proves how obsessed he is with me, so it's lucky we got out when we did, but Donny didn't think it was safe for me to be out of the house on my own. The thing is, I endured those boring days because I knew how wonderful it would be when he came home to me. And it was, it really was, he made me feel like a goddess.

But then, after the first month, his mood's changed, he's tetchy, cold in a way he never has been before, and he's started coming back later and later. When I ask him what's wrong it irritates him. It's the pressure, he always snaps, the pressure to support us. He never told me at the start but the rent on the flat is astronomical. He says he only got the sea view for me but that it's ruining us. He says he's working for Richard in the gallery, spending his evenings trying to network at private views in order to try and get people to buy his work, to get backers for the exhibition. And he says he can't draw any more, he can't paint, there's no time with all the stress of having to make money for us. I offered to get a job but he told me I was being ridiculous. We still make love but it's different now, fast, not gentle like it was, sometimes it hurts. And I know it's because he blames me. I wanted to be the perfect muse for him. I can't believe it's my fault that he can't create any more.

I started leaving him Post-its like he used to for me. Quotes I got from books he has about Van Gogh, Picasso. Something to try and get the creative juices flowing. I'd find them crumpled up on the pavement outside our apartment block. I know he doesn't mean to be so cruel but it hurts so much to see him turn away from me.

In a moment of weakness, I nearly called my mum two days ago, but luckily there wasn't a cent in the house so I couldn't use the payphone. I thought I had some coins stashed away in a bag somewhere but Donny must have known I might be tempted. I miss her, that's the thing. I miss school. I miss sitting next to Lily in maths, I miss the stupid songs she'd make up about Mrs Francis's comb-over. Everything feels so serious all the time now.

And then last night I did something and I'm not sure he'll ever forgive me. But I was trying to make him happy. I swear it. I thought it would make him happy. He was furious when he got home, something about Richard not paying him for a mural he'd done. And, I hadn't spoken to anyone all day and I blurted it out, what I'd been thinking, the thing that might be a solution for us, the thing that might stop me annoying him so much, that might give him the motivation, the inspiration to become the great artist I know he can be. It was something he'd talked to me about, something he'd always painted me with. I thought it would make him so happy.

I told him I wanted us to have a baby.

He stormed out and I haven't seen him since. I want to go and look for him but if he sees me out of the flat it will only make him more angry.

But I do want us to have a baby. I've thought about it every day. It would give us something to live for. Something to bring us together and fight for. No bond is stronger than a child.

But maybe he's right. Maybe I am just a stupid little girl.

36

BRAUNEoverBRAINS

473 posts   78.8k followers   1,758 following

ERIN BRAUNE

This is my contrite face. Because I am stuffed with contrition like a Christmas turkey cushion.

Better half doesn't like me sharing too much of our relationship on here. But I've been reflecting on some mistakes I've made in the last couple of weeks. It's easy to put yourself at the centre of things, particularly when you're tired, busy or when exciting life things are happening. But I've really learned this week that forgetting those around you, family, friends, your support network, not putting them at the heart of your decision-making, is the worst thing you can do. Being a parent is hard. Being a partner as a parent is harder. But I'm lucky to have found a man to spend my life with who can look past some pretty stupid, immature behaviour from me and not get angry, not lash out like I would, but who takes time away and always comes back and forgives me. Which in itself is hard because I just want to have a blazing row and hash it out. But I know his way is better.

Take a minute then today to think about them. Think about baby. Think about partner. Think about your parents. Because, and I'm guiltier than anyone of this, it's so easy to cloud your experience of life through your own narrow perspective.

#theguruwillseeyounow #selfishallergy
#imab•tchimaloverimachildimamotheretc

@trudibell44 THIS. Tiredness is a killer. Since I've had Bodie I feel like everything I do is SO incredibly selfish even though I never seem to get any time to do anything for me. So good to know I'm not the only one.
@ggheorgh you like your baby yet?
@aniiieclarkson QWEEEEN
@periodicalprudence Where are you in your cycle? I often make strange decisions in the week before my period is due. Maybe you can get your husband to track your cycles with you? It's important you don't blame yourself. Be kind. It sounds like your partner is. (eventually)
@leisacrowd where do I find me a man like that?

37

'Manuka honey? That the stuff that's meant to cure all ills?' Caz says, giving her son Stanley a leg-up onto the stern of a wooden pirate ship in the Viking play park on the seafront. Erin nods. 'Bobby's had a bad chest for weeks, hasn't he?'

'What are you trying to say?' Erin snaps, glancing round at Bobby who's picking up clumps of sand and then brushing it violently from his hands. She went through Amanda's kitchen this morning and found a black pot of Manuka honey under the sink and recognised it as the object she saw her stuffing away in her shoulder bag a few nights ago.

'Just wondering if she was trying to help his chest.' Caz clears her throat. Stanley clatters up and down the wooden floorboards of the empty ship, while Imogen toddles towards a wall of rope netting. The winter sun makes the view out to sea so clear, Erin can see a gunship in the distance.

'Are you telling me you'd be fine with someone putting honey in Imogen's bottle without asking you?'

'It's twenty quid a pop that stuff, even in Aldi it's a tenner. Why not use 50p runny stuff if she's trying to turn Bobby against you?' Most of the time Erin loves Caz's brusqueness, her challenging honesty, but right now she wishes she'd just accept what Erin thinks and agree wholeheartedly. Since the pictures were posted, it seems like everyone she's spoken to now doubts her every word. She goes to rescue Bobby who's struggling to scrabble his way out of the sand. She picks him up and walks him over to the baby swing. When she tasted the sweetness in her milk it seemed to confirm what had been at the back of her mind for some time, that perhaps Amanda wasn't just being a helpful Mary Poppins wonder-nanny, but that in fact she wanted to make Bobby look to her as his primary person instead of Erin. The skin-to-skin cuddling, the spiritual songs, the special games with special smiles, and now this, all of it designed to make Bobby like her more.

'Honey is on the NHS list of things you're not meant to give a child under twelve months, I looked it up,' she says.

'They also say you have to cut up a blueberry into about fifteen pieces just in case the baby chokes.'

'Why are you sticking up for her?'

'Look, no one should be tampering with what's going in your one's wee body, no one,' Caz says, plonking Imogen into the swing next to Bobby. Ten in the morning and the playground is deserted. 'But I guess, if you let someone look after your bairn you've got to accept they might not do it exactly like you want, you're not paying her or anything neither.'

'I don't care how she's looking after him. She's worked with babies for years, I'm sure what she's doing with him is much better than me. But he's rejecting my milk.'

'Oh, babe, that's horrible.'

'The only thing I ever felt like I was doing right was breast-feeding him and now he won't, and it's because of what she's done.' Imogen keeps saying something that sounds like 'more' so Caz goes behind the swing and begins pushing her higher. Meanwhile, Bobby clings to the swing's restraint, concern etched into his brows.

'You sound a bit –' Caz hesitates, unable to look at Erin.

'A bit what?'

'Na, listen, forget it. It's not on, you're right.'

'What do I sound, Caz?'

Caz winces, sucks air through her teeth. 'You sound a bit paranoid, which I totally get, you know? If I had some prick taking pictures of me, I'd be paranoid too, but Amanda, I just don't understand why you'd think she's trying to turn Bobby against you.'

'She hasn't got a family, there's some old flame back home who seems to be messing her around, she's spent her life working with children, she obviously likes them, she's of a certain age and she doesn't have them. Women in that sort of situation have done much more "mental" things.'

Caz sighs, turns away from the swings and walks towards the chain-link fence that divides the playground from a mini-golf course that's been allowed to overgrow into disrepair. Erin huffs out a dragon-puff of condensation in the air. She thought Caz would side with her, but she's seen the pictures, she's seen images of Erin looking like she can't stand her own child. In her trial by social media, even her best friend has chosen to believe the photographic evidence. Erin glances all around her at the thought of the troll, feeling like prey searching the landscape for a predator. After being accused of paranoia the thought of telling Caz she thought she was being followed a couple of days ago has rescinded firmly from Erin's mind.

Bobby begins to cough. It's horrible hearing the phlegm on his tiny lungs. She picks him up out of the swing and wraps the collar of his coat tighter around his neck. Raf said he was up a lot in the night and she can see it in the rawness in his eyes. Stanley tumbles off the roundabout in the far corner and Erin watches Caz turn quickly and efficiently, grabbing Imogen out of the swing as she hurries across to attend to her boy. She rights him, gives him a cuddle and he runs off towards the slide with Imogen waddling behind him. Caz sits on a bench and pats the space next to her.

'I'm sorry, babe,' Caz says as Erin sits down next to her, Bobby perched on her knee. 'I've got about eight followers, no idea what it must be like for you. But have you tried talking to Amanda about it.'

'Raf's so angry still, I think if I start throwing accusations about … I don't know.'

'We had a coffee last week, after Joy's.' Joy's is a gym and singing class run at a soft-play centre in town. Erin looks up at Caz, remembering the overheard conversation Amanda, Sophie and her friends were having and trying to suppress the feeling that Amanda and Caz were engaged in a similar form of latte-laced betrayal. 'I asked her why she decided to come here in the winter. She told me she'd been struggling back home. Felt stuck with her life. She's estranged from her family and has this horrible stepdad who's trying to get back into her life. I didn't want to pry but it felt like she'd seen some shit, you know? She said that when her and Raf were friends, it was the last time she was happy really. Sad.' Erin clenches her jaw, nods. Is the stepdad the man she's talked about as some sort of on–off boyfriend? That would certainly explain how guarded she's been whenever Erin's prodded for details. Bobby's turned to her and is giving her the shy smile that he's now wheeling out more often and Erin can't help but be heartened by it. 'Sounds like she's been struggling on her own for a long time,' Caz says. 'I don't know, maybe she's just so delighted to be part of a normal family. She's over-stepped the mark, for sure, but maybe she's just trying too hard to make you all like her. I've got a mate who's a singer in a wedding band and she absolutely swears by that Manuka stuff for colds and coughs and that.'

'She tell you about how she found us?' Caz shakes her head. 'She saw a painting in one of my "stories" which she recognised from Raf's dad's house from when they were kids.'

'No, she didn't mention it.'

'She said "Mercury was in retrograde" and thought it was a sign. You heard of that, Mercury in retrograde?'

'People blame it when everything's going tits up.'

'I've never put that painting in any of my stories.' Erin looks at Caz, challenging. Caz keeps her eyes on Stanley who's try-ing to drag Imogen up a small hill towards the baby slide.

'That right?' Caz crosses her arms.

'I hate it. It's in a dark corner of the room.'

'The pink one with the person in the cloak?'

'I've actively edited it out of posts before. So how did she see it?' Caz looks at her Casio watch. Imogen can't make it up the hill and Caz stands as if she's about to go and help her but she doesn't move. 'How did she find us if she's never seen the picture, Caz?'

'I don't know, Ez, I don't know. Look, I'm sorry about what someone's doing to you with these pictures. It's fuck-ing foul. Maybe you can take a break from the "Gram" for a bit, let the whole thing settle down.' Erin's phone buzzes in her pocket in retaliation and she stands up as if to defend its honour.

'If you two are such good mates now, maybe you can find out why she lied about how she found us?' Caz looks down at the rubbery fake woodchips below her feet. She bites her bottom lip, trying to disguise her irritation. She's only about five foot two but she's got such presence.

'How many Instagram stories do you post every day? Five, ten? How many of those are in your front room? Half of them? How long have you lived there? A year? Eighteen months? That's hundreds of pictures, hundreds of videos you've posted, that you have no way of looking back through, and you are certain, certain enough to make up some conspiracy about Amanda, the nicest person most of us have ever met?' Erin's breath shortens and she shifts Bobby from one arm to the other. 'I'm not trying to be cruel, babe, I'm, I'm here for you, I am, I just can't bear to see you put two and two together and make fifteen like this. I get that you're angry, you're right to be angry, I'm fucking furious on your behalf, and talk to her about the honey. Definitely. It's not on. But, all this – all this paranoia, it'll make you unwell.' She puts a hand on Erin's upper arm before moving off to help her daughter up to the top of the slide.

Bobby swipes at Erin's shoulder and begins to groan up into a cry so she plonks herself down on the bench and, without even considering trying to breastfeed him, gets the bottle of premixed formula out of her baby bag and gives it to him. He pushes it away, probably not sweet enough for his newly tampered-with taste. She shoves the teat further into his mouth. She looks at the walkway above the beach that butts onto the play park. An old gentleman walking a dog that looks too strong for him smiles at her as he passes. Erin blinks, shakes her head to banish the constant feeling that she's being watched. Caz keeps one eye on her as she catches Imogen at the bottom of the slide. She throws her a sympathetic smile, abject concern lingering in her eyes.

38

'All right, pal, it's Caz. You're probably having a beer with Wolf from *Gladiators* or some such shite so don't worry about calling me back, but listen, about earlier, you didn't need me telling you that you're being paranoid or whatever. I should've listened to you and I'm sorry but here, I've WhatsApped you a link to a photo. Was on Facebook wasting my life scrolling and I saw this photo of Claire Porter. She was in town taking a photo in front of that crap local museum no one goes in. Well, Lorna fucking Morgan is in the background with her kids. And it's the day you thought she was in Maidstone, the day the photo was taken from the church group. Anyway, have a look. Thought I should let you know.'

39

Erin pushes the buggy along Wilkes Road. Bobby is covering himself in orange corn dust from one of those terrible Wotsit-looking carrot sticks that are meant to be healthy. Wilkes Road is Lorna's road, two away from her house, and Erin's not one hundred per cent sure what she's doing here. Since the video was first posted on her Instagram she's felt like she's a character in a computer game, a simulation where she's not fully in control of anything she's doing. Perhaps she'll just pass by the house, give Lorna a little glare through the kitchen window, the sort that, if it were her that was the troll, might be enough to say 'I know what you're doing'. And if it wasn't her, could be explained as the smack-arsed expression of someone who's had a long, hard morning.

But Lorna's in her garden pruning perfect flower beds in the small front garden outside her prefab while the twins, presumably, sleep in the covered double buggy behind her. She looks up and gives Erin a wave of her secateurs.

'How are you coping?' Lorna says, voice full of hollow sympathy, eyes fixed on Bobby covered in radioactive carrot dust.

'Saw the pictures then?' Erin says, mouth barely open with her jaw tensed. Why would she ask a question like that? Does she want to know that her devious plan to dethrone Erin is having a harrowing affect?

'Er, yes. Afraid I did. How awful.'

'What, the person doing it or how I feel about my son?' Erin bites the inside of her lip. She's sure someone's following her, someone knows where she is at all times, Lorna could have been in the locality on all the occasions. Why post something on Instagram saying you were somewhere else when you weren't if not to cover yourself?

'No, of course, the man doing this to you.'

'A man is it?' She wants to accuse Lorna, even though she's still not convinced. Perhaps because she can't confront Amanda about the honey, she feels a need to lash out, to get some answers, to find some clarity in her head that's swimming like a pool of frogspawn.

'Oh, I –' Lorna looks round at her buggy, feeling the fire radiating from Erin. 'I suppose I always thought Internet trolls were men. Sure, women can be just as horrible though.' She shrugs a laugh out.

'You tell me.' Erin realises she's doing an impression of the sort of a detective from the sort of shows she had auditions for when she first left drama school.

'Have you got something you want to say?' Lorna says, putting the secateurs on her garden wall and squaring her shoulders.

'You don't go to the church group any more.'

'It's very busy.'

'Heard you were saying I've ruined it for you?'

'Well –' Lorna juts her chin out – 'as it happens, it – I do feel like it's been taken over. I set up that group.'

'So we've all heard.'

'And now it's – Well, no one talks to me, it's sort of cliquey. Not what I wanted to create for the community.'

'One of the photos was taken from the group. Last week.' Erin feels her hands tighten on the handle of her buggy. She's doing it. Why is she doing it? 'Someone in the lobby outside must have taken it – as you say, it's so busy at the group, someone would have noticed it being taken.'

'The twins will be up soon, I'd really like to get this –'

'But you wouldn't know anything because on the day of the group, the day that photo of me was taken, you were in Maidstone visiting your sister.' Lorna looks away, scrunching her nose. 'Or at least that's what your Instagram says, but there's a photo of you on Facebook that tells a different story.' Lorna's lips purse into a tiny 'O'. Erin can see that her tolerance has come to an end and the conversational gloves are on the verge of being taken off and she now seems more intimidating than the sparrow-like woman Erin's always thought her to be.

'I haven't been to see my sister in over a year.' Lorna crosses her arms. Erin was expecting her to be shocked to have been caught out but she seems unabashed.

'On Insta—'

'My mum just joined Instagram. Sister and I aren't speaking and she doesn't know. Mum smelt a rat so I put up an old photo of us. So I could have taken the photo of you at the church group and put it up online. That's what you're saying, isn't it? Well, yeh, I was about. But I don't go to the group any more because it's packed with up-themselves wankers. I know none of you like me. I know I'm not as glamorous and smug as you. I'm not cool. And does it piss me off that I don't feel welcome at the group that I started for the sake of my community, for the sake of the mums who'd lived round here years before any of you turned up, who had nowhere decent to go to get their kids out of the house? Yeh, it does. Makes me sad, actually. But has it affected me so much that I've started following you around, taking photos of you, posting them on the Internet? Why would I, do you think? To bring you down a peg or two?' She intones the last phrase in inverted commas. 'Truth is, I wouldn't want to waste the energy on someone as self-involved as you. Now, if you don't mind.' She grabs the secateurs off the wall and turns to the back of her garden. Erin stands stock-still watching her, seeing a slight tremor across the line of her shoulder blades. That cost Lorna. She didn't enjoy having to be so overt, but she felt impelled to do it. Why? Overcompensating because she's guilty of what Erin was on the road to accusing her of? But it was so vehement, the passion of someone who's just had the final straw placed on their back. If Lorna is lying to cover herself, can she really be that good an actor?

Erin opens her mouth to say something but neither another question defending herself nor any sort of callow apology seems to be worth it now. Lorna bends down to her flower bed and decapitates a clump of dead flowers leaving Erin no choice but to turn on her heel and head back home.

40

The wheel of Bobby's buggy sticks in a hole in the cobblestones outside the Cupcake Society in the old town's minuscule market square. Erin's jaw tenses as she tries to, very gently, ease it back onto the pavement. Bobby screamed for ten minutes before going to sleep and she can't have him wake up again.

As she glides the stroller past the old-school tea shop, the former library that now sells second-hand books and the place that looks like an airport bar on the corner, she feels the eyes of the town burning into the back of her head. She used to like the idea that people were watching her, talking about her. She got frustrated with actors who moaned about the extra trappings of celebrity. She'd always known that when she made it she'd enjoy the feeling of being a person who incited curiosity, who carried their mystique with the elan of someone whose lifestyle is envied. It's the exact sort of flagrant self-involved thinking that Lorna accused her of yesterday. Because now, walking around today, the first time she's ventured into the heart of town since the pictures were posted, she can see what the A-listers are complaining about.

She wants to go into the handicraft shop where she sees the owner point her out to an older customer and tell them that she loves her baby, that being a new mum is hard, to ask them how they'd feel if pictures of them at their most fallible had been secretly posted online to create some kind of false narrative to tens of thousands of people. It's not like she can run away from it, take time away from Bobby to sleep, take a break from Instagram so she can think about what it's done to her, to her relationship. The contract with Phibe is signed, payment should be imminent. Their 'Tinder for mums' app launches in six weeks and they've just sent her the schedule of posts she has to craft and there's a lot. To her surprise, her number of followers has increased in the aftermath of the trolling, but in light of her 'positive mum' tag being reassessed she feels more pressure than ever to respond to the deluge of messages and comments that she's getting every day, and the joy she used to feel making these connections has now curdled into a heavy duty.

Up ahead of her, Sophie Delauney emerges from Phoenix Wines with Mercedes, both without children. They're in big padded coats, Sophie's electric blue, Mercedes' white, over gym leggings. Erin tries to up her pace to catch up with them. Mercedes spots her and says something to Sophie who turns to look. Her permanent expression, somewhere between a grin and a pout, drops when she sees Erin. She looks incredible, Erin thinks, her face has filled out a bit with the due date approaching which suits her and the new orange tint to her pixie cut seems to emphasise her pregnancy glow. She puts out a flat hand to Erin, somewhere between a greeting and the gesture for stop, before giving an empty smile as she turns back the way she was going. Mercedes creases her brow in some kind of apology at their not stopping then follows her friend up the hill away from town.

Erin swallows and turns down a side street, feeling like the whole county has just witnessed the snub. She's just been on the receiving end of the sort of fickle shallowness that's driven Lorna away from her own toddler group and she starts to feel sorry for the woman. She's replayed the conversation they had over her front garden wall many times since and it just didn't seem like she was lying. She could have done it, of course she could. She doesn't like Erin, she doesn't like anything she stands for, but she seemed so upset to be accused, there was no furtiveness, no defensiveness. On the other hand, she is a gossip, she has got a reputation as someone with a streak of cruelty to her, so perhaps that was all for show. Perhaps she's at some other baby group she's started, talking to her old mates about how she's sticking it to the middle-class dickheads who're trying to take over their town.

She flicks onto Sophie's Instagram, hit by the thought that they might be off to meet Amanda. There's a new post, a picture of a flat-white, oat milk probably, with the caption 'Caffeine kick before HotPod launch'. Erin didn't know there was a new HotPod yoga class starting. Clearly no one's felt she should be invited.

She's had so much support online, hundreds of people sharing their stories of how they've shouted at their kids, how bored they've found themselves – many have posted selfies of them looking numb as their baby cries or feeds or plays. There was a hashtag that went around for half a day or so after she made her apology, #boredlikeBraune. The responses haven't all been positive, some of her followers feel as if they've been lied to, but Erin's been relieved that so few people have voiced their disapproval. But the real people, the mums and dads she half knows who she sees every day at the various groups or playgrounds, can't seem to get over the revelation that someone they looked up to as an aspiration of easy-breezy parenting is actually a fraud. Perhaps they're embarrassed, having bragged to their friends about being on first-name terms with someone who's been revealed to be a liar, or possibly it's more personal to them because they feel some collective ownership over her online celebrity and so its tarnishing feels like a deeper betrayal. Whatever the reason, their smiles are strained now; she spots clusters of whispering faces in her periphery and it stings like seawater in a graze.

She walks into the shade of a narrow street, wanting to get away from the busyness of the old town. As she gets down towards the seafront she hears steps behind her and turns, certain someone's following her, but no one is there. She looks in the reflections of destitute shopfronts, hoping to spot a glint of humanity, but the street's deserted. The chill from the sea seems to flood in through the collar of her coat so she heads towards the warmth of the nearby supermarket, trying to stop herself from turning round every few steps to see if whoever it is she senses is really there.

She's tried to apply logic to work out who it is that's doing this to her but perhaps that's where she's been going wrong. There's nothing logical about the sort of people who choose to plague other people online. And Raf's right, there's no doubt that the troll's activity has become more brutal since her crusading speech at Claridge's, so that does point to it being some resentful misogynist, but to what end? Whether it's Lorna, some other jealous local mum or any faceless incel malignity, what would any of them actually gain from doing what they're doing?

Just as she pushes Bobby through the automatic doors into the heat and fabricated bread smell inside the supermarket, she sees something out of the corner of her eye in the car park to her right. A floating flash of aquamarine in the blanket of concrete grey. She reverses back out of the shop and begins to follow the black parka and grey woolly hat as it disappears down the ramp towards the lower level. Erin gets to the top where a silver car has to slow abruptly on seeing her as it turns the spiral of the ramp, the driver giving her a look that asks what the hell she's doing pushing a sleeping baby down a ramp made for cars as it ambles past. She sees the black coat moving through a gap in the concrete pillars and rushes down the ramp to follow it. When she gets to the underground level she sees the figure up ahead, step quickening as they jink between cars. She wants to shout after whoever it is but it'd wake Bobby. The person makes for the exit towards town. Maybe she's imagining it, Erin thinks, maybe this person isn't following her, perhaps it's one of the many slightly dodgy folk who hang around this car park.

A white van swings round a pillar and she has to pull the buggy back towards her quickly to avoid it. The person in the parka crosses into a patch of sunlight and Erin sees a glint of burnt orange coming from below her hat. Erin's eyes drop to the bottom of her coat and she sees a thin band of blue, the aquamarine that caught her attention at the supermarket's entrance, poking out from underneath.

'Amanda,' she calls out, halfway between a shout and a whisper. Bobby stirs in his buggy. The woman stops. She doesn't turn round immediately and it looks to Erin like she might try and run but eventually she turns, cheekbones rendered sharper by the shadows from the spotlight of sun she finds herself in, and raises a hand in greeting.

Erin observes the dark grey yoga pants she wears as she walks over to her.

'Off to Pilates at Phoenix?' Erin says, trying to sound casual. Amanda looks at her watch, eyes Bobby still sleeping in the buggy. 'I saw Sophie in town on her way over.'

'Yeh, that's right,' Amanda says. 'I'll be back home later if you want me to do some food.' Erin puts her head to one side and stares at her, trying to drill into her lie, but it just makes Amanda smile wider. She spots a large tote bag hung over Amanda's shoulder.

'Can I have a look in your bag?' Erin asks.

'What?'

'I want to have a look in your bag — can I?' Erin crosses in front of the buggy. Amanda steps back, holding the bag further into her body.

'Um, why?' Amanda laughs.

'You're following me.'

'What?'

'You're following me. You've been following me. For how long? A week? Two? Since you got here?'

'I'm not —'

'Sophie and Mercedes are going to HotPod yoga. There's no Pilates at Phoenix today.'

'I haven't been following you.'

'Show me what's in your bag?' Erin thrusts her hand out in front of her as she hems Amanda into the corner of the underground car park.

'Shall we —' Amanda points down the ramp that leads into town. 'Doesn't feel safe having Bobby here, the cars.'

'Were you there, at the top of the cliffs yesterday, look-ing down on me on the prom?' Erin knows she's right. It's Amanda. Of course it's Amanda. The trolling started just after she arrived.

'Erin, shall we just go down to –'

'Someone's been posting photos of me, videos of me and my baby on the Internet to make me look like a shit mum, to make me look like a fraud, an absolute psycho. And now you're following me?'

'It's not what you think.'

'So you are following me then?' Amanda opens her mouth as if to speak then closes it. She smiles, ducks her head under the shade covering Bobby to look at him sleeping. Erin finds herself so enraged by it that she grabs at the handle of the bag on her shoulder. Amanda looks at her scared, both hands clutching the body of the tote. She looks around, for help perhaps, but the car park is deserted. Erin doesn't care who sees. Amanda's been following her. She's practically admitted it. She's the troll and Erin knows the proof is in the bag. It's so heavy. There's a camera in there. A lens. A massive smartphone at the very least. And she's going to force Amanda to show her what's on it, what pictures she's been taking of her today ready to post up anonymously to besmirch her reputation further.

'Go ahead,' Amanda says, sliding the bag off her shoulder and into Erin's hands. Now she has the bag it strikes her how aggressive she's just been. All her certainty that Amanda is the troll has vanished as she rests the snatched bag on a low wall. Bobby shuffles around in his buggy and Amanda pulls his footmuff up so it covers his hands.

There's no telephoto lens in the bag. Erin moves a pair of woollen gloves, a thin thread of a scarf, but most of the bag is dominated by a black velvet sack, clearly not a camera case. Erin swallows air as she pulls opens the string of the bag to reveal a mass of pink and white stones.

'Rhodochrosite,' Amanda says, standing over her shoulder. 'I bought them from Marjoram's shop. Keep looking though, see what else you can find.' Erin sees an old flip phone at the bottom of the bag, but little else apart from a packet of what look like hippie throat sweets. She hands the bag back to Amanda.

'Sorry,' Erin mumbles.

'Do you want to get home before he wakes up?' Amanda asks, hoisting the bag back onto her shoulder, sadness in her eyes. Erin nods, riddled with shame. There was fear in the woman's eyes. Erin knows that if Amanda had withheld the bag from her for another moment, she might have done something, pushed her, snatched it roughly out of her hand. Amanda starts to push the buggy and Erin doesn't stop her.

'I shouldn't have lied about Pilates,' Amanda says as they emerge into the light. 'And I – you're right.' She stops next to the main road and lets several cars past. 'I have been following you. For the last few days. But I'm not taking pictures of you. I haven't even got a camera, there isn't one on my phone, you saw.' They cross the road together, onto an expanse of grass that leads down to the sea.

'Why then?' Erin asks, fists balled in the pockets of her mac.

'I think, after Raf saw the video … he said he was worried about you.'

'He's always worried about me.'

'He was worried about, about you with Bobby.' Amanda's words seem to block the top of Erin's throat. 'He said he might have to take some time off, to be with you and Bobby, during the day. He was really stressed about it, said you couldn't afford for him not to be working at the moment. If it makes you feel any better he did say he was probably overreacting.'

'Feel much better now,' Erin says, belittling herself with sarcasm. She feels like she's had three double espressos, vibrating from grabbing at Amanda's stuff, accusing her of something she has absolutely no evidence of. Erin doesn't know what's happening to her, doesn't recognise this rash, suspicious person she seems to have turned into since the pictures were posted just a few days ago.

'I think he wanted me to keep an eye on you, so I have been.'

'He asked you to follow me?' Erin bites her upper lip.

'He seemed so worried about Bobby's safety.'

'He thinks I'm going to hurt my baby? The father of my child thinks I'm going to hurt my baby?' Erin says, but it's to herself as much as it is to Amanda. A hit of cold wind punches them both as they round a corner onto the front. 'Is that what he thinks?' Erin has to shout past the sound of the wind. Amanda shrugs, expression filled with pain. 'That I'm a danger to my son?'

'I'm so sorry, Erin,' Amanda shouts back to her. Another wave of wind hits them and Bobby's buggy begins to blow back towards them. Erin grabs at the handle to steady it, inadvertently barging Amanda away with her other hand. Amanda gives her a look of shock. Bobby wakes up and his scream pierces through the wall of sound.

41

She scours the local council website for the names of child-minders. As she clicks through their profiles she sees all of them have between four and five children a day. That's too many for Bobby. Bobby wouldn't be able to handle three other toddlers prodding him and screaming and demanding their caregiver's attention. It would be the same at nursery, Erin's decided.

After they got home, Bobby outright refused her breast milk and, based upon the tiny quantities Erin's been able to pump recently, she fears that she might have to give up on it completely. He also refused the bottle until she buckled and put a tiny bit of honey in it. Erin can't understand how she's got here. Feeding him was always her favourite bit. A time she could look down at her beautiful little boy and know that, however inadequate she may feel, however con-flicted, she was doing something right. So as she watched her baby hungrily gulping down the sweetened breast milk before putting him down to bed, she felt the anger building inside and she made a decision. Amanda has to go. She may not be the person taking photos of her, but she is the reason her baby doesn't clamour for her, she is the reason that every single day Erin feels like the only mother in the world whose infant doesn't want to be held by them. Amanda offered to help with Bobby's bedtime, offered to make dinner, but Erin said no, so now she's skulking in the studio at the end of their garden. It's not sustainable. Erin can see that it never was.

So now she has two options. Put Bobby into childcare or tell Grace that she's going to have to delay many of her commitments for the next month or two. The PR person from Phibe has got her doing two or three events a week for the next month including quite a few evenings. She knows that trying to get out of them, just as the app's launching, could be terminal for her hopes of getting more big-brand work so she's going to have to make the childcare route work. There is a third option. Raf could take some time off. Although she's never got too involved with the details of their family finances, the Phibe money, whenever they deign to pay her, must be enough to pay the mortgage and their day-to-day expenses for four or five months, at least. But Erin knows that she invited Amanda deeper into their lives, she was the one that set up their unconventional childcare arrangements, and she doesn't think, in light of recent revelations, that she's in a position to demand that Raf switch from being the primary breadwinner to the primary caregiver instantaneously.

She snaps her laptop shut and almost throws it onto the bottom shelf of the coffee table before slurping from her glass of wine – a perk, at least, of not having to breastfeed in the night. She glances at the wine bottle in the kitchen. There's only about a glass left in it and she should probably ease off before Raf gets home.

She's tried to keep her mind busy, tried to keep it rational, logical. Because ever since Amanda told her that Raf wanted her to follow her, she hasn't felt particularly level. As she gave Bobby his cumin-spiced sweet potato, she had to smile at him through the molten oil of rage in the pit of her stomach, she had to sing the saccharine Disney melodies during Bobby's nappy-off playtime with more gusto than she ever has to try and push down the anger that sits in her breastbone like heartburn. As she frothed his Olly Octopus in the bath she had to swallow back the medicinal bitterness at the back of her throat at the thought that her fiancé, the father of her son, thinks she's such a bad mother, so dangerous to her own child, that he has to employ his lackey to follow her about. Why? So that she could intervene if Erin looked like she was going to throw Bobby off the cliff?

The key turns in the lock and Erin gulps the rest of her glass of wine down before going to the kitchen, rinsing the glass and putting it and the rest of the bottle back in the cupboard.

'Smells good,' Raf says, referring to the pasta bake bubbling in the oven as he comes round the corner to see her stood by the sink. His eyes dart out to the lights of studio. Erin grits her teeth, they're going to talk about this and she's not going to lose it. 'You OK?' He still has his big coat on, woolly hat still in place. He looks expectant, tentative, as if he can sense she's anything but 'OK'.

'Yeh, tired.'

'Me too. He wasn't up for ages last night but it was the frequency, you know?' He crosses past her, goes into a drawer to get mats out for the table.

'Done it,' she says. He wheels round, sees the table set and smiles, a surprised smile. He surveys the room.

'Place looks great.'

'Thanks,' she says. He doesn't look out the window but she knows he's thinking that Amanda must have cleaned today, but she didn't. The moment lingers between them. He waits for her to ask about his day, to tell him something about hers, something about Bobby. But she doesn't. She keeps her arms crossed so Raf can't see her hands balled into such tight fists that she can feel her nails leaving dents in her palms. The oven beeps. Raf gets oven gloves out of the drawer and heads towards it.

'I'll do it,' she says, 'you sit down.'

'It's fine, I'm here now.'

'I'll do it, I said. I made dinner so I'll do it.' She thrusts her hand out for the gloves. Raf gives them to her before moving over to the other side of the room, expression split between a smirk and perturbed.

'Was Bobby OK today? Are you OK? You didn't text or anything. I hoped that meant you were managing with him but, but you seem a bit, I don't know, stressed.'

'"Managing with him",' Erin says, almost to herself as she gets the bubbling-hot dish out of the oven.

'You haven't told me anything about your day, Ez, was he all right? You know I like to know.'

'Oh yeh,' she says, through a bitter half-laugh, 'you like to know exactly how my day's going, don't you? Haven't you spoken to your old pal about it yet? Don't you already *know* how great my day's been?'

'Erin –'

'Don't you already know that today, just today, I managed not to hurt my baby. But who knows, there's always tomorrow. Better have a debrief with Earth Goddess out there about keeping close tabs on me tomorrow.' Raf runs his thumbnail over his bottom teeth, starting to look annoyed. Annoyed is the least that Erin wants Raf to be. He had her followed. The temperature of the dish is getting through the gloves and she feels the heat flush through her body, the red wine swelling in the front of her head like a crashing wave.

'Should I do that? You've let yourself get upset by something, so let's sit down and have something to eat.'

'What do you think I've "let myself get upset by"?' she spits. He glances out to the garden. 'Don't look for her. Me, look at me. What do you think I'm upset about, Rafael?'

'What *aren't* you upset about, doesn't take much, does it?' He smiles, a Cheshire cat superior grin and she snaps. Erin launches the dish of boiling pasta bake at him. He sees it coming and manages to slam the corner of it down in front of him, sending the dish flying to the floor where it cracks into pieces, the contents splatting out like a Jackson Pollock. He shakes his head in disbelief, his lip curled in disgust as if she's a drunk who's just been sick. He closes his eyes, a long blink, then walks to the other side of the room. Erin stands, rictus hands inside the oven gloves still held out, miming the food, paralysed with the shock of what she's just done.

'No, you do not do that to me.' His voice is steely but calm, like he's talking to an aggressive dog. 'You do not hit me. You do not throw things at me.' He's put the table between her and him and he paces by the bookshelf at the far end of the room like a captive jaguar. 'What – what the hell do you think you're doing?'

'You had her follow me.'

'What?'

'Amanda, you had her follow me. The video's made you think I'm going to hurt Bobby so you had her follow me.'

'What the fuck are you talking about?'

'I caught her. I thought she was the person trolling me, but she said you told her to "keep an eye on me". You thought your son was in danger. With his own mother.' The truth of that statement hits her all over again, bringing her back into the reality of their kitchen. She sees the mess of food all over the kitchen and it dawns on her what she's just done. She's just thrown food, scalding hot food, in a heavy ceramic dish at her fiancé, the person who's worried that she has the capacity to hurt their child. So is he right? Is she dangerous?

Raf stops his pacing. Then he goes to the back door and goes out into the garden, leaving the door open so the cold rages into the room. He's going to get *her*, Erin thinks. She begins to manically clear up the mess of pasta and vegetables on the white kitchen tiles. The dish has broken in five or six large chunks which she picks up and puts in a local newspaper and into the recycling. She tries to wipe up the mess but then they're there, at the door. Raf and Amanda.

'Oh my goodness, Erin, did you hurt yourself?' Amanda rushes over to help but Erin stands up and walks out of the kitchen.

'I dropped the dinner,' he says. 'But, Mand –' Amanda perks herself up like a meerkat – 'I was hoping you could clear up a bit of a misunderstanding. Erin thinks you've been following her? Around town.'

Amanda seems to be chewing something in the side of her mouth. She gives Erin a nervous side-eye.

'What? No, no I haven't been following her.' Erin looks between them, speechless, she can't believe Amanda's denying it now. 'I wanted to try and be around. I've stayed in when you and Bobby have been here, made sure I'm close by when you've been out and about.'

'And that's not following me?' Erin's exasperated but Raf gives her a warning look.

'She told me that you said I had asked you to keep an eye on her? After I'd seen the video.' Raf says it plainly. There's no anger in his voice, only curiosity. They stand in a triangle, Amanda in the kitchen, Raf by the back window, Erin in the far corner of the room. It feels like a stand-off from an old Western but there are no guns, just calm expressions, the casual, almost soothing words of Amanda and Raf as Erin stands, the perpetrator in this kangaroo court, silent.

'You didn't ask me to do anything like that,' Amanda says. Erin glances between the two of them. She knows that behind her is the painting, the painting that Amanda says impelled her to travel around the world to come and visit them. It's bullshit. It's all bullshit. She's lying. She said that he asked her to follow her, that he was worried for Bobby's safety.

'You said that though,' Erin says, trying to maintain a veneer of civility. 'Down by the front. You told me Raf asked you to make sure Bobby was safe with me.'

Amanda cocks her head, face dripping with concerned confusion. 'I thought you'd want someone being there for Erin.' She speaks to Raf as if she wasn't in the room. Erin looks at her hands, they're shaking. She knows she should feel angry, but her outburst of violence has soaked up any residual feeling she has in her body and replaced it with pure, juddering adrenaline. 'You were upset about it, you told me.' She goes towards him, simpering almost, but he backs away.

'I was worried, yeh.' He darts a stern look at Erin. 'I am worried about how you've been, Ez.' Erin looks at the floor. 'I'm frightened about how you are being, but I never asked to have you followed. That's insane.'

'You said, Amanda, that's what you said. That Raf asked you to keep an eye on me after he saw the video.'

'I thought, he might want me to keep an eye on you. That's what I said. Not that he asked me to follow you. I remember that that's exactly what I said. I'm sorry if I wasn't clear.' She looks to Raf. There's a steeliness in Amanda's tone Erin's only heard her use when Bobby's gone to hit or nibble her. That might have been what Amanda said, she can't remember. 'I'd never want you to think I was spying on you Erin, and –' she glances at Raf, Erin might be imagining it but it seems like something passes between them – 'I've grown really attached to Bobby, and stress, tiredness, hormones, I've seen it with my work back home, it can make mums behave in a way they wouldn't normally. Like the video –' she looks at the mess on the kitchen floor – 'I know you'd never do something like that, something that aggressive, but that was before this person started attacking you. I can't imagine how strung out you must be feeling now.' Amanda has her arms wrapped round her waist and there's something strained in her expression, worried almost. 'I wouldn't have been able to forgive myself if something had happened to Bobby. I shouldn't have skulked around without you knowing. That was wrong –' she takes Erin's hands in hers, her cold fingers massaging her wrists – 'and I hope you can forgive me for that.'

'No harm done,' Raf says curtly. Amanda smiles, touches the crystal on the shelf above Erin's shoulder and turns back to Raf. 'Just a misunderstanding like I thought,' he says. 'No harm done.'

'Let's get this up off the floor,' Amanda says, too chirpy. 'I reckon I could salvage a couple of bowls. Cheesy stuff at the top's the best bit anyway.'

She gets plates and scoops some of the pasta up into it. Erin stares at Raf, desperate for him to look at her, but he just stands in the shadow of the corridor that leads to Bobby's room, jaw tensing, a gale of thought blowing behind his eyes. He snaps out of it, blinking the fact that the mother of his baby has just thrown a boiling dish at him away as he heads across the room to help their guest clear up the mess that Erin's made as if they're all happy families now. Bobby coughs, a whimper comes through on the monitor. Erin wants him to burst into a full-on wail so she can run to him and escape the toxicity that overlays the others' put-on normalcy. She looks at the crystal next to her, sparkling with what seem like dots of some internal light source. She touches it, holds on to one of its spires, grips it harder until her fingers stops shaking.

42

'I don't want to go away for a few days.'

'You assaulted me.'

'I didn't –'

'You don't think what you did was assault? Fuck's sake, Erin.'

'Sorry.'

'It's not OK.'

'I'm sorry,' she says. Raf makes a sound between a grunt and a laugh. 'Are you asking me to move out?'

'No. No, I'm saying exactly what I mean. You need a break from Bobby, from Amanda, from social media, from me even, from everything. You need time to reset. I don't recognise the person that threw a dish of boiling pasta at me.' It sounds like he's saying the word 'pastor' and Erin feels her nose wrinkling with indignant irritation. She's lying in bed, covers pulled up to her neck. Raf stands by the window. It's eleven o'clock. He went for a run after Amanda left them and she's been sat up here in bed, stewing, considering, trying to make sense of everything that's happened in the last few hours.

She's gone back over their conversation and Amanda's right, she never expressly said that Raf had asked her to follow them, but she allowed Erin to believe it. As if she was trying to provoke some kind of contretemps between her and

Raf. And then all her bullshit about wanting to be on hand, in case Erin needed her, but not telling her? It's lies and she wants to tell Raf, she wants to tell him that they need to get rid of Amanda, she needs to tell him that she's worried about her being around them. But then the thought of the two of them, on their hands and knees together in the kitchen clearing up the mess she made, the edginess in his eyes when he looks at Erin now, now that he's been the victim of abuse, her victim, she feels that, for the first time in their relationship, he might not take her side. But she can't help herself.

'She's been putting honey in Bobby's bottle. She tell you that?' She expects him to turn away from the darkness outside in shock but he doesn't. His shoulders slump and he lets out a sigh.

'Manuka honey?'

'She told you?'

'No, but it's from New Zealand, everyone in Oz uses it for coughs and colds.'

'With babies?!'

'Sometimes, yeh.'

'She's trying to turn him against me, she's trying to turn you against me.'

'Would you listen to yourself, Erin? Fuck!' He kicks at one of the cardboard boxes next to the radiator. He leans forward, his arms wide like a bird of prey, and speaks into the window ledge. 'You threw a two-hundred-degree dish at me.'

'I know, I thought –'

'I know what you thought and it's not –' he turns to her – 'rational. What you're saying isn't rational. None of it is the behaviour of someone thinking rationally.'

'No.'

'I want you to cancel whatever Instagram things you have this week.'

'I can't, there's a meeting about a –'

'Say you're ill. Hand, foot and mouth, from Bobby, something contagious. Do whatever it is on the phone if you have to. But you can't go. I've got two projects to finish this week but I'm going to ask Amanda to take Bobby. If you refuse to go to your mum's and have time away, I want you to rest. Here.' He produces a blister pack of pills and throws it onto the end of the bed, keeping his distance as if she were some wounded animal. 'These will help you sleep. Pretty hardcore antihistamines. I think you need to sleep. We all do but, shit, I don't know, Erin. What you've done to me is not OK.'

'I know.' Her voice sounds like that of a chastened toddler. She looks down at the pills. She's never taken any sort of medication to help her sleep before but the thought of a blissful night of oblivion feels quite seductive right now. Raf goes into the bathroom and she can hear him brushing his teeth. She's so angry at herself. By losing it in such spectacular fashion, she's lost her voice. She's lost her right to think or feel anything about Amanda, about what she thinks Amanda's doing. She pops two of the pills from the blister and, when she sees there's nothing in the glass by her bed but the cloudy remains of limescale, swallows them dry. She turns onto her side. Turns off the lamps and listens to Raf's mechanical brushing. What is Amanda doing? she thinks. She can't be the troll if she doesn't have a camera. She was following her, but she did watch Erin screaming at her baby, she has observed her struggling, nearly losing it three or four times. Maybe she was right to want to protect Bobby. Tonight Erin's seen how violent she can be. Perhaps she's lucky it was six-foot-three-inch Raf she attacked and not her son. The thought makes her shudder.

She hears Raf pausing at the door of the bathroom about to say something but then he sighs and leaves the room. Her phone lights up on the bedside table. A notification. She turns it over and closes her eyes.

43

Erin scrolls through the four pictures of Bobby Caz has sent her from baby sensory class in her cocoon of duvet and doubled-over pillows. Her friend has rung a couple of times in the last two days. She wants to come round and visit but Erin's put her off. It feels like she knows that Erin's not really ill, that she's got a sense, perhaps from Amanda at the groups she's seen her at, that there's something much deeper going on than a bout of norovirus.

She's tried to do what Raf's asked. She's cancelled the two events she had this week, though she has one she can't miss for Phibe tonight, and let Amanda take Bobby while she rests, while she, Raf's word, 'resets'. The antihistamines worked that first night but she hasn't taken the others Raf left for her. Both he and Amanda have been treating her like she's mentally ill. Before he's gone off to work for the day and as soon as he gets back, he comes up to her room, hovers by the doorway, and asks if there's anything she needs, asks how she's feeling, whether she's had any thoughts about what happened the other night. His tone is clinical, like he's trying to be her therapist. But reflecting on it, perhaps he's always talked to her like that. He's always approached problems in a clinical manner. She never met his dad but it must be from him. And that's what she feels like to him now, a problem patient he needs to cure. Maybe that's always been the appeal for someone like him.

She looks at the big group photo of everyone with their babies staring at the camera. Lorna's there and Erin zooms in on her. Crow's feet pinch the sides of her eyes, she looks exhausted, spindly arms wrapping the twins with their too-big heads. Kristina's there, her Eden dressed in what looks like an Elizabethan ruff. Then there's Amanda and Bobby at the heart of the photo. She seems older than in real life, her cheekbones softer, hair more mussed than usual, and although there's no resemblance to speak of, Raf's genes so dominating the shape of every one of Bobby's features, no one would think that she wasn't the baby's mother.

Erin's spent hours in the last two days looking at the photostream of Bobby that Raf set up when he was born. The boy always looks concerned in pictures. But there's a few, a few where he's looking at Erin and she's looking back at him and she sees it, love. Pure unbridled love in both of their faces and she knows she would never hurt him, not like she hurt Raf. And she feels so annoyed at herself for not having seen it, amid the screaming and the painful feeds and, to her shame, her eyes glued to the screen of her phone, he loves her and needs her and he's in pain and he's confused and she can be the person to soothe him through all of that tumult.

She notices something on Bobby's wrist at the bottom of the image. She zooms in but she can't see much detail. The class is full of fancy dress, bubbles and all sorts of other baby paraphernalia. There's a bit where everyone's given a little silk scarf so perhaps someone's tied something onto him. Erin takes a screenshot and then zooms in on the image. It's not a scarf. It's a bracelet. The picture has started to pixelate, but it's a bracelet with what looks like beads on it. Or stones.

Erin sits up in bed. Why is he wearing a bracelet? And why hasn't he been wearing it around the house when Erin's been with him? That means Amanda must be putting it on him when they're out of the house. She hadn't wanted to leave Bobby with Amanda but she didn't feel she had a choice. She had assaulted Raf, if he was telling her she needed a break, she couldn't say no, but the honey in the milk, the cuddling, lying about the painting and now this. She has to tell Raf, she has to get him back on her side, make him understand that Amanda is up to something, but if she mentions a bracelet, she can picture the conversation, picture him sighing, turning away from her, clutching the bridge of his nose between his thumb and forefinger, perhaps insisting that she goes to see someone.

Erin looks on Mercedes' Instagram and sees that Amanda is out with them at the playground near the seafront and she bolts out of bed and down the stairs, outside into the garden, the mud soaking into the bottom of her slippers as she gets over to Amanda's studio. There has to be something, there has to be some clue as to what it is she's up to. The first thing Erin sees on the table is Amanda's crystal arrangement, but the stones are different now. The grey obelisk still stands in the middle, the pale pink stones, the bright red rubies, the hot-pink crystals with white, the same ones she found in the bag. But now there are blue stones interspersed, small royal-blue pebbles arranged in a triangle among the lines of stones. She hovers her phone over the top and takes a picture. She looks at the pattern that the stones make on her camera and sees the shape of a star, a five-pointed star. A pentagram, the shape she's seen so many times in schlocky scenes of high school séances. Hadn't she noticed the shape before or is this new? There's nothing here that tells her anything, but these blue stones, what do they mean? And why has the shape changed?

She looks underneath the sofa bed and sees the jar is still there. She pulls it out but it's different as well. The glass has been covered with some sort of purple material that's been taped up with parcel tape. Erin tries to find a chink in the opaque material to shine her phone light into but there isn't one. There's a faint smell from the jar, something furtive. Erin puts it back in its hiding place but then makes a note on her phone of what she remembers being in it, a doll, chilli powder, was there some mud? She writes it down anyway, no idea what this list is for, but it feels good to be out of bed and doing something proactive. Raf might be right. She might be losing the plot. Perhaps all of this, all of her suspicions of Amanda, are driven by some cynical outlook that thinks anything remotely spiritual is in some way suspicious, but ever since Erin saw this woman, this interloper in her house, topless and holding her baby boy sleeping to her breast, she hasn't been able to shake the idea that there's something much darker going on than a lovely friend of the family helping out with some childcare.

The built-in wardrobe behind her is slightly ajar and Erin opens it up to see Amanda's rucksack. Erin rifles her hand through the two main sections but they're both completely empty. She hears a rustling outside and swings round, panicked, face hot with embarrassment but it's only a seagull that's landed on the decking outside the studio. She puts the bag back in the cupboard but as she does she feels something in a pocket of the top flap. She unzips the pocket and pulls out Amanda's passport. It looks brand new. The only stamp in it is from this trip. She flicks to the back page and sees that the passport's starting date is 3 January. Erin tries to think back to when she arrived, it was near the end of January. She checks on her phone to see when the digital detox weekend was and, yes, it was the 25th.

Can that be a coincidence? Is it possible that she got her passport just for this trip? If so, that makes her claim that she saw the pink painting and just got on the plane even more preposterous.

Then she reads something that makes her sit down on the edge of the sofa. Amanda's date of birth. 15 November 1985. She's a few months younger than Erin. She'd always assumed Amanda was at least five or six years older than her. Why? Because she was friends with Raf when they were kids so it seemed they must have been similar in age but Raf's seven years older than Erin.

She blinks three, four times, and swallows the lump in her throat. Seven years' age difference. Raf left Australia when he was around twenty-one, so when they were friends, close friends, a formative friendship as she put it on that first night Erin met her, Amanda was, at most, fourteen.

44

'You OK?' An attractive twenty-five-year-old with skeletal arms and floral tattoos around her neck comes up to the desk at the front of Raf's co-working space. Erin hasn't seen her before.

'Is Raf not here?' Erin points over to his double monitors.

'He was.' She turns to the scrum of freelancers beavering away at laptops. A burly man with a huge beard looks up from his desk that's littered with expensive-looking camera equipment. Sev, Erin's been introduced to him in town by Raf, a photographer who joined the space at the same time as her fiancé, stands up, acknowledges her shyly.

'I think he had a meeting,' he says, a mild hint of an Italian accent, 'at Marine Gallery.' Erin pinches her brows. Why is he having meetings here, in town? All his clients are in London. She sees the girl glancing down at the pyjama bottoms that protrude from her big Puffa sleeping-bag coat. Sev's giving her a strange look as well, something furtive in his eyes. She catches herself in the screen of a huge iMac on the reception desk, and Erin sees why: she looks like she's just escaped from an institution. Her skin looks drawn, red spots around her chin and her hair looks like a pile of straw a farm animal's made a bed in. God, Erin thinks, she must follow my feed. She knows that Sev does, Raf's explained in the past that he's seen this or that post because Sev has mentioned it. She'd ditched her dressing gown and changed her slippers for shoes, but that aside she'd come straight down here from her supposed sickbed. Raf wasn't answering his phone and she was so desperate for some answers, to try and understand why the hell he was such close childhood friends with someone seven years younger than him, that she ran down here without much thought, but now she feels self-conscious.

She thanks them and leaves to walk down on the seafront, away from the main traffic of people, towards the harbour and Marine Gallery. She's been trying to go over the timeline of Raf's childhood, as she knows it, in her head. His mum left them when he was eleven. They moved from Melbourne when he was still a teenager. She can't remember him ever saying an exact age but she's pretty sure that he said he was in his teens. Even if by teenager Raf meant nineteen, that would make Amanda twelve. Erin thinks back to when she was in her late teens, she wasn't the most popular girl in school but she had a good group of friends and they would barely allow a twelve-year-old sibling to hang around with them let alone choose to be close friends with one.

As she walks through the piss-stinking tunnel underneath the promenade above her, she sees Marine Gallery, an asymmetrical modernist building overlooking the harbour. It's not huge, about the width of two shops, but its architecture makes it stand out from the rest of the Victorian terrace across the road from it and marks it out as a destination for all the London day trippers.

Through the window she sees Raf talking to a serious-looking young woman with a sharp Joan of Arc hairstyle wearing what looks like a black smock. Erin walks into the gallery and both of them turn to face her. The woman's face transforms into an amused grin while Raf's falls into chagrin.

'Erin, hi, we were just talking about you.' The woman walks over to Erin and shakes her hand. There's something of the countryside about her despite her chic attire. 'You feeling better?' She holds Erin's eye as if trying not to make a point of looking at her dishevelment. 'Sorry, Carmel, I run the gallery.'

'I know, yeh. Great to meet you. Could I borrow Raf for a minute?'

'You can have him,' she says, a joke but does Erin sense a note of unkindness? 'I've got a thing to be at. I'll let you know,' she says to Raf. 'So, so wonderful to meet you, Erin, and please come in and see us more and bring that gorgeous boy of yours. We could always do with a bit of free promotion.' She squeezes Erin's shoulder and sweeps off.

Raf shakes his head in irritation and sighs before moving past her and out onto the stone terrace outside the gallery. Erin stops at the glass door before she ventures out into the cold and looks at him as he stares out to sea. He's put his maroon hat on and wears the heavy orange waterproof coat, expensive for someone who always claims money is tight, the one he's worn every day in the winter since they first met, that she knows so well, and she wonders if that's all she really knows about him.

'Amanda was born in 1985,' Erin says, matter-of-fact calm, standing a few feet behind him. There's a ripple along Raf's shoulders but he doesn't move. It's just started to spit but there's no wind so she knows he's heard her. He walks down towards the harbour arm.

45

'Her stepdad. Craig. She never told anyone but he, he was, when she was really little, threatening her. When he was drunk. She told me she thought he was going to do something to her, make her do something to him.'

'Shit,' Erin says. They're huddled over in a shelter down on the promenade. The beach is deserted, the concrete walkway in front of them littered with shattered slabs of chalk fallen from the cliffs above them. 'Didn't her mum know?'

'Her family set-up was pretty fucked.'

'Wasn't her mum a doctor?'

'What and that'd make her a saint? Look at my dad. But no, she was a nurse, Janey. Dad took a shine to her at the Tropical Medical centre he got a job at after we moved from Melbourne. I don't know if anything happened between them. Knowing him, probably. Things between her and Craig were pretty rough, they drank a lot, had parties at their house. Pretty sure he hit her.' Raf pauses, clears his throat. The implication that just a couple of days ago he was the one on the end of a spousal assault hangs between them like the smell of burning plastic. 'Anyway, I, er, I ended up babysitting Amanda once or twice when they had a party. She'd come over to Dad's, we'd hang out in the garden. She was smart, bit mad, but quite funny. I felt sorry for her.'

'How old were you?'

He looks at her, back at his hands. He's picking at the cuticle of his index finger. 'Ah, eighteen, nineteen maybe when we arrived there.'

Erin clenches her jaw, bites her upper lip. She wants to press him for more detail, to ask him exactly what date it was they moved. Since finding the passport she realises how vague Raf's always been about his and Amanda's friendship. Those first few days she was with them, Erin was so caught up in the excitement of all the things taking off in her own life, she didn't take the time to interrogate what sort of friendship leads someone to drop in from across the other side of the world. He didn't have many friends, she'd always loved how content, how dedicated to her he always seemed. So who was this friend of her fiancé?

'She started spending time at our house,' he says. 'Amanda said she thought Craig was scared of me, he was short, a real bogun scumbag. I don't know. She was a little kid. She saw me as her protector I think. Then I moved from Dad's place to live in Darwin. She wanted to come and see me but I told her it wasn't allowed, then Craig got wind of it, thought I was trying to get her to run away from home, there was some other boy, from school I think, so Craig accused me of covering for the mystery boyfriend as well. Anyway he started throwing threats around so I told him I'd tell social services what he'd been saying to her unless he left me and her alone. That ended it, I thought. Thought I'd done my bit. He was a piece of shit that guy.'

'She was what, twelve?'

'You went through her bag to find her passport?' He looks at her for the first time since she came into the gallery. She stands up and walks away from him. She needs to stay calm. They'd told her they were family friends, allowed her to think they were two relatively isolated teenagers thrown together by their parents' work. She'd pictured them being fifteen maybe, she thought they would have skulked together at neighbourhood barbecues while the grown-ups talked about health policy or lack of research funding. She's not thought there could be something this complex, scared young princesses, fairy-tale wicked stepdads and Raf the accidental knight in shining armour.

'Amanda's lying about how she found us. Your dad's painting's never been on my Instagram. That's why I was looking in her stuff. And –' she has to swallow hard, swallow down the desire to start shouting, to start losing it – 'I'm pretty glad I did. Because she is lying to us, maybe about everything, and now I hear you've got some weird past where you what, saved her from her abuser? The idea she's come for a winter jaunt to the Kent coast seems a little far-fetched all of a sudden.'

Raf's looking at the ground. Strands of sodden seaweed clog the walkway and he kicks at a jumble of it.

'I told her to say about the picture.'

'What? Why?'

'Craig went to prison. Three years after I left. I didn't know any of this until she got here. One of her teachers flagged that they didn't think she was safe and the police got involved,' Raf licks his lips, struggling to get the words out. 'Craig had been messing with Amanda. It had been happening when I was still there as well. He tried to tell her they were in love. She's, she's fucked up about it. Janey tried to cover for the bastard, but they locked him up for it.'

'God.'

'Yeh, he was released a couple of months ago. That's why she's here.' Erin massages her wrist, only just noticing that the rain's got heavier so she ducks into the weeks-old weed smell of the shelter.

'How did she find us then?'

'She wrote to Lydia's daughter Anya. That was true. That's how she got our address. Lydia had worked in the hospital with Dad and Janey for a while before she moved back to England so Amanda knew her surname. Found her on Facebook I think.'

'Why didn't Anya give us a heads-up that she was coming?'

'She didn't know. Amanda just said she wanted to write to me. Perhaps she did initially. But then she saw Craig in a bar in Alice Springs, he was all full of how he still loved her, I mean, what a mindfuck all those years later, and, ah, I think she, I don't know how she felt, scared maybe, but here she is. She didn't want you to know. She's not told me much, no details.'

'She mentioned an on–off boyfriend who'd come back into her life,' Erin says, voice distant. Raf narrows his eyes.

'I think she thought she'd rebuilt her life, but then seeing him must have thrown it all on its head. Look, I don't know why she came here. Maybe she needed to be somewhere she could feel safe for a bit.'

'With you.' He throws his hands up, *I guess so*, before scratching his head through his beanie. She knows it makes her a bad person, she knows she should feel some sympathy for Amanda and her harrowing childhood, but her first thought, the thought that's now raging in her head, is about Bobby. Is he safe with her? Are they safe with her? Erin knows that she invited Amanda into the bosom of their home but what Raf's just told her has done nothing to assuage her fears about her. She hasn't got a family, her concept of family has been warped by her stepdad, she's broken, she has deep childhood scars that sound like they've been recently reopened. The crystals are one thing but Amanda's been trying to turn her baby against her, trying to make him love her more. A woman whose childhood was taken away, who's sought refuge with the family of an older boy who looked after her for a year or more, is trying to turn her baby against her and, the thought hadn't landed before, perhaps her fiancé too.

'Do you not think …'

'What?'

'Should we not ask her to leave?' she asks, trying to sound as innocent as possible.

Raf looks up from the litter-strewn ground at her, brows wrinkled in confusion. 'That's what you take from this?'

'Everything's been so messed up since she arrived.'

'How do you know? You've barely been here.'

'I think there's something wrong with her and –'

'No,' he says, standing up, and the shelter suddenly feels much smaller. 'I'm not doing this.' He walks out into the open before turning back to her. 'I don't know what's happened to you. I tell you about a woman who's done everything for you, who's picked up the slack at home because you'd rather swan about with your mad new mates, and when you find out she's had an unbelievably tough time as a kid your reaction is to throw her out?' Erin reaches out a hand instinctively, he's twisting her words, that's not what she meant. 'You going to hit me now?'

'No.'

'I googled it. Every single website says that if your partner throws something at you, assaults you in any way, you should walk out. They said that it crosses a line that it's virtually impossible to come back from.'

'I lost it, in the moment, I lost control and I'm sorry, I'm so, so sorry.'

'Sorry doesn't undo it though. Doesn't suddenly make me forget that you burned me.' He holds his hand up, a bandage wrapped around the palm where he batted the pasta dish to the floor. 'I'm too weak. That's my problem, I'm too bloody weak.' He grits his teeth, moves closer to tower over her. She doesn't know what to say, she should have known that he'd react to her saying she wanted Amanda to go like this. But she's his fiancée, he should be on her side. He shakes his head. 'I can't even believe it, can't believe it,' he says, before pulling the orange hood over his head and storming out into the weather.

46

Erin downs a shot of Jägermeister and as Anna Mai claps her on the back in sorority, the aftertaste makes her think of Manuka honey. Amanda in her house, having put Bobby to sleep, having dinner with her fiancé, talking about her.

Anna Mai's drunk. She was steaming into the warm wine at the Phibe pre-launch 'hype' event that was held, somewhat inappropriately, in the crypt of a central London church. It was the first time Erin had met the whole team at Phibe, not all women despite what she'd been told to post when she first signed up, and she'd found their excitement at her being there awkward. People all around the room were still stealing glances at her, but it felt less in admiration and more a sordid curiosity, as if she were a weeping stranger whose sad story they're desperate to know. Every time someone told her how thrilled they were to meet her, how much they loved her feed, how inspirational they thought she was, it seemed hollow to Erin now. There's a line from *The Seagull*, the Chekhov she did at university. A famous writer is given a compliment and he responds that he finds people's admiration of his life sickly, 'like sticky sweets a child gobbles up, to an adult's palate, in some way nauseating'. All of her followers' love, all their adulation, she thinks, what does any of it actually mean?

On the train up it had hit her, what Raf had said. He could leave her. The man she's decided to make a life with, away from her brother and mum, alienating herself from them in the process, the man she's had a child with, the man she's entirely dependent on for money, for support, for a roof over her head, would be entirely within his rights to leave her because she lost control. She lost control because some anonymous arsehole is making her look bad on Instagram, a social media platform, something that she knew nothing about until fairly recently, something that didn't even exist ten years ago. So tonight's had none of the joy, none of the sweet release from domesticity that have made her other Insta nights out so electric.

Anna shakes her shoulders to the beat of the music and indicates they go and sit at a booth in the corner of the seedy pub-cum-club that they've dragged themselves to with a couple of hangers-on from the event.

Erin settles herself into the booth and slurps her Tom Collins. She knows drinking is probably the last thing she should do, but it's been her go-to in good times and bad for so long she doesn't quite know what else to do. Anna Mai's standing up at the end of their table, struggling to pull her gold-sequinned bolero jacket off and mumbling something off-key about paedophiles in relation to how much she's sweating. Erin looks at her friend, with her Farrah Fawcett tumbles of golden hair and wonders what it is about her that's so magnetic. She can't remember the content of a single conversation they've had, only that they always laugh a lot. Which is surely a good thing, and yet now, even that feels meaningless. She has real friends, close friends from school and university, that she's drifted away from in the years since she and Raf got together, because he thought that spending time with them with their success and ebullient contentment was making her sad, but this – however beautiful Anna is, however snappy her incessant wisecracks, Erin never feels remotely nourished by their time together.

Anna Mai sits down opposite and Erin notices a circle of beads wrapped around her upper arms. She pulls Anna's arm closer and looks at them, they're purple, translucent.

'What the fuck? I'm not that kind of girl,' Anna slurs with a laugh in her voice, but she clearly didn't enjoy having her arm jerked across the table.

'Who gave you this?' Erin asks, attempting to still the tone of accusation. The beads are crystals, Erin's sure of it. Has Amanda got to Anna Mai in some way? Is she here? Erin scans the room, a ragtag group of pissed-up students and ropy-looking Hackney locals standing, predatorily, at the side of the dance floor.

'So,' she says, leaning forward as if about to share a secret, 'I've not been allowed to "Gram" it up yet, but I've been seeing this amazing healer, Cariad Bloom, I think she's got like eighty thousand followers or something, she's big, impossible to get an appointment, but my agent hooked me up with her and it's been a bit of a game-changer. These are ametrine. From the Anahi Mine in Bolivia. The genuine ones have so many wonderful properties, focus, self-empowerment, but what Cariad really prescribed it to me for was trying to give up smoking, it's meant to get rid of compulsions.'

'Didn't you have a cigarette outside with that awful Pete guy?'

'Yeh, but that's the first one I've had in three weeks, so I feel like it's really working.' Erin nods. She's surprised Anna

Mai's into crystals. Her whole brand is based on being a sort of nineties-style ladette who happens to have kids. Hungover trips to Legoland, guilty looks to the camera as her children eat McDonald's, and of course, sticking with her smoking habit, which, Erin has to assume, the ending of is soon to feature heavily on her feed.

'Can I show you a picture?'

'Your troll sending you dick pics yet? Has he got a big one?'

'Look,' Erin says, 'crystals.' She gets up the picture of Amanda's collection of crystals from her studio. Anna Mai looks at it, one eye squinting a bit which Erin's sure is more to do with the booze than her eyesight.

'It's a pretty standard crystal grid. Cariad has one in every room of her house and has designed one for me that, I have to be honest, I haven't got round to getting all the things for yet. Because they cost a fortune – at least the ones I've been prescribed do.'

'Do you know what it's for?'

'What, like, what healing properties?' She tries to zoom in on some of the image but shakes her head. 'Na, impossible to tell and I'm really no expert at all. The one in the middle will be a conductor of some kind and the light pink ones are probably rose quartz, just because rose quartz seems to be used for everything.'

'And what are –' Erin's tentative to hear the answer – 'the properties of rose quartz?'

'You fucking name it. Friendship, love, kinship, warmth, peace, tenderness. All those sort of soft, warm, lovely bubbly ones. I think it's used to heal trauma as well. You name it,' she says, having no knowledge she's already said that. 'Send me this.' Anna hands the phone back to Erin. 'I'll ask Cariad next time I see her.'

'That'd be ace.'

'What's up with you?' Anna slouches back into the cricket-green velvet of the booth, a snarl on her face.

'Nothing, I'm fine,' Erin says, taking the straw out of her cocktail and taking a big slug of it.

'You've had a face like a smacked arse-piece since I've seen you tonight. Tell me. If it's that nob following you around and putting pictures up, might help to call him a cunt a few times to someone that understands what it's like. I've had all sorts. Jesus, some bloke DMed me the other day and said, "You've got a face that's begging to be raped." I mean, fucking hell. I've got a thick skin and everything but I just started crying. It's not even the sentiment, what he's saying, it's just how can someone just casually be so fucking horrible to me for no reason? So yeh, tell me. Tell me what the fuck is bothering you because bottling it up clearly isn't working.' Erin looks at Anna Mai and she does want to talk. She does want to tell someone about what she did to Raf. She doesn't know much about Anna's relationship with her husband Tristan, but she's certainly done stories where she's talked about shouting at him, calling him names. She definitely gives the impression that there's a volatility in their marriage. And Anna's got a temper. She often calls out people who are being nasty to her online, by name, talks about how influencers need to fight back, so Erin's sure she'd be OK with it, perhaps she's even done something similar to Tristan before.

'I – I don't know what happened,' Erin says and Anna leans in, scenting something illicit, eyes sparkling with anticipation. 'I've not been sleeping much, there's this fucking twat on

Insta messing with my head, and Bobby's refusing to breast-feed now –' Anna's left eye starts to squint again. 'Anyway, Raf and I, we had this argument. He saw me, losing it with Bobby.' Anna raises both eyebrows so her tanned forehead creases. 'Anyway, I just totally lost control and- I threw something at him.'

'What did you throw at him?' Anna cocks her head, a sideways smile but her eyes look more alert.

'I threw a pasta bake at him.'

'What, like a bowl of pasta?'

'A dish, an oven dish, like the whole thing.'

'Shit.'

'Um, yeh, it was hot as well, straight out of the oven.' Anna Mai pulls her arms off the table and into her lap, edges to the other side of the booth. Erin nods, nervous now.

'Why would you do that?' she asks, all her former lightness dispersed.

'I was so, I was so angry. I thought he was having me followed.'

'What the fuck! He was having you followed?'

'No,' Erin says, 'no he wasn't. I got it wrong.'

Anna shakes her head, blinks a few times and looks over towards the bar. There's someone there that catches her attention, or that she pretends to know. Because then she stands up.

'Lucy Caldwell's at the bar.' Lucy Caldwell (93k followers), a foodie influencer. 'I'm really not sure why you wanted to tell me that.'

'You asked me what's wrong.'

'What do you expect me to say? Well done? You tried to burn your fiancé for what seems like basically no reason. You need to go and talk to someone but I really, really can't help with this.'

'Anna –' Erin's stood now. She can't believe her apparent friend's leapt so quickly to judge her. 'I'm not – It's like the guy who said he wanted to rape you – it, all this horrible shit from people on the Internet, it fucks you up.'

'I've never thrown, like plates, anything at people because of it, Erin. That's what people do in films, not in real life.' She collects her bag, her jacket, the coat she's wedged into the side of the booth. She's trying to shuffle herself out of the booth when she stops. 'Is he going to leave you?'

'He understands how much pressure I'm under,' Erin says, 'forgave me straight away.' She lies to Anna because she wants her to feel guilty for her reaction. If Raf can forgive her, she should be able to be less judgemental. Anna makes a face that tells her how lucky she thinks Erin is, implying that she wouldn't tolerate someone hitting her. Erin feels her stomach crumple. She genuinely thought Anna would understand, would make her feel better. Perhaps she doesn't deserve that.

'I'm going for a smoke.' Anna gives her a grin as she goes but it feels plastered on. Erin sinks back down onto the banquette, drains her Tom Collins and slides Anna's vodka tonic over to her side of the table.

'I can't believe you're Xavi,' Erin says, waving a cigarette in the chill night air a little too close to Xavi, making him duck out the way to avoid it igniting his beard. He's a couple of inches taller than Erin, and wears an elaborate jacket, black with a golden drum-major front panel that he's somehow pulling off. He had swerved the Phibe event but one of Grace's assistants had invited him to join the after-party.

Erin's drunk now. Pete, one of the CEOs of Phibe, had been plying her with mescal and, although she's still compos mentis, her tongue feels thick and she leans heavily on the wide sill of the old pub window. She and Xavi are now on their second cigarette.

'What did you think Xavi would be like?' His English is perfect but he still has the slight sibilance and casual consonants of his native tongue.

'Fat.'

'Right.'

'Bald.'

'OK.'

'Old.'

Xavi laughs, whipping his thick shoulder-length hair behind him. He knows Erin's flirting with him, he's flirted with her, but he also knows she has a child, he knows she has a partner, so it's the purest form of flirtation, untainted by the potential of having to act on it.

'Sorry to disappoint,' he says, finishing his beer, and clinking it on the floor behind him. 'Listen,' he says, turning in towards her, eyes full of sincerity, 'I feel bad that we have not found out who he is, the person taking these photos.' Erin waves him away, *forget it*. 'But have you thought about the names?'

'What d'you mean?' She blinks to try and focus her eyes. She doesn't want to have a serious conversation now. She wants to finish her cigarette, get in an Uber and go back to the hotel before she drinks more and does something stupid.

'Ali-crow, leister-worc.'

'OMG, they're fake!'

'Yeh.' He chuckles at her ribbing sarcasm, sucks hard on his cigarette like it was a shisha pipe. 'Well, anyway, couple of days ago I googled Ali-crow, just to see if anything came up. Nothing.' Erin grips the edge of the sill, the cigarette's making her feel sick so she holds it down to her side and lets the chilly 1 a.m. air smoke the rest of it. Across the street, she thinks she can see someone moving around behind a van. 'There was another name, someone that made a weird comment on one of your posts, "Crowlypoly" and one also called "Leisacrowd". All using the same sort of letters. Which could have been a coincidence, but it seemed weird. So I kept googling and I found a name.' Erin switches her attention from over by the van, where she can't tell if there's someone wearing black walking around or whether it's just the shadow made by people passing under the street light, back to the leonine Xavi.

'Who is it? Why did you wait until now to tell me?'

'Don't get too excited. He's not a real person, well, not a living one anyway. Aleister Crowley. Ever heard of him?' She shakes her head for a few shakes too long, eyes drift back over to the van. She sees a glint of something catching the street lamps, the light catching someone's watch or more likely, the black mirror of their smartphone. 'He was a weird dude. An occultist. Very famous. Into pagan stuff, organised orgies and magic rituals and shit.'

'Do you see someone over there, by that grey van?' Xavi squints in the direction she's pointing. He doesn't see anything, and now he's looking, she's not sure she can either.

'I don't see anyone.'

'No.' She clenches her jaw, swallows back some saliva, regretting the last mescal as the smoky bitterness creeps up the back of her throat. 'You said something about magic?'

'Ah, yeh, this guy, Crowley, he was into real magic, ceremonies, pagan stuff. Orgies. Doing whatever he wants. So, my question was, does that ring your bells about who it could be?'

'What?'

'Is there anyone you know who's into magic or weird pagan stuff?' Erin looks at him and it's like his question takes a moment to seep into her ears because then she starts and it's like she's looking at him for the first time that night. 'There is someone?' he says, seeing the clarity spring into her expression.

'Was he into crystals, this guy?'

'Aleister Crowley.'

'Yeh.'

'No idea. He's into spells, witchy stuff. I just read Wikipedia. I can get Grace to send articles over to you if it helps. Do some digging?'

'No.'

Erin dismounts from the windowsill, cogs stuck by booze suddenly whirring around in her mind. Until she talked to Anna an hour or two earlier, she didn't know anyone that was into alternative, holistic things, no one that would have had anything to do with the occult, apart from Amanda.

'Great to meet you.' She goes to give Xavi a hug, he picks the wrong side, so their faces almost touch, they laugh and shift their bodies so they can hug. 'Got late. Got drunk. Going to head back to the hotel.'

'You getting a cab?'

'It's only ten minutes – I'll walk.'

'Shall I walk you?'

'I'll be fine.' She touches his arm, he looks at her, unsure, perhaps only just realising how drunk she is as he feels her swaying slightly towards him. She looks over to the van again before heading into the night.

She rounds the corner into an alleyway that leads towards a railway bridge, unmitigated darkness beyond. She looks at the map on her phone, a park ahead. The screen lights up her face making her feel like a target. She pockets it and turns, heading back towards the busy road she's come from. She sees a path, a cycle lane, that's well lit and seems to be leading in the right direction. There's some movement to her left, something seems to sweep behind a low wall. A cat, a fox perhaps. Erin flicks her collar up around her face and pulls a hat out of her coat pocket. If she's warmer, perhaps she'll feel safer.

The end of the path leads to a dark road. She checks her map, still some way from the hotel. She hears steps, turns and manages to trip on a broken roof tile in the middle of the path. A hand on the wall, she stops herself falling. There's no one there. The fence at the back of a house creaks. Just the wind. She knows she's being irrational. She's been feeling someone's been following her constantly since the troll posted that video of her. But then someone was, Amanda was. She caught the only person she knows that dabbles in the occult following her. There is someone trolling her, who has made her lose control of her faculties, who's made her violent, has named themselves after some big name in the occult. She feels the rough surface of brick catch at her tights. Perhaps she's not being irrational. Maybe Amanda wanted to catch her, maybe she does have a smartphone, a camera, that Erin just hasn't found yet.

She's in a dark street that leads to a main road up ahead that her map is saying is where she'll find the hotel. Footsteps behind her, the sharp shuffle of feet moving, changing direction – are they breaking into a run? Erin doesn't look back, she can't. She starts sprinting, wedges clipping together as she attempts to accelerate. If she can get to the light on the main road she'll be fine, people are there, she can hear people up there.

A sharp noise, Erin looks behind her and her hips collide with a bin. She crumples forward, lands on her head, her leg twists, shattering pain in her ankle. She manages to crane herself up to sit, looking wildly for whoever it was she heard coming for her. There's no one there. No one's in the street. She slumps down, a distant voice from the busy road ahead slings out of the general noise as she squeezes her eyes to close out the pain.

47

BRAUNEoverBRAINS

502 posts   83.2k followers   1,642 following

ERIN BRAUNE

This is my proud face. Because he is my pride and joy.
This boy is my pride and joy.

I'm not always joyful. The biggest lie they ever got us
to swallow was that we could always be happy, always
be content. Nobody is.

I'm not always proud. I'm mostly not proud of what
I've done, of how I am, of who I am. I don't know if
anyone is.

Am I a 'good enough' mother? The pictures of me
probably tell you I'm not. I know that when he's asleep
like this and his skin looks so perfect he looks like a
little demi-god, it's easy to say how much I love him. I
find him hard. So, so hard. I spit with fury when I look
at other people's babies that never cry. Because he

cries. All the time. And my body tenses up, which I'm sure makes him cry even harder. But, he is my pride and he is my joy. He is. So you can all think what you like about me. You can do what you want to me. But I know what he means to me.

'Holy shit.' Raf's at the door of Bobby's bedroom. He's dressed even though it's five thirty in the morning. He beckons Erin out of the room, shocked by the state she's in but not wanting to wake the baby. Erin smiles, puts her hand out for him to come and join her in staring at the sleeping baby but he shakes his head and his eyes tell her that he wants to know what the hell's happened to her. She's still in her outfit from the club, coat dirtied. She doesn't know if, in the low light, he can make out the blood matted into her hair, or the shredded patches of her tights. She tried to go to A&E after she fell but it was overstuffed with frightening drunks so she came straight home.

'What the hell happened?' Raf asks, as she closes the door of Bobby's room. He ushers her over to the kitchen table, gets her to sit down. She has a banging headache though feels strangely at peace. Perhaps she's concussed.

'I got an Uber from London. Please don't be angry. I'll give you the money when I get paid. You won't have to pay for it.'

'What happened?' Raf goes to put the kettle on, gets a bag of frozen peas out of the freezer and brings it over to her. He doesn't know where to put it until Erin hauls her ankle up on a kitchen chair, takes it from him and winces as she places the peas on it. 'Did someone do this to you?'

'I tripped.' He looks at her, dubious. 'I decided to get the last train back, I didn't want to be away from Bobby for another night. I was sprinting for a taxi to get to the station and I tripped and fell onto a bin.' Raf sits down opposite and puts her hands in his. She realises her fingers are shaking. 'I'm so sorry.' She looks at him starkly, one eyelid slightly closing from the swelling on the top of her forehead. 'What I did to you was unacceptable and you don't deserve it and I hope you can forgive me.' Raf looks down at the floor, he starts breathing through his nose. Erin knows he doesn't have to forgive her, maybe Anna Mai's reaction was right and he should leave her. But his face when he saw her hurt, the compassion, the desire to protect, she needs him, it could be that's all she's ever really needed. She looks at her hands in his. Rather than the adulation of an audience, the likes of tens of thousands of anonymous followers, perhaps she just needs the love, the care and protection of this one man. 'I don't want you to leave us.'

Raf looks up and he's got a big grin on his face, he shakes his head. He goes to hug her, attentive to the fact she's hurt. He's happy.

'Of course I forgive you. You've put yourself under so much pressure,' he whispers into her ear. 'I'm doing everything I can, I'm putting everything I can into helping you cope, but it's got too much. Hasn't it?' She nods. He looks at her with warmth in his eyes for the first time in what seems like weeks and it feels so wonderful to have him back on her side. He is on her side, she knows that, he always has been. It's been her that's pushed him away.

'We should clean that up,' he says, eyeing the gash on her head.

'It's not as bad as it looks. Hair mostly.' He encircles her cheek in his hand and she could almost lean into it and fall asleep. Raf gets up to search the kitchen cupboard where they keep medicine.

A light comes on outside. The security light of the studio at the end of the garden. Erin turns to see Amanda slinking in through the garden gate and towards her room. It's not even six yet. Their guest glances into the kitchen before heading into her lodgings. She doesn't turn the studio light on. Erin thinks back to that dark road in Hackney. Maybe she fell because she was drunk. Maybe she imagined there was someone there watching her. Maybe she imagined the shuffle of running feet that made her sprint into the pitch-black until she fell hard and hit her head. But if she imagined it all, then where's Amanda been in the middle of the night?

48

18 May 1999

We've moved to the suburbs and *everything* is better. Donny and I are clearly not made for city life. We don't need the noise and all the people, we only need space and each other.

He's been so amazing. I thought he'd be angry to have to move out but he's been so kind, so loving, just like he was back at school. It was my fault we had to move so quickly. He'd told me he didn't want me talking to any of the neighbours. He told me, again and again, that sooner or later Jean upstairs would start asking questions about where my parents were. But she always seemed so ditzy to me, I thought she had Alzheimer's and that he was just being too cautious. Well, one day she came looking for me in the day, Donny was home and answered the door. She'd never met him before as she never left her flat after he got back from work. She started shouting at him, threatening to call the police. He told me we'd have to leave that night. I felt terrible, but he was so lovely about it, he didn't blame me even though I knew it was my fault. He went out to get everything sorted and we came straight here.

And now we're in a little one-bed house that has a creek ten minutes' walk away and it feels like when we were getting to know each other again. Donny's still commuting into the city and, for the moment at least, he thinks it's best if I stay inside when he's not here. He's put a CCTV camera above the door so we'll have evidence if Craig finds us here, but I can't see how he ever will.

I was having doubts. It feels almost sacrilegious, with everything we've been through in the last year, to say that, but I did. Our love felt so intense, so pure, it made me feel alive, but when we moved to the city I started to feel as if he thought he'd made a mistake. He seemed so stressed all the time, so paranoid. But now I've got the old Donny back. So loving, so tender. And I feel like our world is everything again. And that's important. People spend their lives striving for money and career, to get married, to have children. But for what? He and I have to put something important in the world. We're on a voyage together. And that's the operative word. Together. Soulmate is a cliché now. But if you find that person who can be enough to satisfy every craving, every desire you have, when you find perfection, you have to do everything to maintain it and never let it go.

He says he still wants me to be the mother of his children. Now he can see what our life can be like, simple, pure, he can see that for us soon.

They say it's always darkest before the dawn and I see now that that's all it was in Darwin. We're safe now. I'm safe.

49

'Hi, is that Cariad?'

'To whom am I speaking?'

'Hi, it's Erin Braune. Anna Mai's friend?'

'Oh. Oh, hello.'

'I got your mobile number from my agent. Grace Fentiman.'

'I have an appointment in a couple of minutes.'

'This won't take long. I wanted to thank you for your message identifying what all the different crystals in the picture were, but I was wondering if you could help me work out what they're all, you know, arranged in that pattern, what they're actually set up to do.'

'Crystals are ciphers of energy. It would be impossible to say exactly what any arrangement is trying to heal.' Cariad sounds tense, not pleased to be cold-called like this. Erin expected her to be nurturing, to have a voice like a children's presenter, but she's not like that at all. She nudges Bobby's buggy with her knee. They're on the seafront. He's not asleep but the movement seems to stop him crying.

'I've googled the individual stones from your message and it seems they could be anything really. Friendship, love, empowerment, confidence. I was just wondering if you could make it more specific for me.'

'This isn't your grid.'

'It isn't, no.'

'Crystals are very personal.'

'They belong to someone who looks after my son and I'm concerned she could mean him harm.'

'Crystals don't allow you to imbue them with any negative energy. I promise you, this grid is not designed to harm anyone. The opposite if anything.'

'What does that mean?' Cariad gives a hearty sigh. There's a pause. Erin can hear her moving some things around on the other end of the line.

'Is your baby very attached to you?'

'Yes. Yes he is.' Erin's not sure why she had to answer so vehemently. She glances down at Bobby who is looking up at her with a dreamy admiration.

'Rhodochrosite has the power to bewitch. It bonds people. Binds them. Garnet has a very sexual energy but, combined with the quartz and the rhody, I'd say it was there to rekindle a destroyed relationship. Rose quartz is the heart stone. It's love. Pure love. So perhaps she's trying to improve her bond with your son.' Erin opens her eyes wide and stares out as a swarm of seagulls swoop across the horizon. 'It's a very powerful arrangement, I was impressed when I saw the picture.' Erin hears Cariad, but she's not listening any more. She thanks the healer and lets her get back to her appointment.

She leans back on the bench she's sitting on, dazed by what Cariad's just told her. Bobby wriggles out of his blanket and she pulls it up over him. She takes off her scarf and lays it over Bobby's lower half. His tiny fingers bat at the felt animal on the buggy-mobile above him. Erin looks up and sees a crescent moon in the afternoon sky. An empty container ship out at sea. 'It is the star to every wand'ring bark.' A line of Shakespeare pops into her head at the exact moment that Erin realises that all her fears about Amanda and Bobby, all her concern about someone taking pictures of her, have clouded her against what Amanda's really here for.

'Let me not to the marriage of true minds,' she recites to Bobby. She knows the poem by heart – she spent a whole term on Shakespeare's sonnets. 'Admit impediments. Love is not love / Which alters when it alteration finds / Or bends with the remover to remove. / O no! It is an ever-fixed mark / That looks on tempests and is never shaken; / It is the star to every wand'ring bark.' She stops and sees Bobby's fallen asleep. She wraps her arms around her body and speaks the words to herself, 'Love alters not with his brief hours and weeks, / But bears it out even to the edge of doom.'

Sonnet 116. Erin hadn't remembered which sonnet it was when she saw it written on the Post-it on the inside of the studio kitchen cupboard, she'd meant to google it to check, but now she doesn't need to and the realisation hurts like a sharp kick to the gut. Amanda's in love with Raf. She's been in love with him for twenty years. Maybe her stepdad being released was the catalyst for coming but she's not here for his protection. Her crystals are there to bewitch him, to heal their broken relationship. Erin can't believe she didn't see it when Raf told her the story of his and Amanda's unconventional friendship. Of course she was in love with him. He was older, he saved her. She can't imagine holding a love like that for twenty years but she also can't imagine pinning a sonnet up like a motivational poster. Maybe the boyfriend she's talked about who's come back into her life, perhaps that's not Craig, perhaps it's her fiancé.

The ice wind picks sand up from the beach and she has to clench her eyes to protect them. She feels numb. Six words repeat in her head again and again. 'Even to the edge of doom.'

50

FROM: grace.fentiman@rfgtalent.com
TO: erinbraune@outlook.co.uk
RE: Post updates

Hi Erin,

Hope you're having a fab week. I just wanted to drop you a quick line because I was talking with my assistants about your content and we were thinking perhaps it might be helpful to pass things by us for a little copy edit before uploading. We do it for most of our clients, but because your posts are always so funny we've never thought it necessary until now. We wanted to help you get back in touch with what people responded to in the early days, your breezy tone that has just the lightest touch of the sardonic. It's totally understandable with what's been going on, but some of your stories have come across a little over-serious?

I can't imagine how personal the trolling must feel, but, thanks to your incredible work and an increased social media marketing spend our end, it fortunately hasn't affected the growth of your followership and 100k is in touching distance. I can't stress again how much of a game-changer it would be to get into the macro-influencer sphere.

I'm chasing payments for you from Phibe and others. It's coming up to the end of financial year so brands often delay things around this time. But I'm on it.

Let me know what you think. So excited to break into the big time with you.

Best,
Grace
X

51

'Poetry instantly turns me off, but some people like it. Maybe it's just that.'

'Caz –'

'And even I've heard of the "marriage of two minds" one.'

'Putting up a Post-it, that's a positive-mind therapy thing. My friend Pete had them all around his flat when we were at drama school. They're like mantras. And hers is "Love is an ever-fixed mark". That's what she's telling herself every time she looks at the inside of that cupboard.'

'Right,' Caz says, plinking a teaspoon around her mug of tea. Erin was waiting outside Caz's three-bed Victorian on a grotty road by the station when she got back from work. She needed to tell someone what she'd discovered and it couldn't be Raf. The way he was last night when he saw how distraught she was, it's been the first time in a week or so that he hasn't treated her like she's rabid. 'I think it's weird,' Caz says, matter-of-factly, 'for sure, everything you're saying is weird. Crystals, jars with old dollies in, weird. But that doesn't make her dangerous.'

'She's been lying to us from the off. She didn't see the picture and fly over here. She planned to come. She's probably been planning to come and claim him for years.'

'People who've suffered childhood trauma, they don't always act in a way that people might see as rational.'

'She didn't have to lie to us.'

'She's ashamed. I had a feeling something like that had happened to her. When I asked her why she decided to leave Oz in their summer to come to this windswept hellhole, she said she'd needed to make a change, she needed a chance to reset. And my fucking sonar went off. I thought it might have been a messy divorce, some prick of a husband that she didn't want to talk about, but this makes so much more sense. Being vague about everything, deflecting, being super nice to everyone, desperate for people's love, it's overcompensating. I've worked with kids that've suffered like her and they all need something to cling on to, so for her it's crystals and herbs, and maybe you're right, maybe it is your Raf, someone who was kind to her at that time. But that doesn't make her a threat to you. She loves you, the way she talks about you.'

'Really?'

'She thinks you're hilarious, always saying it, not sure what she's talking about myself,' Caz says with a wry smile. Erin shakes her head, brow creased. She's told Caz everything Raf told her about Amanda's past, everything Amanda has done, the cuddling, the honey, the crystal grid designed to bewitch, to repair fractured relationships, the sonnet, and Caz thinks it's normal, normal behaviour for someone who's endured a childhood abuser. Erin doesn't know anything about how something like that would affect a person in their childhood whereas Caz has spent her entire career working with those sorts of cases. Her friend gets up and walks to the wooden worktop, still covered in the plastic bearing the name of the DIY shop her husband bought it from.

'Have you heard of Aleister Crowley?' Erin asks.

'No,' Caz says, sounding tired, bored even.

'He was a famous occultist, like the most famous one.'

'Let me guess, Amanda's got a picture of him above her bed and that means she's going to kill you all in your sleep.'

'The troll's handle uses letters from his name. A security expert who works for my agent thinks it's significant and he asked me if I knew anyone who was into the occult.' Caz twists a valve on her sink and water bursts out of a bare copper pipe into a clatter of plates that she begins vigorously rinsing.

'You think she's the troll as well? Christ.'

'Do you know anyone else around here who has pentagrams in their room?'

'The same letters? You mean — You're willing to accuse someone who's looked after your kid for free for two months because of some anagrams?' She shuts off the tap with a clatter, turns and leans back, as if trying to get as far away from Erin as she can without leaving the room. 'Why? Why would she do it?'

'She's obsessed with Raf.'

'And how does making you look shit on the Internet help her with that?'

'I —' She's right, Erin thinks. She's become so fixated on what Xavi said, what Cariad said about the meaning of the crystals, she's become so set on the culprit being Amanda, that she's never stopped to ask herself why she'd troll her. Caz sits down, puts her hands on the table and starts to speak. Her tone is less banterous than normal and Erin can see the authoritative social worker Caz's wards see every day.

'I know you were worried about getting depressed after how you started feeling when you were pregnant and I totally get that. Journaling is a big thing we try and get people with mental health problems to do, and I know it really helped you. But it's gone too far now, surely you can see that in yourself. Even if this guy weren't taking pictures of you. When we've been together, with the kids, when you're not looking at your phone, you're desperate to. I see it in your eyes. You look manic, a lot of the time now. It's scary how much you need it.' Erin thought Caz would tell her to run Amanda out of town, she secretly hoped she might come and do the dirty work for her, she hadn't expected the excoriating spotlight to fall on her. 'I think it's distracting you from the fact that you're not quite right, you know? After Bobby. So many women suffer with some sort of depression or anxiety after giving birth, most even, I'd say.' Erin's breath rattles in her nose as it quickens, she can't believe what Caz is saying. 'I mean, I did. Ask my mum, ask himself, I was a basket case after Stanley. It's just, Amanda? Lovely Amanda who recommended me the supplement for my bad back, which is actually really fucking working, thanks for asking.' Erin looks up at Caz and she softens, smirks and is almost laughing as she says. 'You're saying that mad hippie wants to steal your husband? That she's taking pictures of you and putting them on the Internet?'

Caz grabs a Bourbon cream from the plate on the table and bites into it. 'You're fucking brilliant, Erin. You're a great mum and a great laugh and I miss you.' She reaches her hand across the table and Erin takes it, clinging on to it like the ledge of a clifftop. 'And yeh, get rid of Amanda if it's messing up the vibes in your house. But – Listen, do you wanna know what I think?'

'You've just spent about twenty minutes telling me what you think.'

Caz squeezes her hand. 'Get off your phone, love. Just for a bit.'

As if it's heard her, Erin's phone buzzes loudly in her pocket. Caz can see she's not got her attention any more.

'Don't abstain on my account,' she says, releasing her hand and slouching back in her chair.

'It's fine.' Erin says, ignoring it. But then it starts ringing. 'Sorry.' Erin gets her phone out and sees it's Grace. A sliver of ice runs up her spine. Grace doesn't call any more. All of their communication recently has been by email. Erin goes to the glass doors that lead out to the garden and answers the phone.

'Hi, Grace.'

'Did you do something with Xavier?'

'What? No!'

'There's another photo.' Erin swallows. Dread fills up her insides like a hair-clogged drain. Erin clicks the door handle to try and get out into the garden but it's locked. Caz is there and opens it for her.

'We just –' Erin steps onto the muddy grass. 'He was at the pub and we had a cigarette.'

'You've never mentioned that you smoke on your feed.' Annoyance strains Grace's voice. Caz hands Erin her phone, Instagram open, and she sees the picture. The pub with its blacked-out windows and peeling facade makes it look like a far more sordid venue than it is. There she is, shoulders exposed in her green sequinned jumpsuit, hunched in to Xavi with his mane of hair and thick beard, faces close, laughing, a bead of burning-red cigarette glinting in her right hand. She zooms into her face and one eye is a little squiggly, hair stuck to her forehead. She looks drunk. It could be an Edward

Hopper painting the level of detail the photographer has managed to capture. 'Erin, you still there?'

'We were just talking and I don't really smoke. It's, it's nothing like the photo looks.'

'But it doesn't look good.'

'No.' She hadn't imagined it, Erin thinks, there *was* someone there behind the van. The troll was there, in London, watching her the whole evening. Watching her through windows. Following her down alleys trying to scare her. If she'd knocked herself out when she fell, would they have done something to her? 'Why haven't you taken it down?'

'We took it down but it's been reposted. Three times now. We'll keep doing so but if they keep posting it, continuing to take it down might look worse.' Erin looks down and the photo's gone. But it doesn't take much scrolling through her mentions to see that people have seen it, people are talking about it and, most importantly, some people have screenshotted it. 'It's also calling in quite big favours to get this stuff removed, Erin. They don't just do it for anyone and there comes a point where they just won't any more.'

'Right, I'm sorry.'

'You have to be hyperaware of how your behaviour could look if it's taken out of context. I know it's not your fault.'

'No.'

'We're all on your side. Let's speak later.' They end the conversation and Erin finds herself marooned in the middle of Caz's lawn. She can feel her friend watching her from just inside her kitchen. She's seen the picture. What must she be thinking? That Erin's an alcoholic, smoking party girl? That she's been having an affair? Caz won't but everyone else will.

Raf might. Raf might and it might be the final straw. And who'd be there to pick up the pieces?

'Erin, come in, it's freezing.' She looks at the end of Caz's garden. Two small birds are twitching around a collection of suet balls hung on a bird table, beyond it the door to the alley behind Caz's house, the same as in her garden. She pictures Amanda's lustrous waves of red hair bouncing along and coming through the gate, looking towards the house furtively before going into her little box-home like she did the early morning after she'd come back from London. Caz was right, it didn't make sense Amanda posting the pictures. At least the other pictures didn't make sense, but this one does.

52

Modern Witchcraft Encyclopedia

Jar spells are one of the oldest and simplest forms of magick. Though normally associated with curses and curse-breaking, they can also be a form of love magic if items like honey, flower petals or heart-shaped charms are used.

What you need:

A container – jar, bottle, sealable receptacle
A poppet – a doll that looks like the target of the curse, a photograph of them, some nail clippings or hair.
A medium – the substance through which you'll transfer energy, be it good or bad, to the target. There are many different types of medium.
E.g:
Rusty nails can cause general harm.
Chilli flakes will cause the subject of your spell to become angry.
Honey, petals, heart-shaped charms can encourage your target to love.
Graveyard soil can drive someone away. Fresher the better.
Urine can help you gain power over your target.

Once you have your intention for the spell, pour that into the jar along with the poppet and the medium and then seal the jar tightly. It can make the curse more powerful to paint the outside of the jar so no light can get into it or to hide it in a dark place.

It may take many months for your spell to take effect and if you are putting negative energy into your jar, please consider how to improve the situation for yourself rather than trying to harm someone else.

To break the curse simply break the jar and discard the contents. But make sure you've cast a spell of protection, or you're wearing a protective amulet when you do this, otherwise the spell can come back on you.

53

Raf barely looks at her as he walks from the doorway of their living room over to the sink where he fills up a glass of water. Erin came back from Caz's and put Bobby down for his nap. Then she told Raf that there'd been another photo and could he come home so they could talk about it. She was hoping that he wouldn't see the photo beforehand but his desk-mate, Sev, helpfully showed it to him.

Erin watches him drink the pint of water down in four bubbling gulps before rinsing the glass and putting it on the side. His not looking at her, not talking to her would usually make Erin broil with anxiety but she feels calm. She has no idea whether he'll believe her about Xavi but she knows she did nothing wrong and now she has an answer to what's being done to them. She and Raf can finally be united by a need to remove the malignant presence that's been ruining their relationship. They will be able to get rid of Amanda, together, and move on with their lives.

Raf walks over to her and sinks his long legs back into the armchair opposite. He doesn't look angry, he doesn't look upset. He looks neutral, no emotion shows on his face, boredom, if anything.

'You're going to tell me that that picture is not what it looks like.' He blinks his eyes slowly.

'He's called Xavi. He's the security expert who's been trying to find out who it is that's taking these photos. The photo
makes it look like we're together but we're not, and if you
don't believe that now, there's not much I can do about it.
But I know who it is that's doing this to me and I know I can
prove it to you.' He flicks his eyes up to her. This is not what
he was expecting. He was expecting apologies and simpering
and pleas to forgive her for being such a dissolute and terrible partner but she's not going to let emotion cloud this. A
jar with a curse in is damning evidence. They will rip off the
tape, she will show him what's inside. He'll see that the doll
looks like his fiancée. She'll show him the articles she's found
online, dozens of them, proving that Amanda's trying to curse
her. She'll show him the sonnet declaring Amanda's undying
love for him. She'll tell him that she saw Amanda coming
back to their house in the middle of the night, probably on
the first train, mere hours after Erin had been chased down
the street and fell, nearly concussing herself. And, together,
they will throw her out. Maybe Raf will take all of Amanda's
wacky bullshit and put it out in the street and they'll watch
the wind blow it into the sea and they'll never have to see
her again.

Erin stands up and extends her hand for Raf to follow her.
He looks at her and there it is, the first hint at how angry he
really is about the photo, a glint of jealous rage he's desperately trying to style out with a chill exterior. He stands up,
shaking his head as Erin makes her way to the doors into the
garden. He pinches his eyes into his nose as if he hasn't slept
for weeks. He knows where they're going so Erin marches
out to Amanda's studio before he can object. According to
Sophie's Instagram Amanda's doula-ing for her today so she's

definitely not in. Erin opens the door of the studio, glances at the crystal grid, still on the table beaming its love energy towards Raf as he turns sideways to edge his way through the door. He seems giant in the tiny room, and from the way he sniffs the herbal air and casts his eyes over the brightly coloured throw that Amanda's put up on the back wall, it seems like he hasn't been in here since she arrived.

'I need you to listen to me now. Do you see this?' She points to the crystal grid. 'I spoke to an expert and these crystals are designed to bewitch someone or to repair an old relationship.'

'Erin –'

'Please.' She goes to him and takes his hands in hers, grips them tight and looks straight into his shining brown eyes. 'Please let me finish.' He nods, the anger in his eyes replaced by an etch of concern. Erin slams open the cupboard door and reveals the Post-it, something shimmers in Raf's eyes. He thinks I've lost it, Erin thinks, but she has to make her case.

'"Let us not to the marriage of two minds admit impediments." It's a Shakespeare sonnet all about how once you love, you can never ever let that love go. It's extreme. Too much. And it's Amanda's mantra.'

'How many times have you been in here?'

Erin ignores him, undeterred. 'You know voodoo?'

'What?'

'Voodoo, sticking pins in dolls and causing them pain.'

'I guess.'

'Well.' She goes round to the sofa, bends down to her knees and reaches under. Her hand finds square metal legs. She sweeps again and only finds the edge of the folded mattress. Raf's looking at her down his nose, expression blank.

She gets her phone torch out and shines it under the sofa. The jar isn't there. Nothing's there. 'There was –' She stands up and goes into the bathroom. She looks behind the toilet, opens the bathroom cabinet even though there's no way the jar could fit in there. She looks in the shower. She crosses the room, trying not to look at Raf who's leaning out of the open studio door. Erin yanks all of the cupboard doors, high and low, she puts her head into the deep cupboard under the sink and rustles around the cleaning products. The jar isn't here. She's taken it. She's hidden it.

'There was a jar,' Erin says.

'Let's go back to the house.'

'It was a curse. There was a doll of me in the jar. I've googled it. It's witchcraft.'

'I don't want us in here any more. Close the cupboards, make it look like it did and let's go back to the house.'

'She wants to take you away from me. She's in love with you.' His jaw tenses. 'She's always been in love with you, that's what the poem means. She's going to try and take you away from me. You and Bobby maybe. She put pepper in the jar, chilli flakes, it's part of the spell, to make me angry. And there was some graveyard soil in there as well that was meant to drive us apart. She's planned it all to steal you from me. Now she's moved the jar because she knows I'm on to her. She knows it proves everything. That's why she took the picture with Xavi as well. She's the troll. She has to be. She knows we'll throw her out now we know and she's getting desperate.'

'Get back in the house, now.' Raf says it with such force, such authority that it silences Erin instantly. She almost sits on the floor like a young child. He goes out the door, holding it for her, and she walks past through the tunnel of his arm against the door frame and back towards the kitchen feeling the chilly vitality on her skin that she would have walking back from a big night out at dawn. Everything tingles, her pulse races.

'She's moved it.' Erin sits on the sofa, hands cradled in between her knees. Raf's in the kitchen, staring into the garden. 'She knew I saw her getting back from London, so she moved it just in case I came into her room.' Raf begins moving things from the drying rack and stacking them in a pile next to it. She leans over the sofa towards him, 'I know you can't see it. You still see her as a little girl so you can't see how manipulative she is.' There's a huge bang as Raf slams the stack of dinner plates down on the work surface. He speaks as if his voice was being fed through a mangle, deliberate but strained.

'You're going to go and see someone.'

'What?'

'I didn't want it to come to this but you need professional help. Perhaps go somewhere, away from us for a bit.' Erin laughs. She's knows it's not the right reaction as soon as it comes out of her mouth but she can't help it. He wants to section her. She's never heard anything so ridiculous in her life. He's shaking his head, anger turned to sadness now. He pities her. It suddenly hits her hard. He pities her because he thinks she's gone mad. 'I've been meaning to stage some sort of intervention for months now.'

'An intervention?' Erin stands up and walks to the corner of the room.

'Smartphone addiction is serious. It's just as bad as gambling, worse lots of people are saying.'

'Which people?' Erin turns, bites her lips. The incredulity is switching into indignation.

'You think I don't see what's been happening to you?' Raf comes towards her but Erin backs further into the corner. 'I was worried about losing you to everyone else, everyone you were sharing our baby's life with, but it's worse than I ever thought. It's warped your mind.' Out the window a middle-aged woman looks in on them. 'I can show you the article I read, it can make you delusional. There's some anonymous arsehole trying to ruin your Instagram feed and you're convinced it's happening in real life, in our real life.'

'They're here. They're in town, following me around. She knows where I am at all times. Of course it's Amanda. It has to be Amanda.' Raf's over by her now. He takes her face in his palms, rubs a finger on her temple, but he's shaking his head. He grabs her into him and holds her tight to his body. Erin's eyes dart around the room like a stunned animal.

He doesn't even slightly believe me, she thinks. She sees her reflection in the glass of the painting, that painting she hates, and, does she see what they're all seeing? Caz said she looked manic all the time, Raf thinks she's delusional. Has she been so spooked by the threat to her online persona that she's finding real-world threats that aren't really there?

'I believe you,' he says.

'You do?' She pulls her head away and looks at him quizzically.

'About the man in the photo.'

'Oh.'

'I don't think your head's in any sort of place for that kind of thing.' Erin blinks. 'I know you'd never do something like that to me. That's why I love you. I love you and I want us to get through this.' His hands rest on her shoulders now. 'We'll ask Amanda to go. As soon as you're yourself again, we'll ask her to go.'

'Tell her to go now. Maybe she's not the troll, but she needs to go now. If you want me to get better.' She hates herself for saying it because she doesn't feel ill, she doesn't feel mad. 'She needs to go now.'

Raf breaks from her and goes over to the door. He picks up some junk mail from the console table and begins scrunching it. He seems edgy, conflicted. He's about to speak but it just comes out as an 'ah' sound. But then he does.

'I can't trust you alone with Bobby.' His words hit her like a backdraught, forcing Erin to grab one of the large books on the shelf behind her for ballast. 'Every time I close my eyes,' he says, 'I see you shouting at him on the verge overlooking Hilda's Bay. He's a baby and you're screaming at him.' He sits on the side of the armchair, facing the door, away from Erin as if he can't say what he has to say directly to her face. 'I – Do you remember the thing we watched on iPlayer a couple of years ago, you wanted to watch it, about postpartum psychosis?'

'What the fuck, no.'

'The look on your face in those pictures. You look like you hate him, like you hate our son. And now all this, threatening crystals, curses in jars that don't exist for Christ's sake. You want to know something funny?' He turns round to face her, his shoulders slacken. 'I've not been able to pay the mortgage the last three months. I've been missing deadlines because I'm so fucking stressed with all this, all this shit. You're off spending hundreds of pounds a month on trains, still not earned a penny from any of the "work" you've been doing. So, I'd love

Amanda to go, if it meant you'd suddenly flip back into being the woman I fell in love with, the woman I was desperate to have a baby with, but I honestly don't think her going will make a blind bit of difference. This,' he waves two fingers around his forehead to indicate her mental decline, 'was on the cards as soon as you got pregnant. I could have stopped it but I was too –' he punches his palm with his hand – 'I was too indulgent of your –' he indicates to the phone – 'your ridiculous social network crap. I can't leave him with you. I'm sorry. Not now. It wouldn't be responsible.'

'I'll give up Instagram,' Erin blurts out, not knowing if she means it.

'Really?' Something clears in his expression. She knows that this is what he wants. This is what he's always wanted. He's never said it, he'd never set himself up to be called 'obstructive', but she knows he's jealous of the people that follow her online, she knows he wants to guard what they have from the world rather than sharing it. She doesn't want to give up Instagram but she's scared. She realises how scared she must be of Amanda, or perhaps it's of what's happening to her, because for the last six months, nothing has been more important to her than social media, not even her son. And it hits her how appalling that is. 'I'll give it up but Amanda has to go.'

Raf looks down at the floor, then up to stare out at what's become Amanda's lodging. Her lair where she's hiding a curse – Erin's sure she's hiding a camera too, although perhaps she's moved it all somewhere else now she knows Erin's been in there. She tenses her forearm, she's lost weight in the last month and she can see the tendons vacillate as she does. Her phone buzzes on the hall table between them. Raf looks at her, challenging her to check it, but she doesn't even look down, holding his eye.

'Delete the app,' she says, trying to appear as if it means nothing to her. A smile sneaks into his eye and it's like she's passed an elaborate test he's been playing. He walks over to her phone and picks it up. Presses her code. Deletes Instagram.

'I'll ask her to go,' he says. Erin tries to look grateful but all she feels is relief. Whether Amanda's the troll or not, whether Erin's going mad or is the only sane one, her going is the only way for things to get back to something like they were before. But, as Raf slides her phone into the pocket of his coat, somehow, this doesn't feel like a victory.

54

FROM: grace.fentiman@rfgtalent.com
TO: erinbraune@outlook.co.uk
RE: Great news to brighten up a tough day

Hi Erin,

We did it. We broke 100k followers. I know the circum-
stances aren't what anyone was expecting but you should
take heart from knowing that even with someone out
there trying to smear you, people haven't stopped wanting to follow your and Bobby's journey. The way you've
responded, with grace and charm, is a huge component of
this, so well done you!

I've already had some really interesting brand enquiries but
was holding out until we reached the 100k mark because
it gives me a much stronger negotiating position. Because
it's come quickly I'm going to only raise our per-post fee
to £800, BUT both Debenhams and Peacocks have offered
a full-scale campaign that I'd been putting off telling you
about, we wouldn't be able to do both but I'd hope to be
able to play them off against each other and I imagine we'd

probably be able to get 25–35K if you were happy to do an exclusive tie-in for the season. Anyway. All to be discussed.

Also, a heads-up, a few of the online gossip mags have run with the story, but so far we've managed to put off tabloids. I've waved my magic 'fuck-off' wand at them! It won't even be light drizzle in an espresso mug by next week, and it gives me great delight to declare that BRAUNEforBRAINS is now a *MACROINFLUENCER!!!!*

Speak soon.
Grace
X

FROM: erinbraune@outlook.co.uk
TO: grace.fentiman@rfgtalent.com
RE: Re: Great news to brighten up a tough day

Are you free to chat today? Let me know when works for you.

Best,
Erin
X

55

'You won't recover, Erin.' Grace's voice sounds like a flat clarinet through the phone's speaker. This is the first thing she's said after Erin rambled on to a silent phone line about how she was going to take an extended break from Instagram in light of the trolling. Raf gives a crocodile smile and shakes his head at the phone that stands on the console table between them. 'It makes it look like the troll is right about you. That you're cheating, drinking too much, not being a proper mother.' Grace lets the words hang among the dull fizz of static on the line. 'And we all know that's not true. Is that what you want people speculating? Because that's what fills the void, Erin, speculation, gossip about why you decided to throw it all away.' Erin hasn't heard this tone from Grace. She didn't think that her agent would be happy about her decision but she hadn't expected this.

'Grace, it's Raf.'

'Your idea I presume?'

'I understand this might be difficult for you professionally, but you don't have children, do you? Someone's threatening my family —'

'There haven't been any threats.'

'Is there nothing you people won't say to make money?' Bobby looks up from trying to climb up onto the sofa at his father's forceful tone. 'Someone's following her when she's with our baby. Your so-called security expert knows bugger all, no one on your side's doing anything. Has anyone even called the police yet? I wanted to when I first found out, which, by the way, I do not appreciate you telling my future wife to hide things from me, but you told me not to bother, but now things have escalated, it seems insane they haven't been contacted. Look, I'm so sorry this is going to cut your bottom line but, you know, I'm sure you'll be OK sitting in your million-pound house –'

'Erin, can you take me off speaker?' Erin wants to do as she says but Raf stills her with a glance. She doesn't want to leave Instagram. She has a career now, for the first time in her life she was about to start earning money, really good money. She could start buying the things she wanted, doing the things that she wanted, not always being beholden to Raf, not always asking him for cash to do the most meagre things, she could start to live like everyone else she knew. She was planning to work hard and build her fan base, and who knew what could have happened from there. She's still a bloody good actor, she's not thick, she didn't know where it was going to take her but she knows she could have made something tangible out of her online success. But it's a physical thing as well. The thought of not having it there in her pocket, not checking it, not having that hit of joy every time someone likes one of her posts, every time someone tells her how well she's doing, fills the pit of her stomach with a void. 'I want to make sure you understand –' Grace's voice – 'what it is you're doing at this stage in your career.'

Raf picks the phone up and takes her off speaker. 'Erin isn't well.' Erin's face creases in concern. What's he doing?

What's he telling her? Why isn't she doing anything to stop him? 'And you're filling her head with how she's this great career woman and none of it's real.' Erin wants to grab the phone away, but Bobby's on the sofa now and looks like he'll tumble off so she goes to him and sits down and lets her fiancé handle the conversation with her agent because, the honest reason, she doesn't want to. She doesn't want to leave Instagram even though she knows she should and she doesn't want to have the difficult conversation with Grace because it all feels too grown up, too serious.

Bobby launches himself onto her torso, wraps his arms around her neck and gives her the most nourishing cuddle she's ever had. The noise of Raf storming round the kitchen telling Grace how this whole situation is her fault, how she's failed her duty of care, how he's going to pick up the pieces, melts away. Bobby moves his head from side to side so his furry angel-hair tickles her chin and she thinks to herself that this, this bundle of pudge pawing at her face with his clammy hands, that this is enough. She's spent her whole life wanting to be busy, wanting to be in demand, but the reality is that it's awful. In the last few months, with notifications and emails constantly pinging, everyone looking at her, judging her, wanting something from her, she's never felt more anxious in her life.

She glances round at Raf stood in the corner of their kitchen, legs twined around each other, listening, face crinkled in measured disdain. He's trying to save her. He's trying to smooth things out for her and make things easier like he's always done, because he's right. She can't cope. She isn't coping with what's going on. He's been right all along. She squeezes Bobby into her, almost too hard so he fidgets away. He smiles up at her and she laughs. She doesn't need the love of tens of thousands of faceless avatars, she just needs this.

'You're a cowboy. Erin's been expecting payment every single day. We need the cash that she's been promised and we've had jackshit.'

'Raf,' Erin murmurs, still facing away, not wanting to shout and shock baby Bobby.

'What else is your job? I mean, seriously, apart from creaming off your twenty per cent and sticking the money in your client's account, what is your actual job?'

'Raf, that's enough.' Erin stands, Bobby perched still on the side of her hip. Raf looks up at her, she extends her arm to him. 'Let me.' Raf listens, his face changes. He looks shocked.

'She's gone,' he says.

'Oh.'

'I knew, from the start, I didn't want to say it, but that woman is a piece of work.'

'What did she say?' She bends her head down as Bobby yanks her earlobe.

'Well.' He seems pleased with himself as he saunters over from the kitchen towards her. As the gap closes she gets an image of the pasta bake splattered across the tiles. He laces an arm around her hip. 'You're going to get paid for all the posts that you've already done. Pretty quick I'd say.' He looks like he's just beaten up a smaller schoolboy to impress his crush.

'Great,' she says. 'Well done. Thanks.'

'It's what I'm here for,' he says, planting a peck on Bobby's head that causes him to hug in closer to Erin. 'You and I don't have to deal with money-grubbing harpies like her ever again.' He takes her cheek in his hand and kisses the side of her head. Over his shoulder Erin can see Amanda standing in her studio, watching them.

56

Erin looks down at her 'mum jeans' and sees where the fingers of her right hand have scratched into the denim. She's at the church group and Bobby's struggling up against the pink plastic walker that's so encrusted with dirt it reminds her of a pig rolled in mud. She stands to go and help him and notices the lightness of her pocket, the void where her phone should be. She knows she hasn't got the willpower not to re-download Instagram so she's let Raf hang on to it for her in exchange for an old Nokia he had at the back of a drawer. She's heard people talk about how, if you lose your phone or it breaks, the first hour or two feel weird but then it starts to feel liberating, but Erin's clearly further entrenched in her addiction than most people, because after two days she's feeling the opposite of freedom. She feels edgy, like she's had a line of coke and tried to go straight to sleep.

A dad with a lumberjack shirt and a preposterous beard laughs at something an uber-trendy older mum says to him, she might be called Ellerby. They both glance momentarily her way before falling back into conversation with each other. She didn't want to come today, she spent all of yesterday in the house with Bobby, but Raf said he'd been up all night with him, and although he seemed fine in the morning, Erin knew that she would have to go out and find distraction for her tired boy or face a grave screamathon.

She walks over to the crumbled 'Nice' biscuits in the corner by the plastic jugs of squash, greeting a couple of local mums on the way. There've been a few snatched conversations this morning, but, and it's not her being paranoid, there's been a wariness in whoever she's spoken to. Before, people would find all sorts of reasons to come and sit on a tiny plastic chair next to her, people would offer to get her tea, push their son or daughter in one of the Fisher-Price toy cars over to where Bobby is and make some comment about his Babygro or his perma-frown, in order to open up a conversation, but now, as she looks over at her boy stumbling his way to push the stroller up against a radiator, and the furtive eyes of a mum called Fran as he gets close, it seems like she's put an exclusion zone around the two of them. Perhaps she would have been better keeping them both inside.

Bobby tries to bend over to pick up a piece of Duplo, his tentativeness making him look like an old man picking up a dropped coin. There's no doubt that not having her phone to turn to has made her feel closer to him. He's been in pain, with his teeth or a rattly chest, she's not sure, and he's had moments of being miserable, but Erin hasn't found herself getting as tense as she used to. She's found herself holding the boy into her, shhing rhythmic comfort into his ear as he cries or struggles against her, patiently, until he relents and gives himself to the comfort of his mother's shoulder. Oddly, she has Amanda to thank. It seems she's osmotically absorbed some of Amanda's calm with him, some of her ability to withstand her son's torrential emotional responses.

Amanda's still around. She offered to come to the group with them but Erin declined. She's not sure what she's been up to but, with the responsibility of Bobby taken away after Erin's various commitments were struck from the calendar, she's seemed listless. Trying to cook, trying to clean around them, but she also spends hours at a time out of the house, doing God knows what. It also seems clear that Raf hasn't spoken to her yet. Which Erin hasn't brought up, because he's been in a much better mood with her, much more loving, more caring, and she doesn't want to shatter the veneer of balance that's fallen over their home. But she wants to know why nothing's been said, their deal was crystal clear, and so far, however hard it's been to go cold turkey, she's the only one who's kept up her part of it.

She looks up to see Bobby on top of a tower of soft-play blocks that some large toddlers have been building. The tower begins to lean to one side. Erin rushes towards him and just as he begins to tumble off, Bronwen, the lady who runs the group, manages to grab at him. She doesn't get both hands on him but she manages to manoeuvre him to land on one of the gym mats rather than the floorboards below. As Erin picks him up into her arms before he has a chance to start properly crying, she notices a dozen pairs of eyes watching her – *no wonder* she's *not watching her baby* – they all seem to be thinking.

'Thanks, thanks so much, Bronwen.'

'Boys will be boys.' There's something in her eyes too. A coldness, disdain. Lovely, kind, Christian Bronwen. Can she know too? Has someone snitched to Bronwen about the photos of Erin, about the picture of Erin screaming at her baby? Bronwen glances down at Bobby. She's always loved him, always lavished extra kisses and games of peekaboo on him. She always tried to defend him whenever Erin would complain about his screaming to her. Erin catches more glances around the room. She feels like a car crash everyone's desperate to see so that they can feel safe, content with the calm mundanity of their lives.

Without thinking, she bursts through the double doors leaving her buggy behind. She had to get out of there. She has to get out of this town. She needs to be in London. She needs to be anonymous for a few hours, she needs to soak up the collective energy of thousands, to escape the scrutinising eyes down here, just for a while. As she pounds the streets towards the train station, Bobby bouncing on her chest, grinning from ear to ear, she thinks about how uncomfortable she's always been here. She grew up with the bustle of Croydon, the teeming life of London. It's too quiet here, too bland. There's no colour, no culture. No wonder when the local populace found someone remotely well known, even just on Instagram, they took to her with such parasitic zeal and no wonder they're now enjoying her downfall so much.

She reaches the station, goes to one of the machines on the street and selects a ticket to London. She puts her debit card in the machine and pumps her pin into the keypad. It seems to be taking a long time, Bobby's getting heavy in her arms and restless. The screen on the machine says:

CARD DECLINED
INSUFFICIENT FUNDS

before it cancels her transaction.

'Fuck!' she says. An old dear waiting at the bus stop turns 180 degrees to see who's swearing so loudly in the street and shakes her head when she sees she has a baby. Erin extends a hand to apologise before trying the joint account card in the machine. She gets the same message. Raf normally makes sure there's money in it, but he's obviously forgotten to.

The train is in two minutes. She considers crossing the footbridge to the platform and getting on, hoping that she'll somehow be able to blag the inspector, or phone Raf to put money into the joint account, but she can't. She can't be thrown off a train with a one-year-old and she can't expect Raf to pay for this if money's as tight as he says. She watches the train trundle to a stop across the tracks, then watches it leave. The old woman at the bus stop gives her a disgusted look, then at Bobby. She's not even on Instagram and she's judging whether Erin's fit to look after her child.

She gets her phone out as she turns and makes her way home, and calls Grace Fentiman. This isn't fair. She's given everything on Instagram to try and finally make herself some money, her safety, her sanity potentially. The funds from Phibe have presumably been given back, but she must have earned at least a few grand from the various sponsored posts she's done, as much as ten maybe. All the other influencers moan about how long it takes to get paid, but it seems ridiculous that she hasn't even been paid enough for a train fare.

'Grace Fentiman's office?'

'Is Grace there? It's Erin Braune.'

'Er – she's not.' The hesitation tells Erin that she is but clearly has no time to talk to her ex-client.

'I need to speak to her about when I'm going to get paid.'

'Let me just –' Erin's hip starts to burn with pain from the weight of Bobby perching on top of it as Grace's assistant, Zoe, looks through Erin's file on their system. 'Are you talking about the payment from Slow-Aloe for the selection of hair masks? Because that's come through now. Payroll's not till Thursday if you remember so you won't get it for a couple of days.'

'I'm not just talking about Slow-Aloe, I'm talking about all of it. The hair-mask posts were only a couple of weeks ago, three at most. I'm talking about all of them. I haven't been paid for any of the posts I've done yet. Why would I specifically be talking about Slow-Aloe?'

'Um –' Erin has to endure the sound of Zoe tapping on her computer for a moment. 'We're all up to date up until the Slow-Aloe invoice on our system.' Erin tastes the spit in her mouth. What's she talking about? Erin hasn't been paid for any of those things. Her card's been declined. As of a few days ago, when she last checked, she had about forty quid in her account and had worried about asking Raf to put his monthly £150 in early.

'I haven't got any of that money,' Erin says, shifting Bobby onto her other hip, almost limping along the parade of shops towards home. She needs to put him down. She wishes he could walk.

'That's weird. I mean, the money's left our account so –'

'Can I speak to Grace?'

'She's in a meeting. Yeh, it's been paid into account number 94738382.'

'That's not my account.'

'That would explain it.' Zoe's sunny tone makes Erin actually slap herself on the forehead in exasperation. Bobby thinks it's a game and joins in hitting her so she has to hold his hands down.

'It's a totally different account number, why would you pay it into that account?'

'I've just found the email you sent us with your details, are you able to check your email?'

'Not right now.'

'OK. The 26th of Feb you sent us an email that said, "I've set up a new business account, details below 9473 –'

'I signed with Grace at the end of January. I sent my bank details then, not on the 26th of February.'

'OK. I'll forward the email chain back to you, maybe we should get off the phone so you can check it.'

'I can't –' But she stops herself. Somehow she's too ashamed to admit that she's not using a smartphone.

'OK. Thanks. Let me check.' She hangs up just as she turns onto her road. She almost skips down the hill to her house, opens the door and deposits Bobby onto the play mat. She pulls her laptop out of the kitchen drawer. It's dead. She plugs it in. The minutes feel like hours as she waits for it to turn on. When it sparks into life she logs into her email. There it is from Zoe, a forwarded message.

FROM: erinbraune@outlook.co.uk
TO: grace.fentiman@rfgtalent.com
RE: Account details

Hi Grace,

I've set up a new account for my work with you, details below. I wanted to be able to keep my business income separate from my day-to-day life. Hope you'll be able to amend on your system.

Thanks.

Erin

There's no 'X' at the end. Erin and Grace always end their emails with an 'X'. Erin didn't send that email.

57

'You must be able to tell me when the account was opened?' The middle-aged man with a Don Draper hairstyle that doesn't suit the width of his face grimaces from behind the bank counter.

'Sorry, no. We can't reveal any details about our accounts without the account holder's photographic identification.'

'The identity of the account holder is exactly what I'm trying to find out!' The man in the polyester suit is starting to look uncomfortable. She breathes, tries to calm herself. Bobby's sleeping in the sling on her front and the last thing she needs is him waking up.

When she read the email it suddenly all clicked into place. Raf was right, she was being ridiculous thinking that Amanda was here for him or to steal Bobby away from her. Amanda's in a dead-end situation at home, she found out she has a tenuous link to someone who has tens of thousands of Instagram followers. She could have googled how much money influencers make or maybe she knows much more about the whole thing than she's ever let on. Erin would love to accuse her, she'd love to tell Raf, go through her wallet and find the card from the account, but what if she's hidden it somewhere like the jar? Erin's not sure Raf would tolerate that, it might be the last straw.

But this officious jobsworth isn't giving her anything. She expected it to be an Australian account but the sort code says that this is the bank, the only one left on the high street. Amanda must have set up an account when she got here, though whether Erin's money's still in it, she can't be sure. In heist movies the money's always redistributed to untraceable accounts as soon as it's paid in.

'Can you tell me if there's any money in the account? If there's any forwarding account? All my money, everything I've earned this year, is in that account and I don't have access to it.'

'How has it got in there?'

'Look –' she glances at his name tag, almost double-takes – 'look, Fabian. Someone has stolen my money and put it in one of your accounts. I'm not asking you for the person's address, just tell me when it was set up, tell me if there's anything left in it. I've been a victim of fraud. I'm a mother. I have nothing else. Nothing!' Fabian's staring down and Erin realises she's grabbed the sleeve of his shirt. His eyes are wide with shock. She withdraws her hand and places it on Bobby's head as if that will excuse the indiscretion. Fabian steps back and points at a sign behind him that says 'Any abuse of our staff will not be tolerated'. Erin's winces in indignation and is about to tell Fabian to man the fuck up when someone grasps her upper arm firmly.

'I think you need a coffee, Erin.' Lorna's there, without her mothership buggy. She must have been in the queue behind her. 'Hi, Fabian, how you doing?'

'Er, yeh.' Fabian comes back towards them, his hackles drop. 'Fine, fine, Lorn, how're the kids getting on?'

'Much better than poor Bobby. He doesn't sleep a wink, does he, Erin?' Lorna gives her a nod, she's prompting her to use it as an excuse.

'No, no. Lorna's right. Think I need a coffee. Sorry. Sorry about –'

'Give my love to your mum, Fabian,' Lorna interjects, putting an arm around Erin, levering the broken sliding doors open, and shepherding her out into the street.

'What a mess!' Lorna says, picking out a hunk of melon from her fruit pot. Erin leans on the arm of a sofa in the coffee shop opposite the bank. Lorna marched her in here, bought her a cappuccino, and asked her if she wanted to talk about it. And even though most of it was said in a stage whisper in order not to wake Bobby, it seems that Erin did want to talk. She told Lorna everything and, contrary to her reputation, she doesn't seem to have enjoyed hearing about what Erin thinks has been happening to her. And, like brainstorming a character's motivations with a director, it feels like going through everything that's happened since Amanda's arrived has helped clarify everything for her, if not for Lorna. It makes so much sense, Amanda's plan. Become a fixture at their home, gain their trust; when she saw that Erin wasn't making as much money as she expected, she then actively facilitated her going out to work. She was always ushering her out the door, telling her not to worry. Then trolling her so she was distracted, so she wouldn't think to check why she hadn't been paid yet. But now she's not on Instagram any more. Amanda must know that the money will dry up, Erin thinks. Has she gone already? Did she see Amanda last night? Has she seen her this morning?

'So you haven't got any money of your own?'

'What?' Lorna's question snaps Erin out of her train of thought.

'No savings, no credit cards? Nothing in your account?'

'I've spent my month's allowance.'

'Allowance?'

'I didn't have a job before having Bobby so I haven't had maternity pay. Raf pays into my account every month.'

'How much?'

'Sorry?'

'How much does he give you?' Lorna bites a grape in half. It seems that unburdening everything to Lorna, taking away any chance for her speculative mind to speculate, has changed their relationship and it now feels like she's talking to a mortgage adviser.

'Er, a hundred and fifty a month.'

'That's not much.'

'It's normally plenty. We've got a joint account as well. It must be all the trains I've had to take.'

'So you don't –' Lorna stops herself. Closes her eyes, does a little shudder of her head. 'No, don't worry.'

'What?'

'Well, are you sure it's Amanda that's stole from you?' Erin stands up from the sofa.

'Who else could it be?'

'When we first met, that bloody awful walk on the beach when I was knackered and snippy and being a total bitch about everyone, you told me you'd been in loads of debt when you met Raf and he helped you out with it.'

'I wouldn't have told you that,' Erin says. Lorna shrugs as if to say, then how did I know about it?

'I just know that some men feel threatened if their partner suddenly starts earning lots of money.'

'You think it's Raf?' Erin says, almost laughing, incredulous. What the hell was she thinking telling Lorna all of her problems, unburdening herself to the biggest gossip she knows? Of course she has a theory. There's nothing she doesn't have some wild theory about. Erin gathers her handbag up from the sofa.

'I thought I'd got it wrong about you,' she says, 'but you can't help yourself, can you? It was the same when you saw Amanda and Raf walking together, you were desperate to reveal some sordid affair. But it's not there. Raf has never done anything to hurt me. He dedicates everything, absolutely everything to me.'

'Erin –'

'Thanks for the coffee.' Erin slides past chairs and out towards the exit. Bobby's stirring slightly with the movement. She looks back to Lorna, shaking her head, sadness brimming under her fringe of straw-coloured hair.

58

Erin has texted Raf. She's texted Amanda. Which took an age to do on her terrible old phone. Bobby woke as soon as she went into the cold but has been babbling to himself contentedly as they've walked along the front towards home. They're going to sit down, like adults, and they're going to try and work it out together. Amanda will deny it and that's fine. Erin is going to ask her to leave and tell her that the police will be informed.

She wanders up her street. Bobby seems to recognise it and bounces with excitement, reaching to grab clusters of leaves from the hedge that borders the house on the corner. His joy is almost infectious. She feels she finally has something. Before it felt like she was clutching at straws but, even if she doesn't have proof it's Amanda, she has the email. Someone has stolen from her and who else could it be? When she gets to their bungalow she sees Raf standing at the window, waiting for her. He doesn't look amused. She wasn't expecting him to have got home before her.

'You OK?' He asks the question before she's through the door frame.

'Something's happened,' she says. Raf raises an eyebrow, nods his head and lets out a sigh. He goes to sit down at the table that has a view out to the road and grabs one of the place mats from the table and begins rolling it up into a cigar shape. Erin puts Bobby down on the play mat. She puts *Hey Duggee* on the TV, glances over at Raf to see if he's going to object to their son watching a screen before five o'clock, but he doesn't. Erin observes Amanda clacking her way through the back gate. The sun blares down on their little garden and Amanda, her maroon coat over a flowing powder-blue dress, walks in and out of the shadows caused by the neighbours' overhanging trees, towards the house.

'Hey, guys, everything good?' she says as she heads through the door to face them sitting at the table like they're about to interview her.

'We need to talk about something,' Erin says. Amanda looks at Raf who shrugs back at her. Erin sees his jaw clench, she knows how much not telling him what this is about will be enraging him, but she doesn't care. When he hears what's happened he'll be shocked. He should feel guilty. He should feel ashamed for allowing this manipulative bitch into their home. Amanda's about to sit but, spotting Bobby on the floor, extracts a tissue from her coat pocket and goes over to him to wipe his nose. 'Do you want to sit down, Amanda?' Erin stops her in her tracks. She comes back to sit down, brow furrowed though smiling still.

Erin slides across a printout of the email chain Zoe sent over to her. Amanda reads it and gives a nervous laugh. She looks at Raf for some sense of reassurance.

'What the hell's going on, Ez?' He snatches the papers up and reads what they say. 'What, you got a new bank account?'

'She did.' Erin's index finger flies out from her fist and points at Amanda like a gunshot.

'Sorry, I did what?' Amanda puts prayer-hands to her chest and widens her eyes.

'You sent my agent an email with new bank account details so you could steal my money. That's why you came here in the first place.'

'Erin, stop' Raf puts a hand on her wrist.

'I won't go to the police. But I want to see the card. I want you to show Raf the card. Then I want my money back and for you to get out of our lives today.'

'I – I'm so – I didn't do this, Erin, I swear. I didn't even know –'

Raf stands up and shoves the chair into the table. He walks over to the shelving unit and Erin almost thinks he'll sweep all the books off, but instead he leans against it.

'This is too far, Ez. Too much. You've crossed a line,' Raf says, but Erin won't be cowed this time. She has the evidence.

'The money hasn't gone into my account because of this. Nine thousand pounds, that's how much my agent has paid me, or at least thought they've paid. But it's not in my account. How do you explain that?' Erin's up now. Amanda sits still, looking up at Raf, plaintive, begging him to rescue her. Confess, Erin internally screams at her. Confess to this, she thinks, glaring at her, there's nowhere to hide, I've caught you out. But now she looks sad, pitying almost. Erin would like to slap the light out of her glistening green eyes.

'Come on, Amanda,' she says, trying to smile, cajole her, looking almost sympathetic. 'I'm sure you had your reasons, but please, please don't make this more painful than it already is.' Raf storms out to the hall, almost knocking Bobby as he goes. He comes back with Erin's laptop and places it on the table in front of Erin. He opens the screen up.

'Does she know your password?'

'No, but that's – I could have left it open.'

'When would that have happened?'

Erin glances at Amanda whose gaze is fixed on the surface of the table. Erin hadn't thought about this, hadn't thought about how she might have got into her email. Erin doesn't put much effort into passwords and security so she'd assumed it must be easy but Raf's right. He types in the password, goes straight into her email. He pulls the laptop over to face him. Erin and Amanda both seem to be in a state of paralysis, and with Bobby motionless in front of the television, it's as if Erin's accusations have cast some sort of spell over everyone apart from Raf. She looks at his back as he hunches over her laptop doing something. She remembers what Lorna said in the cafe.

'It was you,' she says. He ignores her, tapping and clicking at the laptop's mousepad. 'It must have been. You're the only one who knows my passwords. Lorna was right. You don't want me to have any money of my own. It had to be –' Raf turns the screen round. There's an email from her sent items, from 26 February. A message to Raf's email address.

Hey babes,

Thinking of setting up a business account for Instagram. What do you think?

Ciao bella

'You just wrote that,' Erin says, squinting at the screen. Raf sighs and walks into the kitchen. He fills a sippy cup with water and takes it over to Bobby. The boy bats it away at first, but after Raf offers it to him a third time, he takes it and sucks water down. Erin looks closer at the screen. Checks the date again. Tries to think about how someone could fake all of these messages.

'I got it when I was on a call. Forgot to go back and reply. Only just remembered. You did it, Erin. You set up the account.'

'Should I go?' Amanda's chair scrapes as she backs away from the table.

'Maybe go read Bob a story, thanks,' Raf says, coming round the sofa towards Erin. Amanda goes to get Bobby and carries him in the direction of his room. Raf takes Erin's hands in his. She looks up at him, hat still low over his hair, and he gives her the same beatific look he gives Bobby just after he's come out of a screaming fit. As if she's a troubled soul who needs his succour. 'Now –' his voice is gentle, his fingers massage up her wrists – 'I don't know if you don't remember doing it or, or if this, acting like this, is because –' he lowers his voice – 'Amanda's still here.' Erin glances over to Amanda who's stopped at the end of the corridor that leads to the bedroom. She's watching them with a worried look in her eyes. 'Which is it?' he says, snapping. Erin hadn't even clocked that he'd asked a question. She blinks, thinking, almost twitching, wanting to scream. What is going on? Is Raf right? Is she suffering from some form of psychosis? Have all the hours staring at the phone made her delusional? Could she really forget having done something like that, something practical that would have involved her getting her ID together, filling in application forms?

'I definitely didn't do this, I couldn't have done this. I wouldn't just make it up.'

'What about the jar? The jar with the doll? I'm not saying you're doing it on purpose, Ez, but, you're tired, you've got this thing about Amanda.'

'I didn't do this. Set up a bank account that I don't remember!'

'You really don't remember? Are you sure? I get how much you want her to leave, and I want her to as well, but I'm not sure you're thinking's right on this, and I'm not sure you're well enough.'

'I've been saying I haven't been paid yet for weeks. You think I've been concocting some elaborate lie for all that time to try and get rid of Amanda?' She flips her hand over and bats his touch away. He gives her a warning look. That night, the night she threw the dish at him, floats between them. He lifts her handbag off the back of one of the chairs.

'Can I look?'

'I didn't do this.' She feels tears prick, the wave of emotion stuttering her words. Because as he gets her wallet out of her bag, as he flicks his long fingers through the card section, she knows what he's going to find. And she knows that he might be right. That the troll might be right about her. She's losing her mind.

'Oh God.' Raf turns away from her and walks to the door, carrying the wallet with him. Erin's breath shallows, she feels herself standing on her tiptoes, almost trying to peak over Raf's shoulder to see what he has. '947383 –' he turns, reading from a bank card – '82. I'm sorry, Ez.' She goes to him and grabs the card from his hand. It's for a business account, her name, 'Mrs E. Braune', written below the long number.

'This isn't mine,' she says without conviction. 'I didn't do this. I know I didn't.' Raf steers her towards an armchair and she sits, staring at the card in her hand. It has her name on it. Not Amanda's, not Raf's, not anyone else's, hers. She throws her head into her hands and begins to weep silently. Raf puts a hand on her shoulder but she shrugs him off.

She rubs the tears down into her cheeks. Through her fingers she sees Amanda half out of Bobby's room watching them. She's staring at Raf. She bites her top lip, shakes her head almost imperceptibly. Erin sees an expression she's never seen before. Rage.

59

'I want you to stay here today,' Raf says. It's the morning after. He's standing in the door frame. He slept in with Bobby last night, as he has virtually every night for the last few weeks. She's stopped asking whether he had a bad night – according to Raf, he's always had a bad night. 'Erin?' She nods.

Amanda took care of Bobby's bedtime last night. Raf got Erin a bowl of cereal and suggested she go to bed. She lay there, eight o'clock in the evening, staring at the water mark in the eaves of her bedroom ceiling. She was trying to process the emails, the card, the jar, the honey, the troll, but none of the thoughts would click over in her mind, as if her brain's starter motor had gone kaput. She feels hollow. Her body, her mind, feel as if there's nothing inside them.

'Will you promise me? Stay in bed today. Rest. Take a pill if you need to. I'm going to see if I can get someone to come and talk to you, a doctor, a nurse maybe. I was googling last night, I think you might be having a stress-related break-down.' He checks her reaction but there isn't one. 'You have been under a huge amount of stress. First Bobby, being so hard those first eight, nine months, feeding him, you weren't sleeping, I wasn't sleeping, we weren't always as nice to each other as we should've been. And I'm sorry, for my part, I'm so sorry about that. Then all this extra work, you were out of your mind responding to everyone, even before the whole thing with Grace and her putting you out to work. And, and the troll.' He looks down at the duvet, reaches his hand towards her but stops short. 'I'm thinking I'll try get a loan. Take time off. To care for you. Anyway, I better go, go get cracking. I think Amanda's taking Bobby to a singing class at the old cinema?'

'Tabby's Rock and Rhyme,' Erin says, flat.

'Probably, yeh. There's a sandwich on the side for you.'

'Great.'

'I love you.' Erin flicks her eyes to him.

'I know.'

She takes half of one of Raf's pills and spends the rest of the morning in and out of sleep. She wakes and looks at her dumbphone. A message from Raf checking in on her. When she looks over to the door, she sees the tray Raf left with a sandwich on it now features a still-steaming cup of tea. Next to the tray there's a pile of magazines, *Vice*, *Wonderland*, they look new. Raf's at work so it must have been Amanda. But they don't seem like her kind of thing. She removes the top two to see it must have been Amanda, because there's a magazine called *Destiny and Soul*. Raf definitely wouldn't have bought that. Erin finds herself touched at the gesture.

She grabs the tea and scooches back into her duvet-cocoon with the pile of magazines and lays them all out on the bed. She flicks through *Destiny and Soul* and, as expected, it's a bunch of claptrap. Then she turns the pages of *Wonderland* until she gets to an interview with Rhia Trevellick, the girl who was given the part in the indie movie that she'd managed to miss out on when she was stuck in a cabin in Connemara.

She's just signed on as the lead in a big Netflix fantasy show. She looks amazing in the pictures, short choppy hair, insanely beautiful clothes but not too Hollywoodified. Erin doesn't feel as envious as she would have done yesterday. Perhaps it's the sleeping pill, perhaps it's the dawning realisation that she might be having a breakdown, but she's almost happy for Rhia – she was there, she was good in the film, she's made good choices since and always seems nice, fair play to her.

She hears Bobby squeaking downstairs and yearns to go and see him, to hold him. But she catches her reflection in the mirror above the dressing table. She looks ill, skin translucent, greasy, hair dishevelled, and she's worried he might be scared of her. She thinks of Amanda last night staring at her after having been accused of stealing thousands of pounds, knowing that the woman accusing her is deranged, the anger in her eyes. And yet she's willingly looking after her son for her. Erin wonders whether she'd do the same. Probably not. Amanda shouts up the stairs to say they're going for a walk for Bobby's nap, taking the choice of seeing her son out of her hands.

Erin flicks through another of Amanda's magazines, this one looks older, more heavily thumbed. The *Journal of Wicca*. It's a cheaper-looking affair. All pentagrams, healing and spells. Erin laughs at an interview with a Druid in a purple robe with a beard down to his feet. It feels like the first time she's enjoyed not having her phone since she gave it to Raf. She turns a few pages and feels a jolt, grabs a pillow to prop herself up.

There's a picture of a jar with a hairless doll in it. The title of the article: 'How to get the most out of your spells'. There's a checklist of ways to 'maximise the reach of your magick'. Erin runs down it, adding crystals, imbuing amulets and giving them to the target, urine. These people seem to be obsessed with urine, she thinks. But then she sees something has been circled in black biro. 'The best way to increase the power of your jar spell is to hide it somewhere in pitch-darkness where no one will ever find it. Burying or a locked safe works best.' Amanda's moved it. Maybe whatever it was meant to do, drive Erin away, make Raf fall in love with her, wasn't working so she's hidden it somewhere.

She cracks the bedroom door open and creeps downstairs. She checks no one's in the house, before putting her coat on over her pyjamas and heading out to Amanda's studio, the wedge of magazines held to her chest like precious treasure. She unlocks the door and lets herself in. She checks under the sofa. The jar's not there. She looks in the wardrobe. No sign. She roots around in the cupboard under the sink. She even goes back out of the studio and looks around for any signs of the earth being disturbed. There's nothing. No sign of it. She goes into the bathroom and sees it. The little screwdriver she saw the last time she was in here, resting on the surface next to the sink. With a tiny screw next to it.

She looks around the room. Nothing in the cupboard, nothing in the shower. Then she looks up at the ceiling and sees it. A flap vent with what looks like one screw missing on the top right corner. Erin grabs the screwdriver and steps up onto the toilet. She unscrews the remaining three screws and pulls the vent out. The toilet shifts beneath her and she steps down, scared her weight's going to crack it off the wall, but she can't reach with one foot down so she steps back up. She puts her hand up into the hole and reaches around the recess like a periscope. She drags out stray plasterboard and dust bunnies but can't find the jar. She pulls her hand out and looks into the hole, cursing not having the torch on her phone. But it doesn't look big enough to house that large pickle jar. She steadies herself on the wall and tries to reach further in. There must be something in here, Amanda's not going to be messing with a vent for fun. Then she finds something, but not what she was hoping for. It's a book, an exercise book. She steps off the toilet and blows some dust away. It looks old, one of those classy notebooks with a marbled cover in yellow, black and cream. There's a snapping noise outside. She goes back into the main room to make sure she's got a view in case Amanda comes.

There's an envelope wedged into the inside cover of the notebook. Erin pulls it out and puts the notebook on the table next to Amanda's crystals. There's a millisecond where she considers the breach of privacy she's committing but she knows she's way past that now. In the envelope there's a single orange Post-it. On it, in block capitals that lean to the right:

34 HILDA'S BAY ROAD
CT8 1BU
UK

It's Erin's address. Why has Amanda got her address written on a Post-it? Erin looks at the envelope. An address in Darwin, Australia. Two large international stamps. A postmark.

East Kent
28.11.2018

It's been sent from here. Raf. Raf sent their address to Amanda in Australia several months ago. She didn't come here because of a picture, she didn't come here because of some fucked-up relationship with her abusive stepdad. She came because Raf told her to.

60

The stick-thin receptionist isn't at her desk at the Lookout. Erin's called Raf but his phone appears to be off so she's come looking for him. Amanda will be at the group for another half an hour and, although Erin hasn't actually thought what she's going to do yet, she needs to have this conversation without having to worry what Bobby may think about how she's behaving. Because she's fairly certain she isn't going to behave well. He's been lying to her, he and Amanda have both been brazenly lying to her from the first moment she set eyes on them together in her front room. He sent her their address. He didn't call her or email her or even write her a letter. He sent a Post-it in an envelope all the way to Australia.

She slaps the desk a few times to get someone's attention. There aren't many people here today. Eventually a burly man with a yellow-checked scarf wrapped tightly around his neck looks up.

'You OK?' he says, a Welsh accent beleaguered by a heavy cold. She's not met him before.

'Is Raf in?' He gives her a sideways look. 'Wears a beanie all the time like he's stuck in the nineties?' She tries to smile but can only manage a grimace. The man breaks into a lopsided grin.

'Ah, no. He was. Earlier. Think I heard him saying something to Sev about going to London for work?'

'Is Sev not here?'

'He went out about an hour ago.' Raf didn't say he was going to London, she thinks. She remembers how he was this morning. Telling her to stay in bed, to take a pill if she can't sleep, suggesting to her that it might be better not to leave the house, that facing people after what happened on her Instagram might make her unwell. She turns on her heels and barges her way out the double doors into the main space. Where's she going to go? To the group. She should go and get Bobby, everything Amanda's told her about how she's here, why she's here is a lie, she has to get her baby and then she can worry about finding Raf. But then something stops her. There's a door with a symbol of a man and a symbol of a woman. The toilets, unisex. She turns round to look through the glass doors, to the corridor behind the bullpen of desks. When she came here after she found Amanda and Bobby together in the nursery bed, Raf came from the back, wiping his hands on a tea towel. She'd assumed he was coming from the toilet, but she's standing next to the toilet. On the wall she sees an old school sign indicating who's in and who's out, desks numbered 1 to 12, studios 1 to 4. Studio 4 is the only one set to 'unoccupied'.

'Who is it that has Studio 4?' she asks the room loudly, head popped back through the double doors. The Welshman looks around and, seeing everyone else entombed in their noise-cancelling headphones, realises it's on him to answer again. He gets the attention of a woman in a hoodie who's making what look like artificial flowers. She pulls her hoodie down, takes her headphones out and smiles at the Welshman.

'Studio 4 – that the big one at the back?'

'That's right, yeh.' The woman nods, then notices Erin by the door. 'Oh, hiya,' she says. They've met before. She's called Sara, moved from Walthamstow. 'Raf was in there this morning but not for long – he left about ten, I think.'

'In Studio 4?'

'We all call it the beast cos it's three times the size of all the others.' Erin blinks. She didn't know he rented a studio. Why does he need a studio? How can he afford the biggest studio at this chichi co-working space? She needs to go and get Bobby, but he's safe, he's at the class, Caz is there. She can't leave without knowing why the hell her fiancé has an art studio he's never told her about.

'I'm locked out,' she says. 'He's not answering his phone, must be on the Tube or something. Any chance I can get in and see if he has our spare in there?' Sara hesitates. The Welshman eyes his desk, keen to extricate himself from any responsibility.

'Sure,' Sara says, coming up to get a set of keys from behind the front desk. Erin follows her through the gauntlet of desks, laptops and computer monitors, air plants and succulents. The place has been done up a little since she was last here. Walls painted, electrical cables no longer visible.

As Sara leads her to the back of the building, she looks at the clock on her dumbphone, the group Bobby's at is on for another twenty minutes. She labours to text Caz and to tell her to call if Amanda leaves with Bobby before the end. If Raf invited Amanda to come over to England then perhaps it has something to do with the baby. Maybe he knew that Erin wouldn't be a good enough mother so tried to recruit someone better.

'This room is so beaut.' One of Erin's eyes twitches with Sara's familiarity. Has he been writing Post-its to her as well? No, she tells herself, this can't be right. He's never looked at another woman. She's never been with anyone who's been so devoted to her. There has to be some logical reason why he invited Amanda to come. Some reason why he lied. Because that's the kicker. There's nothing wrong with inviting an old friend, maybe she'd asked for the address and he sent it on a Post-it as some sort of in-joke, but lying about it, making up a story about Lydia and seeing some painting …

They arrive at the nondescript black door. A numeral '4' has been daubed on it in yellow paint.

'Everyone's super jelz he's got it, but, to be fair, no one else here could afford it, and he lets people store their stuff in it so that's pretty sound.' *They* can't afford it, Erin thinks. And if they can, then Amanda's reason for visiting them is the tip of an iceberg of lies. Sara takes a key from a large bunch and puts it into the lock. Erin realises her breathing has deepened as if she's preparing to plunge into freezing water.

Sara opens the door. It's dark, a curtain drawn over a huge window at the far side of the room, but Erin can see it's huge. She had no idea this was even here. Sara reaches around for a light switch. The lights click on and what Erin sees forces an audible gasp. She turns the noise into a cough and musters a smile for Sara.

'Hope you find your key,' she says as she wheels past Erin and back to her desk.

The walls are stacked with row upon row of canvases. The outside one of each has a picture of a woman with flowing bounds of red hair sat among rocks, turned towards the viewer. Amanda. Erin closes the door, backs into it and slumps down onto her haunches. It's not a woman, she thinks. It's a girl. A teenage girl. Younger perhaps. Amanda as a young girl. Erin closes her eyes and rests her head on her knees. She needs to look again but can't. That girl is thirteen, maybe twelve, is there any way to see them as anything but depraved? When Erin found Amanda's passport, she knew, deep down, there was something deeply wrong about the age difference, but she was so keen to believe that Raf was the man she's always known him to be that she ate up his story.

Erin tries to get her breathing under control. She opens her eyes and stares round the room. On the opposite wall there are more canvases, but these all face the wall. There's a larger one, half finished, on an easel down towards the window, though she can't make it out from where she is, such is the prodigious size of the room.

She manages to get herself up and walks along the row of pictures of the girl Amanda. Raf's attempted to make her expressions ambiguous, Mona Lisa smiles, but he's failed. In one painting her head's lowered and she has a 'come-hither' stare. In another, the face is up and on an angle so she looks wary. In a third, the lips are pursed, it could be fear, it could be hatred. Erin crosses to the other side of the room. The studio is newly painted, the light fittings look expensive. A free-standing metal shelving unit next to the door is heaving with premium-looking art supplies, oil paints, brushes, black leather-bound books, a huge MacBook, padded bags full of what looks like expensive technical equipment. Where has all this stuff come from? Has he bought it? They don't have any money. He's always telling her that they don't have any money.

She grips the top of one of the canvases that face the wall and turns it round quickly, like ripping off a plaster. It's different. Still Amanda, but Amanda now. Most of the painting, the background and the body, has been sketched, only the face is finished. It's disturbing. Amanda's wrinkles have been accentuated and have been painted again and again, smears of black and dark brown, it's chaotic, as if done in a flurry of strokes. From here she can see the work-in-progress at the end of the room. It shows Amanda, the young girl Amanda, reclining on a bench, shoulders bare, an expression of forced joy. There's an ottoman on the other side of the easel. She looks at the girlish pictures behind her and it hits her. They're not from before, he's painted them here, since she's been here. There's dozens of them. When has he been doing it? Is this why he's been so busy with work, spending all his time here, in his studio, working on these paintings? Does he even have a job?

She can't be in this room any more. Can't be surrounded by scores of eyes, scores of Amanda's eyes, her child eyes, staring at her. What has Raf done? What did he do to her? Why would she let herself model for him while he painted pictures of her prepubescent self? Caz has talked about how abuse suffered as a child can drastically alter how you view the world, what you think's normal, your morality. She catches one of the faces, an upturned smile, cruel. Bobby, she's looking after her baby, she has her precious boy. Erin needs to go and take Bobby away from this woman now. She clatters the painting to the floor and bolts out of the room. She must make a lot of noise in the hallway because several freelancers in the main space look up from their laptops to see what the commotion is. Sara gives her a thumb's up. Erin smiles maniacally and nods her head.

As she blunders towards the entrance, she knocks her hip on the corner of a desk that clatters a Lego structure over into the occupant's lap. She puts up a hand in apology and gets an irritated acknowledgement. As she walks off, her eyes fix on a row of different colours lining the top of the front desk's iMac. Post-its. Blue, orange, yellow, green. Green. Sonnet 116. 'It is an ever-fixed mark / That looks on tempests and is never shaken.' Raf wrote that note. Raf's love is never-changing. Raf's love for Amanda is unshakeable in the face of whatever it comes up against. He told Erin to stay in bed all day. He's gone to London. And Amanda's with her baby.

Erin slows her run as she rounds the corner onto the cliff front. She bends forward and puts her hands on her knees, breath heaving. She hasn't run since giving birth, her hip rags, her chest feels clamped shut. Raf's not answering his phone. Nor is Amanda. She sees a group of mums walking out of the decrepit cinema cafe that the singing group is held in. Caz is there, laughing with a woman called Carla.

Erin rushes across the road – a grey Transit van has to swerve to avoid her and hoots his disapproval, which makes the emerging mums and dads look over in her direction.

'Where is she? Did you not get my text?' she gasps to Caz who, seeing her friend's distress, picks up Imogen and comes out of the scrum to meet her.

'Not seen my phone. What do you mean? Who?'

'Amanda, Amanda's got Bobby, she was meant to be at the group.'

'She wasn't there, thought Bob must have fallen asleep at home,' Caz says. Erin looks out to the sea. She shuts her eyes, holds them closed. Her boy is gone. 'Erin, what's going on?'

'Let me look at your phone,' Erin says, eyes still closed, voice robotic.

'What? What's happened?'

'I need your phone.' Caz hands it over. Erin goes into Instagram. Scans Sophie's Insta-feed, Mercedes', Kristina's. She goes onto the feed of the group Caz has just been in to look at the group photo of the class, as if perhaps her friend somehow missed Amanda and Bobby being there. She turns and heads towards home when she realises she still has Caz's phone. She doubles back and gives it to her.

'Come on, get in the car,' Caz says, 'we'll find them.' Erin nods, though she feels catatonic. Where could they be? In London? With Raf? She checks her dumbphone again. Nothing. No returned call from Raf.

'Let's check home first.'

Erin leans her head against the cold glass of the window of Amanda's studio. They're not here. They're not in the house. She clenches her fists to stop her hands shaking but it just transfers the tremors into her arms. She's lost her baby. That woman has taken her baby. Or was it Raf that's taken him? Or, she thinks, and she knows that even back to that moment when she walked into the house and heard the sound of moaning from Bobby's bedroom, there was a seed in her head that this could happen, they've taken him together.

The shakes have spread to her shoulders now, her chest, and as she turns her head on the glass so her hair smears into it, she begins to make a sound that comes from deep inside her. She looks up and screams at the wooden patio roof, slamming her flat palms against the glass. She stops, hands still on the cold glass now, breathing huge audible huffs out of her nose. She steps away from the glass, thinks about sitting down on the edge of the decking, but then doesn't. She gets her dumbphone out, still no messages, and is about to call the police when she notices a smear of something on the inside of the glass door. It looks like glue, a slug's trail of glue, as if a toddler's got excited with the Pritt Stick. She goes into the room and presses it with a fingertip. It's not glue but it is tacky. She looks around the room and then she finds the answer. A pad of orange Post-its rests on the draining board of the tiny sink.

Erin goes over to it and sees a biro indentation but she can't make out what it says. She races back into the main house where Caz and Imogen are waiting for her. Caz must have just watched Erin wailing at the sky because she looks bewildered.

'We should go out and look,' she says, 'something might have happened to them.'

Erin waves the pad of Post-its in front of her and goes into Bobby's room. The smell, she'd never noticed how wonderful her little boy made that room smell. She gets a physical pain in her stomach at how much she misses him. She finds what she's looking for at the bottom of a storage box under his cot. An unopened packet of crayons, a gift from one of her mum's friends, that she wrenches open. She pulls out the purple one and rubs it over the indentation to reveal Raf's message.

Room 332
Premier Inn
Heathrow Terminal 4

61

15 June 1999

He didn't come home last night. It's eleven o'clock in the morning and I've got no idea where he is. Something must have happened to him and I'm terrified. I don't know what to do. We don't have a phone and of course I can't call the police. If he's not back by the evening I might have to go out to the local shop and – I don't know. What if I give away where we are? Donny's said that the police are on Craig's side. That he's enlisted them to look for us. What if Donny's fine, what if he just got stuck somewhere? Then I will have given away where we are and we'd have to move again just as we're getting settled. I can't go look for him myself. If only I had the gallery's telephone number, but then I don't even have money for the payphone. Oh God! What should I do?! Something's happened to him. That's the only explanation. If he's hurt, if he's gone, I don't know how I'll carry on.

16 June 1999

I've been up to our neighbour Colin's house and called the two big hospitals in Darwin and the one in Palmerston. He's not there. I was going to call the gallery but then realised I didn't know what it was called. I rang a couple out of the phone book but I couldn't stay in Colin's house for too long. Donny thought he was creepy and wouldn't have liked it. I'm sure he'll be back soon. He has to come back soon. He never would have left me, so he has to come back. I can't believe that something terrible has happened. I can't.

18 June 1999

The police came today. I begged them not to call my mum but they have. They've been looking for me ever since I left home. I told them that it was me who wanted to go to Darwin, I told them that I suggested moving back out to the sticks, but they keep saying he kidnapped me. They keep saying that he'd abused his position at the school but they don't know what they're talking about, he wasn't a proper teacher, just an assistant, and I didn't even do art.

I keep trying to tell them what Craig was planning, I told them he was hunting me down all on his own, told them what he was planning to do to me, how weird he'd been with me whenever I was half dressed at home. I told them that Donny was just trying to protect me from Craig and that he should be the one they lock up, but they're not listening.

They don't have Donny. They keep asking me where he is and don't seem to believe that I don't know. They say that our old neighbour Jean was found at the bottom of the stairwell and they think Donny might have pushed her. I told them that it was impossible, that Jean wasn't steady on her feet, that the stairs in our apartment block are too steep for an old woman, that they shouldn't have let her live there. But she's unconscious in hospital at the moment so she can't tell them that she fell and they're blaming it all on Donny.

I wish I did know where he is though, even if it meant us going to prison for fifty years. I feel certain something terrible's happened to him. He would never have left me otherwise. I keep telling them to ask Craig. I'm sure it's him. That he found Donny and, when he wouldn't tell him where I was, he did something to him. It's the only explanation. I'm scared. I'm wasting time being held in the police station when I should be out looking for him.

28 June 1999

He's alive. He's alive. He's alive. He's alive. He's alive. Mum said he'd probably left the country. So I rang all of the airlines that operate out of Darwin International. Many of them wouldn't speak to me, but when I started telling them that my husband had gone missing, I eventually found one that told me Rafael Donadoni was booked on a flight on 15 January. When I pressed her for his destination, she wouldn't tell me.

I've found a women's hostel to stay at in Cairns. Mum wouldn't have me when she found out what I'd told the police about Craig. She says he'd never dream of doing what I'd said. But she would protect him. I've got an interview to assist a childminder in three days. So now I just have to wait until Donny gets in touch to tell me how to join him. I can be patient. I can wait. Because that's what you do for love.

Erin puts the notebook down on the train table in front of her. The drama, the passion, the certainty of Amanda's words, the handwriting, they're all so young. She was a child and he did that to her. Convinced her she was his muse, pretend-married her in just the sort of ceremony that a spooky, gothy kid would lose their mind for. He separated her off from her family, her friends, then abducted her, telling her it was for her own safety. You can't tell from the journal whether this Craig guy was a creep, maybe he wasn't that nice a guy, but he never did anything to her. Raf did do something to her – or Donny as he clearly wanted to be called then, prob-ably to hide his Italian provenance. He was a teacher at her school. He groomed her. Abducted her. Raped her. Moved her around to avoid detection and then, presumably, fled the country without a word when it looked like the net was closing in on him. Erin lifts the notebook up and brings it slapping down onto the table. It wasn't Raf's father's indis-cretions with younger students that got them in trouble, that forced him to leave Australia. He was the sick one; he was the depraved one who couldn't help himself. The move from Melbourne – was that the same thing? Was there another underage girl he and his father had to run away from? Is it a pattern of behaviour? She glances at the time on her iPhone – she scoured their downstairs looking to see where Raf had put it, finding it in the side pocket of one of his bags. It seemed ridiculous to delay, but she somehow felt she might need something more powerful than the useless Nokia he'd given her.

Then it hits her. She gave her phone over to him willingly, but only because he made her believe that she was delusional, that she was suffering side effects from some form of addiction to her smartphone and that it was the only way to get better. Just as when she'd chosen to distance herself from her brother, who she'd spent most of her life so close to, she did it to overcome the despair she felt after every time she'd visit him and his perfect family. And when she moved to the sea, away from her dissolute friends and controlling mother, it was because starting a new simple life was the only way to cure her tempestuous mental health. And having a baby, now she thinks of it, there was a motivation for that too. She needed to remove herself from the centre of her universe, start living for something real, something tangible, a deep love, that was the only way she would ever find true happiness. But she'd never been to a doctor, she hadn't spent months having sessions with a therapist to get to these discoveries about herself, to become empowered to enact these various radical curative life changes, no, Raf suggested she needed to do all of it. And none of it was true. Just as the threat of Craig was planted in Amanda's head as a tool to coerce her away from everything that was there to protect her, to blind her to the fact that the only predator in her midst was the man she felt she loved, Raf had made Erin believe everyone she surrounded herself with was damaging her, and when he'd dealt with all of those competitors but she still wasn't entirely his, he had to make her believe that she was losing her mind. All of it to disguise the fact that the only person destroying Erin's life was her fiancé.

There's an acrid taste in the back of her mouth and she wants to spit. She notices a mum in her forties, sitting next to a seven-year-old girl reading a book, staring at her. Erin sits down and looks out the window again. She can tell the woman's a former follower of her Instagram. She's texting someone. Probably one of her mates to tell them that BRAUNEoverBRAINS is sat on a train opposite her, that she looks pale, drawn and frankly terrified, and that she's not with her beautiful baby boy. 'As usual' she'll probably add.

Erin turns her attention back to the notebook and flicks through the next entries. It's clear that marvellous 'Donny' never does get in touch, but, oddly, it seems Amanda is defiant. She creates various reasons why he hasn't been in touch, she's adamant that he will and that she just has to wait. But then the tone changes. The entries become shorter and more factual. Her assertions of confidence in the love of her life become emptier somehow. And then the entries stop.

Erin leans back in her seat, lets the cover of the book fold over onto her finger that remains on the page. She's still half an hour from London. The train thuds into a tunnel. She bites at the side of her thumb even though the cuticle's already bleeding. The hotel, she thinks to herself as she stares at the blocks of black flying past the window, the hotel gives her hope. He wouldn't have booked them a hotel unless they were going early tomorrow, so as long as she can get there, she can stop it. Stop what though? What is it they're doing? Erin's assuming they're planning to try and escape together with Bobby but can that really be what's happening? It seems insane that he could be leaving her, that he could be taking their baby away, but he's done it before, left a woman he claimed to love without a word. And in the last few hours, it feels like everything he's ever told her about himself, every conversation they've ever had, has been total fiction, so why wouldn't this be happening?

The train roars out of the tunnel. She can be at the hotel in just over an hour. She feels the judgey mum glancing at her again so Erin gives her a mania-tinged smile that makes it unambiguous that she doesn't appreciate being stared at and that she's in a mood you could describe as unhinged. The mum pockets her phone and puts a protective arm around her daughter.

Erin holds her shaking hands together, squeezing the fleshy part between her thumb and forefinger, the pain seeming to calm her momentarily. She glances at the little girl opposite, enwrapped in her book. A dull ache comes into her breasts. She hasn't fed Bobby from them for weeks now and her milk is almost completely gone, but the thought of her little boy feels like it's getting it going again. She doesn't know what she's going to do when she gets there. She has no idea what they're going to do, what they're going to say when she finds them in a hotel at Heathrow airport, but she is a mother. It's taken her a long time to come round to it, to understand what it means to be a mother, but that's what she is, and she needs to get her son back.

62

She stares at the pale wood of the hotel-room door. The number '332' in brushed brass in the centre of it. The low light of the hallway, the carpet like blue static, identical door upon identical door. As she holds her hand up to knock, she feels like she's in a horror film. What they've done isn't explicable, it's extreme. It's violent in its extremity, it's criminal. What does Erin think her intervention is going to achieve? The journal suggests that Raf pushed an old woman down the stairs when she threatened him. He's not just going to hand Bobby over and suggest they all head home for a cup of tea and a slice of Battenberg.

Just as her hand goes to knock, the door opens. Amanda grabs her into the room and closes the door behind her.

'Turn off your phone,' Amanda says but Erin ignores her as she sees Bobby on the ground, knocking miniature shampoo bottles together. Erin swoops down on him and cuddles her baby boy where he is on the floor, settling herself next to him and pulling him up onto her lap, both her arms wrapping around him like the bulky restraint of a roller coaster. Before she even looks for Raf she decides to stay like this. To never let him out of her sight again. Her eyes dart around the darkened hotel room like a woodland animal, alert, waiting for Raf to come out and strike, her eyes fixed on the closed bathroom door. But nothing happens. He's not here.

'Turn your phone off please,' Amanda says, her voice firm but kind.

'What the fuck are you –'

'I'm sorry about faking the post-it to get you here, but it was the only way to keep both of you safe. Now please, for Bobby, turn your phone off.' Erin feels the weight of it in her pocket. Bobby's little paws tickle at the hairs on her arm, he wants to get back to playing. She makes a circular pen with her legs and puts Bobby in the middle with his toiletries. 'He uses the Find My iPhone thing, it doesn't work if the phone's off.'

'What do you mean he uses?'

'He always likes to know where we are, to make sure we're OK. But he can't know we're here now. He'll try and stop it.' Erin turns off the phone. She has no idea what the hell is going on but Amanda said that Bobby wasn't safe and, with what she's read on the train, with what she saw earlier in the day, she feels she has to do as she's told. Amanda comes over to her and makes to sit down in front of her.

'Back off. Sit somewhere else,' Erin finds herself saying. Amanda gets back up and walks over to the desk near the window. 'Open the curtains.' Amanda does as she's told, flooding the dingy hotel room with daylight. 'Now, what the fuck is going on? I thought you were abducting my baby.'

'I'm so sorry,' Amanda says, sitting down on the edge of the chair. 'I didn't want to scare you. I would never do anything to hurt Bobby, never, but I needed you to come here and I knew you wouldn't if I just asked you to.'

'You wrote the Post-it?'

Amanda nods, looking proud of herself. 'And I left the screwdriver out so you'd see it. I couldn't risk us being at your house, he wouldn't have allowed it.' She's smiling still as if this is a nice chat they're having.

'So you wanted me to find the other Post-it, the one with our address he sent you?'

'I've started to become concerned about what he was doing to you. It felt, it felt like it wasn't loving any more.'

'What wasn't loving?'

'Making you think you'd set up a different bank account. He – he's always been strange about money. His mother's fault. When she left them she took most of his father's money. It forced them to move from the city. She'd never had a job, and he's always said that if she hadn't been able to take that money, she never would have left and they might have worked it out. It's incredibly traumatic for a boy to lose his mother so young.'

Erin places a hand on Bobby's bare knee.

'He set up the bank account? He's stealing my Instagram money?'

'No, no.' Amanda laughs. 'No, I don't think he needs to steal from you. He set up the account in your name. He felt like he was losing you, with all your Internet stuff. He was scared you might leave if you had the means. I tried to tell him.' She shrugs, with that gleeful grin that Erin would love to smack off her face right now, 'I took your side. I told him that he should let you go. I could see from the moment I walked into your house that you weren't meant to be together. It was so obvious. When I first got there, when you were away, he said that sending me your address was a mistake. He said he'd been feeling down in the dumps, ignored by you, uninspired by his art, and he thought he wanted to see me, but that it had been a mistake. He told me to go and I was going to, but as soon as you walked in, as soon as you sat down and went straight to your phone, I knew you didn't have what him and I have and I couldn't leave after that.' Amanda plays her fingers over what looks like an envelope on the desk. 'I'm so pleased that this —' she gestures to Erin on the floor — 'has worked out so well.'

Erin looks at the door. She should go. The way Amanda's talking about Raf isn't right. He abducted her, he statutory-raped her then abandoned her for twenty years, and she's making excuses for him like she's his long-suffering girlfriend. Erin stands up, bringing Bobby into her arms. Amanda makes a face at him, tongue out and cheeks puffed out, looking faintly absurd in a cream lace dress in this soulless hotel room. 'Miss Havisham' vibes she remembers Caz having said about the way she dresses, having no sense of quite how unwittingly prescient she was being. Erin gets a stab of chill down her back. Why has this woman brought her here? What's she planning on doing to her? Amanda cocks her head to the side, perhaps seeing the dawning fear in her eyes. Erin goes for the door but the handle just flicks down impotently. It's locked. Amanda comes towards her, the envelope in her hand.

'This is for you,' Amanda says, handing the envelope over. Bobby starts using Erin's ribcage as a climbing frame and she nearly hands him over to Amanda before remembering and wheeling him away from her. She crosses to the corner of the room, rests Bobby on the top of the trouser press and opens the envelope. Inside there's a plane ticket. British Airways, to Sydney, for Erin Braune plus an infant.

'I've packed a bag for you with some of your things, some essentials for Bob. Passports are in there too. I checked with the airline and you can take two tubs of formula with you – that should be enough to get you going.' Erin watches Amanda swing a plastic bag with two huge cans of formula up onto the bed. 'Am I right in thinking you've got a cousin who lives somewhere in Oz?'

'Have you lost your mind?' Erin spits the words out with such venom that even Bobby looks shocked. 'You think I'm going to leave my fiancé, leave my home, with a eleven-month-old? How much did you spend on this ticket? Jesus Christ, Amanda? What the actual fuck is wrong with you?'

'You don't want to leave him?' It's a genuine question. 'Did you not read my journal? We're married. If the law was a little more nuanced about age differences in meaningful relation-ships we'd still be together. We've always been supposed to be together, Erin. That's why it's not worked between you. It's not your fault.' She moves towards Erin, hands outstretched as if to take hers. Erin backs into her corner, brings Bobby closer into her neck. 'I know it might seem drastic but it's the only way he'll let you go. He can't go back to Oz after what happened with us when we were kids –'

'You were a kid, Amanda. He was a grown man. How old? Twenty, twenty-one? What he did to you is called grooming.'

'Do you want to stay with Raf then?' She bites the words off like they were a stale biscuit. She's still obsessed with him, after all these years. The crystals, the jar spell, all designed to force Erin away and win him over again. And of course Erin wants to leave him. He's a compulsive liar, a rapist, a paedo-phile for Christ's sake. He's isolated Erin, made her think she's an insufficient mother and partner and that he's working all hours to provide for them, he's made her leave her agent, taken the money she earned, the first proper money she'd ever earned, and made her think she's mad. Now she thinks about it, he was probably days away from committing her to an institution. Has he ever loved her? Why didn't he just run off with Amanda if that's what he wants? Why all this? She has so many questions but right now she needs to deal with Amanda. Damaged, eggshell-fragile Amanda, who has her locked in a hotel room with her baby expecting her to get on a plane to Australia in three hours.

'I'm going to leave Raf, yes. Of course I'm going to leave him,' Erin says and Amanda brightens. 'But I'm not going to get on that flight. I'm not going to get on a plane to Australia.'

Amanda's brow furrows. 'It's the only way.' She sits on the bed, both hands fiddling with a large obsidian pendant she has round her neck, eyes on the carpet. 'He won't let you go. You're engaged. He —' She looks up at Erin and she can see the petulant, precocious teenager that Raf painted in the pictures. The girl he clearly still wants her to be. Has she seen his pictures? Has she seen how he's painted her, how dissatisfied he is with the aged her, the real her? 'I imagined it was going to be easy to remind him why he married me.' In her mind they're married. That crazy little ceremony they had, she thinks they're married. 'I wanted to show him how much better I'd be as a mother, as a partner, and it seemed to be working. He wanted me to spend more time with him, he started painting me again. He said I was inspiring him. He wanted to be an artist again, to get his work out into the world. He said he hadn't felt like this in years.' She looks out the window, a sadness falling into her eyes. 'When he found out about the video, when he saw how you were treating his son, I thought that would be enough, I thought it would make it easy for him to leave. I never wanted to take Bobby.' She flicks back to looking at Erin, the shadows under her severe cheekbones making her look her age for once. 'I just wanted to show him how obvious it was that we were meant to be, how good a mother I'd be if he wanted to have the sort of family he wanted with me.'

'What sort of family does he want?'

'You were never going to be happy just being his wife. It's not your fault, but that's what someone like Raf needs. Someone who will dedicate themselves entirely to him and his baby. He wouldn't have done any of the things he's done to you if you weren't always trying to make a life away from him. We all need different things from our partners and sometimes people get into relationships that aren't right, and they stick with them out of stubbornness or fear. But you can never give him what I can, what he deserves, and no matter how hard he's tried with you, and I can see he's tried so hard, too hard, what he's done to you isn't right, but he has only ever done it for you, to make you something like his first wife —' she puts both hands to her collarbone — 'who he was cruelly separated from. But he can have what he needs now. I'm here to claim him. It's legal now for him and me to be what we always should have been. And you can be free. It's what we all deserve, Erin. We all deserve to be happy.'

Erin's about to try and contradict her, to try and make her see that she's talking like a cult devotee, but she stops herself. The situation feels as if it's teetering on a needlepoint and trying to win over someone so damaged, whose mind is set on an entirely different planetary wavelength, isn't going to get her anywhere. She sees a cool bag, some of Amanda's preparations for her flight, and extracts a banana and gives it to Bobby before plonking him down on the carpet and sitting next to him.

'Why is this –' she holds up the plane ticket – 'why is this the only way?'

'He's really very traditional,' Amanda says, making Erin actually shake her head in disbelief. 'I realised that he wasn't going to leave you of his own accord. I thought about telling you we were still married, that we'd lived as man and wife, about, well, I didn't think you'd understand about the age difference, no one ever did, but I thought about telling you, in the hope you'd leave him. But how he was –' she pauses, glances up at Erin before going back to massaging the pendant around her neck – 'how he was behaving, I could see he was fighting to make things work, so if he found out I'd told you about us I knew that he'd never, ever forgive me. And it would have tarnished things between us, stopped us ever refinding our bond. I thought he'd just gravitate towards me, but –' she hums a half-laugh – 'he's very traditional, I should have known he wouldn't just be able to let you go. He's got such strong principles, and it makes perfect sense, after how his dad treated his mother, her running away, he wants to be the type of husband and father his dad never was.' Erin swallows the lump in her throat. She glances at the window. She doesn't feel safe in the room with Amanda. To her, this isn't a hare-brained idea. This is how she's going to clear a path to Raf so the two of them can be together. What's she going to do when Erin tells her she's not getting on that flight? Amanda's so deeply in thrall to Raf. But no, Erin tells herself, she's got me here to help me, she thinks she's helping. Perhaps the excuses for him come from the way he conditioned her as a child, some scar tissue in her psyche that stops her seeing anything he does as the rest of the world would. But how to shine a light into her head and make her see how brainwashed she is? Erin starts as Amanda looks sharply at the clock radio on the bedside table.

'Bobby will need a nap in half an hour,' she says. 'Probably better to get through security first.'

'What do you think's going to happen, Amanda? Bobby and I get on the flight and then what? You go back to our house and reclaim your husband?'

Amanda tries to smile but she looks annoyed. 'I don't think he's going to just fall into my arms. I'm sure he'll try and get to you, to try and get you back, but he won't be able to because he can't travel back home. He only left me in the first place because of what the police were accusing him of. He's still wanted for kidnapping me, and, um, what happened to our neighbour Jean. I know he wouldn't risk it. And, here it is, he knows deep down that what we had was true, powerful love. I feel sure that that's the reason you and he have never been able to make things conduct between you. So with you gone, I'm certain it will just be a matter of time. And I can wait as long as it takes.' She moves her hands from her pendant to her lap as if that proves her point.

'You don't think he'll want to know why I've gone? If he's that obsessed with my not leaving, don't you think he'll blame you?'

Amanda smiles, one hand twists the thick cord of hair that rests on her chest. 'He knows you've been going through the studio, spying on me, trying to find something to incriminate me. I hid the journal where no one could ever find it, he can't blame me for that.'

'What if I tell him? What if I tell him that you told me everything, that you told me exactly the sort of man he is?'

Amanda launches herself off the bed and down onto the floor with such force, that Erin finds herself almost gearing up to shove her away.

'You can't!' she pleads. 'You can't tell him. There's no need. You want to be free of it. Be honest with yourself, you don't love him. You're not the person he needs, I am. But if you tell him it would taint everything we have.'

'Have you seen the paintings he's done of you? They're sick. He's not in love with you. He's a pervert who abused you when you were a child. He doesn't love you.'

Amanda blinks three, four times. She pulls at the lace on her cuffs. She shakes her head, smiling from ear to ear.

'You don't know him.'

Erin gets Bobby onto her, stands up with him and goes into the bathroom. Raf's been telling her she's deluded for the past few weeks, but now she's witnessing true, profound delusion, the likes of which she's never imagined possible. Amanda needs help immediately, and she needs to get away from Raf, because if he's half as controlling as her journal says he is, he won't forgive her, and although she doesn't know what happened to Jean, Erin can't let him do the same to Amanda. But what's Erin going to do? She looks at Bobby looking at himself in the bathroom mirror. He's starting to look less blobby and more human. He smiles as he makes his huge powder puff of hair shake from side to side. She can't risk Raf seeing him again. She definitely doesn't want to see him again. She doesn't understand it all yet, but Amanda, the studio, the paintings, she knows that everything about their relationship is a lie. Bobby can't have anything to do with someone who could do what he's done.

'We should get you to departures,' Amanda says from the bedroom, her tone eerily flat. Erin needs to deal with her. What Amanda's done today, the elaborate treasure hunt leading her to look for the jar spell, the fucking jar spell! She needs to get Amanda somewhere safe, then Erin can assess what the hell she's going to do with the rest of her life.

'This is what's going to happen.' Erin turns back into the door frame of the bathroom. This is all acting now. The wide stance, deepening the tone of her voice, the firm, commanding words. This is Henry V 'Once more unto the breach, dear friends' stuff. 'We're going to go to the British Airways desk, put your name on this ticket, and you're going to go home. My old agent, Grace, her company has an office in Sydney, they'll find someone for you to talk to. You've been a victim of abuse, you've been groomed, and you've not been able to move on from it. Raf will know that you told me about his past.' Erin pauses, expects Amanda to come up with some objection, but she just stares ahead of her, fiddling with her pendant again. 'Do you understand that, Amanda? He'll think it's your fault that I left him, that I took his boy away from him. If he's so obsessed with being a great dad, that's going to make him very angry. You won't be safe.' Erin can't quite believe it but Amanda starts nodding.

'What will you do?' she asks.

'Go to my mum, I guess.' Erin hasn't thought about it all, she hasn't spoken to her in months, but she can't think of another option.

'He'll find you.'

'I'm going to tell the police about the bank account,' Erin says, biting the inside of her lip, making it all up on the spot. 'Tell them I found out he was pretending to be me. That's illegal. I'll say I'm in a coercive relationship. I'll show them the journal, show them what he did to you when you were a child and they'll be able to protect me.' Amanda turns her head to Erin. She's smiling.

'Us abandoning him like this,' she says, eyes filling, 'it's much worse punishment than anything the police can do to him.'

'You might not be able to understand it yet, Amanda, you might not ever believe it, but he deserves every punishment we can mete out against him.'

'Let's go then,' Amanda says, closing her eyes briefly. Then she whips a key card out of her pocket and opens the door onto the yellow light of the hallway.

63

'Erin?' Her mum's shock scratches curtly through Erin's iPhone speaker.

'Hi, Mum.'

'You've deigned to call me.'

'Are you at home?'

'It's not a great time to be honest, I've got to go into town for –'

'I'm coming over.'

'Um –' The crowded airport swirls around Erin and Bobby as if they're in the eye of the storm and she can barely hear her mum with the noise. She half expects her to say she has some pastoral stuff at the charity she volunteers for that she just can't put off. She hates to be surprised. Bobby grabs a clump of skin. He looks exhausted, panda patches under his eyes. Erin's mum clears her throat. 'Has something happened?' she asks, concern beginning to melt her frostiness.

'Yes.' Erin's chest shudders up at the thought. 'Yes, something has happened.' The admission breaks Erin's banks, she sucks short breaths in, the point of hyperventilation, yelping almost. Eyes in the crowd become fixed on her though no one does a thing. She locks eyes with Bobby who's staring at his mother somewhere between upset and amused and it stills Erin momentarily, gives her the time to rein her emotion in.

'I'll be here,' her mum says. 'I've got stuff for a fish pie.' Erin bursts into laughter, tears streaming down her face. Soon they'll be there. Soon they'll be safe.

Bobby looks tiny sitting on the big train seat next to her. He napped for a while on her chest and he's now dismantling one of those spirals of compressed fruit and sticking bits of it on his face. As the scenery outside starts to adjust from towers of council flats to the flatter rows of suburban terraces, towards Croydon, her mum, sanctuary, everything starts to settle in her mind.

She thought she was losing her grip on reality; that she'd forgotten about a bank account she set up. She glances at her phone on the table between her and Bobby. He almost made her believe that her addiction to it had made her so delusional that she was imagining jars with dolls planted under sofa beds. She never truly believed that she was going mad, but Raf seemed so frustrated with her, so quick to dismiss the things she was saying were going on, that she accepted it. Got into bed, pulled the cover over her head and just accepted it. Looking back on their time together, she can see that the pattern was always the same. He'd suggest she make a life change, not hanging out with certain friends, giving up acting, moving out of London, having a baby, and at first she'd rail against the idea but somehow she always acceded to it. And it would always be because he was 'worried' about her, worried about her mental health. He used her neurosis about her career, her anxieties about her friends making more money than her, her sense of wasted potential, her antenatal depression even, as a tool to control her and she drank it all down like a milkshake.

From the hotel she and Bobby walked Amanda to the British Airways office to put her name on the ticket, checked her in, and saw her off at the security gates. She must have somehow known that this was the best course of action because she had her passport with her but she barely said a word. As they parted ways, she gave Erin the tightest hug and seemed genuinely emotional to say goodbye to Bobby. It was as if she suddenly realised that this whole trip was a fantasy, that the ardour she'd harboured all this time, the lies she'd been telling herself, were a result of being abused. Erin wasn't sure how she'd got through to her, there hadn't seemed to be a road to Damascus realisation but she seemed, in the hotel room, to just give up.

Raf calls again. Only when they got on the train did she turn her phone on. She sent him a text: *I found Amanda's journal. You're sick. I never want to see you again. I never want Bobby to see you. If you try to find us I will have you arrested.*

He hasn't stopped calling since but she doesn't want to hear his lies, she can't bear hearing how she's got it wrong, how Amanda's making it up, how they're all deluded. She looks at Bobby who's moved on to mutilating a small pot of carrot sticks. At least she has a purpose now, at least her life has a meaning. To make sure that her boy grows up nothing like his father. Her relationship is over. She should be distraught but all she feels is intense relief. Relieved she's not lost her mind but mainly relief at being free of him. Because she's spent the last four years just as deluded as Amanda is. She so wanted a saviour, someone that would make sense of how messy her life felt, that she allowed herself to be controlled by a monster. But now the blinkers are off. Bobby cries out as he bites his finger instead of the carrot stick between his four little teeth. He hands it out for her to kiss better so she leans down and smothers his tiny fingers with kisses. It feels extraordinary to mother him like this. It feels natural, perhaps for the first time.

She looks on her phone and sees the icon for the Find My iPhone app. She had no idea what it even did, no idea that you could use it to track your partner, but when she goes into it she sees his phone is there along with hers. She clicks onto his phone. There's a tiny icon of a phone with a pin stuck onto their road at home. He's back from London, whatever he was doing there. There are two other phones on the list. 'iPhone 3', 'iPhone 5'. Raf's old ones probably, Erin's borrowed one of them in the past when hers was stolen on a bus in Camberwell. She sits forward when she sees that one of them is 'online'. She clicks on it. The dot seems to be somewhere on the south side of the M25, heading east from Heathrow. She remembers Amanda in the hotel room saying that Raf used the app to watch 'us'. And Erin had never realised – of course Amanda has a smartphone, she had to have one, the baby monitor they use for Bobby is on a smartphone app. He gave her one of his old ones. Amanda's not on a plane back to her homeland. She's in a car heading back towards Erin's home, back to him.

Erin squeezes her temples. She remembers what Amanda's journal said he did to the neighbour who threatened to break up their relationship. She wrote that the police had made a mistake but she also thought she hadn't been abducted. Erin wants to scream 'fuck' very loudly, but for the sake of the carriage she manages to restrain herself. She glances out the window and sees the spire of the clock tower of the Museum of Croydon. Her mum's house is ten minutes away, fifteen, max. She could take Bobby up to her old bedroom, climb into bed and cover herself in the duvet, just for an hour or so. The train comes into the station. She picks Bobby up and he hugs into her. As she's stepping out into the cold grey of suburbia, she looks into her boy's eyes, like pools of molten chocolate. His dad's eyes. Erin's going to go to her mum's to drop him off, but she knows she can't stay.

64

The ground floor looks like it's been ransacked. The coffee table has been upturned; three empty cans of lager, a bottle of half-drunk vodka stand like sentries on the edge of their dining table guarding a huge bag of crisps popped, spilled and ground into the carpet below. The wire bookshelf has been pulled from the wall and rests on an armchair, its contents mostly on the floor. This is nothing like the man Erin knows, so considered, so neat, so fastidious. But the Raf she knows isn't a real person at all, so perhaps this is him finally revealing his true atrocious self. Perhaps he has to attach himself to vulnerable, desperate women to bring order to his monstrous mind. But even though he clearly has been here, there's no sign he's in the house currently. The Find My iPhone trail has gone cold for both him and Amanda.

She spots the painting of the shrouded figure staring at her and realises that he must have painted it, and that it's probably of her. Erin's stomach sinks like she's dropping in turbulence at the thought of Raf, the grown man, and the poor child Amanda. And he's a fucking terrible artist, she thinks, looking at the immature daubing, feeling a sense of glee. She remembers back in Marine Gallery, the way the curator was almost sniggering at him. Was he trying to get her to sell his work? Erin feels her own laugh building inside her when she hears a desperate sound. A shriek, a keening, mournful shriek. Erin's eyes dart to the window and, though the blinds are down, through the door of the studio she sees Raf holding Amanda up against the wall by her shoulders? Or is it by her throat? Erin picks up the first thing she finds, the twin-spired crystal, balanced on the leaning shelf, and runs out into the garden.

'Put her down,' Erin says, brandishing the rock by one of its columns, the heavy end held up in front of her like a mace. Raf looks round at her through a mop of hair, pupils huge, desperate delight coming into his expression as if she were a rescue ship and he a castaway. He releases Amanda who slides down the wall, holding her throat, gulping big breaths in – he was strangling her? He looks like an entirely different person to her fiancé, pupils huge, face shimmering with sweat. Is he on drugs as well as pissed? Raf has never done drugs, she knows that his house of cards is crumbling around him, but what the fuck has happened to him since this morning? He moves towards where she stands in the door frame but Erin swings the crystal, warning, and he stops where he is.

'Ez, I am so sorry.'

'I don't want to hear it.'

'She's lying.'

'I saw your studio. Your lavish studio that you pay for with, with what money, Raf, because I thought we were skint?'

'Look, I've, I've got – Weird about money but –'

'Shut up! Shut the fuck up! You have lied to me every single day I've known you to make me feel like a piece of shit –'

'Ez –'

'Shut the fuck up!' She screams it at the top of her voice, a power and intensity she's barely ever shown him, and it works. He's stunned into silence. 'Amanda, come on.' Amanda shakes her head on the floor. 'Come on, for Christ's sake. He just tried to kill you, come on.' Amanda looks at Erin, black pupils, large in her eyes too, cheeks streaked with tears and trails of eyeliner. 'Get up,' Erin says, playing the role of an action-movie heroine, puffing herself up with forceful authority because she has to get Amanda away from him. She wants to go over and grab her but she can't get too close to him. 'Come on, Amanda – now!'

'OK, I'm sorry. I'm sorry, I'm sorry, I'm sorry. I thought I was going to lose you. I never would have done any of what I've done, but you were leaving me.'

'What the fuck?'

'You were leaving me, you didn't know it, but all the people online, hundreds of thousands of people, I was losing you to them, Bobby as well. I had to do something. I know I shouldn't have made you scared, I never wanted you to be afraid. But I was angry, angry that the rest of the world got this fun, sunny side of you while I had to listen to you moan and moan, on and on about how terrible you felt, how you didn't feel connected to the baby, how hard it was. I think I was jealous, I was, I was jealous to see you looking at your phone, smiling like you were in love with it while all I got was your misery.'

'Can you – Just shut up. Amanda!' Erin doesn't want to hear this. He looks reasonable again, the shadow of mania seems to have passed, and it's like he's genuinely trying to reach her, to find some kind of rapprochement in this batshit-crazy situation. She doesn't want to hear his excuses, she doesn't want to get sucked back into his logic, his rationality. He's an abuser, a paedophile, it's not just in his past, those pictures were painted in the last few weeks. 'Amanda, for fuck's sake, come on.' Erin roars at her but Amanda only shrugs, blinks away her tears, a sorry shake of the head.

'It was like when you were acting. You were so desperate to get all these jobs that would fly you around the world away from me, that'd make you famous, loved by all these strangers. So excited about the chance of getting one and then so miserable when you didn't. For weeks. Until *all* I ever got from you was misery and despair. You were never as hopeful about our future as you were for these jobs, never so devastated at the possibility of having to leave me for any length of time. I was just funding the fucking roller coaster, a port in the storm, you called me that, a port in the storm. Those first few months you were incredible, transcendent, and that was enough to tie me to you forever, but after that, all I got was your pain. I'm not proud of what I did then and I'm not proud about what I've done now, but I knew you'd never listen to me if I just told you that you were changing. I knew that confronting you and telling you that you were neglecting your responsibilities as a mother and a partner would drive you even further away from us. That's why I put up the video and the photos, I wanted you to see for yourself how toxic the social media stuff is, how it was destroying the incredible woman you are. I know it might seem fucked up, Ez, but you have to see, I was so so scared of losing you. I couldn't see there was any other way.'

'You're the troll,' Erin says as if it's the most obvious thing in the world. Raf looks quizzical, eyes even wider than before, as if he's just revealed something he shouldn't.

'I wanted you back. I love you and I missed you and I wanted you back. I still want you.'

'Then', she thinks, he said he did something 'then', what did he do? Erin's mind races, she thinks back to her acting career, what did he do? She spots the pile of magazines she must have left in here from the bedroom this morning, *Wonderland* on the top, the interview with Rhia Trevellick. 'You whisked me off on a holiday. You fucking – you whisked me off to a cabin in fucking Ireland. Somewhere you knew there wasn't going to be any phone reception. You fucking knew, you knew I was going to get the part, how –'

'It doesn't matter how, I did it because –'

'Tell me how you knew.'

'There was a voicemail.'

'Fuck you!' Erin turns and leans on the table, the huge crystal sweeping the rest of Amanda's crystal grid onto the floor. It was him! All along it was him that ruined everything for her.

'You and me, Ez, we've never needed anyone else. I've always known that but I could never make you see it. I thought when we had Bobby that would prove it to you but even that didn't work. I'm sorry for scaring you but don't you see? We're free of all that stuff, past the lies, we can be what we're meant to be.'

'Donny, please –' Erin wheels up to see Amanda launching herself from the floor and throwing herself towards Raf. 'We don't need her, I can be your muse, I'll be your servant, I'll dedicate every ounce of my being –' Then Raf turns, takes Amanda's arms off his neck, almost picks her up by the wrists and launches her against the back wall. Without a thought Erin swings the huge crystal and hits the side of Raf's head. It makes a dull thunking sound like a pillow hitting a wall. And moments later Raf falls in the same direction as the crystal

Erin immediately dropped to her left, as if he were attached to it by an invisible thread.

Erin begins to breathe out of her nose, loud, forceful breaths. What has she just done? Blood flows down the side of his face; she takes a step closer, peers at it, it doesn't look as bad as she was expecting. She can't have caught him as hard as it felt in her hands. She looks at Amanda, who's nursing her shoulder, facing the wall still. Amanda turns and sees Raf on the floor. She stares at his body and begins to blink, strong, hard blinks, as if she were trying to get something out of her eye, like waking from a dream. Then she looks at Erin. The side of her mouth twitches into a half-smile. Erin stares at Raf for a moment more, eyes closed, chest rising and falling slowly. She hasn't killed him. Of course she hasn't killed him, she's not strong enough to kill someone with one blow of a blunt instrument. She steps over his body and grabs Amanda, pulling her out towards the doorway.

'He'll be fine,' Erin says, voice shorn of conviction. 'We need to get you away from him now. You're not safe. Neither of us is safe once he comes to.'

Amanda nods but she breaks from Erin's grasp, eyes fixed on Raf, the sinister crease of a smile setting on her face. Erin shakes her head, slams the studio door behind her and marches back towards the main house. As she gets to the open door into their main room, she turns to see Amanda trailing behind, staring at her cradled fingers. Beyond her Erin sees Raf's legs prone through the glass. He's going to be fine, she tells herself, hands shaking, he deserved it, it was the only way they were going to get away safely. By the time he comes round, they will both be far enough from him that he can never hurt either of them again.

'Please, Amanda,' she says to the still-dawdling woman. Amanda trots up to her like an obedient child, pupils wide as dinner plates. 'He'll be fine, OK? You're safe. Do you get me? He would have killed you, you're safe now.' She clutches at Amanda's wrists, trying to get through to her, trying to convince her that Erin's not the bad person here, that the man in the studio is the monster and not her.

Amanda smiles, a titter of a laugh, but her eyes, she looks crazed. Erin spots the kitchen knife out of its block on the sink. She's just knocked out the person this woman thinks is her soulmate, she could do anything.

'Let's get you in the car.'

Sitting side by side speeding down the main road that takes you away from the coast in Raf's hatchback, Erin and Amanda haven't said a word to each other. Erin's driving to Heathrow, she has the card for the account Raf set up with her money in it so she's going to buy Amanda another plane ticket, watch her go through security this time, and make sure, somehow, she's on that plane. Then she's going to get home to Bobby at her mum's, call her brother to come round, just in case Raf turns up, call the police and tell them everything. Once they've heard he's still wanted in Australia for what, abduction, manslaughter, murder maybe even, she feels sure they'll make sure she's protected. If they ask her what happened to him, how he hurt himself, she will admit she hit him, say that he was trying to strangle Amanda and it was the only way to stop him. Erin has no idea whether Amanda would back up her story but she's hoping that away from Raf she'll regain some semblance of rationality and see that what Erin did was to protect them both.

She hears a snuffling sound next to her and darts a look at Amanda. She's covering her mouth, eyes watering, attempting to smother the beginnings of laughter. She sees that Erin has clocked her and puts her other hand over her mouth, trying to hide what she's doing like a schoolgirl. Erin turns her eyes back on the road, frightened, more frightened than she's been all day. It seems like the taut cable keeping the ravages of Amanda's trauma under the surface has finally snapped and now she has the aura of a rabid animal, as if she could do anything at any moment. Erin angles her elbow up slightly as a blocker, suddenly hit by the idea that she might grab the steering wheel and send them both careering over the central reservation. The noises from the passenger seat die down. Out of the corner of Erin's eye she sees Amanda's hands are down in her lap now, but she's shaking her head like it's on a spring, face stretched in a grimace.

'What the fuck,' Erin says, not to anyone, as she pulls off sharply, throwing her over towards Amanda. She drives into a lay-by on the slip road she's come off on to. A burger van billows smoke up ahead. Erin stares at her, imploring her to tell her what the hell is going on in her head.

'I'm alive,' Amanda says, her eyes seeming to swell again and again as she stares in front of her.

'Yeh,' Erin says, 'you got out alive, we both did.'

'Atropa belladonna.'

'What?'

Amanda starts laughing again but then catches it in her hand, as if it's naughty. 'Of course I'm alive, I've built up a tolerance. I've been taking it all my life. I – The smoke of that van is making the most beautiful patterns.' Amanda turns her head sharply towards Erin. 'I gave him twice the dose, perhaps more, because I thought, he's at least twice as big as me.' She blinks again, that long slow blink.

'What are you talking about, Amanda? Are you – Have you taken something?' Erin remembers Raf's eyes, she'd never seen them like it. She used to go raving and that's what it looked like – in the moment she thought it must be the adrenaline of the situation, but Amanda's eyes are the same fishbowls now.

'Atropa belladona. Amazing for some bowel issues, asthma, and people even use it for motion sickness.' She grabs at the armrest on the door, as if she feels like she's on a boat in the static car. She leans over, conspiratorial, then points up ahead at the smoke. 'And it can send you on the most wonderful trips in the right proportions.'

'What did you – did you drug him?'

'He always said he'd never leave me, he said we'd be together forever.' Her mouth creases, eyes narrow, and a moan catches in her throat. It looks like she's going to cry now. She grips the sleeve of Erin's jacket and looks into her eyes. 'He didn't want me, he told me he didn't want me. Belladona, deadly nightshade, it was the only way for us to be together, the way it was always meant to be. But I'm still alive.' Erin turns away from Amanda and stares out the windscreen. She takes a big breath in and huffs it out. She pulls the keys out of the ignition, opens her car door and steps out, slams it behind her and then presses the button on the key fob to lock Amanda in the car. She leans her back against the door, unable to look at the woman. In the distance, she can hear the siren of a police car.

65

ANNAMAITRON

789 posts   91.7k followers   7,356 following

OK. I am going to address this because I'm getting hundreds of DMs about it, which is insane. But just once, because this isn't the platform for it IMHO. Hence the uncharacteristically stern face in the pic – though that coral lipstick is popping the fuck out regardless.

Anyway. My dear friend Erin Braune left Instagram some weeks ago due to online harassment. As many of you will know, as has been reported in the press and shared all over social channels, it came to light that it was her fiancé Rafael Donadoni who was responsible for this savage and cruel trolling of his own partner and, following the revelation, he committed suicide at their home. It's since emerged that Rafael has a history of coercive, violent and controlling behaviour including that of an underage girl he abducted back in his native Australia in his early twenties where he was, before his death, still wanted by the police for both his grooming of the girl and for the attempted murder of an elderly neighbour.

Erin has been through a trauma the likes of which very, very few of us can even begin to relate to, which is why I find myself appalled that so many people seem to want there to be more to Rafael Donadoni's death. There are all sorts of theories being passed online and, to be honest, it's made me evaluate whether I want to continue to involve myself in any sort of Internet discourse. I think the people peddling this trash are absolutely disgusting gossip-mongers who have no sense of empathy for someone who's been through something horrific. Donadoni was clearly a deeply disturbed individual with no sense of compassion or concern for other people and it seems ridiculous that people are surprised that he'd choose to take his life when his appalling behaviour was revealed and the consequences of it were about to be meted out. Everything he did demonstrated a craven and egotistical streak and, although my psychology undergraduate degree doesn't make me an expert, suicide seems to be the obvious course of action for someone whose sociopathic behaviour has been exposed.

Coercive control is real. The patriarchy want us to think it's some new thing but it's ingrained in our homes and our society. Examples like this shouldn't be picked apart to see how, in some way, the woman is to blame, they should be seen entirely as they are. A man trying to suppress the ambition, voice and power of a woman who threatens his ego. A man wanting his woman to be some Victorian mother and wife, madonna, whore and nothing else. To those who accuse Erin, to those who think her silence on the matter is some suggestion of guilt, be you whatever gender, I implore you to take a long hard look at the facts and YOURSELF and think about re-evaluating the way you look at the world and other people.

#brauneoverbrave

Comments turned off.

66

Imogen trowels a large mound of soil into a rusted frying pan and takes it over to a pile of sticks that Caz and Erin have assembled to be their stand-in fire at the far end of the garden of Erin's rented house. It's only three bedrooms but its owner is an amazing interior designer Erin knew from her Instagram days who's now moved to Porto, so it looks incredible. She and Bobby have been living here the past four months, since she moved back to the sea from being with her mum. As she looks at Caz helping Bobby make a mud-castle with a bright pink plastic bucket, she realises she's one of the big reasons why she came back. Caz, the sea and the fact that in and around Croydon there seemed to be about four times the amount of people who used to follow her and knew, thanks to the fact that the tabloids ran wild with the story, everything that happened six months ago.

'Not even tempted then?' Caz says down from where she is.

'Nope,' Erin says with a definitive shake of the head.

'Most people probably have some awful reason they got their big break. You deserve something good to come out of it. Now, tap the top, Bobby-boy, that's right, tap, tap, tap.'

Erin squirts some water from her bottle onto the pile of dry soil Imogen's got her hands in and she giggles with the mess. Erin's just been telling Caz about the swathe of offers to audition her old acting agent's had since the news broke. Nothing brilliant, a couple of fringe plays, a Shakespeare in Leeds, *Hollyoaks*, an American network sitcom. It seems so bizarre that people are suddenly interested in her from that point of view but she knows the producers are all thinking of the PR angle. Everyone wants to be seen as the person that gave a traumatised former actor her restart and they'll be thinking how journalists will lap up the chance to rake over the sordid details of her and her late fiancé's relationship. Grace's been in touch as well. A production company are pitching a true-crime documentary about the whole thing, but Erin shut it down, cited the fact that she wanted to move on. She does. They all deserve to move on.

'That ship's sailed I think, Cazabelle, and it's for the best.' Bobby toddles over to his mother, covered head to toe in mud, and hugs at her trouser leg. She bends down and he leaps into her arms getting dirt all over her #gifted couture dungarees and she couldn't care less. 'I'm happy where I am,' she says and she means it. Now Bobby's a bit older, his tummy's not causing him any problems and the screaming has stopped. The couple of months she spent with just Bobby and her mum, trapped in the house while the story about Raf blew over, had been some of her happiest since she was a kid. For Erin and her mum, the feeling of them against a cruel world, the permission to mother and be mothered, erased the guilt and blame they'd felt towards each other, rebuilding their relationship organically; but, more than that, coming back to each other as adults, they've discovered a friendship that had never been there before. Her mum's currently looking at houses, planning on moving down to be near her daughter and grandson. And with Bobby, that time cemented the kind of bond, the kind of intense love and dependency on each other that, for the first few months of his life, Erin didn't think they'd ever have.

As she looks around her huge garden – she won't be here much longer, she needs to buy somewhere smaller as her new job, she's training to be a drama teacher, isn't going to pay for a particularly lavish life – she notices how much lighter she feels now. She'd never realised it before, so grateful was she to Raf for working to support her and put a roof over her head, that trying to please him, trying to second-guess what she had to do to avoid one of his suggestions of how she could do things better, had created this intense anxiety, a weight in her that she'd not felt before they were together.

But perhaps the sense of freedom comes from somewhere else. Raf left over seven million Australian dollars. When Erin got the call from an Australian solicitor she almost slammed the phone down in disbelief. She should have put it together from Amanda's journal and the mention of some huge estate him and his dad were living on, but it seems that Raf wasn't just more comfortable than he was letting on to her, he was in fact from an incredibly wealthy family, a line of Italian factory owners who'd moved to Australia a few years before the Second World War. It also explained why, after getting engaged less than a year after they met, Raf had never pushed marriage in the same way he'd pushed everything else – to try and ensure she had no legal recourse over his fortune. The lawyer told her that all of the money is bequeathed to Bobby and there's no doubt that, even if Erin never earns more than enough to feed them and clothe them, the knowledge that her son will be much more than OK financially is a very, very liberating one. And the very least the boy deserves. Erin tries to dismiss the thought of what she'll tell him about his father when he grows up. When he's old enough, she's decided, she wants to tell him the truth. But how truthful should she be? Should she tell him that she hit his father over the head? Knocked him out? And was it Amanda's poison that killed him? In the months since, Erin's often wondered whether the head wound she'd caused was as innocuous as she'd convinced herself it was at the time.

'Here, look at the state of this,' Caz says, smartphone in hand. She shows her a picture of Lorna. She's had a drastic haircut, perhaps trying to emulate some of the trendier mums. It's Barbie-pink, cut in a long bob, and looks like someone's dropped a vat of candyfloss on her from a great height. Erin shoves the phone back towards Caz.

'Stop it,' she says, tone warning.

'Come on!'

'I mean it, we said we'd be nice to her. We said we'd be nice to everyone. And you should come off that thing as well.' Caz looks at her with an eyebrow so raised it's almost coming off her head. Erin laughs. 'OK, fine, not that, do what you like, but we've all had shocking haircuts. And that is shocking, but write her a message telling her you love it. For me.' Caz smirks and begins typing, then shows Erin the complimentary message to which she nods her approval. Erin owes Lorna. She came forward and told the police that she'd been walking the twins up and down Erin's former road to avoid the wind on the front and she hadn't seen anyone anywhere near the house around the time they suspected Raf died but that she did see him at one point through the window and told them it looked like he was drinking and in distress. With that testimony and in light of everything that Erin could tell them about what he'd done, the police felt it was a cut-and-dried case of suicide and the coroner didn't request an inquest. Erin doesn't know why Lorna lied, and it must have been a lie because Erin and Amanda weren't just there the once that day. So Lorna must have been lying for her, but when Erin went to see her she simply stuck to the story she'd told the police. 'That's just what I saw,' she'd said. But there was something in her eyes, a glint of complicity. Whatever her motivation, it's allowed Erin and Bobby to be here in this garden building mud pies, so she couldn't be more grateful.

It's an hour later and Erin sits on the chair in Bobby's new nursery watching her baby sleeping, hand clutched round a monkey puppet that he's become absolutely obsessed with. Her eyes move to a shelf on the other side of his cot and the two spires of the huge rose quartz Amanda gifted her that first night they met. The stone she'd gone back into the studio to recover from next to her fiancé's body, his dead body. Right after she'd moved the small dining table into a position that would make it conceivable that he'd hit his head on the corner of it on his trajectory to the floor.

Erin had discovered, in an idle moment on Google images a couple of months ago, that its twin spires mark it out as a soulmate stone, which makes more sense of Amanda giving it to her to put in the house, presumably to remind Raf that his true soulmate was her. Erin thought it right she put it in Bobby's room, because he's her soul now, the only one she'll ever need.

She stands up and presses a button on her old smartphone, which she now uses solely as the monitor for her baby boy. She and Amanda haven't had any contact since the photo

Erin insisted she send her from the arrivals hall at Sydney airport. But at this time every day, Bobby's nap time, Erin always checks in on the home section of the monitor app and sees that 'iPhone 5' is 'online'. When she first saw that Amanda was logging into the app every day she was shocked, it seemed so creepy that she'd want to watch her baby on a live feed on her abuser's old phone. Erin thought about getting a different monitor and cutting off Amanda's contact with them for good. But then she remembered how she was in that hotel room, the expression on that little girl's face in those paintings. Amanda won't ever be able to move on from what happened to her. She'll always be 'married' to that man, and Bobby, his son, is the only thing left in the world that can still connect her to him. So Erin did nothing, because Amanda deserves some happiness, whatever form it takes. She also finds it reassuring, because every day before she leaves the nursery to try and return her house to some semblance of order after her now walking bundle of joy has blazed a trail of destruction through it, Erin can go onto the app, click on the icon next to 'iPhone 5' and check the geotag still says 'Sydney, Australia', just to make sure that Amanda's still a long way from them, on the other side of the world, as she watches her baby sleep.

ACKNOWLEDGEMENTS

To my friends and those close to me, thank you for your love and support. Without your belief, very few words would make it onto the page.

To the imperious Juliet Mushens who I'm ever grateful to have as my agent. At times, writing this book was like a heavyweight bout and having Juliet in my corner coaching me through gave me the best chance of delivering a knock-out. Thank you also to Liza De Block for all of her help and kindness.

A huge thank you to my editor Jade Chandler who's helped me craft and hone this book with precision and care and is such a joy to work with. I've always felt in such good hands with you Jade and in uncertain times that means a huge amount. Thank you also to Liz Foley, Sophie Painter, Mia Quibell-Smith, Dan Mogford and the whole team at Harvill Secker. Thanks as well to Sara Adams for her early work on the book at a time when I wasn't sure exactly what it was going to be.

To Sam H Freeman, our conversations about books, film, story are such an important part of my writing. The way in which our careers have evolved from those humble beginnings writing average short plays in the Soho Theatre Café has been beyond both of our hopes and dreams and I'm so grateful for that.

To our wonderful community in Margate, I thank you for your friendship and camaraderie in this sleep-deprived and often manic portion of our lives. The energising conversations and stolen afternoons helping our children build sandcastles and paddling in the water have become a huge source of joy.

To my wife Joanna's family, Tina, Stewart, David and Hannah, thank you for all your warm-hearted interest and support. And on my side, to Al, Lyndsey, Mac and my mum Lesley, to whom this book is dedicated, your excitement about my books and never-ending cheerleading is forever appreciated.

To my daughter Sadie, your sunshine lights up our days and we love you for it. To the boy, Otis, I began writing this book when you were a very screamy little man. But, with your cheeky smile and that giggle, what a little legend you've turned into. We love you both so much.

To Joanna. Thank you for your patience with me and this book. I'm so lucky to have you and the life we've built. You constantly challenge me and our conversations about social media, #metoo, coercive control and the psychology of possession and misogyny have provided the bedrock of this book. I've learnt so much from you.

And finally thank you to all my readers. The reviews and feedback I had about *Happy Ever After* were so gratifying and such a huge part of what kept me chipper while writing this book. I can't tell you how much I appreciate everyone who's chosen to spend their valuable time reading my words.

C. C. MacDonald

C. C. MacDonald is a writer and actor based in Margate where he lives with his wife, two children and dog Frankie. *The Family Friend* is his second novel.